——THE——
DEATH AT THE
VINEYARD

PRAISE FOR
THE SHELL HOUSE DETECTIVES MYSTERY SERIES

'A cleverly plotted and thoroughly enjoyable book about dark deeds in beautiful places.'

—Elly Griffiths, author of the Ruth Galloway series

'A total delight.'

—Sarah Winman, author of *Still Life*

'Exquisitely written, set in Cornwall, great characters, and a gripping plot. Who could ask for more?'

—Jill Mansell, author of *Promise Me*

'This beautifully written cosy coastal mystery packs a real punch! With wonderfully atmospheric prose and twists and turns aplenty, the plot will have you riding a wave of suspense long after you've turned the final page. If you love Cornwall, you will adore this book.'

—Sarah Pearse, author of *The Sanatorium*

'Suspenseful, twisty and unputdownable . . . Loved it!'

—Claire Douglas, author of *The Couple at No. 9*

'Clever, plotty and compelling.'

—Jane Shemilt, author of *Daughter*

'If you're looking for a new favourite cosy crime series, here it is!'

—Libby Page, author of *The Lido*

—Emily Koch, author of *What July Knew*

'The mystery is perfectly paced and the characters vivid and true, inviting us to join in as fellow sleuths as we unravel the secrets of the past. I can't wait to return to Cornwall with Emylia Hall for the next adventure.'

—Emma Stonex, author of *The Lamplighters*

'A treat of a book: immersive, suspenseful, full of twists and turns . . . It's as captivating as a Cornish summer. I loved it.'

—Susan Fletcher, author of *The Night in Question*

'*The Shell House Detectives* is a hug of a book that is transporting and full of love, with a humdinger of a mystery at its big heart.'

—Amanda Reynolds, author of *Close to Me*

'Captures the magic and beauty of Cornwall wrapped within a warm and engaging detective story. I loved it.'

—Rosanna Ley, author of *The Forever Garden*

'An intriguing mystery that perfectly captures how a seaside community is rocked by murder.'

—*The Sun*

'Mystery with heart! Fans of intriguing crime mysteries will adore this brand-new series, which is just crying out to become Sunday evening television.'

—*The People's Friend*

'Engaging and enjoyable.'

—*Daily Express*

THE
DEATH AT THE
VINEYARD

Emylia Hall

THOMAS & MERCER

Text copyright © 2024 by Emylia Hall
All rights reserved.

Published by Thomas & Mercer, Seattle

www.apub.com

Amazon, the Amazon logo, and Thomas & Mercer are trademarks of Amazon.com, Inc., or its affiliates.

ISBN-13: 9781662521775
eISBN: 9781662521768

Cover design by The Brewster Project
Cover illustration by Handsome Frank Limited – Marianna Tomaselli

Printed in the United States of America

For Lucy Clarke

Prologue

He buries the body on one of the last days of summer. As his spade hits the earth, it's parched, hard as granite, almost as if nature is giving him the chance to change his mind. But in this act, he is resolute. This land has been theirs for generations, so it's a safe place, this grave, marked only by an ancient beech tree. A grave? Can it be called that? He gives no blessing as he shovels the earth. Nor does he seek forgiveness.

Overhead, the moon observes the act impassively. It shines from the navy sky, as round and flat as a dinner plate.

Once he made his mind up, it was just another task on the list. You can't be a farmer and baulk at death. He's felt a heartbeat stop beneath his palms more times than he can count. Is this different? Well, yes. But not as different as people might think.

When the job is done, when he's back at the farmhouse, a light rain begins to fall. And it doesn't stop for days on end. Sea mists close in, shrouding the lower slopes, refusing to lift for anything. They're barrelling headlong into autumn now but already it feels like winter. Short days, long nights, an intolerable absence of light. The months that follow are storm-lashed, the harshest he's ever known. The poet in him – the pagan – wonders if his actions have brought it upon them. But if a farmer could control the weather by simple acts of treachery or generosity, then wouldn't they all be at it?

Spring comes late, daffodils pushing through the mud. By the beech tree they're a faultless yellow carpet. He stares at them, glassy-eyed. When he turns, he tries to imagine vines tracking the slopes, just like she said. A fanciful notion, here in this western crook of Cornwall, but then why not?

The years roll by – as do the harvests. Because against the odds, against the rains, against what he probably deserves, the vines he planted flourish. He changes the name from Shoreline Farm to Shoreline Vines.

And some days he goes whole hours without her crashing into his thoughts.

Meanwhile, at the top of the vineyard, the bones lie undisturbed. If only the same could be said for his conscience.

1

After an unsettled morning, the skies have cleared to blue. It feels like a crime to ignore fair weather in November, especially when it's forecast to be short-lived. Ally closes the door on The Shell House and crosses the veranda. She walks past the golden blaze of the magnolia, and the fat-bottomed palm that's more pineapple than tree. As she opens the gate, the clutch of sun-bleached buoys swings back and forth; a decorative touch that Bill grinned and shook his head at, much like her lavender-filled lobster pots.

Ally takes such pleasure in her garden, each day noting the myriad small changes. Her grandsons came over from Australia in the summer, their footballs thwacking the mallow and snapping the snapdragons, but a couple of small boys tearing about had nothing on the ravages of a prevailing south-westerly. How she misses them. And Evie, of course. Evie told her that she and Scott were seeing a marriage counsellor, confirming Ally's suspicion that there was more to her visit than met the eye. It's not that she doesn't like Evie's husband, but for a moment Ally imagined her moving back to these shores and her heart leapt. But for the children to be separated from their father by the span of the globe? It's unthinkable.

Ally's grandsons have Australian accents and Australian passports. Their home is on the other side of the world. And so, now, is Evie's.

When their daughter announced that she was moving to Sydney, it was one of the very few occasions that Ally saw Bill cry. *It's a hell of a long way away, Al.* The two of them pushed their heads together, a pair of old gulls, mourning their baby's inevitable flight. And now Bill is a hell of a long way away too. A hell of a long way away if he's anywhere at all.

Ally is still trying to understand the ways in which grief shapes and reshapes. It's been more than two years since Bill died, and sometimes it's as if she could open the door to The Shell House and there he'd be: tugging his police-issue boots off and throwing her that smile. Other times his absence is unarguable. There's nothing to be done except to keep on keeping on. Try to make the most of it. And give thanks for all that her life has become.

Ally and Fox head up and over the dunes to the beach. The tide is high, and her dog barks at the waves as they explode on the shore. Sand flies at his paws. Wild weather is forecast for the weekend, and she knows how that goes: waves as high as houses, and afterwards a strandline full of riches. Autumn storms are made for wrecking – or beachcombing, as people outside of Cornwall say.

She calls to Fox and the words are whipped from her. It's a funnelling wind and she's caught in it. She wishes she'd brought a hat.

Ally turns and looks back the way she's come, her coat filling like a sail. The beach is all but deserted at this time of year. She can see the blue gable of The Shell House, the last in the dunes, and beyond it the scattering of other wooden houses nestled amidst the marram grass. Gus's place isn't quite visible, though if she pricks her ears, she'll probably hear hammering. Shortly after buying All Swell, Gus discovered that it was all but falling down around his ears. *Turns out there's no such thing as a free lunch, or a bargain beach house,* he told her ruefully. But she knows that nothing can diminish Gus's joy in having gone from holidaymaker to homeowner in the dunes. Even a severe case of rotting timber.

And nothing can diminish Ally's joy that her favourite neighbour – *is that all that I'm calling him?* – is well enough for anything, let alone DIY. Ally didn't realise how much Gus meant to her until, back in the summer, she nearly lost him. Beside his hospital bed, she promised herself that she wouldn't waste another second. And Ally doesn't think she has, not by her reckoning; her and Gus's bond is strong, rock-steady. But urgency can't help but recede when the luxury, the extraordinary privilege, of uneventful daily life resumes.

Over the sound of the sea, Ally can hear the ringing of her phone in her pocket. She pulls it out and sees another name that always comes with a spark.

'Jayden, hello.'

He could just be checking in, suggesting a coffee, asking a favour.

'Al, you got a second?'

And it's there in his voice: he's not checking in, nor suggesting a coffee, nor asking a favour.

'Of course.'

Between the crash of waves there's a moment of such stillness it's as if the world has paused. Even the gulls stop their shrieking.

'Clear your diary,' Jayden says. 'We've got a new case.'

2

Jayden finds his wife in the sitting room, in a yoga stretch he now knows as the cat-cow. He joins her on all fours.

'Hey, babe.'

'Hey.'

Jasmine, getting on for twenty months old, cannons towards him in an approximation of a forward roll. Sound effects – miaowing and mooing – go with her.

'Yoga is so relaxing with you two in the mix,' says Cat, puffing a fallen strand of hair away from her face.

Jayden wraps an arm around his daughter as she scrabbles to get away. Cue more cat-cow sounds.

Cat unfolds from her pose and flops back against the sofa. She rests a hand on her domed belly.

'You feeling okay?' he asks.

Every time Jayden sees Cat's hand go to her middle, he can't help saying it. She's been cool as a cucumber through this pregnancy, but he's worrying enough for the pair of them. Maybe because they got so lucky with Jazz; he can't rest until their boy is in their arms, and wishes it weren't all on Cat to get him there. Maybe because the clocks have gone back, and he knows they're plunging towards another Cornish winter: gales across the headland; night drawing in when the afternoon has barely started. It's not like Jayden misses the bright lights of Leeds that much, but wow does it get dark here in the middle of nowhere. And sometimes, when he wakes up at stupid o'clock and hears rain against the window, he thinks of that time last winter when he clung to a cliffside in the pitch black, the sea exploding below, his life hanging in the balance.

Uneasy vibes? Who can blame him.

'I'm feeling great,' Cat says. 'But Jazzy's got all the energy today.'

'I'm cooking tonight. Your wish is my command.'

'Bolognese. Plus, Jazz will eat it.'

'Done. I'll grab the stuff on the way back. I'm headed up to Shoreline Vines with Ally.'

'Dad's tip? The stolen quad bike?' Cat grins. 'He'll want commission, you know.'

Jayden makes a noise that falls somewhere between a grunt and a laugh. They smashed their first season with the campsite, but that income's got to stretch through the winter now, so while the detective work pays – especially since the Rockpool House case – they'll be living small the next few months. And, with the cottage on the farm, living in continued proximity to Cat's mum and dad – something that Cat loves, and Jazz too. Jayden? He loves that his girls are happy.

'Want me to take Jazz with me? She looks like she could do with a run.'

'She's not a dog, Jay.'

At which his daughter launches into a volley of barks.

'Anyway, not on Shell House business,' says Cat, wrinkling her nose. 'Not this time. Dad didn't tell you the story, I guess? About Shoreline Farm?'

'Shoreline Vines.'

'No, it used to be called Shoreline Farm. Anyway . . . rumour has it there's a body buried up there. Under the farmhouse or one of the barns or something.'

'What?'

'It was in this old book of local ghost stories I had as a kid. It's supposed to be the body of a sea captain whose ship went down in the bay. He made it to shore, only to find a cold welcome up at the farmhouse. And now his ghost won't leave until justice is served. On a dark night you can hear his whistling in the yard.'

'Maybe he was stealing a quad bike.'

'This was in, like, 1840. Or 1900. Or . . . 1710. I don't know, years ago. But there's a weird old pine tree that looks like the mast of a ship. That's where they say he's buried. Beneath the tree.'

'I thought he was buried under the farmhouse. Or a barn.'

'Yeah, no, it's this tree. Honestly, look out for it, Jay. From the right angle, it's a mast with sails.'

'Babe, you know this story's all over the place, right?'

'Anyway . . . it's creepy. I don't want Jazzy up there.'

'You're joking, right?'

Despite Cat growing up in the back of beyond, Jayden generally thinks of her as a worldly individual. *Generally.*

She pulls a face. 'Yes. No. Anyway . . . Mum and Dad are up there on Saturday night for a swanky dinner with the Harpers. Rather them than me.'

Cliff didn't mention that. But then Jayden's father-in-law is not famed for his chit-chat.

'What's the occasion?'

'They're entertaining some VIP and have invited various community people, I think. Who needs that, though? I've got all the glamour I need right here. Jazzy and I have a hot date with some potato printing, so . . .'

'So I'm out of here,' says Jayden, bending to kiss his wife and daughter.

'Don't forget spag bol stuff. But no mushrooms, I hate mushrooms.'

8

'Me hate mushooms too,' pipes Jazzy.

'Got it,' says Jayden, 'no mushrooms. And watch out for the tree of death at Shoreline Vines.'

◆ ◆ ◆

The lane is a steep climb, but Jayden lets the old Land Rover do its thing. Just before they crest the hill, the sign for the vineyard comes into view. He takes the turning, bumping the vehicle down the uneven track.

Jayden's done his research. Shoreline Vines isn't the kind of place that's putting itself out there with tasting tours and terrace dining, but it's been quietly, and successfully, producing wine for the last couple of decades. Before that, it was a farm, and has been in the Harper family for generations. Nowhere did Jayden's research throw up Cat's story of the dead sea captain, the long-buried bones, or the ship-like tree, though. Funny, that.

Decent bloke, Frank, was how Cliff described the late Frank Harper. And for Cliff, *decent bloke* is the highest accolade. Is Jayden a decent bloke? Possibly. After all, Cliff's trusted him with this, erm, sensitive and highly charged case, hasn't he? *I've got some business to send your way. Now, don't bungle it,* was how he put it.

'So, when exactly did they last see the quad bike?' asks Ally.

'They noticed it was missing yesterday morning. It's kept out in the barn. Which was unlocked. Always is, apparently. No tracker on it either. Nothing to go on at all, Al.'

Jayden can't help sighing as he says it. He knows machinery theft is a big deal. As rural crimes go, it's probably one of the biggest. But it doesn't get his juices going.

'Cliff said because we've solved murders, we can definitely solve who nicked a quad bike. I don't think he gets it.'

'Well, we'll do our best.'

9

But Jayden has a funny feeling that, as far as his father-in-law is concerned, their best won't be enough – unless it results in the return of a gleaming red Honda Fourtrax 420. And the thief paying the price for their sticky fingers too. For all Cliff's gruffness and high-handed ways, Jayden knows that he thinks Jayden's solid; that his precious only daughter could, on balance, have done worse. But he'd still prefer not to mess up this case.

This kind of boring, and probably unsolvable, case.

'Why haven't they reported it to the police?' asks Ally.

'They reckon there's no point. That's what Owen said anyway.'

Owen Harper. Son of Ruth, brother of Edwin. Frank, the dad, died two years ago. Jayden got the family tree from Cliff. And Owen is, just like Frank, a *decent bloke.*

The track up to the vineyard is rough, and Jayden takes it slow. He doesn't know much about winemaking, but he can see that the harvest action has been and gone. The vines that run to the edge of the track look like elaborate twigs – not a grape or leaf in sight. Up ahead, the grey stone farmhouse comes into view. There's a patrol car parked by the gate.

'Oh,' says Ally. 'Looks like they've reported it after all.'

As they pull into the yard, they see a second police vehicle. A white-suited CSI passes with their head down. Beyond the outhouses, lengths of blue and white tape flicker in the breeze.

'Seems like a lot of fuss for a quad bike,' murmurs Ally. 'Doesn't it?'

Jayden cuts the engine. 'Yeah, it does.'

A familiar figure taps at the glass and Jayden buzzes down the window.

'News travels fast,' says Mullins.

Porthpella's resident police constable usually has a bit of swagger about him. Not the kind of swagger that'd do much outside of Porthpella, but down The Wreckers Arms on a Friday night, he passes. This version of Mullins who's leaning against the Land

Rover looks depleted, though. His usually ruddy cheeks are pale as butter. His mouth is a straight line.

'I never did like cows. It's the way they look at you, like they're planning something. Best you stay in the car, Ally. It's not a pretty sight.'

'We're here about a missing quad bike,' she says.

'Mullins, what's happened?' asks Jayden.

Mullins suddenly lets out an explosive sneeze. He pats his pockets and brings out a massive cotton handkerchief. Jayden does a double take.

'Bloke got himself trampled by the herd,' Mullins says, blowing his nose noisily. 'He's a right mess.'

At the gate there's a cluster of officials. An older woman in a dark green wax jacket, her iron-grey hair cut as close as a skull cap, jabs at the ground with a stick. Jayden can't hear what she's saying, but she looks angry.

He glances at Ally and sees she's watching too.

'Who's the victim?' Jayden asks carefully.

Mullins grimaces and shrugs. 'Unconfirmed. I told you. Cows. Hooves. Brutal.'

3

Owen Harper takes off his boots at the door. His hand rests against the granite, always on the same palm-smooth patch. As a pint-sized boy he used to sit down to yank off his wellies, or sometimes ask his dad for help: *They won't come off. Pull harder, Dad!* A little indulgence, from a tough man to a tough son.

Inside the farmhouse it's dark and quiet. Is it him, or is it darker and quieter than usual? An interior reaction to what's gone on out in the field. Owen was born in this old house, and he's never been afraid of ghosts. The farm is too much in his bones, his blood. It's not a bad place – how could it be? Because that would make him bad too.

'Karensa?'

She doesn't answer, but then Owen finds her in the kitchen spilling coffee granules into mugs. He reaches to touch her shaking hand, but she flits away. She takes milk from the fridge; slams the door with some force.

'Are you okay?' he says.

'I can't remember if the officer said sugar or not.'

The sight of her in that tatty knitted jumper pulls at something deep inside of him.

'Let me help.'

It wasn't Karensa who found the body – that was Owen's mum – but she was there when the herd scattered, leaving churned mud and a battered body. A man, that much was clear, but he was unrecognisable. Owen could only watch as Karensa turned and hid her face in her husband's coat, as Edwin wrapped his arms around her, murmuring, *It's okay, don't look, it's okay.* Edwin, who was suddenly all composure, who just moments before had reeled from the sight of the body and punched the bars of the gate, bloodying his knuckles. That initial reaction was Edwin all over though, turning his upset upon himself; as a boy he once failed a maths test and came home and struck his head three times against his bedroom wall, ending up with a bump the size of a hen's egg. That Owen should judge his brother at such a traumatic moment shows just how far they've fallen.

Now, Owen moves close to Karensa. With one ear on the rest of the house, he puts his arm around her tense shoulders. She's wearing perfume, something cheap and fruity that doesn't suit her. Edwin gave it to her for her birthday.

'What can I do?' he says in a low voice.

'I can't stop seeing it. His . . . where his face was.'

They spring apart as the front door slams.

Edwin, pounding into the kitchen. Stress has drawn deep furrows in his forehead. At thirty-three he's two years younger than Owen, but he's always looked older. Maybe because Edwin styles himself as a gentleman landowner, Barbour and checked shirts, whereas Owen is more surf-rat-meets-labourer.

'Total bloody mess. And you've got people coming round about a quad bike?'

As Edwin faces him, it feels to Owen like his brother's squaring up. He's not – he already punched a metal gate today, apart from anything, and definitely came off worse – but Owen knows that one day Edwin will undoubtedly hit him, and he'll have every right to. His cheek tingles in anticipation of the strike. Then he thinks of the man in the field, who didn't have much face left at all. Bile rises in his throat.

'You mean the private detectives?' says Owen, turning to the window. 'Cliff Thomas talked me into that one. Said it's his son-in-law.'

And Cliff's naked pride as he said it made Owen think of his own dad; his dad who he loved with his heart and soul and misses every damn day. Outside, beyond the police car, he can see two people: a tall brown-skinned man and a small grey-haired white woman.

'I said the quad wasn't worth bothering with,' says Edwin. 'Mum said the same. Sounded like an order to me, brother.'

'A new ten-grand Honda and it's not worth bothering with?' *It's no wonder the place is in ruins with an attitude like that.* 'You said there was no point going to the police about it, so I didn't. I went to Jayden Weston and Ally Bright.'

'Anyway, I told them we've caught the thief,' says Edwin. 'Or Greg's steers have, anyway. Nature finds a way, hey?' Owen chews his lip. Before he can say anything, Edwin runs on: 'Looks an awful lot like that loser Tremaine, doesn't it? That's what I told Tim Mullins just now.'

Owen hasn't seen Russell Tremaine for a year or two, but he grew up here and his dad still lives in the cottage at the end of the track. Every time Owen passes it, he feels a pang of guilt for the way Shaun has been treated. Sometimes, all this guilt feels like rocks in his pockets. Like the best thing he can do is walk into a storming tide and keep on going.

'Shaun'll be devastated,' says Karensa quietly. 'If it is him. If it is Russell.'

'Owen, go and get rid of your amateur detectives before they charge you by the hour,' says Edwin. 'Unless their special skills extend to getting a dead man to tell us where he stashed our quad.'

'I'm going,' says Owen. He shoots a look at Karensa, but her head's dipped. She's stirring sugar into a mug of coffee; a manic whirlpool. 'I'll carry those out, Karensa. You take it easy. It's . . . a shock.'

'Tell that to Mum,' says Edwin, with a humourless laugh. 'She's busy putting her brave face on. You know, the one she had when Dad died?'

Owen will never forget it; Ruth wore such a hard mask he hardly recognised her. It was part of why he had to leave back then. But he's here now, isn't he? And he's determined to help the vineyard thrive. Even if an independent observer would say he's doing the exact opposite.

4

Instead of taking the seat Owen offered her on the bench, Ally stays on her feet, her eyes on the cattle field. The police tape is stretched across the five-bar gate and flaps in the wind. Beside her, Jayden and Owen are watching too.

Mullins is holding a small, slightly built man by his elbow. The man is wearing tracksuit trousers and an old overcoat; mud-streaked wellington boots. As he looks down at the body he wheels away, bending double and spitting in the dirt. He wipes his sleeve across his mouth and Mullins puts an uncertain hand on his back.

'I should get over there,' says Owen. 'That's Shaun Tremaine. It's his son. I mean . . . it looks like it's his son.'

'We can talk more later,' says Jayden. 'Or come back another time.'

Owen puffs out air from his cheeks. 'The quad was insured. It puts it in perspective, you know? A thing like this.'

And they can't argue with that.

'What do you think happened?' asks Ally.

She doesn't know much about cattle, but to trample a man to death, is that possible, without provocation? Even *with* provocation?

'What happened,' says a new voice, 'is that the thief returned, scoping out what else he could get his hands on. I'd say he was startled and leapt over the gate to hide. And what he didn't reckon on was Greg Sullivan's steers startling too. An Angus bull is getting on for a ton and these boys won't be far off that. Once you're caught in that sort of a ruckus . . . Well, let's say it'll never end well.' She holds out her hand; smiles thinly. 'Ruth Harper.'

'Ally Bright.'

'And you're Jayden Weston, Cliff's son-in-law.'

Jayden nods.

'I know Owen got you up here, but you've been saved a job. It's a terrible shame but . . .' She lets the 'but' hang in the air, and Ally thinks *but what?* What possible 'but' could there be? A man is dead.

'How do you know he's the thief?' asks Jayden.

Ally studies Ruth as the woman contemplates the question. She's strong-featured, with large brown eyes and a full mouth, dashed with bright lipstick. What people might call 'striking'. They haven't met before, but Ally heard that Ruth's husband died not long after Bill. It wasn't Frank's terminal cancer that killed him but a fall on the stairs when he was at his weakest; a mercy, some said. The news of his death took longer to filter through to Ally out in the dunes, as she was pulled up in her own shell, then.

Does Ally feel anything like kinship, knowing they were widowed within months of one another? She's always been compassionate, but since turning detective she's found it a strange sensation, to go from being so private to being enmeshed in other people's lives. Not just observing, or listening, but asking questions. Having opinions. Ruth Harper found a dead man on her land but there's something about her briskness, her very certainty, that sets Ally on edge.

'It's too much of a coincidence,' says Ruth. 'Well, isn't it? Why else would anybody be hanging around here? It's not a public right of way. There aren't any footpaths crossing our land, though it doesn't stop the occasional rambler trampling the vines.'

'Ally, Jayden,' says Owen, cutting in. 'Look, thanks for coming all the way up here. I'm sorry for the trouble.'

Ally watches as Owen goes over to Shaun Tremaine and wraps an arm around his shoulders. Beside Owen, Shaun looks very small indeed. She feels a burning in her throat and looks away.

'Yes, thank you both,' says Ruth, turning to them. 'And I'm sorry for my manner. It's because we're upset. We're much obliged. You must come again when it's a little . . . quieter. Have a glass of wine.'

'You sure you don't want to give us a photo of the quad?' asks Jayden. 'I've got the make and model, but any distinguishing features? We might as well put out some feelers . . .'

'Forget the quad,' says Ruth. 'Why would we care about that . . .' She stops. 'Suddenly I can't . . .' She takes a laboured breath. 'I feel as if I can't . . .'

Ally places a hand on Ruth's back. She gently guides the woman to sit down, but she can feel resistance through her angular frame.

'It's nothing, just . . . shock . . . it's . . .'

Ruth's eyes are wide, bleary, as she pants. Her hand claws at her chest.

'Ruth,' says Jayden, 'it's okay, I think you're having a panic attack. Have you had one before?'

'Yes . . . once . . . Long . . . time . . .'

'We're here. Just take it easy. Deep breaths. Nice and slow. That's it.'

But Ruth's breaths are fast and shallow, the expression in her eyes chaotic.

'Easy now,' says Jayden. 'That's it. Nice and easy.'

Ruth closes her eyes as Jayden keeps talking to her in a low voice.

'Should I call someone?' Ally asks, but Ruth looks to be settling and Jayden gives a quick shake of his head.

'There we go, Ruth, you're okay. Al, can you get one of her sons?'

'Ed . . .' manages Ruth.

Ally looks to Owen, but he's still deep in conversation with Shaun. It feels callous to interrupt. She glances back; Ruth is holding Jayden's hand. Her eyes are closed and she's breathing slow and deep. Ally goes to the farmhouse.

◆ ◆ ◆

'Hello?'

When no one answers her knock, Ally steps inside. The flag-stone hallway is dimly lit. It's a functional space, cluttered only with boots and shoes, a groaning rack filled with padded coats and Barbour jackets. She smells woodsmoke and the tang of something else she can't quite get hold of. Ally feels the weight of other people's lives, and it sits strangely: a low-level sadness in her chest.

Outside, she was quick to write off Ruth Harper as unfeeling. But, despite her front, Ruth's body betrayed her. Ally finds it oddly reassuring.

'Is anyone here?' she calls out.

Edwin Harper, the other brother they spoke to briefly when they first arrived, pads down the hallway. He smiles genially, hands stuffed in his pockets. 'Ah, the sleuth. Still here?'

'It's your mum,' says Ally.

Edwin's face changes in an instant.

'What's happened?'

He looks as scared as a tiny boy.

5

Mullins is ready to call it a day. He's knackered, this cold of his getting the better of him. What he needs is a lie-down. A lie-down, and a mug of piping-hot blackcurrant squash. Sticky-sweet and just the job. That's what his mum used to give him when he was a kid.

He clambers back into the patrol car, taking a last look around the yard. The rambling old granite outbuildings, and the half-finished new-build behind, blue tarp flapping in the wind. It's a holiday cottage project, according to the Harpers, but one they've hit pause on. *You seen the cost of building materials lately? Not sure we want the place crawling with emmets anyway*, Edwin said. And Mullins had two words for him there: *Right on.*

All in all? Funny place, Shoreline Vines. He's not into wine so the various outhouses filled with ruddy great vats – thousands of pounds' worth of grape juice doing its thing, according to Edwin – don't mean much. But it's good business. Must be, if they're willing to shrug off the loss of a quad bike. The quad bike that they figure Russell Tremaine stole, before he made the mistake of coming back to look for more and ended up on the wrong side of a herd of bullocks.

Mullins told them they should have reported the theft instead of going to Ally and Jayden. Not least because there's been a spate of robberies and it looks like the work of an organised gang. Slick operators who come in trucks and cut through chains and make off with whatever your basic Farmer Giles has neglected to lock up or set a tracker on.

No, we'd have heard it if there'd been a truck, said Edwin. *And no chains were cut. More likely it was the work of an opportunist. An opportunist like Russell. And I'm sad to say, Officer, that's exactly Tremaine's reputation round here.*

Though why Owen Harper thought it was worth getting Ally and Jayden involved, Mullins doesn't know. Still, Mullins isn't here about the quad bike. He's here about the dead man. And with Skinner sunning himself on a beach in Gran Canaria, Mullins is in the hot seat. Well, he's done what he can. He's got his statements, and the next of kin has been informed.

Next of kin. Such a bog-standard phrase. And nothing about telling Shaun felt standard. The way the bloke went in on himself, shuffling up the track without saying a single word then doubling up at the sight of his son's body. You grow yourself a thick skin in this job, you have to – that's what Mullins's superior officers told him when he started out. Lately, though, it's like he's been going in the other direction, every case unpeeling him a bit more. If Mullins ever gets to be an ancient copper, he'll be bawling like a baby at every turn if he's not careful.

Now Shaun is back at his cottage, taken there by Owen Harper.

There'll probably be a post-mortem, but Ruth Harper's statement confirmed the horrible truth of it. She saw the commotion: the bumping of flanks, the hooves churning the mud. No wonder the woman had a panic attack. By the time Ruth got to the gate, the bullocks had done their worst.

I did check, said Ruth, *if he was breathing. But anyone could see he was done for.*

Ruth told Mullins she cried out and her younger son, Edwin, rushed over, followed by her daughter-in-law, Karensa. They phoned the police immediately. The cattle don't belong to them;

21

they're renting those fields to a neighbouring farmer, a bloke called Greg Sullivan. Mullins went to school with Greg's younger sister. Might even have asked her to the leavers' disco.

Definitely did ask her to the leavers' disco.

Sharp-tongued lot, those Sullivans, as he remembers.

His next stop is Greg Sullivan's farmhouse, five miles east of here, because he needs to be informed. He'll be called to court; a few more 'Warning: Livestock' notices required on those gates, most likely. And maybe he'll have some light to shed on what Russell Tremaine was doing in that field. Just in case it didn't play out like the Harpers said and Tremaine was adding cattle-rustling to his CV.

Just as Mullins is about to start the engine, Edwin taps on the window. Reluctantly, Mullins winds it down.

'Sorry about that scene with Mum, Tim. Delayed shock. She's perfectly fine now. Did you get everything you need?'

'I did,' says Mullins. 'Cheers.'

He knows Edwin from The Wreckers. Nifty with a dart. Bit of a big mouth. Not as posh as he thinks he is.

'What about Shaun?' says Edwin.

'Your brother's with him. I asked him if he wanted me to send someone round – we've got a new family liaison officer, see – but he said he wanted to be on his own.'

'Poor guy. They're not our beasts, but I do feel responsible. It's a nasty way to go. I wouldn't wish it on anyone.'

'I've probably seen worse,' says Mullins. And he's thinking of JP Sharpe with his head bashed in. Baz Carson floating like a lily pad in his own pool. 'There's no malice in it, is there? Just animals being animals.'

But he's not convinced as he says it, and Edwin doesn't look that sure either. Mullins has never much liked cows. They always look like they're plotting something. Swishing those tails and batting those long lashes; noses dribbling.

'We'll be in touch. . .' says Mullins. But his voice breaks with a cough, and he loses all authority.

Edwin claps his hand on the roof of the car. 'Cheers, then.'

Just as Mullins is buzzing the window back up, Owen trudges into the yard. He didn't spend long with Shaun Tremaine then, did he? As Owen reaches them, Edwin nudges his brother's shoulder, saying something like *alright?* And for a second it makes Mullins wish he had a brother of his own. That easy connection: in it together, come hell or high water.

Mullins buzzes the window back down.

'He didn't want me there,' says Owen. 'Not once he'd got himself together. More or less told me to get out.'

'Well, no one likes to think their son's a thief,' says Edwin.

No one likes to think their son is dead, more like. But Mullins doesn't say it.

'I pedalled back from that. It's not going to help, is it? What's done is done.' Owen turns to Mullins. 'Officer, Shaun used to work for us. He went way back with Dad. But . . . we couldn't keep him on. Not after Dad died and we saw the real picture of the finances.' He rubs at his stubble, says, 'There's probably a bit of ill will there, to be honest.'

'We offered him a different package,' says Edwin. 'We didn't cut him off entirely. But he wasn't interested. All or nothing. He's a stubborn git. Sorry, but he is.'

'That's as may be, but he's in pieces. I didn't like leaving him. But then Ally and Jayden stopped by so he's not on his own.'

'And I expect Shaun told them where to go as well, did he?'

Owen shrugs. 'Dunno, I left them to it. But I think we should look in on him tomorrow. You can go next time.'

23

'Because I'm known for my bedside manner?' says Edwin, cuffing his brother lightly on the back of the head.

Time to go. Mullins thanks them for their time, and then he's out of there. He looks back in his mirror. The two of them standing side by side in the yard. *The future of Cornish wine.* That's what the framed newspaper article in the kitchen said, with a picture of a younger Edwin and Owen, arms around each other's burly shoulders; matching grins. Their parents, Ruth and Frank, standing a little to one side, as if the baton had already been passed to the next generation.

Nice to be born into a family where something's just handed to you on a plate. Or in a wine bottle, in this case. Mullins thinks of Russell Tremaine, ending his days trodden into the mud. He was probably never handed anything much, and now his dad's been left with even less.

He puts his foot down as he takes off down the driveway and rattles over the cattle grid. As he passes Shaun's old cottage – a squat granite place, hiding beneath a spreading yew tree – he sees Jayden's Land Rover parked outside. But Mullins doesn't stop. They're good at the touchy-feely stuff, those two. Unless they're busy rooting around Shaun's shed for the stolen quad bike? He wouldn't put it past them.

6

'It's got three sugars,' says Jayden. 'Is that right?'

''Cause no one ever says I'm sweet enough,' says Shaun. And his attempt at a grin is heartbreaking. Jayden passes him the mug – the least chipped he could find – and Shaun grips it hard.

Jayden was surprised when Shaun invited them into his home. They'd stopped with no agenda other than to check on him. Ally had seen Shaun sagging in his doorway as Owen Harper went back down the path and said, *Jayden, pull over.* She didn't know Shaun, but Shaun knew of her. *You're Bill Bright's missus. Alright, he was. For a copper, anyway.*

Yew Tree Cottage reminds Jayden of Sebastian Lyle's place in the Somerset moorlands, back on his and Ally's first case. There's a similarly neglected air; a slightly sour note. When they first knocked on the door, a dog went mad barking – a scraggy-looking hound – but it's settled back in its basket now. Inside, it's cramped and dark, the low late-autumn sun hardly making it through the grimy window. They sit at a melamine-topped table in the kitchen.

Ally rests a hand gently on Shaun's arm.

'Is there anyone we can call?' she asks. 'A relation, or friend . . .'

He shakes his head. 'Don't need anyone.' Then he looks up sharply, right at Jayden. 'You're not with the police?'

'We're not.'

'Useless bloke, that copper out there.'

And Jayden feels bizarrely compelled to defend Mullins. Mullins with his cotton hanky.

'Writing down everything those Harpers are saying in his note-book. My Russell's no thief.'

Jayden glances at Ally, then says, 'Does Russell live with you?'

He keeps the present tense going, because following Shaun's lead feels like the right thing to do.

Shaun shakes his head. 'He rents a place in Camborne.' Then, 'They're saying he was in that field because he was lifting a quad bike.'

'It was stolen two nights ago,' says Jayden. 'That's why we were up there.'

'You said you aren't police.'

'We're not,' says Ally. 'Jayden and I . . . we take the cases the police aren't interested in.'

Shaun blinks at them. 'Saw you in the paper, did I? Back in the summer? Something about that Rockpool House? Singer drowned in his pool.'

'That's it,' says Jayden.

'Seashell detectives or something.'

Shaun rubs a hand across his bloodshot eyes. His woollen jumper is ripped at the cuff and a loose thread hangs in his mug of tea. He needs looking after, that's what Jayden thinks. Someone to keep the cups of tea coming. Cook a meal. Put fresh sheets on the bed. Shaun Tremaine's son is dead out of nowhere – and he's all alone with it.

'Do you want me to get a few things in for you, Shaun? Groceries?'

Jayden looked for sugar in the kitchen cupboards and he found it, but not much else. A jar of instant coffee. A small tin of beans. A packet of rice, down to its last grains.

'Errand boy, are you?'

'I'm shopping on the way back. It's no trouble.'

Shaun shakes his head. Says, 'Who got you in for the quad bike? Ruth, was it?'

'Owen,' says Jayden.

'All as bad as each other. That Owen pretends he isn't, but he is. Frank would roll in his grave.'

Shaun gets up from the table and moves with unexpected speed from the room. Ally and Jayden send one another a questioning look. He emerges a moment later, holding a photo frame. He lays it carefully down on the table.

'That's my Russell.'

It's a picture of a boy of around ten years old, in shorts and wellington boots. His hair is white blond and buzz-cut. He's got a stick in his hand, like he's about to go off adventuring, and he's smiling the widest smile.

'What a lovely boy,' says Ally softly.

'He was afraid a lot,' says Shaun. 'Pretended not to be, but he was. That's why he got himself in trouble later, you know?'

Jayden nods, suppressing the desire to ask more.

'He had a few problems, but we all do, don't we? And he was a lovely lad, deep down. Good to me. It was Russell that got me Charlie here. Rescue pup, five or six years ago. But what I said about Russell being afraid . . . one thing he hated, one thing he always hated? Cattle.'

He looks at them both, his eyes darting from one to the other.

'He was chased once, as a boy. Not here; seeing his uncle over Bodmin way. Got on the wrong side of a big old bull. He made it out by inches. *Inches.* Had himself a phobia of cattle from then on. See what I'm saying? If Russell saw there were bullocks in that field, he wouldn't have gone in it for love nor money.'

Shaun sits back, spent by his words.

Jayden's seen this so many times before. Sudden death never makes sense to the bereaved. Here one minute, gone the next; the saddest of magic acts.

'Shaun, are there often cattle grazing there?' asks Ally.

'More often than not, last year or two. They rent that field out to Sullivan.'

'The Harpers' theory . . .' begins Jayden.

'I know what their theory is. That he was up to no good and when he heard them coming, he hid. What, jumped over a gate into a field of steers? Russell? No chance.'

Jayden runs it through in his mind. If Russell was quickly hunting for a place to hide, he might not have seen the cattle if they were at the other end of the field. And if he was keeping out of the Harpers' way, then he'd have been focused on watching them, not what was going on behind him. The bullocks could have approached without Russell ever being aware of it.

'Why do you think Russell was up at the vineyard?' he asks.

'Police didn't ask me that question. See what I mean? Useless.' He shakes his head. 'He had no reason to be there.'

'Was Russell here with you beforehand?' asks Ally.

'Hadn't seen him for a couple of weeks. We . . .' he starts, then stops. 'Doesn't matter.'

'What?' says Jayden, carefully.

'The last time . . . I sounded off about the Harpers.' Shaun rubs his nose with the back of his hand. 'Word got around that Edwin was bragging down The Wreckers. That's what he's like, see. Going on about the big plans they've got for the vineyard. So one minute they're telling me they can't afford to keep me on, the next they're going on about all this cash they're getting.'

'What sort of plans?' asks Ally.

'Investment. Some Londoner wants to give them a load of money.'

'When did you stop working for them, Shaun?' asks Jayden.

'Coming up on two years. They let me go after Frank died. It was all water under the bridge, but now that there's new money coming in, it feels like a kick in the teeth. And I know my Russell saw it that way too. We had words about it because he didn't think I should be taking it lying down.'

'And that was two weeks ago?' says Ally.

Shaun nods; looks up suddenly. 'What if that's why he was up there? Fighting my fight?'

Jayden nods, as if it's just as possible as the quad-bike theft explanation. Perhaps it is.

'But ending up in that field?' says Shaun, his eyes burning not just with sorrow now, but with conviction. 'It doesn't add up. I'm telling you he had no reason to be in that field. Not today. Not any day.'

Jayden can feel Ally shift beside him. He knows her mind will be turning too.

Russell was afraid of cattle.

'Leave me now,' says Shaun, his voice terse. 'That's enough talking.'

And suddenly he's out of his chair, hustling them towards the door. He sees them down the steps and along the cracked path. When he pushes open the gate – rotted wood; rusted hinge – the squeal it makes is almost human.

'How long will it take?' he asks.

'What, with the police?' says Jayden.

'No, I don't want police. With you. Seashell detectives.'

Shaun holds out his hand and Jayden shakes it. For a moment, it feels like Shaun isn't going to let go.

'How long before you tell me what happened to my boy?' he says.

7

Ally and Jayden are quiet on the drive back to the dunes, the events of the afternoon settling. The mundanity of the case that brought them to the vineyard, then the shock of what greeted them. Close-up images flicker through Ally's mind: the corpse beneath a sheet; Ruth's stricken eyes as she gasped for breath; Shaun's tobacco-stained fingers tugging at his frayed jumper; the smiling face of Russell as a boy.

She looks across at Jayden and sees he's lost in thought too.

'We had to say yes,' says Ally, 'didn't we?'

'Yeah, I think we did.'

We'll look into it, Shaun. Those were Jayden's words. And Ally found herself adding, *We'll do our best.* When Shaun asked how much they charged, they waved it away.

By the time they reach Porthpella, dusk has fallen. The lights are on in the old stone houses, and The Wreckers Arms has its usual welcoming glow. Ally feels her shoulders relax. But then she thinks of Shaun alone with his grief in his dark cottage. The tender way he showed them that childhood photograph. Ruth Harper just saw a thief, but Russell was Shaun's cherished boy.

'I get it,' says Jayden. 'I get why Shaun's struggling to get his head round what his son was doing at the vineyard.'

'And in that field particularly.'

'According to the Harpers it's straightforward though. He stole the quad, and he was back scoping for more. He saw them coming and hid in the first place he could find.'

'And didn't spot that cattle were grazing, even though Shaun said they were usually in that field.'

'Yeah,' murmurs Jayden, 'because if he had seen them, he'd never have gone in there. Because he was scared of them.'

And Ally recognises Jayden's thinking voice.

The lights of the village fall behind them as they head towards the dunes. Ally winds the window down and takes a breath of salted air. The dark sea unspools ahead.

'The Harpers were quick to drop the quad bike investigation, right, Al? Owen gave no room for manoeuvre there.'

'Well, it would have been insensitive to pursue it, given what happened.'

'Yeah, but they were just so sure that Russell was the thief. When, really, where's the evidence?'

'If I had something stolen from me, and then two days later I saw someone hanging around . . . I think I'd probably put two and two together.'

'And potentially make five.'

'Well, yes.'

'The police aren't investigating the quad bike theft, so they're not going to be fingerprinting the barn it was kept in, or anything like that.'

'Wouldn't they, as part of this investigation?'

Jayden shakes his head. 'They've got witness statements and no reason to doubt them. If the post-mortem confirms that Russell's injuries are consistent with being trampled by cattle, then it's chalked up as an accidental death. Investigation over. What Russell was or wasn't doing in the field is irrelevant.'

They bump slowly along the track, the dunes ghosted white in the headlights, until they reach The Shell House. It's dark inside but Ally will light the fire, fill it with warmth. Fox will be wanting his supper.

'Shaun is convinced that there's more to this,' says Jayden.

'Perhaps part of that is his reaction to the shock.'

'Al, if we can find the quad bike and link it to Russell, then we can give Shaun his answer. He won't like it, but at least he'll know.'

'I can't imagine how we'd begin to find the quad bike.'

'It wouldn't be easy for the police either, unless the theft was caught on camera, or they intercept it being sold on.' Jayden drums his fingers on the wheel. 'I want to talk to the Harpers again. The door's open for us with Owen.'

'And Ruth was grateful to you for looking after her. I think she'd give us the time of day.'

'If they've got a VIP descending, we'll want to get in quickly, right?'

'Jayden, what if Russell did go and ask for his dad's job back? Shaun told Russell he was upset that the Harpers were crowing about their investment. He and Russell argued because Russell thought he shouldn't be taking it lying down. Those were Shaun's words.'

'But they had that conversation two weeks ago, Al. Why would Russell go up there today?'

'Perhaps Russell was deciding how to make his case. Shaun lost his job a couple of years ago. Any business's fortunes can go up and down. There's a danger it could have come across as sour grapes.'

Jayden nods. 'No pun intended. Okay, I see that. So maybe Russell gives it a bit more thought, then goes to speak to them.'

'And considering what happened with the cattle, the Harpers might not have wanted to admit that conversation to the police. It wouldn't make them look good.'

'Shaun really did convince you that there's more to it, then.'

'Well, didn't he you?'

Jayden rubs at his jaw. 'Okay, so . . . let's roll with this. Russell goes to the vineyard. He doesn't tell his dad, because he doesn't want to get his hopes up. Or because Shaun wouldn't appreciate the interference.'

'And Russell sees one of the Harpers in the field, so goes to talk to them . . . although he's not likely to do that if he can see the cattle, is he?'

'He can't have seen them. And hold on, why would the Harpers be in that field? They rent it to a local farmer, right?'

Ally nods. 'And it doesn't lead anywhere either, does it? Ruth said no footpaths cut across their land.'

'That's something we should check out tomorrow, right? Walk the territory. But Al, even if they talked in the field, why would they leave Russell in there on his own afterwards?'

'And Ruth saw the trampling happen, remember,' says Ally. 'She yelled for Edwin.'

'If they gave the police an edited version, they're probably going to stick with it, however nicely we ask. But I'd like to see the scene again. Run through some scenarios. Like, if we are going back to the hiding theory, does it even make sense that Russell would pick that spot when he's got an actual phobia of cattle? Shaun's right. It doesn't add up.'

'What if we told the Harpers that Shaun just wants to make sense of why his son was at the vineyard?' says Ally.

'Thing is, Al, there's already tension there. Shaun thinks they treated him badly.'

'Then isn't it an opportunity to make amends?'

'Or dig themselves deeper.'

They look at each other. So many questions, and no obvious answers. Not yet.

'Do you want to come in?' says Ally. 'We can make a plan for what we're going to do next.'

And it still strikes her as extraordinary, that she can assume Jayden's company. That they're truly a team.

'Let's do it,' says Jayden. Then he checks his watch; smacks his forehead. 'Argh, Al, it's got to be first thing in the morning. I'm supposed to be doing dinner. The shop'll be shut, right?'

'The shop'll be shut.'

'Fish and chips it is, then. I'm going to be in the doghouse. I promised the girls spag bol. Look, let's sleep on it. Talk early tomorrow, okay?'

Ally climbs out of the car. She pauses, hand on the handle. 'Jayden, I know one thing. Shaun's trusting us to help him.'

'And we won't let him down, Al.'

8

Gus tramps along the dunes, his torch picking out his path. The tide is on its way in, and he can hear the rolling surf. The Atlantic Ocean has been his bedtime lullaby for nearly two years now, but sometimes the sound of the sea at night-time makes him feel a bit edgy.

Gus can see the lights of The Shell House up ahead. It'll be so nice to be inside with Ally, so nice to have a glass in his hand, so nice to be between four walls that aren't threatening to collapse on his noggin. Maybe that's the source of his unease; the sound of the sea is but a whisper of its true power, and lately Gus has come to believe that his little beach house could very easily become tomorrow's salvage. A collection of split timbers strewn about the shore.

To think there was a time back in the summer when Gus was afraid that All Swell would be sold from beneath him, his rental agreement worth little in the face of an owner wanting to cash in on soaring house prices. Then the delight, the sheer delight, of realising he could just about afford the asking price. The freakishly low asking price. And the reason for that price only becoming apparent when a survey revealed the extent of the work required.

I've got dry rot, he wrote in a letter to Rich and Clive, to which Rich replied, *At our age, haven't we all?*

And it was a fair point. Most days, Gus feels very lucky to exist at all. To say he had a scare over the summer is an understatement. The silver lining – *Silver?! Gold! Platinum!* – is that the experience brought him and Ally closer than ever before.

Gus is not one for counting his chickens, but their quick kiss under the mistletoe last Christmas – a peck, really – could well be more fulsome this year.

But he stops at that thought, certain he's jinxed it.

Gus knocks at the door and Fox barks his welcome. His *sort of* welcome. Ally's little dog is fond enough of Gus, but every so often he catches the animal looking at him with something akin to appraisal. And he finds himself rather flinching under his glare.

'Oh hello,' says Ally, opening the door. Then she holds her hand to her mouth. 'Oh, Gus! I'm so sorry. You're here. Of course you are.'

Typically, Ally doesn't gabble. But perhaps a forgotten dinner invitation will do that to a person.

'I should have called to double-check,' he says. 'I'm sorry. I—'

'No, no.' She opens the door, ushers him in. 'No, we said Thursday dinner. Of course we did. I haven't forgotten . . .' She shakes her head. 'I forgot. I'm so sorry.'

Fox sits on his haunches. Is it Gus's imagination or is he smirking?

It's toasty inside The Shell House. The fire's going, and Ally's lit candles, those chunky white ones that make Gus think of his churchgoing days of yore, back when he was hanging on to his mother's skirts and kept a snail in a jam jar beneath the pews. If Ally had remembered he was coming, Gus would have felt wonderfully welcomed – this warm light, the plumped sofa cushions – but as it is, he knows Ally just lives well. She makes things beautiful with ease.

'Well, I've bought some vino.' He holds it up, still wrapped in its tissue paper – the stuff Wenna only uses for the posh bottles.

'Oh, thank you. But Gus, my cupboards are bare. I meant to go shopping, then Jayden called with a new case, and . . . it turned into quite an afternoon.'

'A new case?' Gus grins. 'Top secret, or something you can talk about?'

'I should think it'll be the talk of Porthpella soon enough. A man was killed by some bullocks up at Shoreline Vines. It was . . . terrible.'

Gus looks at the bottle in his hand. 'Ah . . .' he says. 'Shoreline Vines, you say?'

He thought he'd push the boat out with a drop of local wine. He didn't get much change from a twenty-pound note, and seeing as he's counting his pennies these days, it was a wild extravagance. But he wanted something a bit special, because it's two years today; two years since he signed his name on the divorce papers, his foolish old heart breaking inside his chest, unable to imagine what life would look like beyond that signature. Gus has never been one for turmoil. Yes, he was unhappily married, but it'd been the case for so long he scarcely noticed it any more. He thought he and Mona were on the same page; a mutual assessment of *it could be worse.* Gus was still in Oxford then, and he can remember the stiff walk he took across Port Meadow afterwards, on that grey and airless day. He knew he had to start again for himself, somewhere else. Porthpella was just a dot on a map. He never dreamt he'd feel so at home here. This life-defining stroke of luck.

'Um, perhaps we should save this one for another day then,' he says, setting the bottle on the table. And Gus feels ashamed by his rueful tone. A man has died, at the hands – the hooves – of some cattle. So what if his special purchase is now less than appropriate? 'Ally, what a shock. You didn't see it happen, did you?'

'No, but we arrived not long afterwards. On the trail of a missing quad bike, would you believe . . .'

As Ally fills him in, Gus understands why she forgot about their plans. For all his interest in her story, though, he feels his stomach rumble. Could he host at All Swell? But with his head deep in DIY plans, his own cupboards are bare too. *DIY.* That's too soft a word, suggesting Saturday morning nips and tucks. No, what Gus needs to do is stop the plywood sky from caving in.

Cosy as it is at Ally's, he has an idea.

'Pie and chips at The Wreckers?'

The door creaks, just like in the Western films Gus loved in his youth, and heads turn as he and Ally walk in. By this time of year, Porthpella has emptied. The intrepid October half-term crowd have been and gone, with their wetsuits, dogs and rain macs. Only quiet washes in.

Gus sees Wenna and Gerren at the bar, perched side by side on stools. Porthpella born and bred, they run White Wave Stores – and sold Gus that Shoreline bottle earlier. Wenna throws up a hand in enthusiastic greeting. Gerren, the more lugubrious of the two, lifts his moustache in an approximation of a smile.

'Dear goodness,' says Wenna, 'what a terrible business. That will have given Ruth a dreadful scare, though she won't let on. Heard you were up there, Ally. You and Jayden.'

Word has clearly got around.

'Just by chance,' she says.

Gus watches Ally, thinking she'd probably rather slink away to a table, but she is a detective. And Wenna knows everyone – which makes her useful.

'Do you know the Harpers well?' she asks Wenna.

'What, Ruth and Frank? God rest him. The two sons? I wouldn't say well, but they're faces round here, aren't they? And they've done alright out of that place. I wouldn't sell the wine if I didn't rate it. Not that I can afford to drink it, mind. You enjoyed your bottle did you, Gus?'

'We're saving it,' he says. And then the colour rises in his cheeks at the use of *we*.

'Course, it did give me a shiver,' says Wenna, 'the accident being at Shoreline. Didn't I say that, Gerren? I wouldn't use the word *cursed*, but it knows death, that place.'

Beside her, Gerren's droopy moustache twitches. 'Nothing but a yarn.'

Gus passes Ally a glass of wine – your standard pub wine – and she murmurs her thanks. They both know that with Wenna, you don't need to ask. You just listen.

'The story goes,' says Wenna, 'that a man was murdered on that land, Ally. His throat slit.' Wenna grins and makes a hacking motion with her hand. 'Poor fellow was a sailor. It was a wild winter's night, and his ship went down. He saved himself by washing up on that straggle of beach down by Shoreline. Got himself together and made it up to the farmhouse. Knocked on the door. He was looking for help and what did he get? The opposite.'

'Wenna, when was this?' asks Ally, her eyes wide.

'Oh, a good many moons ago.'

'Which is code for never,' says Gerren.

'Ask anyone round here. It's a story we all grew up with.'

'Fairy story. Ghost story. Because isn't that the other part of it? You have him as a ghost now, this sailor?' Gerren chuckles into his pint.

'As kids we went blackberrying all over, but never up at Shoreline Farm,' says Wenna. 'That's all I'm saying.'

'What's the ghost bit?' asks Gus. Because he's always rather liked tales of hauntings. Ideally with a crackling fire and a glass of port.

'Savagely murdered,' says Wenna again, 'then buried. But his spirit was doomed to walk the land for evermore. When the wind's up over the headland, you can hear his wailing.'

'Don't forget the bit with the tree,' says Gerren.

'Imagine a tall ship. One of the ones you get over Falmouth way. Mast reaching to high heaven. There's a pine tree at Shoreline that's the spit of that. The story goes that it sprouted on the ground where he lay. I like to think it means he found his way back to his ship, in the end.'

'What business does he have going about wailing, then?' says Gerren.

Wenna laughs and elbows her husband, the two meeting in a look that's so full of a life shared that for a moment Gus feels acutely lonely. But then he glances to Ally, and she smiles.

Wenna pushes her glasses up her nose. 'When the Harpers first took on the farm, they got it for a song. And that's why. Mud sticks. And bones never rot.'

'When did they take on the farm, Wenna?' asks Ally.

'Oh four, five generations ago. The land holds on to its history, see. And though they've done a lovely job of the vineyard, I've never felt easy up there. It's a wild spot, isn't it, Ally? That lonely farmhouse. It's bleak as you like. And with only Shaun Tremaine's tumbledown cottage at the end of the track for company. Poor devil. He was a tearaway, was Russell, but I suppose Shaun loved him all the same.'

And Gus notes that it's the first time that the victim's name – the real-life victim, not some old myth – has come into Wenna's story.

Russell Tremaine. Ally told Gus about the old photograph Shaun showed her. The little boy with his blur of blond hair and skinny knees. A t-shirt as yellow as the sun.

For a moment there's silence in the pub; by chance, probably, the scattering of customers just falling into a natural lull. Ally dips her head, and Gus feels an urge to take her hand. It won't have been easy, being with Shaun so soon after.

'I don't want to say that Russell got what was coming to him . . .' begins Wenna.

'No, you don't,' says Gus, a sharp note in his voice. It even takes Gus by surprise.

Wenna raises her eyebrows, and her glasses slide down her nose. For once, she's lost for words.

'Bullocks turning vigilante,' says Gerren cheerfully. 'Now I've heard everything. Come on, Wenn. We were only stopping in for one. And that gogglebox isn't going to watch itself.'

Wenna and her husband say their goodbyes – rather abruptly – and Gus is left with the unpleasant sensation that he spoke out of turn. He catches Ally looking at him. Did he just derail a potentially useful investigative exchange, or simply ruffle their good neighbours' feathers?

'Gus,' she says quietly, 'well said.'

9

'You coming up to bed, Weston?'

Cat's in her dressing gown, her hair damp from the shower. The smile she gives Jayden is a gentle one. He got a bit emotional earlier, talking about Shaun Tremaine. No matter that Russell was in his mid-twenties, Shaun is a dad who's lost his little boy. Cat knew instinctively that Jayden's mind was running to their daughter – and to their tiny baby boy lying curled in Cat's womb.

Back in the West Yorkshire Police, Jayden was no stranger to death. There was the young man whose body they pulled from the freezing River Aire; the elderly lady who looked like she was sleeping on the number 72 bus; the muggings that escalated and the brawls that didn't stop. And Kieran. His best friend and finest partner, stabbed on a summer's night as the two of them patrolled the city centre. Jayden remembers every single one, because how can he not?

Just like he remembers knocking on the doors and making the notification to a victim's family; seeing a person's world fall apart and feeling like he was the one to detonate it.

'In a bit,' he says, with what he hopes is a reassuring smile. Then he looks back to his laptop.

When they first moved to Cornwall, Jayden's grief was a fog so thick that some days he struggled to see through it. But then a few different things happened. Time was probably the biggest factor: even though his grief was complicated, bound up with his job, eventually he felt it start to lift. There was Jasmine, his daughter: the promise of her, the dad he wanted to be for her, and the husband to Cat. And there was Ally: their first case together; a reawakened sense of purpose, and possibility.

Cat would throw in the Porthpella vibes too – getting smashed in the ocean, breathing in that salted air – but Jayden's not so sure. It doesn't make the top three.

'Are you looking up Russell Tremaine?'

'I'm on his Instagram.'

Cat leans against the door frame; crosses her arms. And Jayden knows what she's thinking: why pore over a dead man's social media when he could be going up to bed with his wife?

In Russell's profile picture he's wearing shades and a baseball cap. He's slightly built, like Shaun.

'Last post two weeks ago,' he says.

It's one of those motivational quotes that people stick up from time to time. *Fortune favours the brave.* Which now reads like grim irony. It has three likes, and a comment from someone called Nicky Ballard: Oh that's why I'm outta luck, with a laughing-face emoji.

'I know why you've told Shaun you'll help,' says Cat, 'but . . . it's kind of hard to prove anything, isn't it?'

Jayden makes a non-committal noise. Cat hasn't asked yet whether Shaun will be paying for their services, but Jayden's sure the question's coming. And it's fair enough, because while they're already getting campsite bookings for next summer, those customer deposits aren't exactly jackpots. But the answer is no; they can't charge Shaun. The abandoned quad-bike case? That would have been rate card all the way. But that case is ditched, as far as the Harpers are concerned.

He keeps looking through Russell's grid. The post before that is from way back in August. A selfie. The baseball cap's there, back to front this time, and Russell's big brown eyes stare back at Jayden. He's wearing an Arsenal shirt from four or five seasons ago. Caption: Winning big. To which there's one reply, Nicky Ballard again, with Baller. The post before that is June: Fistral Beach, the blue horizon on a slant.

'Jay? Just don't be too late,' says Cat from the doorway.

'I won't,' he says. Then looks up, sings out, 'Night, babe.'

Maybe Cat's right to say it'll be hard proving anything, but the question is straightforward: why was Russell in that field at Shoreline Vines? And if he did lift a quad bike two nights ago, why return so soon?

Russell's Instagram gives Jayden the feeling he always gets with this kind of work: sad, a bit uncomfortable with this glimpse inside another person's life, but also a sharp focus at the thought that he might just find something. Russell only posted sporadically, but the last was around the same time that he and his dad had a heated conversation about the Harpers. *Fortune favours the brave.* Could it be relevant? Otherwise, all Russell's posts show is that he liked his beer, liked his football, liked the beach. There aren't lots of pictures with friends and family, but Nicky Ballard is a frequent commenter on his posts. The only one, basically.

Jayden clicks through to Nicky Ballard's profile. He's of similar age, wearing motorbike leathers and wraparound shades. His last post is of a group of guys on a night out. Jayden zooms in, recognising Russell among them. They're sitting at a table in a bar, raising beer glasses to the camera – Russell in the middle. It's dated two days ago and posted just before midnight. Caption: Just getting going.

Wherever it was taken, it's not Porthpella.

44

If Russell was on a night out with some mates, is he likely to have headed all the way to Shoreline Vines to steal a quad bike? *Erm, no.* And if Russell's unlikely to have stolen a quad bike two nights ago, he's even *less* likely to have been out recceing the same spot again this morning.

Jayden takes a screengrab of the post, then clicks back to Nicky Ballard's profile. He describes himself as a 'Grease Monkey'. Slang for mechanic? He taps *Nicky Ballard mechanic Cornwall* into Google and Mackay Motor Services in Redruth appears.

Jayden picks up his phone and messages Ally.

Up for a day out tomorrow, Al?

10

Friday morning and it's a wet one. A quiet one too. The rain splatters the windows of Hang Ten as Saffron wipes down the coffee machine just for something to do.

If conditions were different, she'd be hanging her 'Gone Surfing' sign on the door in a flash, but there's a wicked south-westerly and the waves are a mess. Welcome to autumn in Porthpella: one minute it's picture-perfect, the next it's blowing a hoolie. What was it her mum used to say? *If you don't like the weather, wait five minutes.* Or, if you don't like the weather, plan yourself an all-winter-long trip to Hawaii with your hot boyfriend – that's Saffron's current vibe. They haven't booked flights yet, they're holding out for a last-minute deal, but mentally Saffron's already there, with the insanely beautiful poke bowls, gardens full of hibiscus and waves to die for (maybe literally, if they head for the big-wave breaks that Broady's got his eye on).

Her eyes go to a photo on the wall. It was taken in Sri Lanka last winter and shows her and Broady paddling side by side under a bubblegum-blue sky. She cut that trip short to be in Porthpella for Tom Bawcock's Eve, only to find craziness – and all that unfolded because of JP Sharpe – awaiting her. Sometimes Saffron looks back on those sun-kissed South Asian days with an 'ignorance is bliss' feeling; other times, she's utterly grateful for the enlightenment, and the gift that Ally and Jayden gave her.

She didn't have a dad and now she does. Wild.

It's not like she and Wilson went from zero to best buds, but it's nice knowing he's just along the coast in Mousehole. He's her go-to supplier for fish for her cookouts – and for tomorrow's flash dinner up at Shoreline Vines. Meanwhile Saffron has become his go-to supplier for a cappuccino and a box of brownies, should he happen to be passing this way. Which is every couple of weeks, apparently. *He never trucked with frothy coffee before you, Saffron*, his wife, Dawn, said, on one of the occasions she came along too.

The door gusts wide, and because Saffron is thinking about Wilson, she half expects it to be him. She hasn't seen him at Hang Ten for nearly a month now – and, if he has a regular day, it's Friday.

Not that she's counting.

But it's Edwin Harper, brushing the rain from his shoulders.

Anyway, why would her dad trek over to Porthpella today, when he'll be coming up to Shoreline Vines to deliver the fish tomorrow?

'A port in a storm,' says Edwin. 'Didn't know if you'd be open.' He's wearing his standard rig of Barbour jacket and green welling-tons; a smile that falls somewhere between charming and a bit too slick. 'Double espresso. All set for tomorrow?'

Saffron nods. 'Sure. Though I was going to call and ask if it was still happening? I heard about that poor guy.'

'Course it's still happening. I mean . . . tragic stuff. Really bothersome. I don't think any of us slept easy last night. But . . . it's an important weekend for us. The show must go on and all that.'

Saffron nods. 'Okay,' she says. 'Sure.'

'I don't want to say the fate of Shoreline Vines rests on Celine Chevalier enjoying her supper, that would be far too much pressure for anyone, but—'

'Celine Chevalier? That's the investor?'

'Ah,' says Edwin, 'my bad. Celine wants it to be something of a covert mission. Everyone at the dinner will be signing a non-disclosure agreement.'

'Sounds full-on.'

'Not really. It's more about discretion. She doesn't bandy about her portfolio of investments, and we can respect that. Privately, I think she rather likes the idea of the big reveal down the line. Get Shoreline Vines to the place where we all want to be, and then *ta-dah!*' He grins. 'That's the point at which to shout about it.'

Saffron nods. She's flattered that of all the restaurants Edwin could have taken their VIP to, he's chosen her to cater a private dinner instead. *Keeping it local, keeping it real* was the way he put it. After what happened with poor Baz Carson's party back in the summer, Saffron might have walked away from private cheffing altogether, but the Harpers are offering good money. Money that's going straight into the Hawaii fund. Plus, Saffron likes the thought of supporting another local business.

'I'll be up at the vineyard to prep around midday, if that's okay?' she says.

Scallop salad. Bouillabaisse. Tarte Tatin. A Cornish-Franco menu, for the benefit of the guest of honour, and each course matched with a Shoreline Vines wine.

'The kitchen will be all yours. Karensa will be only too happy to run a mile from the stove, though we might have more trouble getting rid of my mother. I'll do my best to keep her out of your way.'

That smile again. Saffron passes him his espresso and he knocks it back in one.

'Any change in numbers?'

'Twelve. The Morgans dropped out this morning. Flu, apparently. No big loss, he's a bit of a bore. Did you sort your staff?'

'Yep, all good,' says Saffron. And for some reason she doesn't tell him that it's Broady she's pulled in as her waiter for the evening. 'A former silver-service waiter, actually.'

For one summer in college, weddings mostly, until he was sacked for running off with a bridesmaid when he should have been doling out the crème caramels.

'Colour me impressed,' says Edwin. 'I'll see you tomorrow. If anyone can charm our VIP, I reckon it's you.'

Despite herself, she glows a little. 'And I'm sorry about what happened. That poor guy.'

'I sounded glib before, I know. I've pushed it to the back of my mind. It's the only way. We can't afford for anything to go wrong this weekend. Anything *else*.'

'I get it.'

'It's all for Mum and Dad, really. Everything we're doing with the vineyard. Dad's legacy. And giving Mum something to hold on to.'

Edwin looks down, pushes his hair from his eyes.

'You're doing them both proud,' says Saffron.

Wilson spoke highly of Frank Harper, when she told him about the gig. Apparently, Frank's family farmed the same land for generations, then a couple of decades ago they planted vines and tried their hand at winemaking. Shoreline Vines has been hailed as one of Cornwall's pioneer vineyards.

'Proud? You think so?' Edwin looks at her intently, eyes glittering. 'Either way, it's nice of you to say. Saffron, I'm looking forward to tomorrow. Even more than I was before now. I've a good feeling about our VIP.' He grins, and it feels more sincere this time. 'And a good feeling about your bouillabaisse too.'

11

Fox has never been one to turn down a trip to Hang Ten, not least because Saffron keeps a jar of dog treats on the counter. As soon as they turn left out of The Shell House, he knows. His tail waves in the air as he trots over the dunes.

The beach is windblown this morning, strewn with debris, heaps of seaweed and lengths of bone-white driftwood. Ally wants to go slow, pick over these ocean treasures – always with a thought to her studio pieces – but Jayden's waiting for her. And a young man called Nicky Ballard, although he doesn't know it yet, is also waiting. So instead, she walks quickly along the strandline, the tide fizzing at her heels. Sea foam settles on the sand like snow.

'Morning, Al,' says Jayden, rounding the corner to the café at the same time. 'Ready for a road trip?'

Before Ally can answer, a man comes barrelling out of Hang Ten with his head down.

Edwin Harper.

Jayden steps to one side, flashing a look at Ally.

'Excuse me,' says Edwin. Then, as recognition dawns, 'Oh, the sleuths. We've got to stop meeting like this.'

'How are things up there this morning?' Jayden asks.

'Keep on keeping on. That's what Mum says. We'll look in on Shaun later, of course, but the man wants his space. Doesn't want to be bothered by every man and his dog, does he?'

Edwin's eyes go to Fox at that point. He holds out a hand to Jayden, tips an imaginary hat to Ally. 'Got to get on.'

She notices Edwin's knuckles then, the grazing across his fist. And in the same beat, Edwin registers her attention.

'Ah,' he says, 'there's an embarrassing story there. You'd think I'd be used to gore. We were a farm before we were a vineyard.'

'What happened?' says Jayden.

'Took out my shock on a five-bar gate, didn't I? I don't recommend it, by the way. If you want to hit something, use a punching bag. Nothing broken though.' Edwin flexes his fingers; makes as if he's lifting a glass to his lips. 'And this still works. That's the main thing, isn't it? Cheers, guys. See you around.'

Inside Hang Ten, Saffron makes their coffees to go. She explains about her gig tomorrow and how, despite the sad news about the man who died, it's full steam ahead.

'I feel kind of weird about it, but Edwin said the show's got to go on.'

'I didn't know you were cheffing the dinner,' says Jayden with a grin. 'My in-laws are going. Be sure to give Cliff a small portion, yeah?'

'Noted.'

'Another private gig though? I thought you said you didn't want to do any more like that after Rockpool.'

'I know, but I love that we make wine in Cornwall. That's cool,' says Saffron. 'Plus . . . it pays well. I think the idea is that different parts of the community are represented, so it's about the Harpers showing their investor that they'll be putting faith in a whole area, not just one business. Jayden, Edwin said what you guys have done with Top Field Camping reminds him of his mum and dad and the vineyard all those years back. Diversifying, you know?'

She puts the lids on their coffees, then bags their brownies and throws in an extra cookie. Her eyes sparkle as she says, 'Are you two on a case?'

'What, Ally and I can't have a friendly Friday morning coffee together?'

'To *go*, though,' says Saffron. 'You guys are on the move.'

'We were up at the vineyard yesterday,' says Ally. 'The Harpers had a quad bike stolen three nights ago.'

'And you're investigating?'

Jayden shrugs. 'Not the most exciting but . . . got to pay the bills, right?'

'I hear you,' says Saffron. She narrows her eyes theatrically, looking from one to the other. 'I'm just not sure I believe you.'

Mackay Motor Services is on a light industrial estate on the out-skirts of Redruth, and on this wet Friday morning the grey units have a desolate look. Ally and Jayden peer through the windscreen, the wipers squeaking back and forth.

'Nicky Ballard must know about Russell's death by now,' says Ally.

'Not sure. There's nothing on his social media anyway.'

'So, we'll be gentle.'

'Always, right?'

As they climb out of the car and walk towards the garage, somewhere on the estate an alarm goes off. The blaring sound – no less piercing for its distance – follows them as they enter the garage forecourt. There's a sharp smell of engine oil and rubber tyres. A couple of Fords are parked skew-whiff, bumpers all but touching.

Jayden nudges Ally. 'That's Nicky.'

A young man in blue overalls comes out, wiping his hands on a cloth. He's thin as string, with chin-length straw-blond hair tucked in a bandana. He spots them and saunters over.

'Help you?'

'Hope so,' says Jayden. 'We're private detectives.'

Ally feels a flare go off inside of her. She'll never tire of how it sounds.

'You're here about Russ,' says Nicky. He looks from one to the other. 'Aren't you?'

'Yes, we are,' says Ally. 'And we're sorry for your loss.'

'Cheers.' He stuffs the cloth in the pocket of his overalls. 'Private detectives . . . what's that about?'

'Russell's dad can't understand what he was doing in that field,' says Jayden. 'We're trying to figure it out.'

Nicky chews at his thumbnail. Turns his head and spits.

'So you're working for Shaun, are you?'

'Do you know him?' asks Jayden.

'Not really.'

'How did you and Russell meet?'

'Just down the pub, two or three years back. In Camborne. He was . . .' Nicky drops his head. 'Yeah, he was a good guy. A mate.'

'What was he like?' asks Ally.

'Funny. Told a good joke.'

'His dad said he'd had a few problems. That he didn't always find life easy.'

Nicky shrugs. 'He had his hard times. Standard stuff for a lot of people round here though, isn't it? Not enough money. Not enough prospects. Forget getting your foot anywhere near the property ladder.'

'So, there wasn't anything specific?'

He gives a brief shake of his head. 'We didn't get into all that.'

'When did you last see Russell?' asks Jayden.

And Ally notes how he doesn't mention his social media research. But Nicky answers without hesitation.

'Tuesday. We were out.'

'Where did you go?'

'Newquay.'

'Not much happening there on a Tuesday night, is there?'

'If you know where to look.' Nicky grins, and his face temporarily lights up. 'Russ wanted a few beers and one thing led to another. He was amped.'

'Was he often like that?' asks Ally.

'What, a party animal?' Nicky gives a quick laugh. 'Not always. But he was buzzing. Said he had some money coming in and was planning a big holiday. Thailand or somewhere like that. It was his chat-up line. He'd invited half the girls in Newquay by the end of the night.'

Ally can't help thinking of the quad bike, even if the timing of Russell's night out makes the theft look unlikely. A top-of-the-range quad bike – even second-hand, even without paperwork – would pay for a very nice holiday.

'And was Russell often like that?' says Jayden. 'I've got mates who are all about the big talk. Anything to impress.'

'Yeah, not Russ. He was straightforward, you know? But . . . that night he was excited. I liked seeing him like that. It was a laugh.'

'What was his job?' asks Ally.

'The latest was call-centre stuff, but then he lost that. He didn't always stick at things.'

'Where do you think he was getting the money for a Thailand trip?' asks Jayden.

Nicky narrows his eyes, perhaps appraising their intentions. 'He liked a flutter. I figured he must have been counting on winning big.'

'But he didn't say that?'

'No.' He hesitates. 'But Russ said he had something big in the pipeline, so I thought . . . it's got to be a hot tip.' He looks up. 'That's something, isn't it? At least Russ went out on a high.'

Ally nods. 'You're right.' Then, 'Was that the phrase he used? "Something big in the pipeline"?'

'That's it.'

'Nicky, what time did you and Russell call it a night on Tuesday?' asks Jayden.

'Gone midnight.'

'And how did you get back to Camborne?'

'Erm . . . I drove us. It was Russ who was on one. I stopped at a couple of pints.'

And from the look on his face, Ally suspects that's not quite true.

'You dropped him home?'

'Yeah. Probably around one o'clock. He was all over the place. I saw he got into his flat though.' Nicky sniffs; wipes his nose on his sleeve. 'Didn't think it would be the last time I'd see him.'

And his upset is genuine. Ally glances to Jayden but he's looking past Nicky to the rear of the garage. She follows his eyes. She can't see what Jayden's noticed. Then, suddenly, she can. Behind a pale blue Transporter, there's a bright red quad bike.

'And do you think Russell could have left his flat again that night?' she asks carefully.

'I can't see it. With Russ, he'd have a few, get a bit lairy, then fall asleep. That was him.' Nicky shakes his head. 'Why are you asking, anyway? What's this got to do with Russell and a herd of bullocks?'

12

'Okay, close but no cigar,' says Jayden, once they're back in the car.

'I really thought it was the Harpers' Honda.'

'And not a Yamaha in for servicing. Yeah, me too. I don't think Nicky knows anything about a stolen quad.'

'Or he's a good liar?'

'Or . . . he's a good liar. If Nicky was sober enough to drive from Newquay that night, I guess he could have been the one to go on to Shoreline Vines. Nicked it and sold it on fast. Then two days later, Russell goes back to see what else there is lying about. Sure, it's possible. But . . . I'm not feeling it.'

'Do you think Mullins would run Nicky Ballard's name through the system for us?'

'See if he's got any convictions?' Jayden drums his hands on the wheel. 'If we want to pull a favour from Mullins, I feel like I want to hold out for something bigger, you know?'

'Agreed. Alright, what do you make of Russell being a gambler?'

'It's a detail worth noting. If this was a murder case, the police would be looking at financial records.'

'But they won't be, because . . . it's not?'

'Exactly. Not *yet*.' Jayden looks to Ally, wondering if she's feeling it too. 'Al, this chat with Nicky changes things, right? He was down on his luck, but suddenly he's talking about having something in the pipeline. Coming into some proper money. I think Nicky was telling the truth when he said that Russell wasn't into big talk.'

'I think so too. Nicky was thoughtful, the way he talked about Russell.'

'So, there's Russell, going on about Thailand, asking girls along with him. Then two days later he's dead. Is there a connection? That's the question.'

'Nicky seemed fairly certain that any money would be coming from Russell's gambling.'

'Yeah, it's one explanation. But Russell's gambling wasn't anything new, was it? And like Nicky said, Russell didn't always go around talking like this. What if he didn't nick the quad bike himself but he was feeding information? Taking a cut. Getting a fee.'

'Would that constitute a big payout?'

'Could be a large-scale operation, Al.' But even as Jayden says it, it doesn't sound like bragging rights. 'Russell's last Instagram post was from two weeks ago. It was a quote, "Fortune favours the brave." I scrolled back through his posts, and motivational quotes weren't his usual style.'

'But gambling was, remember.'

'Yeah, and maybe that's a bumper sticker for a gambler but . . . the timing of it feels relevant. Two weeks ago, Russell and his dad argued about the Harpers' treatment of him, then Russell proclaimed online that fortune favours the brave. Maybe it was a message to his dad to stand up for himself. Though I can't see Shaun on Instagram.'

'It's these points put together, isn't it?' says Ally. 'Shaun's conviction that Russell had no business being in that field. Nicky saying his friend was coming into money. Russell's Instagram post. Three things out of the ordinary.'

'Exactly. Anomalies,' says Jayden. 'That's where we've got to focus. And we need to ask Shaun about this upcoming windfall of Russell's too.'

They're pelting along the A30, the traffic quiet on this November morning. Up ahead, a tractor pulling a hefty trailer looms and Jayden slows. As the road twists and turns, there's no overtaking.

A sudden flash of memory: Jayden and Kieran, tearing up Crown Point Road by night, crossing the river with its reflected light. Sirens wailing. Kieran had been laughing about something when the call came in. What was it? The recollection, at first so clear, starts to blur. Just the fast tyres on the wet road; the glitter of the city around them. And now a tractor and its trailer – and rain-smeared open country running all the way to Shoreline Vines and then on to his place, where the campsite's emptied for winter and Cliff's fields are full of sprouts and kale and winter cabbage. Is it bad that it cracks Jayden up that Jazzy won't eat her greens?

'You know who else has come into some money?' says Ally. 'Or hopes to, anyway. The Harpers. Do we add that to the anomalies?'

Jayden nods slowly. 'Yeah, we do. Their visiting investor.'

'The same investor who just happens to be dining with your in-laws tomorrow night.'

As the road opens, Jayden sees his opportunity. He puts his foot down, leaving the tractor in the rear-view mirror.

Ally shifts in her seat. 'This case, it's really on, isn't it?'

'Oh yeah. It's on, Al.'

'Then when we get back to The Shell House, there's something I want to show you.'

◆ ◆ ◆

At the end of the hallway, Ally stands outside a closed door. One Jayden's always presumed is just a cupboard.

'Bill's office,' she says quietly. She opens the door and turns on the light.

It's a small room, the square window looking out on to the fronds of the back-garden palm tree. The far wall has a whiteboard on it, its surface faintly streaked with old markings. On the bookcase Jayden recognises the spines of the Blackstone's police manuals; a row of Colin Dexters and Ruth Rendells. The old leather chair has a dip in the seat, as if it's still bearing the weight of the person who used to sit in it.

At the desk, an Anglepoise lamp is tilted low. A pair of tortoiseshell glasses sits neatly beside a jotter. There's a framed photograph in pride of place, showing Ally, Bill and Evie, clustered together on the Shell House veranda. It must have been taken twenty years ago. Evie's a teenager, wearing denim shorts and earrings that catch the sun, one arm draped lazily around her dad's shoulders. Ally stands just to the side, smiling at father and daughter. They all look so happy.

Jayden thinks of his own little three-person family, the fourth on the way. He feels a lump in his throat.

'I love that picture,' says Ally, simply.

'It's a great one, Al.'

'It took me a long time to come back in here. It's where he died, you see.'

And another piece of the jigsaw slots into place. Ally has never talked about the day Bill died.

'I couldn't get past it. But then . . . I told myself I was being silly. I bring my coffee here sometimes. Just to sit. I never stay very long.'

'Because of the memories,' says Jayden.

Ally gives a low laugh. 'Because the light in here's poor, even without that palm blocking the window. And you can't see the sea. It's no good at all, really.'

'I hear you.'

'But . . . that whiteboard. There are pens somewhere too. Could it be useful?'

'Very useful.'

An incident room; the space to put the whole case up on the wall. The big wooden Shell House table has always served them well, but Jayden has never felt like they could print out pictures of suspects and stick them up next to Ally's abstract paintings and beach finds. Even though, if he suggested it, she'd probably be game.

'Bill did a lot of good thinking in this room,' she says. 'Near enough forty years of being in the force. I like to think . . . something remains. If that's not silly. Besides, I think he'd like the idea of us using it. I mean . . . once he made his peace with the fact his wife had turned into a sort of detective.'

'Hey, less of the "sort of". How did the press describe us after the Rockpool case? "Super sleuths", wasn't it?'

She smiles back at him. Jayden doesn't need to ask, *why now?* He knows that, finally, Ally believes in herself as a detective. And this case – thanks to Nicky Ballard and his talk of cash and pipelines – has just ratcheted up.

Jayden rubs his hands together. 'Right, Al, let's do this. Let's get what we know out of our heads, and up on that board.'

13

Mullins pulls his duvet up around his ears. Calling in sick isn't exactly well received at the station, but it would have gone down a lot worse if DS Skinner had been in. As it is, Skinner's on a sun lounger in Gran Canaria while Mullins is on his sick bed on Ocean Drive.

There's a tap at his door.

'Come in,' he croaks. And he's laying it on a bit thick, if he's honest.

'Here you are, Tim, love.'

His mum passes him his hot blackcurrant, in the Garfield mug he's had since he was a kid. He wraps his digits round it, says, 'Cheers, Mum.'

It's been just the two of them since Mullins was eight years old. For a chunk of time, they were sort of distant. His mum lived her life, he lived his, they just happened to use the same front door, sit on the same sofa, watch the same telly. But after what happened out on the cliffs by Rockpool House back in the summer – that night that was frightening in so many ways – something changed. Maybe Mullins let her in a bit more; maybe his mum found more to give.

'You've been running around too much, that's the trouble. You'll burn out, love.'

Burn out. That's a new one. She'll have got it from one of her chat mags. *Ten ways to avoid burnout!* Not that Mullins has been reading them on the loo or anything.

'It was cold up at the vineyard,' he says. 'That didn't help, standing round in the mud up there. All those cows.'

'Never liked cows.'

'Me neither.'

'Poor lad. Nasty sight, was it?'

'Not the best.' A beat. 'Mum, do you know the Tremaines?'

She shakes her head. Her face is as round as an apple, and her hair is carefully set with spray. She looks old-fashioned, his mum. Always has, always will. It makes his throat burn, sometimes. He takes a quick sip of blackcurrant.

'Only bits and bobs,' she says. 'Shaun kept himself to himself. The boy, Russell – well, he'd be a man now, touch older than you I'd say – bit of a tearaway, by all accounts.'

'Never popped up on our radar.'

'Well, that's something.'

'What about the Harpers?'

'The likes of them wouldn't mix with the likes of us, love.'

'They're alright actually,' says Mullins. 'Not as posh as I thought.'

And maybe he's quick to their defence but Mullins doesn't love the *us*. Because in his uniform, he feels pretty upwardly mobile, thanks very much. The law is a leveller; you've got to abide by it, no matter who you are. Sort of. Sometimes. Or it should be like that, anyway.

'Well, Frank Harper was alright. Drank in The Wreckers.'

'One of his sons does too. Edwin. I've seen him in there often enough.'

'You shouldn't spend so much time there, Tim. It doesn't do your waistline any good. Nor your liver.'

Mullins bites his tongue, because his mum polishes off custard creams by the bucketload and she's on the Baileys even when it isn't Christmas. *Pot. Kettle.*

'You know the stories, don't you?' she says, lowering her voice.

And for all that his throat is sore, he wants to laugh at her whisper. Who's going to be listening in at Ocean Drive?

'Bones. Ghosts. All manner of treachery. You can pretty it up with grapevines and whatnot, but the fact remains. It was never a good place.'

And she tells him the story of a shipwrecked sailor. A brutal murder. A wandering spirit and long-buried bones. The kind of yarn the old-timers spin down The Wreckers, when they're three sheets to the wind and holding court.

'Ask me if I'm surprised that the cattle sensed it? Lost their minds and ran riot? Animal instinct, that is, Tim. I'm sorry but it is.'

'Mum,' groans Mullins, 'it was Halloween last week. Pull the other one.'

'I wish I could.'

Which makes no sense. But, in the grand scheme of things making sense or not, Mullins lets it go. And takes another slug of blackcurrant.

14

As Karensa Harper reaches the tall pine, she's breathing hard. She rests a hand against the trunk, and for a split second struggles to get control. As a child she had occasional flare-ups of asthma – puffing into brown paper bags at the sides of sports fields, heart scrambling in her chest – and every so often her airways remind her of this. Karensa didn't see Ruth have her panic attack yesterday, but Edwin told her about it later. *It was over by the time I got there. You know Mum, stiff upper lip. But she was shaken, alright.*

Karensa can't imagine Ruth as vulnerable. Since the day she met her, nine years ago, Ruth has been nothing but rock hard. Like an imposing piece of polished Cornish granite – aesthetically pleasing, but you'd have broken knuckles if you ever tried to go up against it. Not that she's ever tried.

Not deliberately.

Broken knuckles. Her husband showed his true colours yesterday, when he punched that gate. Later he tried to say it was the shock talking, but Karensa knows better; he looked down at that dead man and thought only of the impact on the investment. Because what VIP visitor wants a dead body in the mix? Edwin lashed out in selfish frustration. She almost wishes he'd hurt himself more.

She didn't always feel like this.

When Edwin first brought her home to Shoreline Vines, Karensa couldn't believe it. The vineyard glowed in the early autumn sunshine, vines running all the way down to the sea. He opened a bottle on the terrace, and it tasted better than any wine she'd had before, because it was presented to her like a gift – and a promise. *All this could be yours too.* Karensa's never been greedy, but growing up a bookie's daughter she knew the importance of backing the right horse. And Edwin seemed like the right horse.

Her phone pings, and Karensa knows it'll be him.

You OK? xx

If Ruth knew what was going on under her roof, Karensa would feel the full force of that granite coming down on her. Mothers shouldn't have favourites, but Edwin is so much the golden boy that Karensa sometimes thinks something must have happened with Owen; something that nobody talks about, not even him. Karensa's mind floats all over the place – it always has, a stray balloon, lifting on the slightest breeze – and sometimes she pictures childhood incidents. An unforgivable act. But what?

Or perhaps there is a kind of fairness to it, after all. When Frank was alive, anyone could see that he and Owen were two peas in a pod. A daddy's boy and a mummy's boy, only now Daddy is gone.

Karensa's fingers hover over her phone. She can't think what to reply. Is she okay? No, she's not. Not at all.

After Frank died, Owen did his duty by his mother and by the harvest, then left for the vineyards of Provence. Ostensibly to learn some new tricks, but perhaps he needed to take his grief away with him and lay it to rest. Whatever Owen did in France, he was different when he came back, as if an ocean of calm ran through him. In his absence, Edwin had started, and abandoned, the holiday cottage venture – with the full support of Ruth, of course. If Frank had made a mess of the finances, Edwin only made it worse. But this new version of Owen found it in him to shake his brother's hand and say, *Nice try, Ed.*

Not really, she types. Are you?

The unwed older brother. An outlaw, living in a silver-bullet trailer in a dell beyond the farmhouse, who some days didn't have two words to rub together, and on others told fireside stories like no one else. When Owen left, Karensa realised how much she missed him. And when Owen came back, she realised that she'd fallen out of love with her husband – and was in love with his brother.

The trouble is, Karensa had no one to talk her out of it. She was a lonely child and an introverted woman, happy with her head in the clouds, her feet on the coast path, her nose in a poetry book. Life at Shoreline suits her. It is now just so terribly complicated.

Before she thinks better of it, Karensa taps out another message:

I think we need to talk about what happened.

Then another:

He saw us together.

The three dots, indicating that Owen is typing, disappear. Karensa waits; wills their return.

She sinks down on to the ground. It's damp, and she can feel it seeping into her jeans. She tilts her head back and looks up at the endless branches, the splintering light.

It started a little over a year ago. Edwin was away on a stag weekend, and one evening after Ruth had gone to bed, Owen told her the ghost story – this very tree the mast of a lost sailor's ship; his bones beneath the farm – and although she'd heard it all before,

Karensa shivered. *I won't be able to get to sleep tonight now*, she said, looking at him from beneath her lashes. A moment that, looking back, was uncharacteristically bold. So maybe she's got an age-old murder to thank for what's between them.

An age-old murder to blame for this fine mess.

Her phone pings.

Who saw us?

Her hand trembles as she replies.

Russell. The morning he died.

She'd been leaning into Owen's embrace – lips stinging from his kisses – when she saw Russell watching them from the track. At the time, she didn't say anything to Owen, afraid that it might only stir up drama.

Another ping.

So it doesn't matter now, does it?

Three dots. Another ping.

Don't worry about it, K. Don't worry about anything.

Suddenly the image of Russell's trampled face comes into her head. Only it's intensified, just as it appeared in her dreams last night: a ghoulish mess, blood running free. The image is so sharp it punches the breath from her. Karensa tries hard to fix on the horizon: the band of grey sea; the hulk of a tanker way out west. Above her there's a swirl of birdlife as crows and gulls scrap for supremacy. A street fight in the skies.

In her dream last night, Russell's features slowly re-formed. From his muddy resting place, he spoke the words quite clearly: *I know you're glad I'm dead, Karensa.*

Karensa stands up, not wanting to be here any more. It's making everything worse. A light rain is falling, and she knows she'll be soaked by the time she's back at the farmhouse. The wind's coming in off the sea, hurling over the empty vines. When she licks her lips, she can taste salt.

Her eye is caught by a Land Rover slowly making its way up the track. Not exactly an unusual vehicle in these parts, but it looks an awful lot like the same Land Rover the private detectives turned up in yesterday. Didn't Owen call them off the quad bike hunt?

Karensa avoided them yesterday, and she'll avoid them again today. Just the thought of their scrutiny makes her breath stutter. The unease that's been rippling through her since yesterday threatens to burst its banks.

I know you're glad I'm dead, Karensa.

She deletes her exchange with Owen, message by message.

How she wishes that Russell hadn't seen them together. It feels wrong to exult in the fact that their secret is safe, but is Karensa relieved? Yes. She is. And she knows just how cruel, how callous, that makes her.

15

It's coming up on lunchtime as Ally and Jayden arrive at Shoreline Vines.

Earlier, they spent an hour in Bill's office, setting down everything they know about the case. It didn't feel nearly as strange as Ally had feared. And now they have a timeline of events, written up on the board in marker pen. It's a list of anomalies – and the names of everyone connected to the case.

It felt like progress, seeing it all laid out.

Shoreline Vines is quiet, the yard empty except for a silver four-by-four. A tabby cat sits on the windowsill, eying them with suspicion; it drops to the ground and slinks behind the vehicle's wheels. Ally looks to the large sheds. She doesn't know very much about winemaking, but she presumes that's where it all happens.

'Let's take a quick look before we knock.' Jayden points to the end of the yard, the five-bar gate. 'The tape's gone.'

It's as if Russell's death never happened.

'Okay, imagine I'm Russell,' says Jayden in a low voice, 'and I'm checking out the sheds. Seeing if there's anything else worth stealing. I hear a noise, and . . . I need to get out of here. Why don't I just run down the track? Back towards my dad's house?'

Ally turns, taking in the layout of the house, the yard, the outbuildings. The exits and entrances. The field where Russell was found is at the far end of the yard, to the right of the farmhouse. There's a thick hedge, the side wall of a barn, and the gate. She imagines Russell running, clambering. Then what? Perhaps the cattle were curious, moving as a herd towards him. He panicked; they startled in turn. It wouldn't take much to cause a stampede.

'That field's not going to be my first choice, even with the bullock factor. It's taking me deeper into Shoreline land,' says Jayden.

'Unless Russell didn't know that.'

Jayden points back to the driveway, where there's a simple wooden fence marking the edge of the vines. The same vines that run all the way back down the hill, towards the lane.

'Al, look – why didn't he head into the vines? It's a more obvious exit point if he's coming from any of these outbuildings, just because it's closer.'

'There's no cover in the vines, is there? Not at this time of year. Maybe the field, with its high hedges, seemed the better option.'

'Let's go and take a look.'

Jayden glances at the stern face of the farmhouse, then walks over to the five-bar gate. Ally follows. As they draw closer, they see that the field's empty of livestock, the cattle moved elsewhere.

'Strange, isn't it?'

They both turn at the sound of the man's voice. It's deep, level, and not unfriendly.

Owen.

His knitted beanie is riding high on his head, as if he can't make up his mind about whether to have it on or not. He wears an old surf hoodie with rain-soaked shoulders, and a slightly guarded look.

'As if nothing happened,' says Ally. Then, 'Sorry, we were just about to knock.'

'How can I help you guys? You're not still bothering about the quad, are you?'

'No, no,' says Jayden. 'You told us to call that one off.'

'Yeah, sorry for that. I didn't mention it with everything yesterday, but we've got a VIP guest coming this weekend. Apart from anything else, we don't want to advertise the fact that there are thieves roaming the countryside. It bursts the bubble of the perfect rural idyll, you know?' Owen rolls his eyes as he says it. 'Or makes us look like we can't look after our own gear, more like.'

He shifts on his feet; his black wellingtons gleam like stones in a rockpool.

'That's my brother's thinking, anyway.'

'No worries,' says Jayden. 'It's your call. And we know about the VIP. My in-laws are invited to the dinner.'

'Oh, really? Cool. So . . . how can I help you guys then?'

Ally and Jayden share a look. They agreed in the car to be up front with the Harpers.

'We've been talking to Shaun,' says Ally.

'I don't know what to say to the poor guy.'

'He can't get his head around why Russell was up here,' says Jayden.

Owen nods. 'I can understand that.'

'So, you don't think Russell stole the quad and was back looking for more?'

'No, I reckon that's still likely. What I mean is . . . I get why he doesn't want to think badly of his son.'

'Shaun wondered if the real reason for Russell being here was that he was asking about a job,' says Ally. 'On account of the rumour that the vineyard was coming into money.'

'Russell wanted work?'

'No, but maybe Russell thought his dad was owed his job back.'

Owen lifts his beanie, scratches the back of his head. 'A rumour, huh? Word carries fast. And my brother . . . yeah, he likes to talk. The investment's not one hundred per cent in the bag though.' He

71

looks thoughtful suddenly. 'What, and Shaun thinks Russell came up here to ask about his dad's job? No. I can't see that. Shaun knows the door's open – he can always talk to us. He was a good mate to my dad, and mostly a good worker too. Letting him go was the last thing we wanted. But . . . that was nearly two years ago. And Shaun understood.'

'So, there is a job now if Shaun wants it?' asks Jayden.

Owen looks towards the farmhouse. 'We do want to offer him something, as it goes.'

'Because of what happened with Russell?' says Ally.

It comes out more biting than she intends, but Owen's unbothered.

'Situation like this, we're all asking ourselves what we can do,' he says with a shrug. 'If the distraction – and the pay cheque – help Shaun, then that's got to be good, hasn't it? Besides, if this weekend goes to plan, we'll be able to afford it. We'll be making more hires across the board.'

Jayden nods. 'Owen, you weren't here when Russell was found, were you?'

'I was in my trailer.' Owen points across the fields. 'I've got a silver bullet. Bought it as a wreck and did it up.' He grins. 'Not exactly lord of the manor, but it suits me. So yeah, I wasn't around. I've been thinking about that . . . If I'd been in the yard, I might have been able to stop it. By the time Mum and Edwin got there, it was too late.'

'And there's no way your mum and brother might have spoken to Russell before it happened?' asks Jayden.

'They would have said.' He narrows his eyes. 'Look, if you want convincing, come and ask them yourselves.'

And without saying another word, Owen turns and walks up to the farmhouse.

The Shoreline Vines kitchen is a warm embrace. An Aga throws its heat, and the smell of something good fills the air. There's an old wooden table with mismatched chairs. An elaborate patchwork quilt hangs on one wall, showing green hills, blue sea, and the grey stone farmhouse. It's like a fabric version of one of Ally's collages.

'A good hot lunch,' says Ruth. 'Frank always insisted on it, and old habits die hard.'

'Dad didn't insist, Mum,' says Owen. 'He'd just have sooner had bread and cheese.'

Ruth gives a bark of laughter. 'Whatever you say, Owen.'

'You could set your watch by our dad,' says Edwin. 'Same rhythms every day.'

'And this place ran like clockwork because of it,' says Owen.

And is it Ally, or is there something a little pointed in the way he says it?

'Yeah, that's what we all thought,' says Edwin, unfazed. 'Good with his hands, bad with his numbers, that was Frank.'

'Talking of hands,' says Ally. 'How's yours?'

'Oh, come on, don't rub it in,' Edwin laughs. 'Owen thinks I'm enough of a prat as it is. But thank you for your concern,' and he gives a thumbs up.

'The quilt,' says Ruth, cutting in. 'I can see you looking at it, Ally. I keep meaning to take it down, but the boys won't let me.'

'Owen and Karensa won't let you,' says Edwin.

'It's a beautiful piece of needlework,' says Ally.

'Frank's mother stitched it back when Shoreline Vines was just Shoreline Farm. Owen's sentimental like his father was, and Karensa—'

'Karensa likes pretty things,' finishes Edwin. 'Anyway, you didn't come here to talk about quilting, I presume. I've got to confess, I looked the pair of you up. You got quite a lot of press coverage after the Baz Carson case. Porthpella's rock-star private eyes.' He laughs as he says it. 'Owen had a nerve, hiring you for a paltry missing quad bike after all that glamour. And now you're giving poor old Tremaine the time of day.'

Owen has already told his mum and brother why Ally and Jayden are here, and they were promptly invited in. A warmer welcome than Ally had anticipated, but their only other experience of the Harpers was in the aftermath of Russell's death. No one can be judged in those shock-filled moments; not solely.

'You're more than welcome to stay for lunch,' says Ruth.

And Ally can see Jayden eying the stove. For all his slender frame, the man eats like a horse.

'You sure?' he says, mouth crinkling with a smile. 'We don't want to disturb.'

'There's heaps. And you were so good to me yesterday, when I had my ridiculous little turn. Please stay.'

Ruth whisks a couple of extra plates from the dresser, reaches for a ladle.

'Shall we open a bottle, then?' says Edwin. 'If you're trying to get the measure of us, *in vito veritas* and all that.'

Just then, a woman walks into the room. She stops dead as she sees them, and it strikes Ally that if she could have turned round and gone straight back out, she would have.

'Karensa, where have you been hiding?' Ruth says brightly. 'Could you fetch some glasses, darling? We're introducing our guests to the Sauvignon.'

'I'll get them,' says Owen, getting up. And while Ally sees the look that Owen gives Karensa, try as she might, she can't decipher it.

'My wife pulled the short straw and is on cleaning duty this afternoon,' says Edwin. 'Our dusty farmhouse needs to sparkle like it's got a galaxy of Michelin stars.'

'For your investor,' says Jayden.

'That's it,' says Edwin.

'My in-laws are looking forward to it.'

'Good to hear. Cliff and Sue Thomas. Nice example of pastures new, from struggling arable to thriving glamping.'

'Don't let that be your introduction,' laughs Jayden. 'Cliff's veg is thriving just fine.'

'Perhaps we should have invited you and your wife,' says Ruth. 'I hear you're the masterminds behind the glamping.'

'Not sure *mastermind* is the word,' says Jayden, 'and it's definitely more camping than glamping.'

'The idea,' says Edwin, 'is that we show our investor just what an innovative community we are down here. Easy to turn your nose up, think all we do in Cornwall is cider and pasties.'

'While it's wine and pasties.' Owen grins. 'Different kettle of fish entirely.'

As the conversation runs on, Ally watches Karensa as she slides into a chair. Everything about the woman's posture suggests she doesn't want to be here. She wears a baggy knitted jumper, her hands lost inside the cuffs like an awkward teenager. As Owen pours the wine, Karensa drinks it fast.

'See what you make of this,' he says. 'It won a medal at the Cornwall Food Awards, three years ago. Dad's last vintage.'

'I thought we were saving that for tomorrow,' says Ruth.

'I'd like Ally and Jayden to taste the best.'

'Just a drop for me, mate,' says Jayden, putting his hand over the glass.

'Tomorrow's all about the future, not the past, Mum,' says Edwin. He winks at Ally. 'As you can see, there's still some fighting to be done over the wine list.'

'Talking of fighting,' says Jayden. 'Was there any with Russell?'

'With Russell?' Ruth gives a shrill laugh. 'That can't be a serious question.'

'Shaun would give anything to know the truth,' says Ally, as Jayden coolly sips his wine. 'He's having some trouble believing that Russell was here to—'

'. . . case the joint,' finishes Jayden. 'For, allegedly, a second time. He doesn't think it stacks up.'

'I think you'll find,' says Edwin, 'that Shaun's fine mind is a little addled by . . . well, any number of things. Not least grief. And probably a fair bit of shame, if he accepts the writing on the wall.'

'Easy . . .' says Owen, in a low voice.

'Russell had gambling debts, is what I've heard. Back in the day, Shaun was always bleating on to our dad about his son's errant ways. Probably jealous of what me and Owen were doing. Maybe Russell wasn't dealt that great a hand, but he had every opportunity to come good. It's about personal responsibility at the end of the day, isn't it?'

'The gambling was a rumour,' says Owen. 'That's all.'

'A rumour that would be corroborated by one look at his bank statements,' says Edwin. 'Good job it's not a police inquiry, because I suspect a lot more would come out than Shaun wants.'

Ally sets her glass down with a loud chink. The Sauvignon is crisp as a just-picked apple, but, somehow she's lost her taste for it.

'Ally, Jayden,' says Ruth, 'there's something you should know about Shaun Tremaine. I'm afraid he's not an honest man. I say that as someone who's known him for a great many years, so I'd be careful accepting his word too readily. No doubt, the man's heartbroken. It's a tragedy. I won't deny that. But there's such a thing as being taken advantage of. If you pair give him the time of day, if he so much as suspects for a moment that you've got great big bleeding hearts, he'll be like a hound on a fox. Mark my words.'

Silence follows Ruth's impassioned speech. Karensa stares deep into her wine glass as Edwin and Owen swap a look. Is it consternation? Or tacit agreement?

'So how come you're offering Shaun a job again?' asks Jayden.

16

'I know I went in hard,' says Jayden. 'But there are mixed messages, don't you reckon?'

'They didn't seem to hold it against you,' says Ally. 'If I was being sceptical, I'd say . . . what's the phrase? Charm offensive?'

'Yeah, and not that successful, all things considered. They didn't exactly hide how they feel about Shaun, did they?'

'And they consider Russell a write-off,' says Ally. 'That was nothing but snobbery.'

Ally once said how she distrusted certainty, and Jayden thought that such a good way of putting it – the fine but crucial line between conviction and blinkers.

'Owen seems gentler though,' she adds.

'He's definitely got more of a conscience about doing the right thing by Shaun now. Question is, where does that come from? Guilt? If we're running with the idea that Russell came asking for his dad's job back, maybe it was Owen that he went to, because he seems like he's the most sympathetic. But looks can be deceiving, right?'

'Agreed.'

'You know what, I thought it was strange that Owen hadn't put it together that Cliff and Sue are my in-laws.'

'Perhaps he hasn't paid much attention to the guest list,' says Ally. 'That struck me more as Edwin's domain.'

'Maybe. Or maybe Owen is set on his "I don't know anything about anything" jag.'

'I've been thinking about Edwin's hand injury, too.'

'He said he punched the gate.'

'And was clearly embarrassed about it. It's rather an ugly reaction, isn't it? Edwin told us before that it was shock, but I think his first instinct on finding Russell was anger.'

'Because with this investor incoming, Russell's death is an inconvenience,' says Jayden. 'Yeah, agreed. It's not a good look. Unless Edwin's lying, and he didn't punch a gate at all.'

Ally lets the thought settle. 'He's a smooth operator, if that's the case. At Hang Ten, he was the one who drew attention to his injury.'

'Only because he saw you notice it, Al.'

'And Ruth's hardly hiding the fact that she dislikes Shaun. She's not at all conscious of how she comes across.'

They're bumping slowly back down the track, the chimney of Shaun's cottage just coming into view. After Ruth's outburst, Edwin took over, explaining that their dad, Frank, had been a soft touch. That he kept Shaun on even though the guy didn't pull his weight – frequently taking sick days, apparently, and turning up late and knocking off early. Harvest was, according to Edwin, a joke. Shaun would be the one wandering the vines like a foreman, instead of getting busy picking. *Bad back, apparently. It came on just as the grapes ripened and eased up when the vines were picked clean. Funny that.*

'With Shaun, it sounds more like a bit of laziness than dishonesty,' says Jayden. 'Or maybe a totally legitimate injury that he was trying his best with.'

'Shaun might decide he doesn't want to go back to work there.'

'Maybe choice is a luxury he can't afford, Al. It doesn't seem like there's a whole lot of money around.'

The job offer has been made by voicemail and then text message, according to Owen, but the Harpers are yet to hear anything back.

Least we can do, Owen said. *There's no pressure with it. But if you're seeing him later, maybe you can sound him out.*

They park in a patch of rough ground, just along from Shaun's cottage, and their feet squelch in the mud as they make their way to the gate. As the wind gusts, drops of rain fall from the thick canopy of the yew.

The cottage has an abandoned feel to it. It's early afternoon but upstairs the curtains are closed. There's a crack in one of the windowpanes, like a cartoon lightning strike. Jayden shifts the bag of groceries in his hand as he knocks on the door.

The dog barks, just like before.

Care package, Jayden said to Ally earlier; just a few things he took from his own store cupboards and some other bits. Chocolate Hobnobs and pasta and pesto. Some ready-to-bake baguettes with a decent shelf life. *You don't think it's patronising?* To which Ally replied she wished she'd thought of it herself.

The door opens an inch, and the smell of cigarettes greets them.

'Who is it?'

'Shaun, it's us. Jayden and Ally. We wanted to check in.'

The door pushes wider, and Shaun stands squinting at them, a cigarette with a long tail of ash quivering in his hand. He wears the same brown knitted jumper and sagging tracksuit bottoms as yesterday. He looks as if he's barely slept. If Jayden had to guess his age, he'd struggle. Anywhere between fifty and seventy? Russell was twenty-five.

'Got anything to tell me?'

'We've been asking a lot of questions,' says Jayden. He hands over the bag. 'Here you go. A few bits and pieces.'

Shaun takes it without looking at it, and shuffles through to the kitchen. He deposits the bag on the sideboard and goes to the kettle. His dog, Charlie, winds through his legs; a constant companion.

'I can do you tea, but I'm out of milk.'

'There's milk in the bag,' says Jayden. 'Want me to make it?'

Shaun drags a couple of mugs from the sideboard and gives them a cursory swill. 'I'm not useless yet. Sit down, boy. You want one too, do you, missus?'

Ally hesitates, but Jayden sends her a look and she quickly says, 'Yes, please.' Considering she's basically an introvert, Ally's pretty good with people, but sometimes she forgets the basic tricks of the trade, like 'always accept a cup of tea'. A small thing, but it shows willing; slows things down and keeps it friendly. Jayden drank a whole lot of tea as a PC, in a whole lot of kitchens and living rooms; with the wife of a drug dealer, a teenage arsonist, the neighbour of a car thief – and more victims of crime than he likes to think of.

Slowly, over their chipped mugs, they fill Shaun in on what Nicky Ballard told them. His account of the night out in Newquay. Russell's upbeat mood, and his talk of holidays to come.

'He liked knocking about with Nicky. He was a good pal.'

'Shaun, any idea what this "something big in the pipeline" might have been?' says Jayden.

Shaun pats at his pockets. 'I don't know anything about that,' he says, distractedly. 'Pipeline? What does he mean by that?'

'According to Nicky, that was how Russell phrased it,' says Ally. 'He seemed to be suggesting he was coming into some money.'

'What, Russell?' Shaun gives a quick shake of his head. 'Hang on, are you on about this quad bike again? Because if you're trying to say he nicked it and flogged it . . . that's not Russell.'

And Shaun doesn't sound angry this time, he just sounds tired. Jayden looks at him, wondering what on earth's holding him up. He feels a nudge at his leg and looks down. It's Charlie, stretching out beneath the table, his head resting on Shaun's foot. Jayden reaches his hand down to stroke him, glad that Shaun has this friend, this other heartbeat in the cottage.

'From Nicky's account it seems unlikely that Russell would have been anywhere near here on the night the quad was stolen,' says Ally.

'Well, I could have told you that.'

'Do you know if Russell was into gambling, Shaun?' Jayden asks carefully. 'Nicky thought he liked a flutter. Said that maybe this pipeline talk was about a hot tip.'

Shaun pulls out his pouch of tobacco. He starts rolling another cigarette. 'You mind?' he says, before he lights it.

They shake their heads, and this time Ally is quick to the cue. Tea and cigarettes; it's all good.

'I used to like the horses. As a kid, Russell would help me pick the winners. He'd go for the names, never cared for odds. It was just a bit of fun. Never proper money.'

He draws on his cigarette, blows smoke sideways.

'I never thought I was getting him into a bad habit. It was just me and him having a laugh. And they were proper beautiful, the horses. I took him over to Trebudannon a couple of times, as a bit of a treat. He wasn't the biggest, Russell, I could see him as a jockey one day, but . . . couldn't stretch to riding lessons, could I? The buzz of it stayed with him though. That's what I didn't reckon on. Got so that he'd bet on anything. Bet on the weather. Bet on you having red socks on under your boots. Always wanted to take his chance and ride his luck. If I'd known what I was getting him into . . .'

It's the most Shaun's said since they met him yesterday. His eyes have a faraway expression; his cigarette is running to ash in his hand again.

'That guilt's mine to live with,' he says quietly.

'I used to do the same thing with my grandad when I was a kid,' says Jayden. His dad's dad, his white grandad, at the bungalow in Whitby. Glasses of Vimto and the racing pages open on the kitchen table. 'I loved it too, Shaun. You weren't to know.'

But Shaun doesn't hear him.

'He chucked away a fair few wage packets, that way. But he'd had a win, had he? Least there's that.'

'Nicky didn't think Russell had won yet,' says Jayden. 'But he was feeling optimistic about something. How connected was Russell with the horse racing world, Shaun? Could he have got some inside information?'

Shaun shakes his head. 'All I ever said to him was "Son, don't bet what you can't afford to lose." But that would have meant not betting at all, most months.'

'Gambling was just Nicky's guess.'

'Well, that's a better bet than anyone saying he was going round stealing things.'

'We've got to look at all the angles,' says Jayden, levelly. 'Even just to rule them out.'

'I know he didn't have a hand in nicking that quad, Jayden. The mystery is why he ended up in that bloody field. That's what you seashell detectives are supposed to be on.'

'And we are on it. I promise. The more we know about Russell's behaviour in the days leading up to his death, the better chance we've got of finding the answer to what he was doing at the vineyard.'

'It's about building a picture,' says Ally. 'At the moment we've got all these little pieces, and we need to work out how they fit together.'

'The fact that Russell was talking like he was on the cusp of something big, that's potentially an important piece. Shaun, does the phrase "Fortune favours the brave" mean anything to you?'

'Not especially.'

'It wasn't a catchphrase of Russell's?'

Shaun shakes his head. 'What I'm telling you is that I don't trust those Harpers. Or what about that bloke Sullivan? He's the one who's got the herd. He could be mixed up in it.'

'We're going there next,' says Jayden. 'What do you know about Greg Sullivan?'

'His steers killed my boy.'

'Shaun, have you heard any more from the police on the post-mortem yet?' asks Jayden. 'They should be in touch when they have the results.'

'Don't count on it, not with that lot. And how's that going to help, anyway? Anyone could see he'd been trampled. Doesn't take a brain surgeon, or a post-whatnot, to work that out.'

Jayden looks to Ally. He's wondering whether to mention that they walked the yard, and how the field where Russell died didn't seem a natural hiding place. But he doesn't want to fan Shaun's flame.

'We talked to the Harpers earlier,' he says instead. 'They said they've offered you your old job back.'

Shaun gnaws his lip. 'What, because they're suddenly getting a load of money in? They can afford to throw me a few scraps? Nah, they can stick it.'

'How much do you know about this investment of theirs?' asks Jayden.

'Only what Edwin's been bragging about. Word travels on the grapevine.' Shaun gives a thin smile. 'It'll be Ruth who's made it happen though. She's the canny one. Never understood what Frank saw in her, but happen it was that.'

'You and Frank used to get on?'

'He was a good bloke.'

'And you liked the work?'

'Well enough. Standing up on those terraces – that's what Frank called the vines – it was like we weren't even in Cornwall any more. When the sun shone, we could have been anywhere. I was his odd-job man, really. The wine was down to Frank. And those sons of his, later on. With the two of them about the place you'd think I'd be a spare part, but I did the jobs no one else wanted. Edwin never got his hands dirty. And Frank's health was failing for a while, so Owen picked up the slack there. Owen and me. Though I had my own share of problems. Dodgy back. Labour takes its toll, doesn't it? And if you're not firing on all cylinders, well, you're for the knacker's yard.'

He tosses what's left of his cigarette into his undrunk mug of tea.

'What good's this talk anyway? Doesn't tell me what Russell was doing in that field.'

'What do you make of Ruth, Shaun? Other than being . . . canny.'

'Battleaxe. That's what Mum always called her, even back when she was a young one.'

And Shaun explains that the cottage they're in now used to belong to his mum. That when Russell was born, Shaun moved in here with his girlfriend, and started working at Shoreline Vines – or Shoreline Farm as it still was then.

'We did it for the baby, really. Neither of us had the space. But Jackie, she didn't like it. This place, the sea, my mum, *being* a mum. She upped sticks. She came and went a bit over the years; I

85

wanted Russell to know her, though a fat lot of good it did him. She died ten years ago now. My mum passed on the same year. Mum left us this place though.' He blinks. 'I couldn't have done any of it without her.'

Jayden pictures Shaun as a young, single dad, and the thought pulls at him. He's always been emotional – *in touch with your emotions, babe, and that's a good thing*, says Cat – but having a child has changed him in ways he couldn't have imagined. Jayden knows he'd fight to the death for Jazzy, take on anything or anyone. When their baby boy comes along in four months' time, Jayden will love and protect him with all his heart and bones. He's never regretted turning down the offer on the County Lines squad that came his way in the summer. Not for one moment. But if Jayden ever wonders if he's doing enough here – and he does sometimes; he knows the campsite in summer and the detecting when crime calls sounds like a holiday to his Leeds mates – Cat reminds him that his biggest job, his most important job, is being a dad. *And you're smashing it, Jay.* Okay, she's biased, but he'll take it.

'I'm only glad Mum's not here for this,' says Shaun, pulling at the cuff of his old jumper. His voice fractures. 'It'd have broken her heart. And I tell you what, she'd have been knocking down the Harpers' door asking for the real story. But then, she always had more guts than me.'

Jayden looks to Ally. She rests her hand lightly on Shaun's arm, and Jayden sees him send her a look of surprise. Then gratitude.

The real story. All Jayden knows is that Russell was a young guy who liked to gamble, who was chatting up girls in Newquay with talk of something big in the pipeline, then two days later he was trampled to death by bullocks, on land belonging to the vineyard he held a grudge against on his dad's behalf. A place he had no obvious reason to be.

Whatever the real story, it's buried deep.

17

Nobody knows Celine Chevalier is staying in St Ives. Ruth Harper offered her a room at the farmhouse Saturday evening, but that's not going to work. Not least because Celine imagines Shoreline's styling will be shabby-chic at best. And, these days, Celine doesn't do any variation on shabby.

This is what she tells herself: she won't stay because of the home furnishings.

She has accepted Ruth's offer – it would have been strange if she didn't – but she won't tell her she has a backup out of town. *A luxurious coastal bolthole* is how the boutique holiday company described Castaway. Celine didn't spend long considering its virtues; the price – four figures, for three nights, out of season – suggested it would meet her needs. In a break in the rain, she stands on the terrace and drinks her coffee, wrapping her cashmere cardigan a little tighter around herself. The location is unequivocally charming. The cascading slate rooftops are embroidered with a curious yellow lichen, lending colour even on a miserable day like this. The church tower is neat as a chess piece, and in the far distance an island lighthouse completes the quaint setting. The sea is far bluer than it has a right to be.

She must have visited St Ives all those years ago, but she can't remember it. According to her numerous exes, Celine enjoys the power of selective memory. Or, more precisely, she sees memory as a fabrication; no more than a storytelling mechanism. And that's scientifically proven.

Shoreline Vines, then. *Okay.*

A family-run vineyard idyllically set on the Cornish coast. A West Country microclimate, the salted air of the Atlantic, the vigour and vim of those two strapping boys at the helm. Under Frank Harper's eye, the vines had borne fruit, but with the right kind of investment – not just cash, but business acumen – they could truly flourish.

This, thinks Celine, is how it all reads on paper.

It was Ruth who made the initial approach, passing Celine to Edwin as soon as the terms of the offer were understood. Smooth-talking Edwin, so eager to prove his credentials, telling Celine he had considered an MFA stateside, but decided there was more to gain by learning on the job. And what better job than vineyard owner in a Cornish paradise, on land his family has owned for generations? His sell had bluster – something she finds so pathetic in men, and so common – but he's got potential.

Celine has no idea how the wines measure up. Ruth offered to send her a selection in advance, but it felt superfluous. *I'd rather taste them at source*, she said.

And the keyword there? *Source.*

Because Ruth's carefully worded invitation to Shoreline omitted more than it conveyed.

> *You are the only person who can save Shoreline Vines. If we fail to secure investment, we will have to sell. The land will likely be redeveloped; we've already had people sniffing around. I can't stand the thought of it turning into a building site. Diggers turning over our precious soil, destroying our vines.*

Frank would be rolling in his grave. Shoreline has been in his family for generations and it's our job to both protect the past and secure the future. Your investment is the only way we can do that. I know you will understand this, Celine.

Celine needs to look the woman in the eye, Edwin and Owen too, and only then will she get the full picture. Only then will she evaluate then strategize. Any student of business should know the numbers 7-38-55: Mehrabian's theory that when one communi-cates, just 7 per cent of meaning is conveyed by the words them-selves, 38 per cent by voice, and 55 per cent by body language.

So that letter of Ruth's? Arguably, it holds just 7 per cent of the truth. And Celine would claim that, given the circumstances, 7 per cent is probably a generous estimation.

Celine slips back inside and settles on the sofa. Through the vast window the view is framed like a picture. It looks unreal.

She closes her eyes and, despite all the work she's done, an image of Frank drops in. His broad grin and soulful eyes. His deep voice, with its soft Cornish flow; nothing like the brisk, clipped speech she's been surrounded by since.

Vines, she remembers saying. *Have you thought about planting them here?*

The rich sound of Frank's laugh; then the look he gave her, when he realised that she was serious.

So Shoreline Farm became Shoreline Vines and now Ruth wants Celine's money. Perhaps she thinks she's owed it. Maybe she has a hell of a bargaining chip. Celine overheard them talking once. Or rather, Ruth hissing at her husband, as feisty as a barnyard cat. *I can see the way she looks at you.* And Frank murmuring something indecipherable in response.

Now, Celine knocks back the last of her coffee just as her phone goes. She frowns, seeing Edwin Harper's name.

'Celine,' he says, '*ça va?*'

'Very well. Edwin, how can I help?'

And her inflection suggests that it's improbable that her help is required at all, because haven't they already dotted all i's and crossed all t's? She will be at Shoreline Vines tomorrow at 3 p.m. Further conversation is unnecessary.

'Purely a heads-up,' says Edwin. 'There's been a death at the vineyard.'

Celine gets to her feet. Out on the roof terrace an outsized gull is stalking the perimeter. She watches it take off on wings as wide as a prop plane's.

'Did you hear me?' says Edwin, his voice sounding very far away.

'It's a bad line. Did you say a death at the vineyard?'

'Afraid so. Nothing to worry about. A local ne'er-do-well had a run-in with some frisky bullocks. The kicker is it was on our land. I didn't want you to hear about it elsewhere.'

'The perils of rural living aren't widely reported in the metropolis, Edwin. But I appreciate the intelligence.'

'The police have been and gone.'

'Poor man,' she says. 'Bullocks, you said?'

'Herd of fifteen. God knows how many took a pop. Anyway, like I said, a heads-up. We're very much looking forward to welcoming you tomorrow.'

'Thank you,' says Celine, set to hang up.

'We're hosting a simple supper. Mum mentioned that, did she? Last-minute idea. A few local characters. Give you a taste of the community you'll be investing in. We'll be doing NDAs, of course.'

So the Harpers want to show her off, do they? Flash the cash? She briefly considers the meaning of this, but is unable to draw a conclusion.

She has no doubt that the Harpers take the credit for everything, all the way back to the very beginning. It was Frank's idea to plant the vines, so their story goes. And much like memory, stories are manipulations too.

Well, this is Celine's story. She was a pliable teenager, green as a new shoot. The kind of girl who poured out her heart to her diary; drew love hearts in the pages of jotters. She was beautiful and hadn't yet seen the danger in that. When she was nineteen, she hardened. She had to decide what she wanted her life to be – and every path she's taken since is a result of that moment. Her first marriage, and her second, were both tactical, giving her a financial jump-start. But she took those extensive divorce settlements and doubled them, trebled them. She put herself through business school and graduated top of her class. She rose through any rank that came her way, until she built her own, and sat at the very top.

Celine is used to people wanting a piece of her.

Her eyes go once more to the view. The grey sky is full of gulls now. What's the word, a *flock*? It's a murder of crows. A murder of bullocks, as it turns out. Up above, the birds wheel and float aimlessly.

'What is the name of the man who died yesterday?' she asks suddenly. Sternly, too, as if cautioning a small child to tell the truth or else.

'Russell Tremaine.'

And it means nothing to her. But then she didn't expect it to.

'See you tomorrow, Edwin,' she says. 'Send my regards to your mother.'

And she hangs up.

Celine will go to Shoreline Vines tomorrow and she'll do the job as required. The figure the Harpers are asking for is, comparatively, a drop in the ocean. And so, they've assembled the local gentry, have they? The movers and shakers of the back of beyond? She won't have a problem saying the right things – *son fameux charme*. But Celine will be watching her host carefully. Ruth's right about one thing: this investment is about protecting the past and securing the future. Okay, Celine will drink to that. But one question remains: how much does Ruth really know about that past?

18

Greg Sullivan's farm lies about five miles outside of Porthpella, on high ground. The yard is cluttered with old vehicles: a weary-looking trailer with its back yawning wide; a rusted truck, half-loaded with sacks of feed. Two rangy collies strain at their chains, leaping and barking, protecting their castle. Ally thinks of Fox back home at The Shell House, probably snoozing contentedly. He's an old boy now, getting on for twelve. But Ally doesn't want to dwell on that.

Greg is sluicing the yard with a hose as they arrive, but as soon as he knows they're here for Shaun, he's happy enough to give them the time of day.

'Come on in then,' he says, waving a hand. 'The police were up here yesterday. Said I'll likely have to appear at a coroner's court.'

'That's what usually happens with a case like this,' says Jayden.

'It's a body blow,' says Greg. 'Sorry, but it is.'

Ally and Jayden follow him through the stable-style door into the kitchen. He gestures to a couple of high stools by a counter that still bears the remnants of lunch: a loaf, a knife planted in a block of butter like an axe in a log.

'PC Tim Mullins, it was. Molly said they were at school together.'

'We were at school together,' a girl's voice calls from another room, 'not that I'm eavesdropping or anything.'

Greg rolls his eyes, but his face creases with a smile.

'She lives in Bristol now. You were at art college there, weren't you, Mol? Got herself a First and stayed on. Just down for the weekend to see her old man.'

Molly takes her cue and pops her head around the door. She's in corduroy dungarees, her hair in two long plaits; her face is friendly and open.

'Not much of a welcome home. Poor Dad. He's blaming himself.'

'Someone's got to take responsibility,' says Greg. 'I tried getting hold of Shaun yesterday, but he wasn't picking up. I should drop by, really, but I don't want to push it.'

'I think he'd probably appreciate the gesture,' says Ally.

'Russell Tremaine must have done something to really freak out the bullocks,' says Molly, leaning against the counter. 'I mean, if he had a dog with him, I could see it. You hear about that, don't you? Idiot walkers having their dogs off the leash then acting surprised when livestock try to protect themselves. But a guy on his own—'

'Herd mentality,' says Greg. 'If one gets spooked, it's catching. And they're big boys. Young, but big. If they're corralled together . . .'

He lets the sentence drift.

'Greg, the day it happened, were you up at the field at all that morning?' asks Jayden.

'I dropped some feed off round nine.'

'And you didn't see anything?'

'I didn't hang about. Just did a quick head count. What sort of thing are you talking?'

'Like Russell Tremaine,' says Molly, 'skulking about or something, right?'

Greg shakes his head.

'The metal feed thing,' says Jayden. 'Is it at the Shoreline Vines end of the field?'

'No, it's down the other end. There are two gates, but I only use the lower one. They rent me the field, but not the access off their yard. Not that I'd need it anyway. I rent the bottom field too, so it makes sense.'

Ally's just fixing the geography in her head when Jayden says, 'Greg, could we go in the car and take a look with you?'

'You want to see the field? Sure. Let's go.'

'What do you think you'll see?' says Molly, following her dad. 'Clues or something?'

'It's really just to understand the lie of the land,' says Ally.

They head out to the yard, all four climbing into Greg's pickup. They swing down the potholed drive, then out into the lane. Five minutes later and Molly's hopping out to get the gate. They pull into the first field, the vehicle covering the slight incline with ease.

'That's the one we want,' says Greg, pointing.

At the end of the field, Molly jumps out and opens the second gate. Greg takes them into the next field, then kills the engine.

'Here we are,' he says. 'And there's the feeder. You can see the other gate up top.'

Ally gets out and looks where he's pointing. The roof and chimney pots of the farmhouse are just visible beyond the hedge. Around the feeder the grass is churned to mud. Hoof prints and cowpats abound. She can't help but think of the size and weight of the animals as they pushed and pressed and trampled Russell.

'Where are the bullocks now, Greg?' asks Jayden.

'Stuck them in the barn back at mine.'

'Do you want to question them?' grins Molly.

Ally walks away a few steps, feeling her feet sink into the soft ground. It wouldn't take much to slip and fall. And if the cattle moved in, it would be hard to get up. Especially if you were scared.

She looks again to the Harpers' farmhouse. A wisp of smoke rises from the chimney and disappears into the grey sky.

'Greg, yesterday morning, when you came to feed the cattle, were any of the Harpers out and about?' asks Jayden.

'Not that I saw. First that I heard was a phone call from Edwin saying there was a man dead, and the police were on their way. Look, all these questions . . . Shaun can't work out what his boy was doing here, can he?'

'Exactly that,' says Jayden.

Ally turns back. There's a current in Greg's voice; the question was loaded.

'I don't know Russell myself, and I'm not speaking out of turn, but machinery theft's a big problem.'

'No one would want to nick your gear, Dad. It's all too knackered.'

'And that's tactical, that is,' says Greg, nudging Molly. 'Look, Edwin said they had ten grands' worth of quad taken the other night. Best will in the world, that can't be a coincidence, can it?'

'The Harpers think Russell was involved,' says Jayden.

'And far as Shaun is concerned this is about clearing his name then, is it?'

'Shaun doesn't think his son was a thief,' says Ally. 'And he can't for the life of him think why Russell would have been in this field.'

'And if Mol got herself in trouble in Bristol, I'd be saying the same,' says Greg. 'Protective instinct, isn't it?'

'Russell was afraid of cattle,' says Jayden. 'That's what Shaun keeps coming back to.'

'Growing up in the country?' says Molly. 'Come on, man up.'

Ally looks at her sharply. 'If he'd seen there were cattle in the field, Shaun's certain he wouldn't have entered it. And the terrain is more or less even, isn't it? No hidden dips. From here, I can see all corners.'

'Slight incline,' says Greg. 'So yeah, if Russell was looking from the Shoreline Vines end, he'd have seen the boys, alright.'

'Is it a short cut?' asks Jayden, turning on the spot. 'Would someone use it as a cut-through, if they knew where they were going?'

Greg rubs at his chin. 'Well, if you were at the top gate, you could come the same way we did. But it's not exactly an arterial route, that bottom lane. Russell grew up here but if the kid was proper scared of cattle, I'd say he wouldn't chance his arm going cross-country.'

'Unless he was desperate,' says Ally, looking to Jayden.

'The police didn't ask any questions like this yesterday,' says Greg.

'That's Tim Mullins for you. Slobby Bobby,' Molly laughs. 'I seriously can't believe he's ended up as police. I wish I'd been here when he came by.'

While there's no malice in Molly's tone, Ally can't help feeling she's taking it all a little too lightly.

'I should think it was a rotten house call for Tim to make,' says Ally. 'Although nowhere near as bad as the one Constable Mullins had to make to Shaun Tremaine.'

'Yeah, sorry,' says Molly. Even though she's still smiling, she looks a little chastised. 'I know it's serious. It's just . . . my memories of Tim aren't. If you know what I mean.'

'Mol's always listening to these podcasts,' says Greg. 'She lets her imagination run away with her, that's the trouble . . .'

'True crime podcasts,' says Molly. 'I'm obsessed. You two should do one. I'd listen.'

'We'll add it to the list,' says Jayden.

'I mean, if I was looking at theories for why Russell ended up in this field,' says Molly, 'I'd be thinking outside the box.'

Ally wonders whether it's time to be going. Fox will be getting restless. And after the weight of Shaun's grief, Molly's brightness feels like a jolt.

'Go on then, Molly,' says Jayden, 'what have you got?'

'Well, what if he was meeting someone? He could have been told to come here. Like, ordered or something. You don't know who he was working with.'

'We don't know that he was working with anyone, Mol,' says Greg.

'People look at a place like this and they get all misty-eyed, but there's plenty of dark deeds. You two know that better than anyone, right? Maybe for Russell, going in a field full of bullocks was a less scary prospect than not following an order.'

'Or maybe it was a less scary prospect than what was on the other side of the gate,' says Jayden, turning to Ally.

Ally looks back up the field to the gate. She pictures the yard beyond it. The outbuildings and barns. The low fences that trim the vineyard and run all the way back down by the main track. *Why this field?* She imagines Russell sprinting, hunting for somewhere to hide. Or perhaps he knew he could clear this first field, go through one more, then be out on to the lane – and nowhere near his dad's cottage. Maybe that was part of Russell's thinking – if he was thinking at all.

If he was thinking at all.

On this tide of thought, a sudden idea washes in. Ally bends to pluck it; holds it tight.

She looks to Jayden. If she whispers it within Molly's earshot, Ally knows the girl will swoop down on it like a gannet. Because it's absolutely the stuff of the crime podcasts that she says she loves.

And it might just be horrible enough to be true.

19

Mullins is dozing off when his phone rings. He jumps out of his skin – then curses. His grandad Jack swore by a good snooze as the cure for all ills, and Mullins needs to kick this nasty cold. Otherwise, he'll get it in the neck when Skinner swans back in with his suntan. *You thought you'd have a little break too, did you?* Mullins's relationship with his sergeant was always a bit iffy, but in recent months he's felt like he's gained Skinner's respect.

Maybe. A bit. In the right light.

It's the station calling. And, instinctively, his heart sinks.

'Hullo?'

'Wake you up, did I, sweetheart?'

Skinner.

'Sarge? You're supposed to be on holiday.'

'Good job I cut it short, considering.'

Skinner skimping on his holiday? That doesn't sound like him.

'So, what are you dying from, Mullins?'

'Running a hell of a temperature.'

'So was I, in Las Palmas.'

'Flu, the doctor reckons.'

His mum. Who said nothing of the sort, but Skinner doesn't need to know that.

'I've read your report, Mullins.'

Mullins feels his cheeks burn – on top of his temperature. 'I wrote it pretty quickly. I was feeling rough, but I wanted to get it in, and—'

'Nothing to suggest foul play.'

'No, sir.'

'Well, wait and see what the pathologist says. Meanwhile, in other news, we've had the Newquay lot crowing on. Late last night they raided a warehouse full of hundreds of thousands of pounds of farm machinery. Anyone'd think it was a drugs bust, the way they're talking. Mind you, John Deere . . . John Bleeding Expensive, more like.'

Mullins wonders then if Skinner's actually missed him this last week; missed bending his ear, anyway.

'Ruddy great tractors, ATVs, even some variety of threshing equipment, by all accounts. Some shady gang from Plymouth, but they were stashing the gear in a hangar out towards Bodmin. And a bunch of it's from farms in our manor.'

Mullins stifles a yawn and shifts on his pillows. Good job it's not FaceTime; Skinner doesn't need to see his tartan pyjamas. Or his sweaty forehead. Though at least then his temperature might be a bit more believable.

'Hang on, did you say ATVs? I'll tell Ally and Jayden. They're on the trail of the one Russell Tremaine is supposed to have nicked.'

'Ally and Jayden? Thought they'd be hibernating for winter.' Skinner chuckles. 'Into grand theft auto now, are they? Murder and missing persons not enough for them?'

'Ally and Jayden were up at Shoreline just as Tremaine's corpse was getting hauled off. Owen Harper called them in for the quad.'

'Why did he go to them?'

'Didn't want to bother us. Thought there was no way we'd trace it.'

'There's confidence. They clearly didn't reckon on the might of our friends in Newquay, Mullins. Besides, they've got their culprit, haven't they? It's in your half-baked report. One Russell Tremaine.'

'That's it.'

'If the Harpers can ever be bothered to get off their behinds and report it to the professionals, we'll run the details against the Bodmin haul. Though if it's there, that'll put Tremaine in the clear. Different crowd.'

'You following up with the Harpers, are you, Sarge?'

'It's your case, PC Mullins. I'm simply obliging you with the details.'

'But I'm off sick, Sarge.'

'And I'm on holiday.'

And with that, Skinner rings off. Mullins turns the phone in his clammy hand. The trouble with Skinner – one of the troubles – is that Mullins can't tell when he's being sarcastic.

The missing quad isn't his case anyway; it's Ally and Jayden's.

Mullins sighs – a sigh that dissolves into a coughing fit. He *is* sick, thank you very much. And if Skinner had half a heart, he'd be sending him a bunch of grapes, not giving him aggro. He taps out a quick message to Jayden, then gets back to that doze he was trying to have.

But as he drifts, a thought bursts through the haze.

If a gang from Plymouth did nick the Harpers' quad, what was Russell Tremaine doing in that field?

20

'Al, you're saying you think Russell was dead *before* the cattle got to him?'

'It's possible. Isn't it? If his presence in the field makes no sense?'

Out beyond the dunes, the sea is a deep blue. Sunset can't be far off, and while the sky's thick with cloud, an electric outline picks out the formations beyond the lighthouse. Jayden thinks of the CSI at the vineyard; Russell's body taken away for the post-mortem.

'But there was a vital reaction,' he says.

'Vital reaction?'

'It's what you call it when the body shows signs of trauma, and how you know that trauma occurred during life. There must have been bleeding and other wound marks on Russell's body, or the crime scene would have been treated differently. Which means Russell was breathing when he went in the field.'

'I knew it was too much,' says Ally.

'No, wait,' says Jayden, 'you could still be on to something, Al. It's possible that Russell was lying unconscious in the field. If the cattle trampled him in that state, then at first glance there'd be nothing to say any different. He'd bleed. He'd bruise. It'd look like he'd been trampled to death. Because he *was* trampled to death.'

'So something could have happened to Russell in the field before the cattle came anywhere near him?'

'Or before he was in the field. Because otherwise we're still stuck on Shaun's point. Why was Russell there?'

They pull up outside The Shell House.

'Shall we take this thinking to the incident room?' says Jayden.

He sees a flicker of a smile. 'Yes, let's. Though it feels strange calling it that. I think we need a new name.'

Bill's room. That's how Jayden thinks of it, though it's not his place to call it that.

'It's where we're going to crack our cases, Al – starting with this one. Though "crack den" doesn't have the right ring to it . . .'

'What about "the thinking room"?'

'I like that. The thinking room.'

Ally smiles. 'Now we've walked the land we can draw it up, perhaps. The layout of the other buildings too.'

'And I want us to keep going with this thought of yours, Al, that Russell was unconscious when the cattle got to him. We're going to need another whiteboard.'

'I'll get some paper from my studio,' says Ally, climbing out of the car.

'And I'll get the kettle on.'

Inside The Shell House, Ally clicks on the lamps and the place is suffused in warm light. Fox lifts himself from his basket and comes towards them, stretching his legs and yawning. As Jayden bends to stroke his pointed ears, the little dog leans against his shins.

'Did we wake you up, mate?' says Jayden.

Ten minutes later they're settled in the thinking room: Ally sitting in Bill's chair, facing the board on the wall; Jayden on his feet, pacing. His mind ticks over as he looks at the plans they've drawn of the vineyard and its surrounding land: the other hiding places; the more obvious exit points; the unlikeliness of Russell striking out cross-country when a herd of cattle were in plain sight. Ally was right when she wondered what Russell was thinking – and if he was even thinking at all.

Unconscious before the cattle got to him? Try unconscious before he got to the field.

'You know what, Al. It's a great cover-up. Stir up the herd, and they'll do the rest.'

'You mean if someone wanted Russell's death to look accidental?'

'He could have been knocked unconscious elsewhere. And then deliberately put in the field.'

Ally holds his eye. 'I don't know a huge amount about cattle, but it does feel more likely that something – or someone – startled them, rather than them stampeding for no reason.'

'Agreed.' Jayden taps the plan they've stuck to the wall. 'And think about where Russell died. The exact spot.'

'Close to the gate.'

'Exactly. Close to the gate. If the cattle were so far away that Russell didn't see them, then why didn't he just jump back over the gate when he saw them coming? He'd have had time.'

'And if Russell was afraid of cattle, that's the likeliest option, isn't it? That they were grazing at a distance. Or, like Molly said, they were a less intimidating option than what he was already facing . . .'

'Al, I think we need to take this to the police. Why was Russell in a place that he never should have been? Answer: someone put him there. It works for me.'

But even as Jayden says it, he knows it raises more questions than answers.

'If Russell was unconscious before he ended up in the field, would that be apparent in the post-mortem?' asks Ally.

'Depends,' says Jayden. 'Mullins said the cattle made a right mess of him.'

Jayden remembers how Mullins's face was paler than usual; no quick jokes coming from the PC that time.

'The true story could be disguised to an extent,' he goes on, 'but . . . every contact leaves a trace, right?' At Ally's questioning look, Jayden expands. 'Locard's exchange principle. It underpins all forensic science. If anyone else was involved in Russell's death, then there'll be evidence of that. If this case is upgraded to suspicious death, then there'll be a forensic post-mortem, and they'll be looking at everything then.'

'But if it isn't . . .'

'Exactly, which is why I think we need to share our thinking. Including the fact that Russell thought he was coming into money.'

Jayden feels his phone buzz in his pocket. He draws it out.

'Al, it's Mullins. His ears must have been burning.' He scans the message then looks up. 'The police have recovered a load of stolen farm gear. The Harpers' quad could be there. *Could* be. Not guaranteed.'

'And if it is, what does that mean for us?'

'They've nicked a gang from Plymouth. Which makes it nothing to do with Russell, by the looks. I'm calling Mullins now.'

Ally scoops up Fox and buries her nose in his red fur. This is an important development.

'Mullins? It's Jayden.'

'Alright, Jayden.'

'Hey, you sound rough, mate. You okay?'

'Flu,' says Mullins. 'Or a bad cold. I don't know. I feel like death warmed up. What is it anyway?'

'So, if we get you the deets of the quad, you can run it against the stuff that's been recovered?'

'Yes, Jayden, we're clever like that.'

'And if it's there, that's Russell in the clear, right? In which case, the theory about him casing the joint doesn't stack up.'

'Not necessarily. He could have heard about the theft and thought "they're sitting ducks, I'll go and have myself a pot shot".'

'Mullins, Ally and I have got a wild question for you. Have you had the lab report yet?'

'That's your wild question?'

'No, this is: do you think there's any way that Russell could have been knocked unconscious before he ended up in that field?'

Mullins chooses that exact moment to unleash a massive sneeze. Jayden holds the phone from his ear. He looks to Ally, who's listening intently, her eyes bright.

'Bless you, mate. Did you hear me through that?'

On the other end of the line, Mullins is blowing his nose noisily.

'Tell me how that would work exactly, Jayden. Because I don't think cows can jump gates. Or dead people climb over them.'

Jayden sees Ally bite down a smile.

'Oh . . .' says Mullins. 'Unless . . .'

'Caught up?'

He hears Mullins sigh. 'Is Ally in on this too?'

'She is. The thing is, the results of the initial post-mortem could still be consistent with being trampled by cattle.'

'And if I was a betting man, I'd say they will be.'

'Would you tell us when you get the results?'

Mullins grunts. Then says, 'Sometimes people just get dealt a rubbish hand, Jayden. I reckon that's Russell.'

'Yeah, okay. But sometimes people get murdered, only it's made to look like an accident.'

'Jayden, Jayden, Jayden.'

'I'm serious. And on that rubbish hand, Russell allegedly had some good fortune coming his way. Got a minute to hear about that?'

21

Edwin watches as his wife yawns and stretches. There's a performative element to Karensa's gestures and he waits for her to speak her next line. Her plate of crackers and cheese – a simple supper, no one had much of an appetite after the drama – is only half-finished, and she's pulled her napkin over it like a child hiding the evidence.

'If no one minds, I'm turning in,' she says, rising from the table.

There it is.

She does look tired though. And pale. A vein at her temple glows soft blue, and Edwin has the urge to lightly press his thumb to it; caress it. Karensa has always been attractive – her eyes wide and green as a cat's, the soft curls of her dark brown hair – but on their wedding day she was strikingly beautiful. A film star in a silk dress, posing in front of the gleaming vineyard backdrop – he'd never felt prouder. That day feels like a long time ago now.

'It's only eight o'clock,' says Ruth, looking up sharply. 'You're not sickening for something, are you?'

Karensa's been on edge all day; flighty as a bird. Russell's death has shaken her and that's fair enough, but she needs to get it together before Celine arrives.

Have you ever seen a dead person, Edwin? she asked him last night, her voice as broken as a line of Morse code.

You mean apart from my own father?

And she clapped her hand to her mouth. *I'm an idiot.*

And she really is, because Karensa was the one to find Frank after he fell down the stairs. Edwin will never forget the desperate look on his wife's face as she ran into the kitchen. *It's your dad. Oh God, your dad.*

Edwin suspects that Karensa's desire for an early night is more about her wanting solitude than rest. He knows she finds his mother overbearing at the best of times – welcome to Ruth Harper – but it was always the deal: Shoreline is Ruth's home, and it's Edwin's home too. He'll be carried out feet first, just like his dad, and that's a promise.

'Go on then, get your beauty sleep,' he says to her. And there's a terseness to his voice that he's not proud of, but Karensa has no idea how much depends on this investment. It's not like Edwin isn't shaken by what happened to Russell Tremaine, but they can't afford to let anything derail Celine Chevalier's visit. His mum knows that. His brother knows that. And as Edwin's wife, Karensa should sure as hell know that.

Karensa had nothing when they met. A two-bit bookie for a dad, who drank his profits, such as they were. A degree in poetry. *What kind of a gig is that?* Though she wrote a poem for him once, and it made his eyes sting with tears as he read it. Not that he let her see. Maybe it wouldn't have hurt, to show her his soft underbelly, but she fell for a different sort of Edwin and that guy doesn't get misty-eyed over words on paper. That guy has it together.

'We all need to be on form tomorrow,' he says. 'Mum, I'm going to the office. I want to go over a few things.'

'Celine isn't an exam, Edwin, no need for last-minute cramming.'

Edwin musters a laugh. 'I know that. Don't worry, I've got Celine wrapped around my little finger.'

'As you wish,' says Ruth. She pours the last drop of wine into her glass and holds it up. 'Ah well, alone again.'

'Oh, come on,' he says, setting his hands on her shoulders. He can feel the tension and gently massages her. 'We're always with you, Mum.'

Ruth swivels in her seat and grabs his hand.

'Edwin,' she says, eyes glistening. 'Everyone thought your father was so damn wonderful, but he left me with nothing but mess.'

'I know, Mum.'

Edwin feels ten years old again: his mum's moods seeping into him, heavy as a stone in the middle of his chest; something to carry all day, every day.

'I never stopped loving him though,' she says. 'For better or for worse.'

'I know.'

Someone else might be afraid Ruth will run on like this tomorrow in front of Celine, but Edwin knows that when she needs to, his mum finds another gear. For now, he must let her have this moment. Overhead, the ceiling creaks, and he wonders if Karensa is listening in.

'Your dad will be watching us tomorrow. I know he will.'

'Yes.'

'He's watching us now. Edwin, I do believe that.'

Edwin doesn't. When you're gone, you're gone. And maybe it's a good thing, because if the ghost of his father is stalking Shoreline Vines, he'd have it out with him. He'd have to, because what kind of a man would Edwin be otherwise? But his dad's six feet under – bones and dust – and that's that.

'Why didn't your brother join us tonight?'

'Two dinners in a row at the farmhouse – you're joking, aren't you?'

Ruth lets go of his arm and rests her gnarled hands in her lap.

'I'd have liked to raise a glass to tomorrow. Just us.' Then she shakes herself. 'Oh, you go and do what you need to do, darling. I'll be alright here.'

As Edwin leaves the room, he can smell the distinct whiff of burning martyr. Nevertheless, guilt curls inside his stomach, just as it did when he was a little boy. *No child should feel responsible for a parent's happiness*, Karensa said to him once, with one of her deep-as-a-well looks. But Edwin said he didn't know what she was talking about. He'd had a fantastic childhood; a regular little prince, with a whole kingdom to play in. And didn't it feel glorious to be the chosen one?

◆ ◆ ◆

Instead of going to the office, Edwin trudges across the yard. He scales the fence, and cuts across the squelching field. The wind's gusting over the headland and he pulls up his collar. Eventually, his torch beam picks out Owen's trailer. The hunk of silver junk. If this is what independence looks like, you can keep it.

He knocks sharply, and as the door opens, Edwin sees how Owen's face changes.

'Who were you expecting?' he snorts. 'Celine sneaking in early, wanting to rough it with a Cornish toy boy?'

And in classic Owen style, he can't take a joke. Anger scuds across his brother's face.

'What do you want, Edwin?'

It's another little knife wound – that he presumes Edwin's only here because he wants something. Even if it's true.

'Instructions from Mum,' says Edwin. 'Go easy on the memory-lane stuff tomorrow.'

'But it's why she's coming. She wouldn't look at us twice otherwise.'

'That's charming, that is. We're a decent proposition for any investor. If we make Celine feel like she's doing us a favour she could lose faith. Business is unsentimental, Owen.'

'It doesn't have to be.'

'And that's why we'd be destined to fail if you were at the helm, brother.'

Like father like son. But he doesn't say it. He doesn't need to go into tomorrow with a bruise on his cheek. Want to know how to press Owen Harper's buttons? Diss Daddy. They should have all been on the same team, but somehow they got split down the middle: two versus two. And now Owen's on his own.

'How's Mum handling everything?'

Edwin hesitates. If things were different, he'd have brought the whisky out with him. They'd have talked brother to brother. Shared the load of being the Harper boys. But that's never been them.

'Mum's fine.'

'And how's Karensa doing? She wasn't herself earlier.'

'Noticed, did you? She's spooked.'

'Course she's spooked.'

And there's an uncharacteristic catch in Owen's voice. Edwin looks closely at his brother. Why does it suddenly feel as if he's hiding something?

He thinks of the whisky again. Two glasses. But Owen's so guarded, he'd see it as a trap.

'I'd give her a pass for tomorrow but it's important for the image,' says Edwin, brushing the thought away. 'Family business, the future of the vines, all that. Too bad she's not up the duff. That'd make for a good picture.'

Owen goes to close the door. 'Goodnight, Edwin.'

111

Edwin shoves his foot in it. 'Tell me it's message received? Don't bring up the past unless Celine goes there first.'

Owen looks pointedly at Edwin's foot, and he moves it.

'Why the hell wouldn't she?' says Owen. He grins. 'I can't speak for you, but I was an angel as a kid.'

And if that's an invitation for reminiscence, Edwin doesn't take it. Because when it comes to the past, he and Owen will never be on the same page.

22

Jayden's woken by the sound of his daughter's shrill voice, and the feeling of her pulling at his big toe.

'Daddy! Daddy!'

He misses the days when Jazzy used to call him Dadatz. He also misses lie-ins, but the memory of those is more distant. Beyond Jazzy's high pitch, rain drums on the windowpane.

'Granny's here.'

Not exactly a newsflash, seeing as his mum-in-law lives just across the yard.

Jazzy drags at the duvet, and the rush of air is disproportionately chilling. Jayden yelps, in a way that doesn't become a one-time city-centre response officer.

'Daddy, Grandpa dying.'

'What?'

At that, he's up and off, scooping his daughter along with him. He calls out Cat's name, taking the stairs two at a time. Jazzy bounces in his arms, giggling.

'Easy,' says Cat, meeting him at the bottom of the stairs. 'Jay, don't run with her like that. If you slip, you're both screwed.'

He frowns. 'Jazzy said . . . something about your dad.'

'He's got man flu. Mum's here with a proposition for you.'

'First, you can't say "man flu," it's prejudiced. Second, our daughter said Cliff was dying. That's not a great way to wake someone up.'

'Least you had a lie-in, babe. Every silver lining has a cloud.' She puts her hand on her domed belly. 'This guy was turning somersaults all night.'

'Course he was. He's an athlete.'

'Jay, please just say yes to Mum.'

'Yes to what?'

'And just like that,' grins Jayden, 'I've got myself an invite to dinner at Shoreline Vines.'

Jayden raises his coffee and Ally chinks mugs.

'This could be useful.'

'You bet. I'm going undercover as a dutiful son-in-law.'

'I think you're a very dutiful son-in-law, actually.'

'Then maybe I'm going undercover as a detective who, erm, knows what's going on.'

Down by the hearth, Jazzy is curled up next to Fox, pretending to sleep. Every so often she opens one eye, tickles the dog's tummy, then settles back down.

'You know what,' says Jayden, 'she might nod off there for real. Cat reckons she's ready to drop her morning nap but I'm not so sure.'

'My boy's adding naps. He's old, Jayden. And so am I.'

'You're joking, aren't you? You're both spring chickens.'

'I woke up feeling about a hundred years old this morning,' says Ally. And Jayden hears a key change in her voice. 'I spent half the night thinking about whether this really could be murder. And what if we can't prove it? What if the police can't prove it? Won't we only be making it worse for Shaun?'

'You can't think like that, Al.'

Jayden can see why she is, though. Shaun's certain that there's more to it, that people might be lying – but he's never said *murder*. But if Russell was unconscious when he was put in that field, and if someone intentionally stirred up the bullocks? That's murder.

'But what if the post-mortem only confirms the trampling,' says Ally. 'What then?'

'Every contact leaves a trace, Al. We've got to keep the faith.'

'Do you think Mullins will tell us their findings?'

'Yeah, I do.'

After the events at Rockpool House, something changed in their relationship with the constable. Mullins will always be Mullins – chest out, blowing hot air – but fundamentally? Jayden considers him a mate. Perhaps, when it comes to cracking cases, he's even an ally. Jayden can't quite say the same for Skinner. For all that the sergeant has softened, Jayden knows he didn't love the fact that, after the Rockpool case, plaudits – and column inches – came the way of the Shell House Detectives.

'Why Russell was in that field is going to eat at Shaun, until there's nothing left,' says Jayden. 'If we can help him understand what happened, then he'll eventually accept it. He'll move on with his life as best he can.'

'I don't see how anyone can move on from losing a child.'

Jayden looks to his daughter; her thumb in her mouth, the other hand draped across Fox.

'No,' he says, quietly. He crouches down to her, lays a hand on her dark curls. Feels the climb of his heart in his chest. Will this love he has double, or divide, when their boy comes? He knows one thing: it better be split fair. 'Al, she's asleep. Check out these two.'

Ally shakes her head. 'What a picture.'

'Look, I've left a message with Owen to call in the quad's model code to the police. As soon as they've run that, we'll know for definite that Russell wasn't involved in any theft.'

'And then what?'

'Then . . . we work on the basis that Russell was up at Shoreline Vines for some other reason. The Harpers say he wasn't there to see them. If they're telling the truth, then perhaps he was meeting someone else.'

'But why would he use the vineyard as a meeting point?'

'He grew up there. It's land he knows,' says Jayden. 'But . . . yeah, okay, it doesn't stack up for me either. Which brings us back to Russell being at Shoreline Vines to see the Harpers. So they're lying. Or one of them is.'

'But why? We don't have a motive, do we?'

Jayden presses his hands to his temples. Outside, the rain taps on the roof, and beyond the hearth where his daughter's snoozing, the wood burner emits the occasional crackle and pop. The Shell House is a cocoon. Is it dulling his senses? They need to get back in the thinking room, but he doesn't want Jazzy seeing all their workings-out. Because while on the one hand it's a cosy office, it's also looking a whole lot like an incident room for murder.

'Okay, what about this? Russell's up there to ask for his dad's job back. The Harpers don't want to hear it, they've got bigger things on their minds. Russell gets mad at them, charges off across the field, doesn't see the cattle.'

'I thought we said that was unlikely.'

'I was just saying it out loud – strength-testing it. And agreed, it's weak. So how else could it have gone down? Let's run with the same opener. Russell's at the vineyard to ask for his dad's job back.'

'Perhaps there was a fight,' says Ally. 'Starting as a difference of opinion and . . . escalating.'

'Any wounds inflicted by a person would be covered after the bullock attack.'

Ally nods. 'And . . . someone would need to know that. They'd need to know that, in the right circumstances, cattle can startle.'

'Cattle as a murder weapon? I don't think that'd jump into the mind of the average criminal. Plus, they'd have to know what they're doing, because there's plenty of room for that tactic to go wrong.'

'Do we need to look more closely at Greg Sullivan?'

'See if there's any possible connection between Russell and him? Yeah, maybe.'

'He struck me as a straight arrow,' says Ally.

'But even the straight arrows should go on the board.'

'The Harpers were farmers before they started making wine.'

'Way back. Yeah, they were. And I'd say Wenna is a good bet for finding out more about them. Need anything from White Wave Stores, Al?'

She nods, mission understood.

'If we're talking a physical altercation, then Edwin and Owen are more likely than Ruth or Karensa,' says Jayden.

'But it could have been an accident. A slip, a trip, then someone panics and looks to cover it up.'

'Okay, so Russell goes to talk to . . . any one of the Harpers. Perhaps all of them. And his timing's way off. They've got bigger things on their mind. They're thinking about their investor's visit. Russell loses his temper. There's a confrontation.' Jayden stops and thinks. 'Edwin's knuckles, right? That gate he said he punched? Or maybe they're just arguing, there's a bit of shoving, Russell slips and hits his head. The Harpers look down at him—'

'Which Harpers?'

'I'm still thinking any Harpers. They look down at him and . . . panic. And someone has the bright idea to put him in the field with the cattle.'

'But if it's an accident, wouldn't they check his pulse?'

'The vital reaction,' says Jayden. 'He was breathing when he went in that field. You're right, if it was just an accident, they'd have been terrified that Russell was dead. But then as soon as they found a pulse they'd be calling 999. But they didn't call 999 until he was already dead.'

'So they must have had a reason not to.'

'So we're back to it not being an accident – at least not completely.'

Ally's on her feet. She dips her head, as if she's walking the shoreline, looking for that glimmer of promise.

'It's so calculated, isn't it? It wouldn't have been easy, getting him into the field.'

'If the police were thinking like us, they'd be dispatching CSIs right now. They'd be walking the whole scene, testing out different scenarios. Footprints, fibres, blood spatter. If something was used to move him into that field, they'd find it.'

'They could be doing that now, for all we know.'

Jayden shakes his head. 'I think Mullins would tell us. If there's anything inconsistent in the initial post-mortem, they'll do a forensic post-mortem. That's when the big guns come out.'

'Well, could we do it in the meantime? Walk the site again?'

Jayden considers it. A major part of him would love to zoom up there. 'Not without drawing serious attention from the Harpers. I think our best play is to keep them on side.'

'What about when they're busy entertaining tonight? You could tell me what to look for. No one's going to notice someone like me poking around in the barns, are they?'

'I hear you, but you could contaminate the scene, Al. Skinner wouldn't thank us for that.'

'But it might never be considered a crime scene unless the post-mortem shows something.'

'And that's a worry. The more time passes, the more evidence could be lost. We need that post-mortem to show something, so the police catch up to where we are, right?'

'I know we're speculating,' says Ally, staring at the board, 'but I don't think it's baseless.'

'Our theory makes more sense to me than Russell randomly going into a field of cattle. I mean, what thief returns for second helpings in broad daylight? Al, if that quad of the Harpers is sitting in that Bodmin warehouse, we've got the ammo we need.'

Jayden looks to the hearth and sees Jazzy stirring. Nap time over; abort case-chat. He drops his voice, says, 'This dinner tonight. I'm going to be watching the Harpers big-time.'

'Just remember, if they're hiding anything, they're going to be watching you too.'

23

'That sounds amazing,' says Saffron. 'So cool.'

She wants to concentrate on her prep, really. It's not a complicated menu but Edwin's made it clear that the pressure is on. Pressure, though, is something Saffron can handle. Dropping in on a concrete bowl on her skateboard, straight into a fakie tail stall on a vertical wall? Easy. Stroking into an eight-footer on her surfboard, where if you don't ride it out, you're going under? No sweat. And she can sure as hell execute a pitch-perfect bouillabaisse, even if she's working in someone else's kitchen, the owner looming over her, yammering on about his business plans.

What's slightly thrown Saffron is that, instead of her dad delivering the fish this morning, he sent his sidekick Trip instead. He had some kind of appointment, apparently. Which is fine, obviously, but shouldn't Wilson have let Saffron know he wasn't coming himself? Whenever she has these little flickers of disappointment, all Saffron can hear is her mum's voice: *See, I told you so.* Even if those are words she never said.

'Competition will be hot for the head chef role,' says Edwin. He's leaning against the counter, cradling his espresso. 'We'll be looking at Cornwall's best and brightest. Play it right tonight, and you could be a contender.'

Saffron looks up. 'Oh, I'm not looking for anything.'

Edwin raises his eyebrows.

'I mean, it sounds great, and you'll be flooded with applications, but . . . I've got my hands full with Hang Ten.'

And her heart is full too. The ocean as her front garden. Her surfboard propped against the back wall, for whenever she flips the sign to 'Closed'. Her flow of regulars, the coffee shop part of their everyday. The flocks of holidaymakers – people making memories, and how she loves that Hang Ten is part of them. Saffron can't imagine ever wanting to give that up.

'I had you down as a little bit more ambitious,' says Edwin. 'Celine's money's going to change a lot around here. Equipment upgrades across the board. And the jewel in the crown? "Dine at Shoreline Vines." Don't get left behind, Saffron.'

And he throws a salute her way, then strolls out.

Quiet at last.

Saffron washes Edwin's coffee cup, then checks her notes. Time for operation tarte Tatin. She did a dummy run two nights ago, and Broady declared it next-level.

Her phone pings then, and she checks it, wondering if it might be Wilson apologising for his no-show.

Guess who's coming to your dinner tonight? Stepping in for a sick Cliff.

She smiles. It's always a pleasure hanging out with Jayden. Except when he and Ally are dragging her into their investigations, that is. Rockpool House still pops up in her dreams sometimes, an unsettling element, showing that maybe she hasn't processed everything that happened in the summer quite as well as she thought. Sometimes she wonders if Ally, Jayden and Gus dream of it too. And Mullins. Not that the constable would admit it to her.

Sweet, she messages back. **Come hungry!**

She gets to work on the apples, the peel unspooling in one long ribbon, just the way her mum used to do it. Her mum would cut them into crescents, dust them in cinnamon and sugar, then toast them over the fire. *Magic apples, Saffron.* Saffron bites her lip; three years gone, and the loss still catches her out of the blue.

Her phone starts ringing, and this time? It's Wilson. She wipes her hands on her apron.

'Hey there, Wilson.'

'Oh, love hello, it's Dawn.'

'Are you okay?'

Because Dawn never calls her.

'Oh yes. I'm only using his nibs's phone because your number's programmed in. It's not in the book, you see.'

'Sure.'

Saffron waits, but on the other end of the phone, Dawn seems to be waiting too.

'Is everything okay, Dawn?' she says again.

'Oh love, there's no easy way to say this, but it's Wilson.'

After Saffron hangs up the phone, she slips off her apron. She just needs a few moments to reset, that's all. She hurries out into the hall, looking for the bathroom. She tries a door on her left but it's a cupboard. She glances at the stairs. All is quiet. It feels too intimate to just go up. In a farmhouse as big as this, surely there's a toilet on the ground floor? She walks to the end of the dimly lit passage, and peers into the sitting room. Flagstone floor, a big oriental rug, two saggy-looking sofas. There's a faint smell of woodsmoke from the vast fireplace, a huge beam spanning it, the mantelpiece loaded with family photographs.

Tears prick at the backs of her eyes.

She heads on down the hall and sees the dining room with its long wooden table and whitewashed stone walls. She tries another door and it's locked. She turns and, at the bottom of the stairs, she calls up tentatively. *No answer.* She nips up, feeling like she's intruding; the creaky floorboards make music as she goes.

Saffron hears, suddenly, a sob. She freezes. Further down the hall, a door flies open.

'Karensa, wait.'

A man comes out behind her.

'Darling, please!'

Karensa spins on her heel. 'Why can't we have this conversation here? We need to have it somewhere, Owen.'

Saffron tries the door right beside her and, mercifully, it opens. *The bathroom!* She throws herself inside, and quickly, quietly, closes the door. She slides the bolt across.

And breathes out.

She met Edwin's wife, Karensa, earlier. A nice but nervous woman. Saffron met Owen too, and instantly liked him more than his brother.

She hears their footsteps. They stop outside the door, just inches away.

'We have to come clean,' says Karensa. 'It's dangerous . . . it's—'

'You know we can't,' Owen cuts in. Then he says something that Saffron can't hear. And the footsteps quickly recede.

Saffron stands for a moment, as if the intensity of Owen and Karensa's exchange has rooted her to the spot. Was it her imagination, or did Karensa sound frightened?

She goes to the sink and splashes cold water on her face. Alone again, the drama ebbed, the fact of Dawn's phone call rushes back in. *Wilson.* Saffron looks at her face in the mirror. Tears run down her already-wet cheeks.

24

As Jayden approaches All Swell, he sees Gus standing outside, attempting to position a stepladder against the wall. He watches as Gus stands back and peers up at the roof. Nothing about his posture beams confidence.

Jayden slows. It's a gusty day, and only four months ago Gus was in intensive care in Truro. Not a bright idea, going up a ladder.

He buzzes down the window of the Land Rover. 'Alright, Gus?'

'Jayden!' Gus's face lights up. 'Good to see you, my friend.' He peers into the back. 'And hullo, little Jasmine.'

The look that Gus gives them is pure warmth, as if Jayden has just turned his face to the sun. Warmth and gratitude. Jayden has had to stop Gus from saying it all the time though, because *I can't thank you enough* became Gus's constant refrain.

Jayden has never been one to big himself up, and when others do it for him, he's quick to wave it away. *No need. It's all good.* Gus's continuing life on earth? No, he can't take credit for that. Not without caveats. Like the fact that Mullins would have done what he did in a heartbeat; that the emergency services were fast to respond, paramedics descending in a blaze of blue lights and efficiency. *Gus, it was a team effort.*

But occasionally – in the middle of the night, mostly – it feels more complicated. Jayden is very, very happy that he was there in

Gus's hour of need. He just wishes he could have done the same for Kieran. He could save a thousand lives, and he'd still feel the same.

It's okay for it to feel kind of weird, Cat said to him once, slipping her hand into his. It was late summer, and they'd run into Gus outside White Wave Stores. Gus had thanked him. Again. Jayden didn't have to ask his wife what she meant; she just got it.

Now, Jayden looks pointedly at the ladder, says to Gus, 'Tell me you're not thinking of going up that.'

'Have you seen the forecast? Gales on the way. I don't trust the roof not to lift off, Jayden. I was thinking I could fashion some kind of' – he waves his hand – 'temporary fix.'

'The ladder doesn't look tall enough.'

'I've guesstimated, and I reckon if I go tiptoe on the top rung, I should be able to just—'

Jayden kills the engine. He turns to Jazzy, 'Give me two secs, babe,' then climbs out.

'Here, let me, Gus. I'm taller than you.'

Cat would love this. *Not.* Jayden repositions the ladder, planting the ends firmly in the sand.

'Hold it steady,' he says.

And to be fair to Gus, it's not the worst plan. All Swell's not exactly high-rise. Jayden reaches the limit of the stepladder and leans on the roof. He's no DIY expert – he can hear Cliff's laughter at the thought of it from here – but even he can see the roof is patchy at best. As he touches the wooden gable, it comes off in his hands.

'Ah,' he says. He swivels, holds it up. 'Sorry, mate. It's rotted through.'

'Same story with every timber, I reckon. How are the shingles?'

Jayden looks back. Taps one.

'Could do with a bit of TLC. I'd get it sorted before winter.'

'Cash flow no flow,' says Gus, cheerily. 'Might have to wait until I sell the book.'

Gus's detective novel. The same novel he's been writing since he first came to Porthpella as a holidaymaker, almost two years ago. As far as financial strategies go, that plan is about as watertight as Gus's roof.

'I hear you,' says Jayden, testing one of the looser-looking shingles. 'I reckon you want to get it seen to sooner rather than later though. Truth is, Gus, I don't really know what I'm looking at.'

'You and me both. Ah well. For now, I'll batten down the hatches and hope for the best.'

Jayden jumps down the last couple of rungs, and Gus claps him on the back.

'Come from Ally's, have you?'

He nods. 'She told you about the new case?'

'She did. She seems . . . affected by it. I mean, Ally always wants to do her best by everyone, but this poor Shaun Tremaine fellow . . . it's all quite thrown her.' Gus gives a small laugh. 'You know, she clean forgot we had dinner plans the other night.'

'If it's any consolation, I did the same with Cat and Jazz. I was on cooking duty too.'

'Ah,' says Gus, 'so it's a Shell House Detectives thing, is it? Well, now I feel better. I was taking it rather personally.'

And the look that Gus gives Jayden is a door held open.

'Come on, Gus, you know better than that.'

Does he though? Gus isn't the most self-confident guy in the world. But Jayden knows how much Ally likes him. Over the summer they spent more time together than ever before, as if each other's company was the natural go-to. Jayden hasn't speculated beyond that; he and Ally talk case work, not romance. Though he's here for any kind of talk, really. Including with Gus, by a rickety stepladder, sand blowing around them.

'I'm just so . . . out of practice. You know, at reading the signals. I mean, we're good friends, Ally and I, and I'm grateful, deeply grateful for that, but . . . I almost thought by now we'd be . . . more.'

126

Not that we need to be more. I sound presumptuous even saying it, which I'm not. Not at all. But . . .'

'Gus, have you said any of this to Ally?'

'Good God, no.'

What should Jayden say to Gus? Seize the day? But he's all too aware that while Ally cares a lot for Gus, Bill still looms large for her. Take the thinking room: Bill's office. Jayden didn't even know that room existed until yesterday.

'To be honest, I'm . . . tentative, Jayden. More so than before the knock to the head. You'd think something like that would make one throw caution to the wind. But, instead, it's made me . . . rather wobbly.'

'You're not getting dizzy spells, are you?'

'No, no. All grand, in terms of recuperation. Clean bill of health, there. It's just . . . physically. I've lost my confidence a bit, I suppose. Don't quite trust myself to . . . not mess it all up.' Gus offers a brave grin. 'The thing is, Mona and I, well, it was over a long time before it was actually over, if you get my drift. A very, very long time.'

And now Jayden gets it. *Catch up, Weston.*

'Anyway, enough of all this,' says Gus, quickly turning his attention to the stepladder. 'I need to get this put away. And I've kept you long enough, wittering on like an embarrassing old fool, when you've a case to solve.'

Jayden touches him lightly on the shoulder. 'You're not an old fool.'

'No?' He turns a half-hopeful look to Jayden.

'I think you're someone who just really cares. And Gus, without speaking for Ally, I reckon that's one of the things she likes about you.'

25

'Just those bits, is it, Ally love?'

Wenna rings through Ally's groceries, her crusty loaf and salted butter, the wedge of Yarg and pound of bacon. She darts a look at Ally over the top of her spectacles.

'I let my tongue run on the other day. You know how I am. Gerren's always on at me for my ghost stories. Only yarns though, aren't they? No harm meant.'

But it wasn't the old story about Shoreline Farm that bothered Ally and Gus, and looking at Wenna's contrite expression, she knows it too.

'Poor old Shaun Tremaine. He must be in bits. I heard you're helping him.'

'We're trying to.'

Ally doesn't especially want to talk about the case with Wenna – not after her easy condemnation of Russell Tremaine – but, on the other hand, the woman is a source of information like no one else. Even if a pinch of salt – *make that a shedload, Al,* Jayden likes to say – is often required.

'Nothing to prove though, is there, Ally? Beyond him being in the wrong place at the wrong time?'

'Shaun wants answers,' says Ally carefully.

'Well, if anyone can give them to him, it's you and Jayden. I hear he's squiring his mum-in-law about tonight. Off to that fancy dinner.'

Ally smiles to herself. *Is there anything Wenna doesn't know?*

'Gerren and I aren't smart enough for an invitation. Though I do stock the wines, which you'd think would be enough. Oh well. I shan't lose sleep over it. And like I said, I've never felt comfortable over at Shoreline. Not as a girl and not now. Look, there they are on the shelf, the wines. Little bit dusty this time of year. We don't get the money coming through like in the summer, and they're not cheap, are they, Ally? But your Gus bought one the other day. Nice drop, was it?'

Your Gus. For a moment, Ally's distracted. Is that how people see him? He messaged her last night, asking if she wanted to accompany him on 'a minor hike' today. Part of her wanted to say yes – she always enjoys his company – but she couldn't, not in the middle of such an important case.

'If you ask me, they should have cancelled the dinner,' says Wenna. 'It's common decency.'

Call her cynical, but Ally wonders if Wenna's view is largely due to her own lack of an invitation. Ally thinks of Shaun in his cottage at the bottom of the track. Will he see the smart cars passing? The farmhouse all lit up for the party? It's an uncomfortable thought.

'It is unfortunate timing,' she agrees.

Timing. Ally's brain fires. Means, motive, opportunity. Is the timing relevant to the motivation that they're missing for the Harpers? Could Russell's death somehow be connected to the vineyard's future plans?

'I should think that Edwin will be in full swing tonight,' Wenna runs on, 'showing off to the money men. He's been going on about it down The Wreckers for weeks now. Couple of million they're getting, that's the rumour. Said he's been practising his French,

129

but I should think anyone'd know how to say "merci beaucoup" if they're being handed two mil. Suppose it makes sense that it's French money, doesn't it? I think of wine, I think of France. Reckon they'll invest in White Wave too, while they're at it?'

Ally holds the thought up to the light; turns it slowly. Shaun said that he'd been upset about the Harpers' change in fortune, given that not so long ago they couldn't afford to keep him on. Russell was angry on his behalf too. Then the day before the big weekend, Russell was killed. What if the Harpers were afraid Russell was going to embarrass them in front of their important guests?

'They had a French girl staying up at Shoreline years ago. Au pair, she was. Glamorous creature. Tall as a supermodel. Turned a few heads down here. And enjoyed the attention too. Left under a cloud though, as I remember. She brought the kids down The Wreckers one day. Got herself chatted up by the barman – Paddy's son, lovely-looking lad, to be fair – and meanwhile little Edwin's helping himself to someone's pint and then goes puking his guts up.' Wenna laughs. 'He was only a toddler. Poor tyke. Didn't put him off though, did it? He's got a taste for it now. Course Ruth was spitting blood after, though Frank will have smoothed things over. That was his way. That was the end of that though, and the girl left soon after. You can't have an au pair who lets the kiddies get drunk, can you? I should remind Edwin of that next time I see him.'

Ally makes an encouraging sort of noise, then says, 'Wenna, I must be getting on.'

'Here I am, gassing away. You take care, Ally love. And give my best to Shaun when you see him next. No one should have to go through what he's going through. I don't see how you and Jayden can fix this one, but at least you're trying.'

As Ally heads out into the square, she thinks trying is all very well – but it's not enough for Shaun.

She takes out her phone and calls Jayden.

26

Celine sees Owen Harper crossing the yard, his arms already wide in welcome. She raises her hand from the wheel and gives a quick wave, despite herself. He is, unmistakably, the same boy. A thatch of straw-blond hair. An easy grin. *Son petit Owen.*

Celine's relationship with time is supremely well-managed: she makes excellent use of it; is punctual to a fault. She wears a Patek Phillippe and loves the reassuring weight of it on her wrist, this one watch costing almost as much as the vineyard's annual turnover. But, on the rarest of occasions, she feels her grasp of time slip. For instance, before her now is a grown man – and yet she sees a boy. The boy he was thirty years ago, tearing about in shorts and wellingtons.

Then time performs another skip. There's something in the way Owen walks across the yard. That gesture of the open arms; an easy manner that belies a tough interior – in Frank's case, anyway. He draws closer, and Celine takes in his dark jeans and brown leather shoes; a shirt that's probably supposed to be smart, but she can see the creases, and knows that if she touches its fabric, it'll feel cheaply manufactured. His hair is damp from the shower.

Owen has grown up to look an awful lot like his father.

He didn't, in the pictures she found online. Because Celine did her due diligence; every emotion managed in advance.

She looks down at her hands on the steering wheel. The platinum rings, rubies and sapphires. The glint of diamonds. She sees, too, the creases in her skin. She is here; this is now. The year is 2024. She knows if she flips down the mirror there will be creases at her eyes too, and lines across her forehead. Botox? *Non, merci.* She's only too happy for her youth to be lost. Celine would not be nineteen again for a kingdom.

She turns off the engine and climbs out of the car; the toe of her leather boot hesitates before it touches the ground.

'Celine,' he says, 'welcome.'

'You must be Owen. I'd recognise you anywhere.'

She shakes his hand. It's a firm handshake; a good handshake. *Mon Dieu.* Up close, he is so much like Frank.

He looks disarmed, then grins widely. 'Welcome back, I should say.'

'Do you remember me too?'

'Erm, of course,' he says, and his hesitation amuses her. 'Of course I do.'

'It's okay,' she twinkles, *son fameux charme*, 'you were five, Owen. Nobody remembers anything from when they were five.'

And inside she wills this to be true.

'*Bienvenue*, Celine!'

And it's Edwin. Edwin who has led this charge to bring her here, along with Ruth. Edwin who cried all the time as a child; had eczema in the creases of his elbows and knocked out his front milk teeth falling in the yard. Edwin, who stole the beer in the local pub and then blamed it on her. He was sick for days afterwards – or pretended to be anyway. Are three-year-olds capable of deception? Is he, now? She eyes him keenly. He holds her gaze right back; clasps her hand, as if he's afraid she might disappear.

'How was your journey?' he says.

'Horrific traffic getting out of London.' She checks her watch; breathes slowly. 'At least I'm not late.'

'You're perfect,' he says. 'And I should think you'd like a drink. Let me take your bags.'

As he retrieves her Rimowa case, she stands back and looks at the farmhouse. It's just as she remembers it. A grave face. Imposing. Joyless. It was Frank who brought the colour and light.

She breathes evenly. *I am in control.* She feels the spit of rain on her face.

With a magician's flourish, Edwin produces an umbrella and holds it over her head. He dumps her case at his brother's feet, and escorts Celine towards the house. Ruth appears, standing at the threshold. She wears a plum-coloured silk blouse and pearl earrings, her silver hair as sleek as a skullcap. Her lipstick is claret, and when she pulls her mouth into a smile there's a smudge on her teeth.

The first time Celine ever met Ruth, she immediately felt superior to her. It wasn't intentional, but on some subconscious level, Celine was pitting herself against her – woman to woman – and found herself easily coming up trumps. Was she expecting the power balance to have shifted, now? On paper, it's clear that Ruth needs her. Now, in person, Celine feels this too.

'Ruth,' says Celine, with all the appearance of pleasure, and holds out her hand.

But, improbably, Ruth hugs her – and it's as swift, and startling, as a slap.

'Come in. I'll show you to your room.'

Up the stairs. Creaking boards on the landing. All the way along the dark corridor. The room at the very end.

Of course.

Ruth gestures to the narrow single bed, the duo of towels folded on the coverlet. Even the Laura Ashley-print curtains, red and blue sweet peas, are the same. Celine remembers lying staring at those curtains on her last night in this room; how the colours of the flowers bled together. She kept expecting a knock at the door – but it never came.

'Thank you,' she says.

Ruth tips her chin and her eyes flash like amber. Celine's initial assessment of the situation falters a touch.

'I'm sorry for your loss, Ruth,' says Celine. 'I haven't said that yet.'

She doesn't say his name. She doesn't need to. She watches, waits. Ninety-three per cent of meaning is communicated non-verbally.

'Thank you,' says Ruth. 'I know how much he meant to you. And how much you meant to him.'

Celine is reminded of the playground staring contests she used to take part in. She didn't blink then, and she doesn't blink now.

'He was a good man,' she says.

'He tried. But like all men, he had his weaknesses.'

At this Ruth looks Celine up and down – her eyes tracking over her hips, her breasts, her almost-fifty-year-old face – as if Celine's presence in this room, in this house, is the same affront now as it was then.

Belle, Frank said to her, two weeks in. *I looked it up in the dictionary. Très, très belle.* Other girls might not have known where to look – cheeks turning red as cherries – but Celine just laughed. *Your French is very good*, she said. *But you should say 'vous êtes'. Otherwise you could be talking about the view. Or that bird in the tree. Or my dress.*

'To err is human,' says Celine.

'To forgive is divine,' finishes Ruth. And she smiles, showing all her teeth.

Celine goes to the window. The leafless vines track down the hillside, rows and rows and rows of them: orderly brown tangles of stem and shoot. Beyond, the sea is a band of dark teal. The sky above it pewter.

'What a view,' she says.

'It hasn't changed.'

She turns, unsure if Ruth's joking.

'Yes, it has,' says Celine. 'The vines. The vines weren't here before, were they?' Then, before Ruth can answer, Celine says, 'Ruth, I left a book here, all those years ago. A book that's very important to me. You don't happen to have it, do you?'

'I have no idea. Feel free to check the bookshelves.' A hard smile comes over her face. 'I suppose you did leave in rather a hurry, didn't you?'

Again, Celine holds Ruth's eye.

'Thinking about it, if you'd left anything, I probably would have sent it to the charity shop. Or, I'm afraid to say, binned it. You see, at the time I probably thought we'd never be seeing you again, Celine.'

Ruth sets a hand on Celine's shoulder, and she can feel the press of each of her fingers. It's all she can do not to squirm.

'But my sons and are I immeasurably glad that you're here now.'

27

Gus is lost in thought, barely registering his surroundings as he walks. It's not that he's become immune to the beauty of his adopted home, it's just that he can't stop thinking about his conversation with Jayden. And how much he said to him.

Too much? Oh dear, probably.

It's true that, for Gus, Jayden will never be ordinary. That's what happens when you save someone's life. *Sorry, that's just the way it is!* But he can't go dragging him into his love life too. The trouble is, Jayden's so easy to talk to. Much easier than his oldest friends, Rich and Clive, with whom he enjoys a spirited pen-pal correspondence. Perhaps it's a generational thing and young men these days are better listeners.

He stops for a breather, wrestling his Thermos from his backpack. The coffee's tepid, and tastes faintly of plastic, but the act of stopping finally makes him take in the view.

He can see all the way back to Porthpella from here: the cluster of rooftops, the crescent bay and the undulating dunes; the island lighthouse, straight as a matchstick. Everything in miniature, like the model railway he longed for as a boy. Gus would snip out advertisements and keep them in a notebook; note down the parts he wanted to save up for. He eventually bought an engine and a carriage and kept them on the windowsill in his bedroom – *The*

Wolvercote Express! – never expanding the set beyond that. It was as if the possibility was enough; these two pieces no less treasured for the fact they'd never run on rails, nor thrum with electricity.

He's always been easily satisfied, has Gus. Take All Swell. He'd have been happy renting it until the end of his days, if the owner hadn't had other ideas.

The end of his days. And how close he came.

Gus vividly remembers being in intensive care; Ally weaving her fingers through his, murmuring such gentle and fortifying words that, lying there, he felt a good deal more fortunate than appearances might suggest.

All Swell is all his now. The work is less renovation and more resurrection. An albatross? He's bitten off more than he can chew, certainly. But nothing will steal his lucky feeling.

And Ally? Ally is not all his. He would never stake a claim over another human being in that way. Besides, he knows that with Ally it's complicated. Bill's shoes – enormous police-issue boots, as it happens – are not available to fill. Gus is something different to her.

And most of the time – even as much as 95 per cent, or certainly 90 per cent – he's happy with that 'something' being undefined.

Now, he screws the lid back on his Thermos and studies his map. The wind tugs at it, and he turns his back to protect it. Terming this outing a *hike* was probably a stretch. The doctor has advised him to simultaneously take it easy and keep strong – and so Gus has upped his commitment to sedate rambling. A far cry from his fell-walking days as an intrepid geography student, but nevertheless he likes pulling his old boots on and getting a few miles under his belt.

Round this next point, Gus will reach the beach from which Shoreline Vines gets its name.

And this is where his outing gets whimsical. He was rather taken with Wenna's account of the tree at the vineyard that looks

137

like the mast of a tall ship – even if he didn't appreciate Wenna's draconian tone – and Gus wouldn't mind seeing it for himself. He didn't tell Ally he was walking out this way; mostly because the exact idea formed after she declined to come. He'd have loved her company, but in the absence of it, Gus wonders if he can perhaps be useful. Like verifying Wenna's account of the tree – crucial detective work, that. And perhaps pocketing a shell from the beach for Ally, a good luck charm for the case.

See? Whimsical.

When he spoke to Ally earlier, she was a little despondent. Usually, a new case lights her up, but, this time, she said it felt different.

Because of Shaun? he asked.

And she nodded. It was different with their last case, she said. There was no one at Rockpool who took Baz Carson's death to heart like Ally would have imagined. For all her grief, Tallulah – Baz's first love – had a kind of energetic confidence and grace about her. Shaun, on the other hand, feels overlooked; forgotten.

He thinks no one cares, said Ally. *His emotions are so raw, Gus. And his anger. The responsibility . . .*

You'll get it right, Ally, he said.

But Gus doesn't really know what 'right' is. Not when it's a pack of bullocks in the dock for murder. Unless Ally and Jayden are on to something with their theory that there could be more to it.

Gus takes the steep path down to the narrow beach. It's a messy affair, strewn with great clumps of seaweed and loose shingle. Far out, the sea is the colour of his smart jeans, but up close, it's swirling with white water, and when the waves pull back from the shore there's an eerie clacking of stone. Put it like this: he wouldn't bring a picnic here. He imagines at high tide the beach might disappear entirely. For the captain of the wrecked ship in Wenna's story, it would have been a place of refuge – until he got his head bashed in by the farmers, anyway. Gus looks back up to the cliff. The vine-yard's land apparently runs right to the edge, and he resolves to cut back that way. But first, a shell for Ally.

He wanders down to the strandline. Tangled in the inky-brown bladderwrack there are gull feathers and ends of driftwood that look a lot like bones. He pokes one with his toe, hoping for the pearlescent glint of a top shell, or better still one of those tropical little things – a cowrie. His vocabulary has expanded since he met Ally.

The sharp yapping of a dog startles him. The beach is a public space, but Gus suddenly feels as if he's trespassing.

The dog – a scrappy thing – pelts out on to the sand. It appears to be entirely on his own, and the effect is disconcerting. For a moment, man and dog stare at one another. For all its diminutive size, Gus has a ridiculous feeling it might charge him. And of the two of them, he'd come off worse.

Too much thinking on bullocks.

'Easy, boy,' he ventures.

Just then, a man pushes through the tangled briars at the far end of the cove. He walks with his head down, wearing what looks like an old ski jacket – a voluminous 1980s number – and a tweed flat cap. He's presumably the owner, but he's oblivious to the dog's interest in Gus.

A wave cracks on the shore and the shingle clacks in protest. Beside him, the animal growls.

Then, as quickly as he came, the dog pelts towards his owner. Gus watches the man pick up a hunk of driftwood and throw it half-heartedly.

Time to make his escape.

'Afternoon,' says Gus, as he passes. Because it would be per-verse to ignore this other person's presence in so wild a spot. The man lifts his head and looks at him. And Gus is alarmed to see tears streaming down his cheeks.

Is that the sort of thing one should draw attention to?

There's a gust of wind, then, and the man staggers. Gus holds out a hand to steady him and is surprised when he takes it. Takes it and hangs on.

Somewhere down the beach, the wretched dog lets loose a volley of barks.

'Oh,' says Gus. 'Oh dear. Are you . . . Can I help?'

28

'Ruth, I hope you don't mind me subbing in my handsome son-in-law,' says Sue.

Jayden smiles his most innocent smile. 'Hi, Ruth. Thanks for having me.'

'It's a pleasure to see you again so soon.'

And is it Jayden's imagination, or does she put an extra little weight on the words *so soon*?

'And do send Cliff my best,' Ruth adds.

'Cat swears it's nothing but man flu,' laughs Sue. 'Oh, hello, Broady, love. You scrub up beautifully.'

'Broady. Hey, dude.'

Saffron's boyfriend holds the tray of glasses in one hand, and with the other dispenses a knuckle-bump to Jayden. His long blond hair is pulled back in a half-mast topknot. He's wearing a Hawaiian shirt and a black bow tie and, because it's Broady, he pulls it off.

'The jewel in our crown,' says Ruth. 'Sparkling Pinot Noir. You won't taste better.'

'You're not wrong,' says Sue. 'That's absolutely delicious.'

Jayden smiles at his mum-in-law's enthusiasm. That's how Sue walks through life: always on the sunny side of the street. And good thing too, because if Cat took too much after her dad, Jayden's sure they wouldn't have got past the first date.

'It's 2018,' says Ruth. 'A wonderful year. These are our first bottles. Edwin wanted it ready for Celine. Didn't you, darling?'

And Edwin's at his mum's elbow, a questioning look on his face as he takes in Jayden.

'Cliff is ailing, Edwin. Jayden's done the gentlemanly thing.'

Jayden raises his glass to Edwin.

'As I said yesterday, it's a big night for us,' says Edwin. 'It's important for Celine to see that she's investing in a community.'

'Oh, and I do see that.'

It's as if the woman stepped out of nowhere. She's as tall as Jayden. Hair in a chic dark bob, lipstick as red as her nails. She takes a glass from Broady's tray and sends him a wink.

'It's a marvellous community.' Then, deftly, addressing no one in particular, 'Good to see you.'

Edwin immediately positions himself beside her. 'Celine Chevalier,' he says, as if announcing an act at a festival. Jayden feels like he should let loose a whoop, but his modus operandi tonight is to lie low – and see if he can pick up on anything that adds up to a motive for the Harpers.

Ally called him just as he was about to jump in the shower earlier.

The investor's weekend visit, Jayden. The Harpers stand to gain a lot, don't they? Which means they also have a lot to lose. What if they were afraid Russell was going to ruin it for them somehow?

A decent line of enquiry, for sure. They just need the 'why', and the 'how'. And for someone to either discover a conscience – or let slip the truth. Otherwise, they're back to him and Ally piecing together something out of nothing. Well, they've been here before.

'Celine,' says Edwin, 'this evening we have with us not just the cream of West Cornwall's food and drink industry, but a genuine slice of the community too. Morris Gordon is one of the most innovative fish wholesalers in the area. Jago Perkins and his wife Kathy make a Camembert that has to be tasted to be believed.'

'Camembert?' says Celine, with a smile. 'Next you'll be calling your sparkling wine Champagne.'

'Sunita Singh is a gallerist. What began as – and I'm sure she won't mind me saying – something akin to a souvenir shack, the Bluebird is now fast extending its reputation beyond West Cornwall's art world. Meanwhile, the salt-of-the-earth farmers, my dad's compatriots, they're finding ways to diversify now too. You opened Top Field Camping last year, didn't you, Sue? Out with the cauliflowers and in with the camper vans.'

Sue tips her head back and laughs. 'A good job Cliff isn't here to hear you say that. The cauliflowers are very much alive and well. And the campsite is all my daughter Cat and Jayden here.'

Jayden levels a look at Edwin, but he's oblivious to it. Wheeling out Cat's parents like they're relics from a bygone era dabbling in something new? *Not cool.*

Just then, Owen joins the group. He chinks a glass with Celine, as though she's an old friend.

'The smell from the kitchen is out of this world,' he says with an easy grin.

'Isn't it always, Owen?' says Ruth, with a theatrically sharp tone.

And they all laugh, in that way that people do when they're being polite.

'Ruth, when I was here all those years ago,' says Celine. 'I remember you making the most delicious Sunday roasts. You gave this girl from Provence her first experience of Yorkshire pudding.'

'Ooh, you've been here before, have you, Celine?' asks Sue.

'Oh yes,' says Celine. 'Otherwise I wouldn't be standing here now.'

'Though we're very glad that your romantic attachment to Shoreline is also supported by a genuine belief in its business potential,' says Ruth.

'Oh, one hundred per cent. I come with both my head and my heart, Ruth.'

'Cheers to that,' says Owen. 'It's how Dad lived.'

Edwin lifts his glass. 'Head and heart.'

And they're all raising glasses, Jayden suddenly looking at Celine in a different way.

'When did you last come here, Celine?' he asks.

'It must be thirty years ago,' she says. 'I was an au pair.'

'So, our French should really be a lot better than it is,' grins Owen. '*N'est-ce pas*, Edwin?'

'I hoped you boys would learn Spanish too,' says Ruth. 'You'd just returned from a year in Spain, hadn't you, Celine? My trilingual boys, I thought. Only it didn't work out like that.'

'Frank taught me some words of Cornish though,' says Celine. 'Which of course I can't remember now at all. So please don't test me.'

As everyone laughs, Jayden looks to see Karensa hovering in the doorway. Jayden throws her a smile, but she takes one look at him and walks back out.

◆ ◆ ◆

Jayden peers into the kitchen. Saffron's leaning against the counter, staring into space.

'Not disturbing, am I?'

She smiles at him, but it doesn't quite have its usual dazzle. He imagines the Harpers are taskmasters.

'You okay?'

Saffron hesitates, for a second looking like she's about to say something. Then she pops a thumbs up.

'All good. How's Broady doing out there?'

'He's a pro. I dig the bow tie. And the smell in here . . .'

'Just your standard bouillabaisse, mate.'

Although she laughs as she says it, Jayden can tell Saffron's stressed – and that's rare. So, he cuts to the chase.

'So tonight,' he says, 'I'm here on a bit of business, as it happens.'

'I knew it.' Saffron sets down her spoon; wipes her hands on her apron. 'Jayden, you're not talking about the man who died, are you? He was trampled by cows.'

'He was. But Ally and I are trying to build up a picture of events before that. So . . . how's the mood been up here today?'

'With the Harpers? Kind of tense. Celine's a proper VIP.'

'More tense than you'd imagine, in those circumstances?'

Saffron turns back to the stove. She lifts the lid, and the delectable smell amps up. 'I guess there is a bit of a weird energy.'

'Weird energy?' Jayden glances to the door. 'What kind of weird energy?'

'Owen and Karensa. I heard them talking earlier.'

Owen's manner seems relaxed, easy-breezy, but Karensa? She couldn't have left the room with more speed just now.

'Saffron, what were they saying?'

'I can't remember exactly. Karensa said something about coming clean.'

Jayden steps closer. 'Seriously?'

'Yeah, but . . . if I had to call it, I think they're having an affair. They were intimate, the way they spoke. Not like a brother- and sister-in-law, you know?'

Jayden digests the info. An affair under this roof would account for some weird energy, for sure. It's interesting, but how relevant is it?

145

'And you're sure that Karensa was talking about the affair when she spoke about coming clean?'

He watches Saffron consider it. The answer to a question like that is going to be guesswork, but Saffron is one of the most emotionally intelligent people he knows.

'I can't call it,' she says, 'but . . .'

'But what?'

'With Karensa, it was more about the way she was speaking than what she was saying. She sounded . . . she actually sounded kind of scared, Jayden.'

'Scared of Owen? Or scared that her affair with her brother-in-law might be discovered?'

'I don't know,' says Saffron. 'Are they the only options?'

29

It's dark as Shaun makes his way up to Shoreline Vines, but he knows the path like the back of his hand. He's got a fire in his belly after talking to the bloke at the beach earlier. And yeah, okay, a splash of whisky too. His eyes burn in their sockets: tractor beams, showing the way. And that spindly moon's throwing a bit of light too, when the clouds aren't whipping through like smoke.

His boots squelch in the mud, and he stumbles in another pothole. It needs redoing, this track. When they've got their money, they'll put in a three-lane highway, probably. All roads leading to Shoreline bloody Vines.

Frank was his friend. His boss, but his friend too. Shaun didn't expect to get anything when he died, but it hurt to not just be ignored, but thrown out with the rubbish when the boys took over. Maybe Frank did make a mess of the finances, but Shaun's pay packet wasn't exactly a fat one, was it? That's the cruel joke of it, that he needs so little to scrape by – and he can't even manage that most months.

Russell must have been fighting Shaun's battles up at the farm. He loved his dad, and he had a strong streak of justice in him, did Russell. Even as a little kid he'd get himself riled up. A shove from another boy and he'd always shove back. A righteous scrapper – but never with the heft to carry it off.

Like his pathetic old man.

A sob catches in Shaun's throat. He lost himself a bit, that boy of his, but he was still his little Russell William Tremaine. Throwing his schoolbag down in the hallway, wrenching off his tie like he was slipping the hangman's noose. Yelling out *Home!* like he'd just scored the winner in the cup final. Fish and chips every Friday teatime, trays balanced on their knees; something silly on the box.

Any homework this weekend, son?

And his boy's face would split with a grin as he said, *Funny thing is, teacher didn't give us any again.*

Again, eh? Fancy that. You should have a word with that teacher of yours. Tell her to pull her finger out.

Yeah. Or she'll never get on in life, will she?

And they'd laugh together like a couple of herring gulls.

Should Shaun have pushed the homework? Got on at him for his algebra and spelling and capitals of the world? Should he have said no to Russell stretching those scrawny wings of his and flying off to Camborne – said he needed him here, that he couldn't do without him? That first time Russell came home with his winnings, should Shaun have sat the boy down and had a stiff word, instead of the two of them dancing round the living room like lunatics?

Now he'll never dance again. And it's true: Shaun can't do without him.

He rounds the corner and there's the farmhouse. Light gleaming from every window, smoke curling from the chimney like it's a Christmas card. And they'll be making merry inside alright.

Can't stomach it, he told the bald bloke on the beach earlier. *That lot going on up there like nothing's happened. Showing off to some rich Londoner with a great big party.*

It doesn't seem right, does it? the bloke said, as he gave Shaun a little plastic cup of coffee. *Sorry I've nothing stronger.*

And Shaun thanked him and meant it. A friend of the seashell detectives, he said he was. Shaun got a bit teary in front of him, which might have bothered him once, but he's stopped caring about the things that don't matter.

Doesn't seem right. That bloke on the beach wasn't all revved up on emotion as he said it. It was just a sane reaction from a sensible person, and it did Shaun good to hear it. Without those words, Shaun would be home alone, sinking a bottle in front of the fire, crying his eyes out. Not here, holding people to account.

Shaun crosses the yard, where light streams like ribbons on the wet stone. He doesn't look twice at the gate to the field. Sullivan's moved his steers; there's nothing of his boy there. Out front, he counts six cars. One of them is a convertible. He knows those rounded headlamps, that grille like a laughing mouth. As a kid it was Russell's favourite Top Trump card: Porsche 911.

Shaun goes up to the window and presses his face against it. The kitchen. There's a big table, but it's not fancy enough for tonight's crowd. He sees a pink-haired girl at the stove, and when she turns, she must clock his face at the window because she jumps a mile in the air.

That's done it.

He gives a small belch and presses his hand to his mouth. Whisky has never sat well with him, but as an anaesthetic it's the best he could do.

He goes to the front door and makes to pound with both hands. Then he stops; tries the handle. He walks right in.

Straight away Shaun's hit by the warmth of the place. And the smell. The smell twists its way around his nostrils. His stomach wrenches; he doesn't know when he last ate.

He makes to pull off his boots – old impulse – then straightens up. He clumps mud over the flagstones as he makes for the dining room at the back. He can hear their braying from here.

He strides in, easy as a talk show host.

The silence trickles. Some bloke at the end is still telling a story, before he's shushed. Then all eyes are on Shaun. One hundred per cent attention, like he's never had in his life.

Ruth's face is white as a death mask. Edwin's is beetroot red. Only Owen says, 'Shaun. Evening, mate,' and starts to get to his feet.

'That's it,' says Shaun, his voice higher than he'd like. 'That's it, you carry on. You carry on with your drinking and eating and laughing.' He clears his throat; tries to sound louder, bigger. Now he's getting personal, the confidence of his entrance is ebbing fast. 'My son died. My son Russell died just steps from where you're sitting, and you're all carrying on like it was nothing. Like he was nothing.'

There's a movement at the end of the table but Shaun doesn't care. He's staring at the Harpers. At Ruth and Edwin and Owen. And Karensa – who's covering her mouth with her hand as if she doesn't want to catch something.

His gaze flicks to another woman who's sitting statue-still. The VIP? She looks expensive. And frightened of him. He's not used to that, and for a second, he wavers.

Shaun can feel a lump in his throat, and he knows he's on borrowed time now. His vision blurs as the tears come.

'I want to know what my boy was doing in that field. That's what I want to know. Because you're lying if you say he was stealing.' He jabs his finger. 'One of you lot, at least one of you, is a bloody liar.'

He feels a hand on his arm and shakes it off.

'Shaun, it's alright.'

And he can't believe it. It's that young bloke. Jayden. The seashell detective. He's one of them, is he? Sitting at their table, drinking their wine and eating their food. *Double-crossing*. And Shaun throws a punch before he knows what he's doing; feels it land too. There's a scream from the table: some high-pitched lady. Then there are more hands on him, and he sinks under the weight of them. Crumbles, really, into dust.

30

Ally opens another cupboard and finds the box of teabags that Jayden brought. The kettle whistles, and in the quiet of the cottage the sound feels impertinent. She takes it from the stove and fills three mugs. Then she steps back and peers through to the sitting room.

Shaun sits curled like a mollusc, head in his hands. Jayden talks in a low, soothing voice, every so often dabbing a tissue to his own split lip. In the grate, the fire Ally lit is finally jumping into life.

Strange to be moving around someone else's home like this. As soon as Ally got the message from Jayden – *it's kicked off* – she drove fast to Shoreline Vines. By then, Jayden and Broady had brought Shaun home to his cottage. Jayden quietly told her what happened: how Shaun threw his punch and then Owen dragged him back. How Owen was probably trying to help, but Shaun fell, thumping his head on the flagstone floor. Shaun said he wasn't hurt, but by the time Ally got there a bump was rising.

What about you, Jayden? Ally asked. *Are you okay?*

His lip was puffy, and there was a patch of dried blood on his chin.

He grinned then winced. *Me? I'm fine. But I've had to spend the last twenty minutes convincing Shaun I'm on his side. I think he believes me. He defo feels bad about the right hook.*

Now, she carries the mugs through. 'Here you are, Shaun. Three sugars.'

Shaun peers up at her, his eyes red.

'Of all the people to have a go at,' he says, shaking his head. 'You won't believe me, but I don't go in for fighting. Never have. But I was that riled up . . .'

'Shaun, it's okay,' says Jayden. 'I get it. Apology fully accepted. But if you'd struck one of the Harpers, you could have been looking at charges. You don't need that on top of everything.'

'Did something happen?' asks Ally gently. And she realises how foolish that sounds. *Of course something happened.* 'To go to the house, I mean. To confront them.'

Shaun folds his hands around the mug and lowers his head.

'It's not right, is it? That they're living the life of Riley up there with Mrs Moneybags and Russell not three days dead. The bloke at the beach agreed. It was him that made me see I couldn't take it lying down.'

'What bloke at the beach?' asks Jayden, leaning forward.

'Didn't get his name. Bald bloke. Said he was a mate of yours.'

Jayden darts a look at Ally. 'Was it Gus?'

Shaun shrugs. 'He said it wasn't right. After that, I felt like I was letting Russell down, if I didn't do something . . .'

But surely Gus would have cautioned against anything drastic.

'That lot up there. They're lying.'

'What makes you so sure of it?' asks Jayden carefully.

Shaun stares into the fire, chewing at his lip.

'Frank wouldn't have stood for it. He had skeletons in his closet, but he was honest as they come.'

Ally sits forward in her chair. 'What sort of skeletons?'

They wait.

'Years back,' Shaun says eventually, 'Frank said there was a body buried on the farm.'

'That old story about the shipwrecked sailor,' says Jayden. 'My wife told me about that. She grew up round here.'

'No, not that,' says Shaun. 'That's a tall tale. No, Frank said there was a body buried and that no one could ever know.'

There's no sound but for the crackle of the fire. Then a sudden whoosh of wind in the chimney. How could Shaun have not mentioned this before? Ally looks to Jayden. He's casual in his chair, but she can see the energy coming off him; the sparking light of new information.

'Must have been twenty years back that Frank told me.'

Or, as it happens, old information.

'This is me breaking my word, this is,' says Shaun. 'I swore I'd never tell a soul. But what does it matter? Frank's gone. Russell's gone. And the rest of them are running around like everything's smelling of roses.'

'What did Frank know about a body?' asks Jayden.

'He knew where it lay, because he buried it.'

Ally instantly feels goosebumps. 'Did he tell you where it was buried?' she says.

'No. And I didn't ask.'

'Why was he telling you, Shaun?' says Jayden.

He lets out a sigh. 'I did think on that. Frank was in one of his low moods. He got them from time to time. We'd just lost a harvest to blackfly, a year's work come to nothing. Then his old dog Maestro died within days of it. He called it a haunting. A punishment.'

'A punishment?' Ally's brow wrinkles. 'Did Frank hold himself responsible for the death?'

'Are you asking me if he killed someone?' Shaun looks from one to the other. His eyes are red-rimmed and bleary, his voice slightly slurred. 'Yeah, I reckon he did.'

Shaun says it like it's simple, straightforward. Perhaps for him this twenty-year-old truth has lost its sharp edges; a piece of sea glass, smoothed by time and tide.

Frank Harper killed someone, and the body's buried at the vineyard.

'Shaun, didn't you ask who died?' asks Jayden. 'Or when?'

'I didn't want to know. That's what I reckoned at the time. That sort of info's dangerous.'

'Didn't you think you should go to the police with it?' says Ally, trying to keep the judgement from her voice.

Shaun shakes his head. 'Frank was my friend. But he was my boss, too. I needed that pay packet from the vineyard. Russell was just a little kid; all we had was Mum's pension otherwise. I wasn't going to rock that boat, was I? And anyway . . . what you've got to understand about Frank . . . he was a good bloke. When he said this to me, he forgot I was there, I reckon. He was just rambling on. But later he came to me and said, "What I told you, will you forget it? What's buried should stay buried." I gave him my word that day.'

Shaun rests his elbows on his knees, pushes his face into his hands.

'Perhaps this is what this is all about,' he says in a muffled voice. 'A haunting, just like Frank said. Because I did break my word. Didn't matter that I took it back after. I broke it.'

'You told someone about the body?' asks Ally.

'My boy.'

Ally shivers involuntarily. She looks to Jayden.

Russell knew.

'When did you tell him, Shaun?' asks Jayden quietly.

'Couple of years back. It was just after Frank died and they let me go. I was gutted. I was ranting on to Russell and I just came out with it: "I've kept Frank's dark secret for twenty years." Russell near enough laughed, he couldn't believe it, said he couldn't imagine old Frank killing anyone. The next day I regretted it big-time. I told Russell I'd been talking rubbish, bad-mouthing for the sake of bad-mouthing. I reckon he forgot all about it. Probably because he didn't believe it the first time.'

Ally and Jayden swap a look.

'So, Russell never brought it up again, after you first told him?' says Jayden.

'Never. I told you, I said to him it was just bad-mouthing.'

'But it wasn't?' says Ally.

'No, it wasn't.' Shaun rubs his hand across his mouth; his stubble crackles. 'Frank killed a man. And for twenty years I never told anyone about it. Except for Russell.'

◆ ◆ ◆

Outside the cottage, a light rain's falling and the leaves of the giant yew tree rustle with the wind. Beyond, the countryside unfolds in darkness. They can't see the farmhouse from here.

'Man, I'd love to be a fly on the wall up at Shoreline right now,' says Jayden.

'It's coming up on midnight. Too late to call in.'

'Al, can I grab a lift? I told Sue to take the Land Rover home.'

'Jump in,' she says.

They turn into the black lane, silver rain dancing in front of the headlights.

Jayden takes a deep breath. 'Alright, Al. Let's do this.'

And it's the moment she's been waiting for. She and Jayden alone, this remarkable information washed up on their shores.

'Because Frank Harper killing someone is a hell of a skeleton in a closet, right?'

Ally grips the steering wheel; she can't help feeling a thrum of excitement.

155

'Do you think Ruth knows?' she says. 'And his sons?'

'If they do, they've kept it hidden for at least twenty years. That's some cover-up.'

'Just like the bullocks could be.'

'Exactly. Okay, let's get the timeline straight. Two years ago, Shaun's angry with the Harpers, and he tells Russell about Frank burying a body. Then he wakes up the next day and regrets it, so he quickly takes it back. Do you buy that Russell would forget all about it?'

'Or believe his dad when he said it didn't really happen?' Ally shakes her head. 'I don't think so. And I don't think Shaun's a gossip. If he tells a story, I'm inclined to believe it. And I'm sure his own son would feel the same. Even if his initial reaction was to doubt that Frank would be capable of something like that.'

'It's like Nicky said about Russell; he was a straight talker too.'

'Jayden, when Shaun said he'd told Russell about this, I thought he was going to say it was two weeks ago, not two years ago.'

Jayden nods. 'Yeah, me too. That would have been a slam dunk. But I still think it's relevant. Because it's a tangible connection between Russell and the vineyard.'

'A highly charged connection.'

'Knowledge of a murder? Or at least an unreported death, and an illegally buried body. Yeah, I don't think it gets more charged than that.'

Ally takes the drive slowly. The lanes are narrow, the hedges high, the night dark and wet. But, also, she doesn't want to hurry this part. The part where they wander the strandline, looking for the fragments that might just make a full picture when assembled.

Ally looks sideways at Jayden. Sees him press a finger gingerly to his lip.

'It hurts, doesn't it?'

'Could have done with some frozen peas, probably.'

'Oh, Jayden.'

'I wasn't going to make Shaun feel any worse, was I? It was bad, seeing him up at Shoreline like that. The sorrow just . . . pouring off him.'

'I think it must have been Gus that Shaun spoke to down at the beach. He did say he was going for a hike . . .'

'So, I've got Gus to thank for this fat lip, have I? I'm joking. I think we do have Gus to thank, in a weird way. Shaun wouldn't have spilled that story about Frank if he wasn't feeling so churned up.'

'Do you think Shaun was trying to give us something more to go on? I don't think he breaks promises lightly.'

'I don't think he saw the connection. He's hurting. He feels badly treated by the Harpers. And he doesn't think that's fair, given what he's done for them, keeping this secret of Frank's.'

Ally shakes her head. 'I can't understand how Shaun could work alongside someone for the best part of two decades, knowing that they've killed someone and . . . do nothing about it.'

'It's like Shaun said, Frank was his boss. He really needed that job. And fundamentally he trusted Frank. Put yourself in his shoes, Al, and you can see why he'd choose to forget it.'

'But wouldn't it have bothered him? Every single day he turned up to work on that land?'

'I think it did. More than he realises, probably. That's why when he lost his job with the Harpers, it was the first thing that rose to the surface.'

'And he told Russell,' says Ally.

'Exactly. Shaun might have backtracked later, but Russell knew. Maybe Russell thought it was time to tell. Because think about the timing. The investment in the vineyard.'

'The Harpers landing on their feet. I can imagine Russell thinking that good fortune wasn't deserved.'

They climb the hill towards Upper Hendra, headlights dancing over the briars. As they reach the top, Ally looks seaward. The dark skies are blotted with darker clouds, but a thin crescent moon is just visible. A thin fizzle of light moves over the water.

No more than a glimmer. But sometimes that's all they need.

'Alright,' says Jayden, 'let's play this one through. Let's say that Russell remembers what his dad told him about Frank, and he sees it as ammunition. At this point, maybe Russell's thinking it doesn't even matter if it's true or not, because mud sticks, right?'

Ally nods. 'And his motivation's . . . what, to stir up trouble?'

'Maybe he wanted to blow things for them. The satisfaction of wrecking the deal.'

'Or . . . to get his father's job back, perhaps. Use it as a bartering chip.'

'Or a payout for Shaun? A percentage cut of the investment, and some for Russell while he's there. That could be the "pipeline" thing. Plus, he's a gambler, remember. The thrill of the chase. Thing is, Al, why would someone like Celine Chevalier listen to a guy like Russell? Moving in her world, she'll be used to chancers. If she's serious about Shoreline Vines, she's not going to be put off a lucrative investment because of a local kid with an axe to grind.'

'But perhaps the Harpers couldn't be sure of that,' says Ally.

'A risk they weren't willing to take. Yeah, maybe. When Shaun gatecrashed the dinner tonight, he said Russell's name loud and clear. I saw Celine's face. She was shocked, scared even, but far as I could tell, the name didn't mean anything to her.'

'But you weren't looking for a connection between Celine and Russell at the time, were you?'

'True, but I was on the lookout for anything out of the usual. And if Celine reacted to the name Russell, I'd have clocked it.'

Ally nods. 'So perhaps Russell didn't go so far as to make contact. But the theory could still hold, couldn't it?'

'And however you cut it, it implicates the Harpers. Question is, which one of them? All of them?'

Jayden then tells Ally about the conversation that Saffron overheard between Owen and Karensa. The weird energy and the talk of coming clean. The fear that Saffron thought she heard in Karensa's voice, and whether that fear was about something more than their affair being revealed.

'Cheating with his brother's wife? But Owen seems, well . . . decent.'

'Agreed. On the face of it, an easier guy to trust than Edwin. But he could just be a better liar, right?'

They wondered before whether, with Owen, looks could be deceiving. Ally thinks of how he found them at the entrance to the field the other day. He seemed to come out of nowhere. Was he watching, as they scoped out the barns?

'Jayden, I don't like that Saffron said Karensa sounded frightened.'

'I was keeping an eye on Owen and Karensa all night. They seemed easy in each other's company. Perhaps it's Edwin's reaction that Karensa's afraid of. Or Owen's reaction to Edwin's reaction.'

'Coming clean,' says Ally. 'Owen could have been talking about Russell, and not the affair at all. Or even about what Frank Harper did . . .'

'Yeah, that's where my thinking's going, too. And who are they talking about coming clean to? Edwin? Ruth? The police?'

They drive on. Around them, questions swoop in the dark like bats at dusk.

'You know what we're not questioning, Al? Whether Frank really killed someone. Whether there's a body buried at the vineyard at all.'

'I believe Shaun. And why would Frank lie about a thing like that in the first place?'

As they pull into the farmyard, a security light clicks on. Beyond, the Thomases' farmhouse and Cat and Jayden's cottage lie in darkness.

'Who could it be?' says Ally. 'Someone connected to the farm?'

'That's the million-dollar question.' Jayden turns to her. 'If someone went missing it would have been reported. Shaun's going back twenty years with this story, and he's been here at least twenty-five himself. If there'd been a local drama, he'd have known.'

'Perhaps he does know. Perhaps, on some level, he's still keeping his word.'

'So that's our job for tomorrow,' says Jayden. 'Missing persons from the last two decades or more.'

'Where on earth do we begin?'

'We start here,' says Jayden. 'In Porthpella. And then we cast the net wider. A whole lot wider. Up for it, Al?'

It sounds an awful lot like looking for a needle in a haystack. But if it proves to be the needle that can stitch together the facts of this entire case, then every second of the hunt will be worth it.

31

Ruth wakes in the night with a start. She lies still, listening in the dark. Beneath her nightdress her heart hammers. She's used to the complicated music of this old house, but the death on their land has set her on edge.

The noise comes again. A *tap-tap-tap* at the window.

She swings her legs from the bed. The dark is so absolute that for a moment she loses faith in her bearings. Which way is up? She reaches for where her bedside table should be, and her hand meets thin air. She casts around, panic fluttering in her chest. Ruth isn't afraid of much on this earth, but the thought of dying chills her to the bone. What if it's like this: infinite darkness, reaching out and meeting nothing? Endlessly looking for something to hold on to.

Her fingers find the oak edge of her table and she grips it tight. She feels towards where the lamp should be, and something falls to the floor with a clunk. Liquid sluices over her bare toes. Only her water glass.

She curses under her breath, and clicks on the lamp, light immediately flooding the room. The wardrobe, the bed, the dressing table; they loom at her with an intensity that makes her blink fast.

Ruth makes her way over to the window. She battles with the stiff latch, then pushes it open. Cold air surges in like the tide. She reaches out, her teeth chattering involuntarily as her hand fastens around a stem of wisteria. She yanks it hard.

Ruth made Owen cut the wisteria back, ahead of the autumn storms that sweep the headland, the ones that tear at anything that's not nailed down. But Karensa was watching, her hands pressed to her cheeks, crying *don't decimate it, Owen, it's such a beautiful old thing.* So, Owen did half the job he should have. And now the wretched wisteria is creeping up around Ruth's bedroom window again – scratching at the glass. She pulls harder at the stem, but try as she might, she can't snap it. She gives up. In the morning, she'll take a pair of secateurs to it. Or get Owen to do the job properly.

Ruth leans back. From here all is darkness, but there's no question of lost bearings; she knows just how their land unfolds all the way down to the sea. She can taste salt; there's a stiff onshore wind blowing tonight. The trees will be straining from their roots. The tall pine – the one her mother-in-law loved to harp on about as a ship's mast – will be tilting like it's on the high seas.

This is their *terroir.* She can remember Frank explaining the word to her: the environment where wine is made, the qualities that make it particular to not just a region, but a hillside. Which at Shoreline means the sunshine, the salt air, the minerals in the earth; the apple blossom and pine resin; the drifts of Atlantic mist and downpours that feel like the earth's slanted, the sea tipped on their heads. At dinner tonight, before that sorry little man Shaun Tremaine stormed in and made a fool of himself, she heard Owen describe the Shoreline Vines terroir to Celine in just the words that Frank used. Small wonder, for wasn't he always traipsing at his father's heels? Wanting so desperately to be like Frank that sometimes Ruth thinks Owen missed out on being his own man entirely.

But Celine seemed to like it. And she liked the wine too. The woman glugged at the Pinot Noir like it was shandy. She'll have a head on her tomorrow.

How utterly strange to think of Celine under their roof again.

Ruth applauded herself earlier, for keeping her emotions in check. She has managed to disassociate Celine the investor from Celine the brazen girl who moved into their home thirty years ago; to separate the woman of means, who can – who *will* – provide, from the girl who simply took. Ruth didn't know how stupidly fallible a man she'd married, until their au pair's presence revealed it: lust disguised as chivalry. Ruth's own tragedy is that she loved Frank anyway.

Now, Ruth wonders how she must appear to Celine. Desperate? Grasping? Or a cool-headed businesswoman, looking for recompense?

The fact is, without Celine's money, they'll have to sell. And if they sell, then everything Frank worked so hard for – all the sacrifices he made; *yes, Celine, sacrifices* – will be for nothing. Because Shoreline Vines is, despite everything, their safe space. Ruth has been happier here than any place in her entire life, and perhaps that's not saying much, but still. If the gates swing wide, if the family crest is dismantled, then who knows what will happen?

No one here wants Frank's name to be dragged through the mud.

The fact is, they simply cannot lose the vineyard. And it'll take more than an over-the-top scene from their neighbour to derail their plans. Edwin said as much as he kissed Ruth goodnight, and she's always had confidence in her younger son. Except for the day he married Karensa. His only misstep. But perhaps all mothers secretly feel that way.

Ruth shivers, tiredness coming over her in a gust.

She pushes at the window, but the swollen wooden frame resists. She slams it with the heel of her hand, a sudden sob of frustration rising, and that does the job. Spent now, she goes back to her bed. She snaps off the light and, just like that, the tap-tap-tapping at the window starts over. Ruth pulls the covers up over her head, but claustrophobia swoops in. She pushes her face out, panting like a crone.

That heart of hers is going like a drum, and her thoughts skate back to the same old same old.

It took a great force of will, to invite Celine Chevalier back into this house. That she came is its own kind of reward. But it's not without its tax: the reminder that she, Ruth – even in her prime – was not enough for her husband.

But she tells herself that it's a small price to pay, considering.

32

Gus sits at his desk beneath the glow of a lamp. He hasn't written at night for ages. After his spell in hospital in the summer he found he was tired by sundown. But, tonight, he wants to set thoughts down on paper; he wants to breathe life into the deadened pages of this novel of his, and he won't sleep until he has.

That's the Shaun effect.

Because here's the thing: Gus is writing a detective novel, and like it or not that means serving up a murder or two. It means death.

After Gus got back from his walk, he opened his laptop. He read back over a scene he'd written, where the brother of the victim talks to Gus's detective, DI Larkin. Gus remembered thinking it was pretty good, that scene – or at least not terrible. But now he knows it hardly touches the sides. In fact, he's ashamed of how it skirts the heart of the matter. *I want justice for my brother*, Gus's character says at one point, but the guy says the line as if he's asking for full-fat milk in his tea instead of semi-skimmed, or chops for tea instead of shepherd's pie.

Gus had no more than a passing conversation with Shaun on the beach, but even he could see how raw that man's grief was. How palpable his anger. And that was a combination that scared Gus a bit, because how could someone be feeling all of that, and still be standing? Walking about on this earth, just like Gus, but feeling all of *that*?

Gus has never been around for the pointy end of grief before. When his old mum crossed the river, it felt quietly like the right time. She was ancient, tired; life as she knew it had long since ebbed. Gus mourned her with love, not fury.

Now his fingers pause on his keyboard and he's staring into the middle distance and thinking of Ally. And Bill. The road she must have walked.

It's a privilege – a wonder, really – that she's let Gus so far in.

Jayden's calm assurance earlier did buoy his confidence, but it's no good thinking and not doing, is it? Tomorrow is a new day, and Gus intends to seize it; mostly by doing something extra-nice for Ally.

33

Sunday morning, and Jayden, Cat, Jasmine, Sue and Cliff are at the large table in the farmhouse kitchen. Cliff sits at one end, a box of tissues planted beside him. He's wearing a ratty old dressing gown, and according to Sue should still be in bed, but nothing gets between Jayden's father-in-law and a full English.

Cat and Sue have started a new thing: Sunday morning breakfast at the farmhouse. This is then followed by Sunday lunch at the farmhouse, which seems a bit much to Jayden, but hey, he's rolling with it. So, he's here, eying a mountain of fried food, while thoughts of a body buried beneath the vines thrum through his head. Frank Harper as a killer. *How many other lies have the Harpers told? What else are Owen and Karensa hiding, beyond their own deception?*

'And here's your hash browns, Jayden,' says Sue, setting a separate plate by his side.

Hash browns: a point of contention in the Thomas household. As far as his in-laws are concerned, they have no place in an English breakfast. Cat sits on the fence, in the style that he's grown used to where her parents are concerned. So, Jayden brings his freezer bag over, and Sue deigns to pop a few in the oven.

Cat leans over and makes eyes at him. 'You're not going to eat all those, are you?'

Every time. 'Help yourself, babe.' Then, 'Cliff, sure I can't tempt you?'

Cliff grunts and spikes a mushroom.

'Me want tato,' says Jazzy.

Jayden obliges, because when has he ever said no to his daughter? The Weston women appear to have him wrapped around their little fingers. He looks to his wife, her belly nudging the table. He's looking forward to this boy of theirs, not least to even things up a bit round here. Cliff never takes his side, and even the cats are girls.

One hash brown left. He eats it fast, before Sue changes her mind too.

'So, what's all this about you taking my wife out, drinking and fighting, eh?' Cliff chuckles, which promptly turns into a coughing fit.

'It was a memorable evening,' says Sue, 'that's true enough. I must phone Ruth and thank her.'

'Shaun Tremaine sounds dangerous to me,' says Cat. 'I really don't think you should be helping him, Jay. Not after last night.'

And Jayden knows it's his wife's protective instinct talking, not her lack of empathy.

'I think he needs our help now more than ever, babe.'

'It didn't seem to put that lovely French lady off, though,' says Sue. 'You should hear what they're planning, Cliff. Upgrading all the winemaking equipment. A fancy new restaurant.'

Cliff grunts. 'Who's going to go to a restaurant all the way out there?'

'Destination dining,' says Cat. 'It's a thing. Farm to fork.'

'Farm to fork? Hiding to nothing, if you ask me. Frank would never have gone for it.'

'Oh, I don't know,' says Sue. 'He was ahead of the pack, planting those vines in the first place. It was one of Cornwall's first vineyards, you know, Jayden.'

'It sounds like Owen and Edwin are proud of his legacy,' he says carefully.

'I told Frank it was madness at the time,' says Cliff, buttering another piece of toast. 'Shows what I know.'

Cat grins. 'Appetite not dinted then, Dad?'

'Feed a cold, starve a fever,' says Sue.

Jayden takes a sip of coffee and wonders how to slip a line like *So, Frank – reckon he ever killed anyone?* into the conversation.

'What a nightmare though,' says Cat. 'The Harpers are pulling out the stops trying to impress, and Shaun storms in.'

'I honestly felt for him,' says Sue. 'It's a terrible business.'

'No good going about slinging mud,' says Cliff. 'Frank wouldn't have stood for it.'

Jayden sees his way in.

'Shaun and Frank were good friends, weren't they, Cliff?'

Cliff nods. 'A lot of years working together.'

'Through good times and bad, huh?'

'That's farming. Though it was winemaking by the time Shaun came along.'

'It's a hard life either way, isn't it?'

Jayden can feel Cat's eyes on him. He's not known for driving conversation with his father-in-law. Not through want of trying, but after living on Cliff's patch for the last two years Jayden's learnt that he likes his fences.

'Shaun reckoned Frank had his highs and lows over the years.'

'Jay, just say it. What do you want to ask Dad?'

Jayden glances at Jazzy. She's bent over her hash brown, picking off every potato flake and eating them one by one. The girl's busy.

'Did Frank ever confide in you, Cliff? Tell you the kind of thing he wouldn't tell just anyone? Around twenty years ago?'

Cliff narrows his eyes. 'Not sure that's any closer, Jayden.'

Jayden looks to his mum-in-law. Says, 'Or what about you, Sue, with Ruth?'

'Oh, Ruth and I have never been close like that,' she says. 'I shouldn't think Frank was much of a talker, was he, Cliff? And I know you're not. A fine pair. What sort of thing are you thinking of, Jayden?'

'I heard a rumour that there was a death at the vineyard a few years back.'

'That's a ghost story,' laughs Cat.

'No, this was twenty years ago.'

'No one's died up at Shoreline. Not since Frank was carried out feet first. And now Russell Tremaine. If you're going back further, Frank's mum was in a hospice at the end. Shaun's spreading these rumours, is he?' Cliff shakes his head. 'Knew it. You're not the only one capable of detective work around here. But mark my words, no good's going to come from listening to Shaun right now. He's not in his right mind. And fair enough, with what's on his plate.'

'Okay, what about dramas around here? Has there ever been a missing person reported? Going back a couple of decades?'

'Jayden,' Sue laughs, 'what tree are you barking up?'

'Helena Hunter last spring,' says Cliff. 'And you know all about that. The only thing that's gone missing lately is the Harpers' quad. And that's why I had you going up there in the first place. Not to stir up trouble.'

Jayden holds up his hands. 'No trouble stirred. Just questions.'

'You've got a big heart, Jayden,' says Sue. 'I know you and Ally want to make Shaun feel better. But sometimes life just doesn't make sense.'

'I don't want to hear from Ruth that she's lost her deal because of any of this,' says Cliff.

Jayden looks his father-in-law in the eye. *Any of this.* Russell inconveniently dying on their land?

'I shouldn't think that'd happen, Cliff,' says Sue. 'Celine seemed very enthusiastic. And she had lovely memories of staying all those years ago. Ruth apparently wanted the connection kept hush-hush, she seemed to think it made them look like Celine was doing them a special favour with the investment. She's a proud woman, is Ruth, and she wants the vineyard to be taken on its own merit. But I think it's a super story, personally.'

'Is she a family friend then?' asks Cat. 'Nice to have mates in high places. We could have done with that, setting up the campsite, hey, Jay?'

And he'd forgotten about Celine's connection, in the flurry of everything that followed.

'She was their au pair,' Jayden says. 'She looked after Edwin and Owen when they were kids. Now she's an angel investor.'

'I remember her,' says Cliff. And even though he's haggard with his cold, his face lights up. 'The French girl.'

'Funny you should remember her,' says Sue, rolling her eyes. 'Beautiful-looking woman like Celine.'

'Well, don't you remember her, love?'

She wrinkles her brow. 'I suppose so, now I'm thinking about it. Thirty years ago, wasn't it? You'd have been a baby, Cat. *Hazy* is the word for my memory there.'

'But not Dad's, apparently,' says Cat.

'Talking of the French,' says Sue, 'don't forget we've got Old Fran and Bernard coming for lunch.'

Jayden's just reaching for another slice of toast, and he changes his mind. He's got a lot of time for Old Fran and Bernard; Cliff's cousin who lives in Mousehole, and her husband, a jovial guy from Brittany with an epic moustache.

'No one's forgotten, Mum,' says Cat. 'Least of all Jazzy.'

'Love dem,' says Jazzy. And she does. Though mostly for their pea-green parrot and fully stocked biscuit tin – neither of which will be coming with them to lunch today. Though you never know.

'I remember her turning Bernard's head,' says Cliff, with a throaty chuckle.

'Who?' says Cat.

'The French au pair.'

'Dad, we've moved on from the French au pair.'

'It just goes to show though,' says Sue, standing up and starting to gather the plates. 'There she was running around after those little boys, doing the cooking and cleaning too, I shouldn't wonder. Next thing she's turning up in her Porsche, offering them her millions.'

'Working on that basis, maybe we should get an au pair for Jazz,' laughs Cat.

Jayden gets to his feet and starts helping Sue. He's deep in thought, because he wouldn't mind talking to Celine Chevalier. To what end though? And he's pretty sure Cliff would call that stirring up trouble. No harm in some desk research though.

'Was her surname Chevalier back then, Cliff?' he asks innocently.

34

The waves are a mess this morning, so Broady's going nowhere. He is, instead, sitting at his laptop at Saffron's kitchen table. Pulling together a new business plan. A business plan he intends to send the way of Celine Chevalier.

'You're snaking the Harpers, Broady. Not cool.'

'Hey, that's low, Saff.'

Comparing this move to stealing someone else's wave has hit home.

'Celine told me to get in touch. She thinks I've got something.'

'But babe, you were there working for the Harpers. Not to convince their investor to back you instead.'

'Instead? It's not instead. The woman's loaded.' He shakes his head in genuine surprise at Saffron's reaction, and his shaggy blond hair – freed of his silver-service-grade topknot – moves with him. 'And I wasn't working for the Harpers, I was working for you. As a favour.'

And Saffron knows it's true. She knows, as well, that her frustration with Broady for talking surf school investment with Celine is more about the stress of the night. The call from Dawn. Then the incident with Shaun.

When Saffron saw Shaun Tremaine's face peering in the window, she had no idea who he was. She screamed – *who wouldn't?*

Face at the window? Oldest trick in the horror book – but then settled herself. He could have been one of the guests slipping out for a cigarette, or a late arrival, so she just carried on pouring cream into two large Cornishware jugs, then plucked her perfectly caramelised tarte Tatin from the oven. But if she'd spoken up about the face at the window, Jayden could have intercepted Shaun outside – and avoided that punch altogether. So that's on her.

Saffron passes Broady a coffee, and he catches her hand. Kisses it.

'I'd be stupid not to follow it up, Saff,' he says. 'But if you think the timing's off . . .'

All the timing feels off. The tragedy of Russell Tremaine. The look on his dad's face as he stared at everyone sitting around the table without a worry in the world. Saffron standing with her mouth dropped wide, as if the shocking bit was Shaun caring enough to get mad. The way Ruth clapped her hands and said, *Onwards*, after the drama was over.

It all feels off.

And what about Dawn? Phoning to say that the reason Wilson didn't bring the fish, the reason he hasn't been over to Hang Ten lately, the reason he's been lying low all round, is that he's been having tests. They're waiting on the full diagnosis, but it's looking a lot like prostate cancer.

Cancer. *Again.*

And while they're on the topic of things being off, what about Broady's response to the news about her dad? Broady cheerfully said that prostate cancer is *one of the better ones*. That he had an uncle who had it; it never gave him much trouble, so they didn't even treat it and he died of something else in the end. Why can't her boyfriend see that, after her mum, Wilson being connected with any kind of cancer – even one with optimistic cure rates – breaks Saffron's heart?

'No, you know what,' she says, shaking herself. 'Edwin told me I should be more ambitious. So . . . follow his advice. If Celine showed interest in the surf school, you should follow it up.'

Broady's soulful eyes lock on to hers. At least, she *thinks* they're soulful – or did he just get lucky, when eyes were being handed out?

Apparently, Saffron is the first girl he's ever said *I love you* to. *That guy's married to the sea*, that's what everybody told her, but now he sleeps most nights at her house on Sun Street. Waters her house plants and brings her triangles of toast. Makes a mean dhal, when the mood takes him. And they're planning a whole winter together, just the two of them in a tiny beach house – bleached boards and jungle palms and star-loaded nights. Nothing to do but surf.

But how can she enjoy any of it when she's thinking about Wilson?

'Thing is, Saffron, it feels like . . . what's that word you always use? Serendipity. Being pulled in to help and then striking gold with meeting Celine. It's serendipity, right?'

'Serendipity. Yeah, it is. Glad someone had a good night.'

He pulls a weird smile. 'Really? That's not you.'

'What?'

'Moody.'

'Moody? I'm not moody, I'm just . . . I felt bad for Shaun. If the Harpers weren't calling off the dinner, maybe I should have pulled out anyway.'

He shrugs. 'You were just doing your job. Anyway, Jayden was there, wasn't he? If he thought it was alright to still go, then that's a good marker.'

But Jayden was there undercover.

'I might take Shaun some brownies later. Or give them to Ally and Jayden to take.'

'Good as your brownies are, babe, I don't think they're going to do much for that guy right now,' and his eyes are back on his laptop screen.

Saffron feels a prickle of frustration.

'It'll show I'm thinking of him though,' she says. 'It's a gesture, isn't it? Right now, he thinks no one cares at all.'

She watches Broady for a beat more. A beat more for him to look up, show her that he gets it. That Shaun Tremaine's pain might not be her pain, or his pain, but to ignore it altogether feels a little bit inhuman.

A beat more to say something better about her dad. Because maybe Wilson will be totally fine, but how do they know that? Saffron's only just found him. She doesn't want to lose him.

Broady looks up. He smiles kindly and her heart lifts.

'Hey, question for you. Should I ask Celine for fifty grand, or show her we mean business and make it a hundred. Or two hundred. What do you reckon?'

Really?

And before she can stop herself, Saffron says the words she's been thinking ever since Dawn called yesterday.

'Broady, I don't think I can go to Hawaii any more.'

35

'Post-mortem's in on Russell Tremaine.'

Morning, sir. Yes, a tad better, thanks. Nice of you to ask.

Mullins is sitting up in bed. He's had three Weetabix and the best part of a pint of orange juice, courtesy of his mum. He wouldn't say he's enjoying himself, but it's not the worst morning of his life. Not by a long chalk. And today is his day off anyway, which means licence to take it easy.

He glances at the clock. Ten a.m.

'Tremaine died from multiple traumatic injuries to his chest. Fractured ribs, spinal cord. Those cattle meant business.'

'Yup.'

'So far so consistent with the witness statements, wouldn't you say, Mullins?'

And there's something in Skinner's tone. A jibe, probably, that that report of his wasn't his best work.

'Yup,' he repeats.

'But here's the interesting bit.'

Mullins waits. In the end he says, 'Sir, you still there?'

'That was a dramatic pause, Mullins. Because while Russell Tremaine's injuries are consistent with a trampling by cattle, there is also evidence of intervention of a rather more human sort.'

'Sarge?'

'Bruising on the side of the head suggests a human boot print.'

Mullins's jaw drops.

'And there's another partially discernible boot print on his right flank.'

'Someone kicked him?'

'Glad to see your illness hasn't affected your brain power, Mullins.'

'Sorry, it's just . . .'

'I know. It's a turn up for the books. See, there I was in Gran Canaria, going out of my mind with boredom. I knew there'd be something worth coming back for.'

'What about skin under his fingernails?' asks Mullins.

'Sadly not. If he was in a fight, he didn't put up much of one himself.'

'But he was still trampled by cattle, wasn't he?'

'He was. Hoof prints a go-go. Hell of a way to check out.'

Mullins nods. Then says, 'If that *was* how he went.'

'Now you're thinking like a copper.'

Now Jayden's thinking, more like.

'Here's the thing, Mullins.' And Skinner's slowed right down; he can imagine his boss kicked back in his chair. 'Our job is to distrust everybody.'

Is it?

'You're still wet around the ears, you are. But me? I think everybody's lying, all the time. Take you and your sick day . . .'

'Sarge, honestly I'm—'

'And my ex? Oh, yes. I was right about that one.' He gives a hard little laugh. 'And just about any member of the public we have cause to question. *Convince me.* Before they even open their mouths, that's what I'm thinking. And even then, I don't buy it.'

Mullins settles back on his pillows. Closes his eyes. Not that Skinner's voice is any kind of a lullaby but . . . he's got a feeling he's going to run on.

'Ruth Harper tells you she saw the poor bloke trampled to death? Well, maybe she did. But what's she leaving out? What happened prior to Tremaine getting on the wrong side of a herd of bullocks?'

'You think someone knows more than they're saying?'

'Edwin Harper tells you he ran over the second he heard his mum cry out. Ran like the wind! But it was too late by then, wasn't it? Tremaine was a goner. The herd scattered. Same question. What were you doing before you heard that cry of your mum's, Edwin Harper?'

'He was in the bottling shed,' says Mullins.

'Yes, Edwin says he was in the bottling shed, doesn't he? Owen Harper? Karensa Harper? What about them? By my count we've got four people's movements to account for.'

Mullins drains the last drop of orange juice. Says, 'Did the report state when the different injuries occurred? As in, if he was in a fight, how long after did he end up in the cattle field?'

'Ah, for that we'd need a crystal ball. Or a time machine.'

'So . . . Tremaine could have been in a scrap elsewhere, and ended up at Shoreline Vines, couldn't he? Like, what if he ran away to Shoreline Vines, thinking it was a safe harbour? And ended up in the field, where he met with the cattle? That'd be some bad luck.'

'It's an interesting angle,' says Skinner. And he genuinely sounds as if he's considering it. 'What, with his dad, for instance? Some kind of falling-out at the cottage? Maybe Shaun's a bit of a bully. Chases his son up the track.'

'I dunno. His dad was heartbroken. He doesn't seem like a bully.'

Though Mullins has met a fair few in his lifetime; met a fair few at school too. It's not always obvious, is it?

'And Shaun might well be heartbroken, if he's had a set-to with his son and then the next time he sees him, he's dead in a field. Let's rule nothing out. But if you ask me, the smart money is on the vineyard lot. Because there's one more detail from the post-mortem, Mullins. Traces of yeast were found in the weave of Russell's jumper.'

'Yeast?'

'We're talking minute traces.'

'Amateur baker, was he?'

'Could be. But do your research and you'll find yeast is used in winemaking too.'

Mullins stares at his window. The curtains are partially drawn, and thin morning light filters in. A standard bleary autumn day. It's all happening in here though. *What Ally and Jayden would give to know this.* For a minute Mullins contemplates telling Skinner that he talked to Jayden the other day, and he was already thinking in this direction, wondering if it was possible that Russell was unconscious before he ended up in that field.

'You and I need to have another little chat with those Harpers. A chat and a swab – while we're at it.'

'Down the station?'

'No, let's keep it informal. The pathologist is still citing probable cause of death as trampling by cattle. Despite evidence of there being, shall we say, more to it. What you and I need to find out, Mullins, is if there is, in fact, a lot more to it.'

'Count me in, Sarge.'

'I've got to clear it with the powers that be, but I'm officially upgrading this to a murder investigation. It's a damn sight easier to go in with that, than try and escalate it down the line. So murder it is. That worth getting out of your sick bed for?'

36

'Gosh, Ally. If that was my doing, then I wholeheartedly apologise. I mean, the bloke was in bits. I just said what I thought he wanted to hear.'

Gus stands in his doorway, looking sheepish.

'And I know you'd have been very kind to him,' she says. 'You weren't to know what he'd do. And as it happens, his trip to the vineyard threw up some interesting information.'

Gus's eyes sparkle with interest. 'Top-secret Shell House business?' he says wryly.

'Well,' says Ally, 'it's nothing more than a whisper from Shaun. But we're looking into it all the same.'

Fox bumps at her ankles, as if to remind her.

'Fox and I were planning on a coffee and a biscuit at Hang Ten,' says Ally. 'Jayden's meeting me there. Could you be tempted?'

'I'll be ready in a jiffy,' says Gus, darting back inside. 'Coat and a hat and I'm set.'

She smiles to herself.

Then they're making their way over the dunes, marram grass brushing at their legs. They follow a rabbit path – or a Fox path, more likely. There's a lively breeze and Ally feels her scalp tingle through the wool of her hat. Every so often, the wind tugs away the clouds and the light bursts through; a gap that closes just as fast as it opens.

She glances to Gus.

'How was the rest of your hike yesterday?'

'I felt rather rattled after meeting Shaun. Sad. I don't know.' Gus thrusts his hands in the pockets of his coat. 'Seems an isolated sort of chap.'

'I think he is. He was close to his mother, but she died years back. He saw Russell every couple of weeks. But friends . . . a support network . . . after Frank Harper died and he lost his job, I think Shaun withdrew a little.'

I could disappear and people would never know it. That's what Shaun said to her and Jayden. And Ally knows how that feels. Because before she met Jayden, before she met Gus, wasn't she pulled up in her own shell? Perhaps Shaun's isolation is part of what has drawn her to his cause; that in this sorrowful man in his run-down cottage she sees a part of her own self.

'This whisper I mentioned,' says Ally.

'Go on.'

And she tells Gus that, decades ago, Frank Harper killed someone and buried the body at the vineyard.

'Ally, you're joking?' Then, 'Presumably you've told the police?'

'Well . . . not yet. We want to investigate it a bit more ourselves first. Because the thing is . . . Russell knew about it too.'

They've arrived at Hang Ten – a flash of colour in today's muted landscape – and Gus stops dead at the door. By the look in his eye, Ally sees that the possible significance of Russell knowing isn't lost on Gus. She feels a ripple of connection with him.

'Oh dear. You will be careful, won't you?' he says, with such tenderness that for a moment she's back in that low-lit room in the ICU – Gus lying sleeping, Ally saying things out loud that she'd scarcely voiced inside her own head.

182

She takes his hand in hers and it's warm, strong. A good hand. 'I promise,' she says.

◆ ◆ ◆

They sit with their coffees at the corner table. The first time Ally ever went in Hang Ten, she and Jayden sat in this very spot. The jungle-like cheese plant has grown even bigger since then, and she adjusts her seat so her head doesn't nudge the leaves. Saffron is playing the kind of music Ally has grown used to, has come to like, in fact: a fast beat, an unintelligible vocal. Beside her, Gus drums his fingers on the table in appreciation.

Ally and Saffron have already talked about last night. It seems Saffron woke up this morning feeling guilty for her part in the dinner that gave Shaun so much pain. At least that's what she said it was, and it's clear something's bothering her. Ally tried reassuring her, but it was only when Gus said, *To be honest, Saffron dear, I think it probably did him good to vent*, that she looked heartened. Gus is good at reassuring other people, even if he can't always turn his own wisdom on himself.

'You don't have any of your wonderful croissants, do you, Saffron?' Ally asks.

'Ah, sorry, I haven't. They're only good for one day, and it's so quiet this time of year I don't bother. Lemon drizzle?'

'Yes, please.' And she gets a hunk for Gus too.

'Sorry about the croissants,' says Gus. 'You're partial to them, aren't you?'

'Oh yes. Especially with lashings of apricot jam.'

Just then, Jayden comes through the door, a gust of cool air following him in. He gives Saffron a hug and shakes hands with Gus. Fox leans against his legs, and Jayden bends to pet him like he always does.

'Al,' he says, slotting in beside her with a knuckle-bump. 'Cold light of day, how's it looking to you?'

'Like what happened to Russell, and what Frank did, are connected. But . . . how? And how on earth do we prove it?'

'Cool. Same page as me, then,' he says with a rueful grin.

'How's the lip?'

'What lip?' he says, touching the tip of his finger to the cut. Then, 'I've been thinking about Celine Chevalier. And the fact that she was the Harpers' au pair thirty years ago.'

'That's rather wonderful,' says Gus.

'I think the Harpers think it's wonderful too, given what she's become.'

'What exactly are you thinking?' asks Ally.

Jayden shrugs. 'That I kind of wish Celine was their au pair twenty years ago. Then we could join a few more dots . . .'

Ally nods. 'Jayden, I told Gus about what Shaun said.'

'But it stays between these walls, right?'

'Oh yes,' says Gus brightly.

'What did Shaun say?' asks Saffron, coming out from behind the counter. She leans against the wall, her hands in the pocket of her apron. 'You mean about the Harpers lying?'

'About there being a body buried at the vineyard,' says Gus, through a mouthful of cake.

Ally and Jayden swap a look. Would the thinking room have been a better bet for this meeting? But old habits die hard.

'These four walls, Gus,' says Jayden.

'Oh, hang on, I've heard this one before,' says Saffron. 'I'm pretty sure Mum told me the Shoreline story one Halloween.'

'The sea captain?' says Jayden. 'Yeah, not that story.'

'I hoped to see the pine yesterday,' says Gus. 'The ship's mast? Nicely evocative, that. But running into Shaun rather derailed me . . .'

'So, there's another story?' asks Saffron, a confused look on her face.

And, after a moment's hesitation, Jayden fills her in. 'But don't say a word, Saffron. Not to anyone.'

'Of course. My God. You're telling the police, right?'

'We want to go to them when we've got a bit more than a vengeful man's drunken rambling,' says Jayden. 'Because, unfortunately, that's how they'll see it. Al and I have got a few ideas about where to go from here.'

'Bucket-and-spade time, is it, Jayden?' says Gus.

And Ally suddenly has a horrible vision of the reality of it. The hard-packed soil. The secret buried. She hopes, suddenly, that Shaun has very much got the wrong end of the stick.

'I still think you should tell the police,' says Saffron.

'That makes two of us.'

No one heard the door open. But now they all turn to see PC Mullins standing square in the middle of the coffee shop. He has one hand on his receiver, looking for all the world as if he's about to call it in.

37

'Come on, cough up. What should you be telling the police?'

So he didn't hear.

'Shaun's trip to the vineyard last night,' says Jayden. 'We wondered if the Harpers reported it.'

Nice save, Weston.

Mullins narrows his eyes. 'Not to my knowledge,' he says, with some self-importance. 'First day back on the job for me. I've been sick. 'Ere, make it the usual please, Saff. To go.'

And Saffron dips her head, busying herself with Mullins's coffee. She'll be uncomfortable with telling Mullins a half-truth. Or, okay, an outright lie. For all that she moans about him, Saffron has a quiet allegiance towards the PC.

'Anything about it I should know?' says Mullins. 'Hullo, Ally. Gus.'

'Shaun Tremaine punched Jayden,' says Gus, over the whirr of the coffee machine. 'He didn't mean to, though. And then apparently Owen Harper took Shaun down as if he'd caught an assassin.'

Mullins's face breaks into a goofy kind of grin. 'You took a punch, did you, Jayden?' He shakes his head. 'Hate to say it but it was going to happen sooner or later. Always thought you and Ally were playing a dangerous game. You haven't got the badge, see. You haven't got the authority. When you start meddling, this is what happens . . . the public don't have the same respect, Jayden. No offence, Mrs Bright, but they don't.'

Jayden can feel a smile of his own coming on, a smile and an eye roll.

'Shaun misread the situation,' says Jayden. 'That was all.'

'He felt terrible afterwards,' says Ally.

'Can't go round punching people,' says Mullins.

The constable's face suddenly changes. With Mullins, you can literally see the cogs whirring.

'Violent type, is he, Shaun?'

'Normally? I don't think so.'

'Basing that on what, Jayden? He could have a record as long as your arm, for all you know.'

'He clearly hasn't though, or you wouldn't be asking me the question.'

And Mullins screws up his nose like a bulldog.

Why is Mullins suddenly interested in Shaun's temperament?

'Here you are,' says Saffron, passing Mullins his mug of coffee.

'Sorry, Saff, I need it to go,' he says. 'Didn't I say that? This is a drive-by. Headed up to Shoreline Vines, as it happens. Here, are you alright? You look knackered.'

'So they've reported Shaun?' says Saffron, ignoring the question. 'That's unfair. Okay, so maybe he shouldn't have charged in like that, but he's distraught, and—'

'Bigger fish to fry than Tremaine's fisticuffs with Jayden,' says Mullins. 'No offence, mate.'

'Some taken.'

'What fish?' asks Ally.

Mullins's hand goes to his receiver, and he turns to her. Whenever Mullins speaks directly to Ally, he's more courteous than standard.

187

'I can't really say, it being a current case and all. But . . . there are a few inconsistencies.'

Some new information must have come to light.

'Come on, Mullins,' says Saffron. 'Don't hold out. They're just trying to help Shaun.'

'Well, what if they're backing the wrong horse there?'

It has to either be a witness or something the post-mortem has thrown up. As much as Jayden respects Mullins's professionalism – *okay, combination of professionalism and bloody-mindedness* – the guy knows by now that he and Ally aren't trying to get in the way of the police. Or compete. They're just trying to get to the truth.

Which is what Jayden's going to try to do right now – providing Mullins plays ball.

'Look,' says Mullins, as if reading his mind, 'I know you two cracked the Rockpool case.'

Jayden nods.

'And JP Sharpe. I mean, that was my collar fair and square, but . . . I know you helped.'

Cracked the case.

'And everything that Lewis Pascoe started . . . you weren't completely useless.'

Cracked the case.

'But this one's different. We need to tread carefully. And there's a reason people say "too many cooks".'

'A problem shared is a problem halved, remember,' says Gus.

'I heard teamwork makes the dream work,' says Jayden with a grin.

He sees Mullins look to Saffron, waiting for her to chime in too, but her head's down behind the counter.

'So, it's not cut and dried, then,' says Ally, with a deliberate innocence. 'The bullocks killing Russell?'

Mullins sighs. He takes a sip of his coffee, now in its takeaway cup.

'I'm meeting Skinner five minutes ago,' he says. 'I'll get it in the neck if I'm much later.'

'I'll walk you to your car,' says Jayden, and he's on his feet, holding open the door. The wind gusts in, scattering beach sand on the boards.

Mullins juts his chin. 'Yeah, alright,' he says. 'If you have to.'

◆ ◆ ◆

Back at The Shell House, Ally and Jayden settle in the thinking room. The look on Ally's face mirrors the one Jayden had when Mullins finally told him.

'So, a boot print,' says Ally.

'Two. One on the side of Russell's face, and one on his flank. One more defined than the other. But they were clear enough to stop the pathologist in their tracks.'

Ally shakes her head. 'We were right . . .'

'I'm kind of amazed that Mullins let us in on this.'

'He trusts you, Jayden.'

'He trusts us both. I told him about Edwin's knuckles, by the way, and his story of how he got the injury. That was new to Mullins.'

'Because they've had no reason to suspect Edwin, or anyone else, until now.'

'Exactly.'

Jayden moves his marker pen from hand to hand, studies the board.

'So, all the police know for sure is that Russell was in a fight at some point before he ended up in the cattle field. A kick to the head? That's brutal. What happened afterwards, that's still guesswork. Putting our doubts aside, it's possible that he was involved in this fight, then escaped into the field.'

'If he'd been kicked in the head . . .' Ally pauses, takes a breath, 'then he could have been disorientated, couldn't he?'

'Yeah, and if he was confused, maybe the cattle field did look like a good place to hide. That's where Mullins's head is at. They're talking to the Harpers again and getting DNA swabs. There'll be a full-scale forensic post-mortem now.'

'And what does that mean?'

'It means they'll have CSIs back on the vineyard. No stone unturned. Mullins said they're treating it as murder.'

Ally's eyes widen. 'Are they really?'

'He said they don't think it *is* murder, but Skinner has a theory that it's easier to scale down a case than to scale it up at a later date.'

'Jayden, did you tell him Shaun's story about Frank?'

'No. I want us to hold on to that. It's up to us to build a connection, otherwise there's a risk it won't be taken seriously. And it does connect, I'm sure of it. So, let's do some digging.' He opens his laptop, grins ruefully. 'Not literally.'

'Where do we start?' Ally sits with her notebook and pen. She has her reading glasses on, which means she's ready to get down to it.

'There's a register which any member of the public can access, but that shows people who've . . . been found.'

'Dead?'

He nods. 'And that's obviously not what we're looking for here.'

Jayden looked late last night though. He was wired when he got home, and Cat was already in bed. He should be desensitised, shouldn't he? He's had all the training; it wasn't that long ago that he was right in the mix of inner-city policing. But seeing people reduced to their basic statistics – the sum total of a life listed as gender, estimated age, appearance, and where the body was found – is never easy to take. Jayden closed the laptop in the end, trod quietly upstairs and lay next to his sleeping wife; his eyes wide open, his head full.

'There are various round-ups in the media, too, showing people who've been missing for a long time. I looked at one of those for Cornwall. I mean, there's nothing to say this person – this possible person – was reported missing in this area, but we've got to start somewhere, right? Otherwise, it's impossible. And even focusing on Cornwall, it's hard to see a connection. No one leaps out, Al.'

'But that's what we're good at, isn't it? Seeing connections. I know it's what you're good at.'

'But the only way we could properly investigate whether there is a link between any of these missing people and Shoreline Vines is by talking to their families. And . . . I don't think we can do that. Even if we put in the hours and hours of desk research, I don't think we can just knock on those doors and open it all up for the families again.'

'Because of false hope,' says Ally quietly.

'It wouldn't be fair. You and I believe Shaun, but that's just our instinct. His story's light on specifics.'

'But what if one of these people . . .'

Jayden sees their faces then: the young and the old; the smiling and the sullen. Missing persons, mourned without closure. He feels a surge of emotion. What's worse? The fragile hope that someone might still be out there, or the irrefutable knowledge that they're lost for ever?

Ally squeezes his arm.

'I bet you're wondering how I was ever a copper,' he says with a half-smile.

'Bill never took it in his stride either. How could he? *Why* should he? Caring like that made him the officer he was. I rather think it was his super-power.'

'I thought that was his BBQing.'

'Oh, well, that too, obviously. Red mullet kebabs, Jayden. Had to be tasted to be believed.'

They sit for a moment. The fire roars in the burner. A gust of wind draws the sound of the sea closer.

'So what do we do?' asks Ally. 'There must be something.'

'I think we keep talking to the people round here who are happy to talk. Cliff didn't know anything. Or Sue. Is Wenna, aka the Oracle, worth a shot?'

'I think Wenna might have already told us everything she knows. That old ghost story was uppermost in her mind. If there was even a whisper of something more recent, or more plausible, she'd have volunteered it.'

'With relish.'

'A lot of relish,' smiles Ally.

'We could find out from Shaun who else was close to Frank. I'd like to go back up there anyway, because if Mullins and Skinner are on their way to the vineyard, they'll be calling on Shaun too.'

'That question about Shaun being violent. They can't really suspect him?'

'All the post-mortem revealed was that there was evidence of Russell being kicked by a human, as well as all those cattle. There's nothing to point to the Harpers, other than the fact that he was found on their land.'

'I hope to God they're not heavy-handed with Shaun. He'd hardly hire us to investigate if he had something to hide, would he?'

Jayden shakes his head. 'No. Shaun wanted us involved because he didn't trust the police to give him answers. Specifically, the answer to why Russell was in that field. But now things have changed. The police are investigating, right? The discovery of that boot print changes everything.'

Ally slowly takes off her reading glasses.

'So, you don't think we're needed any more?'

'They've got the resources, Al. They've got the authority. But . . . we've got something different. We've got Shaun's trust.'

'I don't think he'd have told them Frank's story, would he?'

'Frank's story only came out because we took the time to be with him at the cottage. He knows we're on his side, Al. We just need to keep making connections. Calling out the anomalies.'

Ally looks to the board.

'Like the fact that Celine Chevalier used to be the Harpers' au pair. And Owen and Karensa are having an affair.'

'And Russell was going around telling people he was coming into money,' says Jayden.

'And Edwin Harper was doing the same thing in Porthpella.'

'And Frank Harper killed a man and buried him at the vineyard.'

They look at each other across the table.

'It has to come back to that,' says Ally.

'Because Russell knew. He knew that dangerous piece of information, and now he's dead. Yeah, that's the end we start from, Al. Not the second death at the vineyard, but the first. That's the part the police aren't looking at. Who did Frank kill? And why?'

38

Owen's pulling on his boots, set to head back to the silver bullet, when Celine catches him at the farmhouse door.

'Owen, wait. I need your help with something. Is that alright?'

'Sure,' he says, straightening up. 'Of course.'

Is it alright, though? Owen's head is full of Karensa and their argument earlier. And it was an argument – the first they've ever had. She's put him in an impossible position. *No, that's not fair.* Owen's put himself in an impossible position.

He sees Celine glance back down the hallway. Knowing she's sought him out specifically makes him feel both flattered and uneasy. But that's a combination he's familiar with.

He tries to focus in on the present moment, no more, no less, but his mind darts here and there. Breakfast was a success, all things considered. Celine said she slept like a baby, although Owen imagines she's used to much grander surrounds than the farmhouse. She was unsettled by Shaun's entrance at dinner, but no more than anybody else would be. It didn't seem to have dented her commitment to investing in the vineyard. *You couldn't possibly be blamed,* she said. *Don't worry on my account.*

As Shaun raged, Karensa couldn't bear to look at him. And Owen understands that; the rawness of human suffering is hard to witness. Everybody knows it lies waiting, like a crouching tiger, coming for everyone eventually. But you've got to carry on regardless, pretending you can't see it, not until it lands on you – claws, teeth, the whole damn weight of it – and then you've no choice but to face it. But Shaun? The poor guy broke the basic rules. He brought his suffering to their door, laying it on all of them. And Karensa couldn't cope.

That's why she's making things difficult now. She's joining the dots and she's getting it all wrong. Just because Russell died, it doesn't make it D-Day for everything. But Owen can't get through to her. He has to remind himself that her sensitivity is part of why he loves her.

'I know you and your father were very close,' Celine says quietly.

Owen nods. Voices drift down the hallway, and Celine looks back. Considering her power, in this moment there's a vulnerability to her that surprises him. As does the line in conversation.

'That's why I'm coming to you.'

'Okay.'

'I'm about to have a tour of the vineyard,' she says. 'Before I leave.'

Owen's the head of the vineyard; Edwin's the head of the winery. The vines are Owen's domain. But Edwin thinks he's got the better patter, and Ruth said that Celine shouldn't be crowded with attention. Honestly? Owen's got bigger things to worry about. Like talking Karensa down.

'Great,' he says. 'This time of year, it's a bit bleak. But then you know that.'

Because she's from wine country, Celine. Aix-en-Provence. And, so the story goes, it was Celine who first said to Frank *what about planting some vines here?* And his dad – immovable in so many ways – looked at this young woman and thought that maybe she was on to something. Owen loves thinking about the moment

195

when their farm went from a standard kind of mixed arable and livestock to something remarkable. Magical. And Owen will do anything to preserve that magic. That's one thing he has in common with his mum and brother.

But is it all for nothing? If Owen does as he should, as Karensa insists, he stands to lose it all anyway.

'Owen, I don't want to ask Ruth because it might upset her,' says Celine, circling back to her original request.

'Okay.' Owen rubs his face with the heel of his hand. *Where's this going?*

'Could we step outside?' Celine glances back down the hall again.

And he gestures through the open door.

It's a wild sort of morning, with an uneven, rushing wind. Out on the ocean, drifts of rain move across the horizon. Directly overhead, the sky's full of threat. But across Shoreline land, the colours are richly autumnal. The leaves might be dying, but they're going out in a blaze of glory. This was always his dad's favourite season. And what Owen said to Celine just now about the vines looking bleak, he didn't even mean it. They're a miracle, those stems. Leafless, but far from lifeless. This time of year, they look like forked lightning.

His argument with Karensa spears back in. The thought of having to leave all this behind? It's unbearable. But so too is the alternative.

'I lent your father a book,' says Celine. 'Years ago.'

'Right.'

'It was very special to me. It was only after I left that I realised I never got it back. I always meant to write and ask him to send it, but with one thing and another . . .' She lets the sentence drift. 'Perhaps I'm sentimental about it now because I'm getting old . . .'

Owen shakes his head. Celine glitters with a youthful energy and intention. He can imagine her in one of her city boardrooms; when this woman wants something done, she'll get it done.

'I'm fifty next year,' she says.

'A baby,' he grins.

'This book . . . it's become enormously important to me.' The wind gusts, heavy as a push, and Celine pats down her sleek dark hair. 'My mother gave it to me, you see. She wrote in it. And . . .' She looks at Owen meaningfully. 'She's gone now. I did mention it in passing to Ruth, and she said I'm free to check the bookshelves. Which I have, of course. But . . . I suspect your father would have kept it somewhere . . . more private. Owen, what I want to ask is, did you hold on to all of your father's things?'

'Not all of them, but most. I guess I'm already sentimental. Dad, though, he was never much of a reader. What was it called, this book?'

'The ridiculous thing is that I can't remember the title. Isn't that absurd? But I know I'd recognise it. I'd recognise it in an instant.'

'The other question is whether Dad would have kept it. We're talking thirty years ago, right?'

'Oh, he'd have kept it.'

And Owen can't quite read the look on Celine's face. But there's something in her tone – her absolute conviction – that gives him pause.

Owen was five when Celine came to Shoreline Farm. His mum and dad were never much for snapping photographs, and Celine didn't make it into any of the few family albums or the gilt-framed prints. She existed in his memory as a notion, rather than an individual: their French au pair. Over the years, if Owen thought about her at all, he probably overlaid other French women: Vanessa Paradis, Françoise Hardy, Brigitte Bardot – obviously beautiful, obviously glamorous, obviously famous.

197

But what about his dad? Frank wouldn't have been much older than Owen is now. Married with two children – unlike Owen – but perhaps not immune to Celine's charms.

'We were close,' says Celine, as if reading his mind. 'Your dad and me.'

And Owen can feel his brow furrowing, but who is he to think about fidelity? *Add hypocrite to his list of failings.*

She gives a small shake of her head, but the gesture does nothing to dissuade him. 'No, no, just . . . a connection. We talked about books, films, music. I found your father easy to get on with. More so than Ruth, actually. And I think, at the time, your mother was all too aware of that, unfortunately.' Celine tucks a strand of hair behind her ear. 'That's why I feel uncomfortable telling her that I lent the book to Frank. I'm afraid she might take it the wrong way.'

'I'm sure she wouldn't,' he says.

But Owen knows his mother. And didn't he notice a weird energy about Ruth ahead of this visit of Celine's? He put it down to the stakes of it – the vast sum of money they're asking for and what it will mean to the vineyard if they get it. What it will mean if they don't, too. Owen thinks of the abandoned cottage project, the money sunk. The outdated equipment in the winery. A new press and a new labelling machine are basic requirements, but the proposed restaurant would take them to a whole new level. Not just get them out of a hole but allow them to scale a new mountain. No wonder his mum is a little tense.

Asking for money from a woman who might have been too close to her husband, though. What is that – an evening of the score? A sense of a debt paid? Or a shameful thing, to go cap in hand to Celine of all people?

Owen groans inwardly. Why does everything have to be so complicated? Sometimes he feels like a fly caught in a web. Others, it's like he's the spider, bristling and venomous.

'I don't want to distress Ruth,' says Celine, 'asking her to look through your father's things. It'd be a terrible imposition. But I thought perhaps you might be the man for the job, Owen. Or better still, let me do it. I don't want to inconvenience you. And as I said, I'll know the book when I see it.'

Celine speaks with the quiet confidence of someone who is used to getting their way. Well, fine. They need her a lot more than she needs them. And if his dad's head was turned? If he got soppy, borrowing books from a French woman – a girl; and the thought makes Owen squirm, nineteen-year-old Celine and his forty-year-old dad – so what? Celine appears to bear no ill feeling.

And Owen's got enough to worry about.

'Okay, sure,' he says. 'No probs. How about after the tour?' He rubs the back of his head. 'What time are you heading off today?'

'It's flexible. I said to myself that I really didn't want to leave without the book.' She lowers her voice again. 'I don't know if you've found this with your father, but the most ordinary possessions seem to take on an almost ferocious level of meaning after somebody's gone. Do you understand at all?'

'Yeah, I do.'

Is this where he tells her he's wearing his dad's old coat? With its lining hanging in shreds and a handkerchief folded in the pocket. But no. He hasn't got the heart for it today.

He swerves the conversation to safer ground.

'Hey, the tour of the vines . . . I thought you'd be putting us through it a bit more. Soil analysis, stem analysis, the works. I can give you the log of the crops for the last three years.'

'Don't worry, Owen, I'm doing due diligence.'

'I wouldn't doubt it for a second. But I'm proud of what we've done here. I'm up for the interrogation.'

'They say the proof is in the pudding, and the wine I tasted yesterday was delicious.'

'The sparkling Pinot Noir? I think that's the best we've made. We disgorged it just for you, you know.'

Always a messy business, clearing the second sediment, angling the bottle just so. The winery splattered with that pale red matter, and usually the winemaker too.

'Well, it was worth the trouble.'

He turns his head at the sound of an approaching engine.

'Talking of trouble, what's this about?'

And he makes his voice light, as the police car rattles over the cattle grid and docks in the yard. He briefly closes his eyes. It feels, suddenly, like everything's coming to a head – just like Karensa said. He wonders if she's watching from the farmhouse.

'Did Ruth report the disturbance last night?' says Celine.

'She said she wouldn't. I told her it wouldn't be fair on Shaun.'

'And she listens to you does she, your mother?'

'Yeah, okay, good point,' says Owen.

And he walks towards the car with one objective: to get rid of them.

39

'So,' says Skinner, 'we'll need to speak to each of you.'

'Can't this wait, Officer?' says Ruth. 'We're rather in the middle of something.'

They're gathered in the farmhouse kitchen and Mullins is looking at everything differently this time. Like how Ruth's mouth is twisted with irritation. And Karensa's chewing on her nails, and maybe that's just habit, or maybe she's extra nervous. Then Edwin, hands deep in his pockets, hiding that bruising across his knuckles, no doubt. Alright, Jayden gave him that one, and Mullins is kicking himself for not noticing it himself when he took the statements, but why would he? At that point in the process there was no reason to suspect foul play.

'No, I'm afraid it can't wait,' says Skinner. 'We're building a picture of what happened in the lead-up to the incident with the bullocks.'

'But why?' says Owen. 'Is this Shaun doing the asking?'

'It's Devon and Cornwall Police doing the asking,' says Skinner. 'And they'll take a cup of tea while they're at it, thanks very much.'

Mullins grins inside. Outside? Straight face all the way.

'Perhaps I could be excused, Officers?' asks a glamorous-looking woman.

And she doesn't even volunteer who she is, or why she might be free to go at this point. Mullins looks her square in the eye. She's probably used to people dropping and licking her boots. Is this inverted prejudice? You bet.

'Celine only arrived yesterday,' says Edwin. 'She came down from London.'

'On holiday, are you?' says Skinner.

And it's a play, because they know all about the investor's visit.

Ruth makes a click of frustration. 'Celine Chevalier is helping us bring the vineyard into the twenty-first century. We're a little behind in that regard, you see.'

'You can go, madam,' says Skinner.

Mullins sees the look that passes between Celine and Owen. There's something in it, but he doesn't know what.

'I'll take a walk,' Celine says, turning to her hosts. 'No problem at all.'

All four watch her saunter out. Nice to be Celine Chevalier right now; nice to be her any time, probably.

'And then there were four,' says Skinner, taking the mug of tea from Karensa.

The liquid slops as she passes it to him. A shaking hand? Maybe.

'My colleague here, PC Mullins, he took your statements on Thursday, when the victim was found.'

'And he was very thorough,' says Edwin.

'There are, however, some inconsistencies, which mean we can't quite draw a line under anything yet. Primarily the suggestion that Russell Tremaine might have been involved in an altercation of some kind, prior to the incident with the cattle. There might be details you've forgotten from that morning that could prove significant. So, we'd like to ask you to cast your minds back.'

Diplomacy from the detective sergeant.

'An altercation? Well, that should hardly surprise anyone,' says Edwin, shaking his head. 'A guy like Russell doesn't just walk a fine line with the law, he crosses it left, right and centre. Sorry, but it's fact.'

Mullins turns to Owen, 'On that . . . we haven't received the model number of your missing quad yet.'

'What's that?'

For a second, it's as if Owen has no idea what Mullins is talking about. He's chewing at his lip; eyes faraway. He looks, Mullins thinks, like a kid caught staring out the window at the back of the class – and now Teach is picking on him.

'We need the model number of your quad. If you want us to pursue that, sir.'

'Oh yeah, course.' Owen rubs the side of his face. 'With everything that's been happening it hasn't been top of the list.'

'We didn't want to waste police time,' says Ruth. 'Though perhaps you have it to spare, given the fact you're here now—'

'We'd like to talk to you all separately,' says Skinner, cutting in.

'That's awfully formal,' says Ruth.

'It keeps things focused,' he says. 'Is there a room we can use?'

'Sure,' says Edwin. 'The lounge.'

'I expect you heard about the little incident we had here last night, Officers,' says Ruth. 'Shaun Tremaine rather letting himself down.'

'He's lost his son,' says Mullins. He feels the heat of Skinner's eyes on him but refuses to look in his direction.

When they called at Shaun's cottage earlier, Mullins couldn't figure out the swirl of different emotions the bloke was caught up in. *What was your relationship with your son like?* they asked. When what they were really getting at was, did they ever come to blows? *He was my boy.* That was how Shaun replied. And the way he said it made Mullins drop his head, suddenly very interested in the toes of his boots. Like, no further explanation needed – love non-negotiable. Isn't it possible, though, to have conflicting emotions when it comes to family? For Shaun to both love his son and, maybe, get it badly wrong too? This morning, there was a bruise and a slight bump on Shaun's forehead. He said it was from falling over in the farmhouse. Could it have come from a run-in with his own flesh and blood? While it looked fresh, Mullins couldn't swear that Shaun hadn't had it on Thursday.

'The lounge,' says Skinner. 'That'll do nicely. Ruth, let's start with you, shall we? Seeing as you appear to have a lot to say.'

◆ ◆ ◆

Mullins shifts in his seat and crosses his legs. So far, each Harper has stuck with what they said in their witness statements. Ruth: check. Karensa: check. Owen: check.

Can he detect anything different in their mannerisms today? Are the Harpers smelling a rat? Ruth is basically the same as she was three days ago. But Karensa is rattled; she kept squirming in her seat. And Owen, he looked like he was carrying the weight of the world on his shoulders.

Now Edwin sits in front of them and, sure enough, he's parroting his witness statement too.

'So, the most likely explanation you can think of,' says Skinner, 'is that Russell was scoping out the premises, with a view to further thefts, and then hid in the field?'

'He must have seen one of us,' says Edwin. 'I was working in the winery. I wouldn't have been aware of him because when I'm in there it's one hundred per cent focus. But it's possible he saw me and panicked.'

'What were you doing in the winery?' asks Mullins.

'Disgorging,' says Edwin. 'Readying the Pinot Noir for Celine's visit. Owen will have been down in the vines. That's where he always is, though this time of year there's not much to do. Maintenance, mostly. Bit of pruning.' He laughs, runs his hand through his hair. 'He actually talks to the vines, Officers, like an absolute lunatic, but I suppose you can't arrest him for that, can you?'

Skinner smiles thinly. 'Not today.'

Owen told them he was working on his own among the vines. If Russell saw Owen, he might have felt his exit was cut off, which made the cattle field the better option for lying low.

'And your mother?' says Skinner.

'Mum was tidying the yard up. Look, Celine's visit is a big deal, so if we're a little on edge, you'll have to forgive us. We're not being hard-hearted about Russell's death. It's just . . . the timing. Selfishly speaking, it's not great.'

'What sort of tidying?' asks Mullins.

'Oh, absolutely insignificant things,' says Edwin. 'The kinds of stuff you or I would never notice, Officer. Smoothing gravel. Bit of weeding. Not to patronise Mum but it makes her feel useful.'

'And your wife, Karensa?'

'Who knows? She's been twitchy about Celine's visit too. She's of a nervous disposition generally, my wife, she . . . ties herself in knots. She went to the doctor about it, and they prescribed physical exercise, so she's taken to walking a lot. All hours, she's up and out, all weathers too. But if it helps settle her nerves . . .' He shrugs. 'And it does keep her in shape, so I'm not complaining.'

Maybe Mullins has been hanging out with Saffron Hippy-Dippy Weeks too long, but he shoots Edwin a look.

'*Mental* shape,' says Edwin, as if reading his thoughts.

Talking of Hippy-Dippy, she didn't seem her usual self this morning at Hang Ten. She didn't just look tired, she looked distracted. Like she was only half in the room – and she's always fully in it. Lighting it up.

Skinner points to Edwin's hand. 'Tell us how you got that. Nasty bit of bruising.'

'Do I have to? It doesn't make me look very good.'

Then Edwin recounts the same story he told Jayden. That on seeing Russell's body, he snapped and punched the gate.

'I know, I know, hardly noble of me. I probably deserve a fracture, frankly. But . . . we've been in the doldrums for some time, and Celine's investment . . . it means everything. I just saw that body and thought . . . this poor guy's blown it for us.'

Edwin pushes his hand through his hair again; looks down.

'And I know just how rotten that makes me sound. The ridiculous thing is that Celine's taken the whole thing in her stride. I mean, not her stride, that doesn't make her sound great either. But she understands the bigger picture. So, I shouldn't have panicked, should I?'

And does Mullins's lie detector go off? The one that's supposed to be inbuilt, as an officer of the law? No, it doesn't.

'I think we're about done here,' says Skinner, getting to his feet. 'Thanks for your cooperation. Oh, one last thing. A quick swab, if you're willing. Just to rule you out.'

Mullins proffers the wand. Steps up to Edwin with a friendly grin.

'There,' he says. 'Done.'

'Okay, then,' says Edwin. 'Done.'

On the way out to the car, Skinner shakes his head.

'Mullins, I know your mate Jayden reckoned he was on to something with those knuckles of Edwin's, but, as usual, that Shell House pair are getting overexcited. The gate story is just stupid enough to be true.'

'You mean we can't charge Edwin for being a selfish prat?'

'Let's see what these swabs tell us. I've a feeling we'll be back here questioning one of this lot again. I just don't know who yet.'

40

'Ally, I don't need any more food,' says Shaun. 'I'm not planning a party like the Harpers.'

But as he takes the box of brownies that Saffron sent, he immediately lifts the lid; bites into one.

'I'm popular today,' he says through a mouthful. 'The police have been here drinking my tea.'

'We heard they were heading out this way,' says Jayden. 'What did they tell you?'

'Tell me? Third degree more like. Wanting to know when I'd last seen Russell, what kind of mood he was in, that sort of thing. I told them what I said before, back when they weren't interested. That I hadn't seen my boy for a couple of weeks. That I've still got no idea what he was even doing in that field. And there's no need for them to suddenly pull their finger out, because I've got others working on it now. That's what I said.'

His eyes flit between them.

'Unless you're here telling me you're backing out.'

'No way,' says Jayden. He shoots a look at Ally. 'We've got you, Shaun.'

'We've been thinking about what you told us yesterday. About Frank. Did you tell the police just now too?' asks Ally.

Shaun shakes his head. 'Didn't see the point.'

'We think it could be important,' says Jayden.

'Don't know about that.' He tosses the last of the brownie in his mouth, chews thoughtfully. 'It was years back. Anyway . . . I don't trust them like I trust you. No one in their right mind does, do they? It's always in the papers. Police corruption, sexism, racism.' He looks to Jayden. 'Tell me I'm wrong.'

'PC Mullins and DS Skinner, they're good guys.'

Would Jayden have said that about Skinner a year ago? Unlikely. But perhaps; Jayden's one of the most diplomatic people Ally's ever met.

'Even if we don't always like their style, they're trying to do their jobs right,' he adds.

Shaun grunts. 'They tried making out that my boy and I had a falling-out.'

Ally's ears prick up. 'How so?'

'Wanted to know what our relationship was like. Like . . . did I ever lift my hand to him. That's what they were getting at.' Shaun darts a look at Jayden. 'Now I know I gave you a bit of a tap, but that wasn't like me. You've got to believe me there. And I'd never touch a hair on Russell's head . . .' Shaun's eyes fill.

Jayden and Ally look to one another. It's one thing Mullins telling them about the post-mortem, but another sharing that information with Shaun.

'They said they knew about me socking you last night, Jayden. They used it as ammunition. Wanted to know if I did the same to my boy.'

'Jayden didn't report it, Shaun,' says Ally.

He could have done, but he didn't.

'I know he didn't. Don't think I'm not grateful.' Shaun wipes his sleeve across his face. 'But why would they ask a thing like that? About me and Russell?'

'I think,' says Jayden carefully, 'that they're exploring what Russell might have been doing before he ended up in the field.'

'So, they've caught up, have they? And, what, they reckon he got himself in a fight, do they? Is that what this is, Jayden?'

'It could be.'

'I've seen my fair share of telly. Post-mortems and that. It's telling them something different, is it?' He rubs at his chin. 'But they'd come out and say something like that, wouldn't they?'

Not if they're harbouring suspicions about you.

'Shaun,' says Jayden, 'remember how Nicky said that Russell was talking about having something in the pipeline. That he was excited about coming into some money, planning a holiday.'

'I never stuck my nose into what Russell did,' says Shaun, 'and I don't want the police poking around in it either.'

'If the police are starting to think there might be a bit more to this than a simple accident, they'll want access to Russell's bank statements and phone records. It's standard procedure,' says Jayden.

'It helps them build a picture,' adds Ally, as Shaun shakes his head.

'Shaun, if someone's talking about coming into money and then they die, the police have to investigate the possibility that those two things might be linked.'

'What about you two building a picture?' he says, his jaw set hard. 'What happened to that?'

'We're working on it,' says Ally. 'And what you told us about Frank feels like it fits in. We just don't know how yet.'

'Alright, I'll give you a picture. Because I can sit here talking about my boy to the end of time. I can tell you that he liked a shiny new pair of trainers. That he always had three Weetabix, even when he was a nipper. That he had a cracking singing voice when he wanted to turn it on. Really cracking, it was. And every bed he slept in, he made sure he had his Arsenal scarf hanging on the wall above it.' Shaun's voice cracks. 'But how's any of that going to tell us why he died? And how's any of it going to bring him back?'

Ally looks down, feeling tears at the backs of her eyes. Jayden says, in a clear, kind voice, 'Shaun, any chance we could take a look at Russell's flat?'

Shaun abruptly gets up and leaves the room. Ally looks to Jayden, and he gives a small shake of his head. Perhaps they've pushed him too hard. But then Shaun comes back in, holding up a Yale key on a single string.

'71A Elwood Terrace. I'll go in at some point, but I'm not ready for it. Not yet. But if anyone's nosing about in bank statements, then I want you two to get there first.'

Russell's flat in Camborne.

Does anyone still have paper bank statements, these days? Wouldn't someone of Russell's age prefer to do everything online? But Jayden's taking the key, closing it in his hand.

'Top drawer in his bedroom,' says Shaun. 'That's where he kept his passport and wallet. If he held on to bank statements, they'd be there too. He was always quite neat, was Russell. You wouldn't think it, but he was.'

'Okay,' says Jayden. 'Thank you. Shaun, is there anything you want us to bring you from his flat?'

Shaun drops his head. 'I can't think,' he says. 'Not now.'

Outside the cottage, Ally looks back at the window. There's a twitch of a curtain as Shaun watches them go. He holds up his hand in a wave.

'To Camborne, then?' says Jayden, a look of determination on his face.

She nods. 'To Camborne.'

Jayden checks his watch. 'Oh, hold on. I've got lunch back at the farm. Sue's doing one of her roasts and Old Fran and Bernard are coming. Al, sorry. Regroup later? I'll eat fast.'

'Jayden, don't worry. It's your family, it's important.'

'Cat's family,' he says with a shrug. 'But yeah.'

Ally thinks of Shaun on his own. His mother long dead, his wife long gone. His son – the boy he saw as a ray of light – gone too. At least he has Charlie; never underestimate a canine companion. After Bill died, and Evie flew back home to Australia, Fox saved her in untold ways.

They're just about to get into the car when Ally sees a flash of red moving through the next-door field. The Harpers' vines.

'Jayden, look,' she says. 'Is that Karensa? Edwin's wife?'

'No, that's Celine Chevalier. The VIP. Now, what's she up to?'

'Mullins and Skinner must still be with the Harpers.'

'Yeah, that'll do it,' says Jayden. 'Hey Al, you haven't met her. Want to? Remember, it's all part of building that picture, right?'

And they're past the yew tree, a little way up the track and heading towards the vines.

'Celine!' calls out Jayden.

Celine jumps. Startled, perhaps, that anyone should recognise her here. For a moment she looks at Jayden like he's a complete stranger.

'We met last night,' he says.

'Of course.' She smiles, holds a finger to her lip. 'How is it?'

'All good. Nice day for a walk, right?'

In less than a minute, their shoulders are wet with drizzle. The sky overhead is streaked with bands of blue and grey, like a painter's drawn a palette knife clean through it.

'It's beautiful nevertheless,' says Celine, her hand trailing over the gnarled stems of the vines. She looks from one to the other. 'You both live locally?'

'Porthpella,' says Jayden. 'Ally's been here for, what, forty years, Al?'

'Getting on for forty-two,' says Ally. 'All down in the dunes.'

Celine wraps her coat around her more tightly. Her eyes look faraway. 'Some places . . . there's a connection that can't be broken. A layer of meaning that only certain people understand. That is what Shoreline Farm is to me.'

'And that's why you're investing?' says Jayden.

Celine gives him a studied look. 'Ruth's powers of persuasion are . . . impressive. I must warn you, if you're on your way up to the vineyard, the police are there. Asking questions about the man who died.'

'Why do the police need to ask more questions?' asks Jayden, all innocence.

'Oh, I suspect they're just paying lip service.'

And it makes sense that the Harpers would downplay things as far as their investor is concerned.

Celine smiles suddenly. 'Last night Owen said something about the pair of you being private detectives. A place like this, I wouldn't have thought there would be enough crime to keep you busy, but I suppose it just goes to show. Too often, people mistake beauty for goodness.'

They hear the distant sound of an engine as a patrol car comes rumbling down the track. *Mullins and Skinner.*

'That's my cue to return to the farmhouse,' says Celine. 'It was good seeing you again, Jayden. And meeting you, Ally.'

They watch as Celine makes her way back up the hill, following the line of vines. Meanwhile the patrol car steams down the track. Mullins and Skinner either don't see them or don't care.

Jayden turns to Ally, says, 'So Celine said she knows we're detectives, but she didn't ask the obvious question.'

'Which is?'

'What we're doing here.'

41

'Jay, you're late,' says Cat, catching him at the door.

'How's my little one?' He lays a hand on her belly, then kisses his wife on the lips. 'Sorry, we got caught up.'

'Dad's got a serious crisis. It's put him in a right mood.'

'What's happened?'

She grins. 'He's lost his taste with this cold. Said Mum's Yorkshire puddings are like rubber, and the beef might as well be a bit of old carpet.'

'Well, speaking as a Yorkshireman, I can confirm your mum's Yorkshire puds kick ass.'

'Make sure you tell her that then.'

Cat takes his hand and leads him into the dining room, and he squeezes her fingers as they walk. He thinks for a moment of what his own mum and dad are doing right now. They do a Sunday roast from time to time, but when they feel like it. *Wednesday teatime, why not?* Once, when he was a kid, his mum declared it an upside-down day. They had macaroni pie for breakfast – his great-grandmother's Trini speciality, always his favourite – then breakfast cereal for tea. Jayden and his dad wore their pyjamas for a kickabout in the garden, and later he and his sister, Ella, did their homework – okay, they still had to do their homework – in the treehouse, working by a storm lantern. Jayden grew up in a home where they made their own rules, and he's eternally grateful for it. Cat's family? They live by fixed rhythms, and ideas of what the 'done thing' is. Being five minutes late for Sunday lunch? Not the done thing . . .

'Ah, here he is at last,' says Cliff. 'Jayden's been chasing wild geese over Porthpella all morning.'

'You know it,' says Jayden, with a sturdy grin. He kisses Old Fran on the cheek and shakes Bernard's hand. Sue passes him a heaped plate.

'Terrible thing about the young man up at the vineyard,' says Old Fran. 'You think there's a bit more to it, do you?'

'He's listening to ghost stories,' says Cliff, shaking his head. 'And all I wanted you to do was find a missing quad bike, Jayden. Instead, you're going on about missing persons.'

'*Yes*, Sue,' says Jayden, getting stuck into his Yorkshire pudding. 'This is your best ever. And the beef. The flavour!'

He feels a sharp kick from Cat under the table. Across the tablecloth, Cliff glowers.

'Shoreline Vines,' says Bernard, holding up a bottle. 'Fill your glass, Jayden?'

'I'm driving later. But hey, nice bottle. Topical.'

'Driving?' says Cliff. 'Not more wild goose chasing? Here, I'll take a drop, Bernard.'

'Go easy, Cliff,' says Sue.

'Dad, if you can't taste, it's kind of wasted on you,' says Cat.

'That's insult to injury, that is, daughter. Red wine is medicinal.'

'Cliff's right,' says Bernard. He raises his glass. 'Cures all ills. It's why I'm fighting fit at seventy-eight.'

'I think we know with Jayden now,' says Sue, 'that what other people might think of as a wild goose chase often turns out to be the opposite.'

Jayden winks at her. 'Cheers, Sue.'

'People in Mousehole are still talking about JP Sharpe and everything that happened last Christmas,' says Old Fran. 'They will be for years to come, I reckon. So, what's it about this time, Jayden?'

'Honestly?' he says, setting down his knife and fork. 'I don't know.'

'But you and Ally always get there in the end,' says Sue. 'You do, you know.'

'A man died in a field, trampled by bullocks. And we want to know what he was doing in that field in the first place. The victim's dad hired us.'

'The same dad that gave Jayden that fat lip,' says Cliff. 'That's gratitude, wouldn't you say? Wonderful job you must be doing.'

'It could be no more than a case of wrong place, wrong time,' says Jayden, ignoring him, 'Or—'

'You'd think it'd be a case of wrong place, wrong time as far as Ruth's investor is concerned,' says Sue, 'but she doesn't sound put off, by all accounts.'

'Well, the wine is okay,' says Bernard. 'Really quite good. For English wine.'

'Cornish wine,' says Old Fran. 'That's different, remember.'

'Or . . . what?' says Cat. 'If it's not wrong place, wrong time, then what is it, Jay?'

'There's a few coincidences,' says Jayden. 'And detectives don't like coincidences.'

'It's a coincidence you bought a bottle of Shoreline wine today,' says Sue. 'A lovely coincidence.'

'Not a coincidence,' says Old Fran. 'We knew you were going to the dinner last night.'

'Anyway, the police aren't done with it,' says Jayden. 'They were back at the vineyard this morning.'

Cat narrows her eyes. 'So they're treating it as suspicious?'

Jayden nods.

'Jayden wanted to know about missing people over the years,' says Sue, turning to Old Fran and Bernard. 'But all we can think of is Helena Hunter. And we all know how that turned out.'

'Why do you want to know about missing people, dear?' asks Old Fran. 'What's that got to do with that poor chap in the field?'

'Exactly nothing,' mutters Cliff. 'Which is what I'm tasting of this wine. Nothing. Cat's right. It's wasted on me. Crying shame.'

'We don't know yet, Fran,' says Jayden. 'But we're talking twenty years ago. Not recently.'

And Jayden says this partly because it's true, and partly because he doesn't particularly want to bring incident-room vibes to the table – not with the scattergun conversation, and Cliff quipping and grumbling at every turn. He thinks of Ally in the peace of The Shell House and checks his watch. There's still a crumble to get through – *that's not fair, Sue's crumble is always a win* – then he can make his excuses. Next stop Camborne. Maybe it's worth a trip back to see Russell's mate Nicky Ballard too.

'You've got a cracking memory though, Fran,' he says, 'if anything stirs, you know where to find me, right?'

'Out chasing geese,' says Cliff. 'Wild ones.'

'What is it, Bernard?' says Old Fran. She's watching her husband keenly. 'He's ruminating. I can tell.'

Bernard lowers his glass. 'There was someone. A long time ago.'

'How long ago?' asks Jayden.

'He's playing you,' laughs Cliff.

'Don't, Bernard,' says Sue.

'Bernard doesn't play games,' says Old Fran. 'And he never forgets a name or a face either. Do you, love?'

'Well, I wouldn't forget this, *ma chérie*, because it was the same day that I proposed to you.'

Old Fran covers Bernard's hand with her own. 'Then it was twenty-nine years ago, wasn't it?'

'*Oui, chérie.* Twenty-nine wonderful years ago. Jayden, a man was here searching for his brother.'

'In Porthpella?'

'In Mousehole.'

'Well, that figures,' says Cliff. 'Harbour lights, was it? When the emmets swarm in, anyone can get lost . . .'

'The brother wasn't lost in Mousehole,' says Bernard, sitting back in his chair and steepling his fingers. 'In fact, the guy wasn't even sure that he was lost in Cornwall. But he was desperate, I suppose. Looking everywhere.'

'What brought him here then?' asks Jayden. 'There must have been some kind of Cornwall link.'

'He had a postcard from Torquay. Yes, it's all coming to me now. The guy had it with him. His brother had made a joke about the palm trees on the card, said that was where the comparison with Barcelona ended. He was Spanish, you see.'

Jayden's brain scribbles frantically, storing the details.

'On the postcard he wrote something like "next stop Cornwall", and that was the last they heard. He was travelling in the UK. An . . . itinerant sort, I think.'

'Why didn't you ever tell me this?' asks Old Fran.

Bernard shrugs. 'I don't know. My mind was on the question I was about to ask you, Frannie. And afterwards . . . afterwards we only had eyes for each other, didn't we?'

And Jayden swears Old Fran blushes.

'But I remember it clearly. Because of the day. Thinking how happy it was for us, but for this poor guy . . . something totally different. I took his flyer because I felt sorry for him.'

'Bernard,' says Jayden. 'This is a total longshot, but you don't remember the man's name, do you?'

Bernard shakes his head. 'I'm sorry, no. The mists of time.'

'But you always remember names,' says Old Fran.

'I'm sorry, *ma chérie*. Not this time. You're forgetting I'm seventy-eight.'

'And? That's nothing. The flyer though, wouldn't you have kept that?'

'That'd be a bit creepy,' says Cat. 'Ooh, Mum, that crumble smells amazing.'

'Can't smell either,' says Cliff. 'Absolutely nothing. You could be bringing a dish of manure to the table for all I'd know.'

'Well, I don't think that's very nice,' says Sue, setting the crumble down in the middle of the table.

'Bernard doesn't throw anything away,' says Fran. Adding with almost a note of pride, 'He's a hoarder.'

'I am,' says Bernard. 'But something like that . . . I wouldn't keep it.'

The flare of hope that Jayden felt starts to wane. He accepts a heaped bowl of crumble and, as the conversation swirls around him, attempts to order his thoughts.

Twenty-nine years ago, there was a missing Spanish man in Cornwall – maybe. His brother was looking for him – in Mousehole, and possibly in other places too. Is any of this information potentially more relevant than those entries that Jayden scrolled through online? Rightly or wrongly, it feels like it is. Because the difference is, this information has come straight to him. Landed in his lap. And he can't wait to discuss it with Ally and see if together they can find a way to take it forward.

'Jayden, you're worse than Jazzy, playing with your food,' laughs Sue.

He looks down, realising he's churned his crumble into something resembling Cliff's remark earlier.

'That's because Jayden has his thinking face on now too,' says Old Fran.

'I know what he's thinking about,' says Cliff.

And Jayden beats him to the punchline.

'More wild geese, Cliff. A whole flock of them.'

'Not a flock, son. A gaggle.'

And this minor triumph gives Cliff his first true smile of the day.

42

'I know something's up with you, Karensa.'

Karensa can feel Edwin's eyes boring into her, and she huddles deeper inside her cardigan.

'I don't understand why the police came back again,' she says. 'That's all. And why they needed to swab us like that.'

'What did you say to them?'

'Who?'

Edwin gives a click of frustration. 'The police, Karensa.'

'Exactly what I said before. The truth.'

Karensa knows Celine's waiting for him outside – Ruth too – and Edwin won't want to be late. She sees him hesitate at the door, his features knotted as he scrutinises her.

'So why do I feel like there's something you're not telling me?'

Historically, Karensa's husband has never been good at reading her; that's been at least half of their problem, his inability to observe her feelings – much less comprehend them. Why this sudden flash of emotional intelligence now? Is her dishonesty that startlingly obvious? And if it is, why haven't the police got Karensa under caution down at the station? She knows one thing: she's a lot more practised at lying to Edwin than to anybody else.

Her mother-in-law thinks she's as insignificant as an ant. Her husband thinks she's as pliable as willow, as timid as a mouse. Did she want to fall for Owen? No. But the fact that she did – that she so brazenly goes to Owen's caravan when Edwin and Ruth think she's walking off her anxiety – is a delicious secret. *Was.*

Until Russell saw them. Then he died, and everything changed.

She bites down on the inside of her mouth as she says, 'Edwin, you don't care about him at all, do you?'

'Who?'

'The dead man, Edwin. The dead man. *Russell.*'

This is what Karensa tried to explain to Owen earlier: the toxicity of the whole situation. The burning shock of Edwin's callousness when faced with the tragedy of Russell Tremaine. Her own shameful feelings of relief, knowing that with Russell's death her and Owen's secret is safe. Whether it's for love or money, she realises now that all they're concerned with is saving their own skins – and it's come to disgust her. Why can't Russell's death spur them to honesty? Some scrap of good be taken from it? *It's time to tell Edwin,* she said to Owen earlier. *It's gone on long enough.* But Owen said he doesn't want to be rushed into saying anything before the time is right. All because he doesn't want to face the consequences of falling in love with her.

Karensa sees Edwin cock his ear at a creak from the floorboards above.

'Look, I don't want to distract myself from what's important right now with . . . *this.* But you're worrying me, Karensa.'

He throws an almost hopeless look at her. Dejected Edwin. Hurt Edwin. It's one he uses sometimes when he reaches for her in bed and she rolls away, saying *I'm just so tired,* or *this headache,* or *can we another time?*

Uses sometimes. That's unfair of her.

Karensa can't say the exact moment when she stopped loving Edwin, but she knows that it wasn't a simple case of transferring her feelings to Owen. Does that make it better? In the scheme of their deceit, she suspects not.

'What are you bloody hiding?' And just as fear so often does in men, in boys, it turns to anger.

For one wild moment she imagines telling her husband that she and Owen are in love. Setting a bomb under this entire farmhouse and blowing the place sky high, and all of its secrets along with it.

'I can't do this now. I've got to talk to Celine about our future. That's what this is all for, by the way. Safeguarding our future. Whatever that is.'

And she has to give him something, doesn't she? Because Edwin is stepping dangerously close to the truth. And it needs to be Owen who says it. Karensa would walk away from Shoreline Vines in a heartbeat, but this is Owen's home. He loves every inch of it. And he'll lose every inch of it when he tells them the truth.

So she takes a breath. Says, 'I saw Russell the day he died. I told the police I didn't, but I did.'

'You saw Russell?'

A foul-weather cloud moves across Edwin's face.

'I . . . was rude to him.'

'You spoke to him?'

Edwin's voice is shot through with disbelief. She nods. After all the lying, this bit is easy.

'And why didn't you tell the police this, Karensa?'

Because it would open up a can of worms. A Pandora's box. It'd be that bomb, blowing the vineyard sky-high.

For just one second, a thought rises, and it cuts Karensa like a knife. The police are talking about an altercation – that's the word the detective sergeant used. Owen told her he hadn't seen Russell watching them. He said he'd had no idea.

Karensa's hand goes to her head. Blood pounds in her ears.

Owen's a good man. Isn't he? He's between a rock and a hard place, that's why he's running scared now. That's all it is. And she's just anxious, which makes everything unstable. Worry jetting in from all directions.

'Hold on, what were you rude to Russell Tremaine about?'

She shakes her head, her train of thought derailed. 'Um, just . . . me being me.'

And her husband clearly thinks so little of her – and of Russell – that he accepts this. It's only natural that Karensa would be rude to someone like Russell Tremaine. Because Edwin grew up with a snob for a mother, and is a snob himself.

'And what did Russell say back?' says Edwin.

'Nothing.'

And here she's telling the whole truth and nothing but the truth, because Russell never said a word. He just stared at them from across the vines – his face as blank and cold as a snow field – then walked on up the track. Actions speak louder than words, and Russell saw Karensa kissing Owen in the vines.

Then that stabbing thought comes again. It twists this time, right between her ribs.

What if Owen lied to her? What if he saw Russell too?

43

'Tell me what we've got,' says Skinner.

They're back at the station, a cup of tea apiece. Skinner holds up a packet of biscuits.

'But first, try one of these.'

Mullins squints at the Spanish writing. Did Skinner bring back a holiday souvenir?

'Almonds,' says Skinner, pulling one out and taking a delicate nibble. 'Absolutely delicious. Whatever you do though, don't risk a dunk. They don't hold up to the soaking.'

'Gotcha. And don't mind if I do.'

Mullins takes a bite and it's a pretty bog-standard biscuit, if you ask him. It's got nothing on a Jaffa cake, that's for sure.

'Tasty,' he says. 'Really tasty. Thanks.'

'Don't say I never give you anything.'

'Why did you cut your holiday short, Sarge?' he asks through the biscuit.

'Because one of us round here is dedicated to the job. Now go on, tell me what we've got.'

Mullins sits up in his chair. But he imagines himself standing in front of the whiteboard, a marker in his hands. A sea of eager faces turned towards him.

'Okay. We know that Russell Tremaine was trampled by cattle, and that was probably what killed him. But we also know that he was involved in a fight with someone beforehand. We don't have any information on the time between these two events, but the pathologist reckons we're talking hours. Maybe even minutes. Definitely not days. Not going by the bruising.'

'Go on,' says Skinner, taking another bite, then catching a crumb from his moustache.

'Russell's dad, Shaun Tremaine, claims to know nothing about any scraps. We've only his word that Russell didn't go by the cottage that morning. And we've only his word that their relationship was . . . cordial.'

Nice. Mullins gives himself a little pat on the back for the use of that one. But then the satisfaction ebbs and he's left with a feeling of mild betrayal. Shaun loved his son. He must have done, because Mullins could feel the sorrow coming off him like heat.

'Carry on,' says Skinner.

'We also know that all four Harpers were present at the vineyard when Russell's body was discovered. And despite Edwin Harper's claim that he had no interaction with Russell at all, his right fist bore the evidence of having recently struck an object.'

'Yes, it did.'

'But he claimed it was a five-bar gate.'

'Yes, he did.' Skinner folds the biscuit packet shut. 'Now, the right thing to do is keep our powder dry. I want to see if we get a hit on the DNA. If there's any skin cells, any saliva, belonging to any one of the Harpers on Russell Tremaine, we'll soon know about it.'

'But what if there is a match? Say it's Edwin, and he's lying about hitting the gate. Maybe he confesses to a bit of fisticuffs, but we still can't prove how Russell died, can we?'

'Go on,' says Skinner.

'Well, how are we ever going to know if Russell's heart stopped in that field, or somewhere else? Or maybe the fight was even in the field, and the cattle came over to see what was going on and accidentally finished the job?'

'*Came over to see what was going on?* What are they, nosy neighbours?'

Mullins frowns. He was doing so well too.

'But you're right,' says Skinner. 'Perhaps science will only take us so far, in this instance. Perhaps we'll have to rely on good old-fashioned interview techniques to find the truth. If we get a hit on the DNA, we've enough to arrest somebody on a charge of at least ABH, if not GBH. And then we'll go from there.'

'What's your gut-feel about Edwin, Sarge?'

'Like I said, I think everyone's lying until they prove to me that they're not.'

'Assume nothing. Believe nobody. Challenge everything.'

He's done his training, after all.

'Exactly. Take you and these biscuits of mine, Mullins. "Very tasty," you said. But I didn't believe it until I saw you take a second one. So, you proved you were telling the truth.'

'I could have just been hungry.'

'Plus, they're delicious by anybody's estimation,' says Skinner. 'So that's that. Edwin though? Against my better judgement, I believe he punched the gate. Mostly because it makes him look like an idiot. But it's not about my judgement, not solely. Enter DNA.'

'Karensa Harper was jumpy.'

'As a frog. Mind you, I would be too, mother-in-law like that. I believe Ruth is of the iron-glove, iron-fist school. She doesn't mince her words, but I wouldn't put lying past her either.'

'I quite liked Owen the first time. There was something different about him today. He looked knackered. Stressed.'

'I agree with you there. He had the old panda eyes. Bloke looked like he hadn't slept a wink.'

'How do you think he likes living out in that little caravan though, with the rest of them in the big house?'

'That's not a caravan, Mullins, that's an Airstream. An immaculately restored silver bullet. That's a lifestyle choice, that is, not a comedown.'

But it's not Mullins's cup of tea. He knows enough kids from his school who ended up in caravans; and that's not a lifestyle choice, that's a housing crisis.

'The hierarchy in the family's obvious. Mother rules the roost. Two sons, each in charge of a different part of the business. Karensa's a bit of a spare part on the face of things, but apparently she helps Edwin with the marketing.'

'And Shaun Tremaine used to work for them in the vineyard. Odd-job man really, but he knew his way round the vines too. Owen said they've offered him a job again, but he doesn't want it. What about the French lady? She obviously trusts them if she's investing. Two million, I heard.'

'Well, she might change her mind after all this,' says Skinner. 'Right, listen up. Get on Russell Tremaine's phone records, Mullins. Might as well do bank statements too, while you're at it.'

'I told you that Jayden reckoned Russell had a windfall coming, didn't I? Or Russell reckoned he had a windfall coming, anyway.'

'I think you'll find they're two quite different statements, Mullins.'

Mullins wrinkles his nose. 'Russell reckoned he had a windfall coming. Least that's what his mate said to Jayden. Bloke called Nicky Ballard. Works at a garage in Camborne.'

Skinner's face hardens. Mullins can't figure out what his boss thinks about the Shell House Detectives these days. He's got more respect for them, for sure, but not enough to actively bring them in on anything. If he knew that Mullins passed on the post-mortem findings? Yeah, Mullins doesn't want to dwell on that one. Hippy-Dippy would say it was for the greater good, wouldn't she? Something like that.

'Check it out, Mullins. Check it all out. And I want you looking at Tremaine's social media. His dad reckons he was a little angel, but then they always do.'

'Roger that.'

'Give it half an hour and we'll start badgering the lab,' says Skinner, pulling out another biscuit. 'I don't know about you, but I can smell a DNA hit cooking – and the aroma's very tasty.'

Skinner really is in a chirpy mood. Maybe he did just miss the job, and that's why he quit his holiday early.

'Are Newquay getting involved?' asks Mullins suddenly.

The Major Crimes lot. Whenever anything juicy's going down, they're straight off the blocks. And Mullins's to-do list is suddenly looking a tad long.

'No,' says Skinner. 'This one's all ours.'

And Ally and Jayden's. Obviously.

44

Elwood Terrace is a sloping street on the outskirts of Camborne, and number 71 a once-substantial family home now divided into flats. The outside railings have a bicycle lashed to them, its front wheel missing. The windows of the ground-floor flat are obscured by a patchwork of large, patterned throws.

On the drive from Porthpella, Jayden told Ally about Bernard and the missing person. And how, despite the sparkle of Bernard's memory, it leaves them with frustratingly little to go on. But it's still a connection, and Ally keeps thinking of the brother and his flyers by the harbour in Mousehole. And who else might have taken one.

'Shaun said it's the first-floor flat,' says Jayden, turning the key in the lock, '71A.'

She refocuses. As they go in, they're met by a carpet of take-away menus and junk mail. Jayden bends to go through it.

'Anything for Russell?'

He holds up a white envelope with a NatWest logo, addressed to Mr Russell Tremaine. 'Bingo.' He looks at the postmark. 'Sent two days ago. Though . . . Russell was talking about coming into money, not having it already. I'm not expecting it to show.'

'But it'll help build that picture of ours, won't it?'

'It will. Okay, let's go on up to the flat. We'll call Shaun there.'

Jayden places the rest of the post on a window ledge at the end of the hall, then they tread quietly through to the stairwell, the musty smell deepening the further they venture. The carpet is dull maroon, the shade of a school jumper, and thin with the comings and goings over the years. One wall is mottled all over with black mould, a print as delicate as pressed seaweed.

'Here,' says Jayden, '71A.'

The key sticks in the lock but then it shifts and the door swings wide.

Russell's home.

Ally stands carefully, reverently almost. She's always believed that houses have energies. The first day that she and Bill stepped inside The Shell House, with its pale washed boards and rooms full of the sound of the sea, Ally felt all the good currents. When she and Bill looked at one another, they both knew instinctively that they were home.

Russell's flat is, Ally thinks, extraordinarily empty. She struggles to feel anything here at all, beyond a sadness for its former occupant. Her eyes take in the simple sitting room with its navy-blue couch and the television. The glass coffee table, its surface uncluttered: a catalogue for a sports retailer, an elaborate-looking remote control. A narrow galley kitchen leads off this room, and that, too, is as neat as a pin. The only mess is a pizza box on the sideboard. Ally lifts the lid, and two congealed slices of pepperoni stare back. An Arsenal mug is upturned on the drainer, and above the sink a window the size of a porthole looks out on the grey pebbledash wall of next door.

'Shaun? It's Jayden.'

Ally looks back through to the sitting room, where Jayden's on his phone.

'So we're at the flat, and there's a bank statement, freshly arrived. Technically I can't open it, it's against the law, but . . .'

Ally can't hear what Shaun says but Jayden's nodding. 'Okay,' he says, 'okay. Sure. Sure.'

He hangs up and comes through to the kitchen; takes a knife from the drawer and slits the letter cleanly. 'Shaun says he authorises us. That he's the "bloody father". Okay, let's see. Transactions up until 31 October. That's five days before Russell's night out in Newquay.'

Ally moves closer, looks over Jayden's shoulder. Her eyes scan the statement. Russell is in his overdraft at the start of the month, and by the end he's even deeper into it.

'No wonder he was excited, if he was expecting a windfall.'

'Nicky said Russell lost his job at the call centre.'

'Yep. And see these, they look like bets. Online, mostly. There's a lot of them. But he wasn't placing massive amounts. Look, twenty pounds here, forty pounds there. To win big, you need to be putting up the cash too. Unless he goes for a rank outsider and gets lucky. So maybe that's the pipeline bit, then. A hot tip.'

'He could have been placing bets in cash too, couldn't he?'

'It's possible.' Jayden looks to the bedroom. 'That top drawer of Russell's . . . let's check it out.'

As Jayden pushes open the door, Ally stops.

It's the duvet cover; that's the trouble. Blue cotton, with black and white footballs dotted over it; the kind a child might pick. Matching pillowcases too. It's faded, the material faintly bobbled, as though it's been through the wash many times. When Russell left his dad's cottage, did he take his boyhood bedspread with him? A piece of home.

'You okay, Al?' says Jayden.

She nods.

There's an Arsenal scarf hanging over the mirror, and on top of the chest of drawers a photograph in a blue plastic frame. Ally leans closer to look. An elderly lady, skinny as a peg, stands next to a much younger-looking Shaun. Between them there's a small boy with a fuzz of blond hair and they each have their arms around him, holding him close. He's missing his two front teeth, and his grin has a roguish quality. He looks as if he's yet to discover the world has any weight at all.

Ally feels Jayden's hand on her shoulder.

'Look at the dear little boy he was,' she says quietly.

'We're going to figure this out, Al,' he says. 'We're going to do it for Shaun.'

She takes a breath. 'So, this is the drawer, then?'

Together they go through it. On the left side, Russell's socks are paired and balled, and to the right is a stack of papers. More bank statements, his passport, some old insurance paperwork. Together they scan the most recent few statements. Beyond supermarket transactions, pubs and online betting, Russell spent little – and earned less. The only thing that stands out is an ongoing monthly payment, a direct debit of £200, to an unnamed bank account.

'Wonder what that is,' says Jayden. 'A childcare payment?'

'Shaun didn't mention Russell having a child.'

'Maybe Shaun didn't know. It's not his rent, look, that's marked separately. The police could run a check. It'd take seconds.'

Ally hears the wistful note in his voice.

'Come on, Al, let's go. I don't think we can get any more here.'

Ally takes a last look at the bedspread, then follows Jayden out.

'Seeing as we're in Camborne, why don't we go and see Nicky again? Might as well, right?'

Jayden still sounds dejected. He's probably thinking of the police resources still: bank statements, phone records, emails . . . they've access to the lot, should they want it.

'Would the garage be open on a Sunday?'

'Oh yeah. Probably not. Okay, we'll phone him.'

'Hold on,' says Ally. 'Let's bin that old pizza. When Shaun does come in, he doesn't want to find it festering.'

Jayden waits by the door while she nips back into the kitchen.

She opens the pedal bin and shakes the ripe-smelling pizza slices into it. She closes the lid on them quickly.

Then she frowns, opens it again. She stares down at Russell's rubbish.

Ally takes a plastic spatula from a pot on the sideboard, and pokes deep into the bin. The contents collapse in on themselves, the pizza slices obscuring her view. It's as if she's walking the strand-line, raking through a heap of bladderwrack, flies rising from ocean detritus as she searches for that glint of treasure. She rolls up her sleeve and reaches in; extracts the object and holds it up to the light. She reaches again and draws out another. And another. She arranges them on the countertop, trying to form a picture. Or a sentence.

'Jayden, I think I've got something,' she calls out.

45

Saffron has stuck a 'Back in ten minutes' sign on the door and is down on the beach. It's a slamming wind and her baggy jeans flap against her legs; her hair blows horizontal. The waves are a mess and there's no one out there. She walks to the edge of the water and lets the incoming tide skim the tips of her trainers. Seafoam blows along the shore.

If she phones him now, he'll barely hear her over the wind. But she's always felt braver out in the elements. And the sea gives Saffron her bearings.

She hits his number. She lets it ring and ring but then it goes to voicemail. There's no recorded message, just the standard phone company one. *The number you've called is not available.*

He didn't want to worry you, that's what Dawn said, *but I thought you'd want to know.*

Saffron shoves her phone back in her pocket. Five minutes later, it rings. She answers – heart in her mouth. Back to the wind; hand shielding the receiver.

'Wilson, hey.'

'I didn't want her bothering you,' he says. And it's a gruff voice, without the twinkle of his eyes to go with it. 'She had no business.'

'I appreciated Dawn telling me.'

'Did you? Well, alright then.'

'Wilson . . . I'm sorry.'

'No need for sorry. Nothing's set in stone.'

'How do you feel?'

'Grand. I feel grand.'

And how Saffron wants to see his reassuring smile. But her mum gave her plenty of them – *oh, I'm fine, just a little tired, that's all* – and see how that ended up.

'So . . . what's next? Dawn said more tests.'

'More tests. More waiting. No point worrying about what you can't control, is there? Hey, how was the fish yesterday? Trip said you were pleased with it.'

'It was great. The bouillabaisse stole the show.'

'That's my girl.'

Saffron's eyes fill. 'I wondered why I hadn't seen you for a while.'

'Well, there's your answer. Cappuccino sales dropped off, did they?' He gives a little laugh.

'I'd like to see you.'

'I'm not much to look at.'

'Just . . . to hang out. If you want. Waiting on results . . . it messes with your head, doesn't it? So, if you ever want to . . . talk . . .'

'Anyway . . . I thought you told me that you and that bloke of yours were going to Hawaii. Gone until spring, you said. Sounds alright to me.'

'Broady's going, but I'm staying here. I want to see if I can make a go of Hang Ten over the winter.'

She hadn't thought of that part until now, but it makes her decision sound more convincing.

'What, keep it open? Good luck. You'll be bored out your brain.'

'So, I'll want company then, won't I?'

Wilson doesn't say anything. Saffron looks to the water, watches the waves explode on the shore. She didn't mean for her voice to crack – but crack it did.

'Saffron, listen,' he says, eventually, 'I know what you went through with your mum. I'm sure as hell not going to thrust that on you again. No way. You don't owe me that. You don't owe me anything.'

Then he hangs up.

46

Jayden lets out a low whistle.

'Good find, Al. Good find.'

He moves the letters with the tip of his finger. They're of varying sizes and types, cut from a newspaper, maybe some from the kind of junk mail flyers they found in the hallway. Jayden holds up a snatch of a headline – *record sales* – the *e* and the *a* missing.

'Poison pen letters,' says Ally, 'isn't that what they're called? Years ago, Bill told me about a case in the village. An elderly man was receiving anonymous letters, made of letters cut from the paper just like this, telling him that if he didn't prune his hedges he'd be in big trouble. Of course it didn't take much to work out that the only person who cared about the state of those hedges was his next-door neighbour.'

He laughs. 'And who says rural policing isn't a thrill?'

'Jayden, what do you think?'

What does Jayden think? He's racking his brains for an everyday reason why Russell might have been cutting individual letters out of newspapers. And he can't think of one.

Russell wasn't a collage artist – not like Ally. He's seen the way Ally sorts her finds in her studio: the shells, and then the plastics that she uses in her artwork. The trays of blues and reds and yellows. Her glue gun and palette knife and stack of broad canvases.

There's no evidence of any kind of work like that at 71A Elwood Terrace.

Could he have been following some kind of college course? Was this a random assignment? That feels a longer shot than the obvious one.

'Al, that's got to be it. Russell was writing a letter, and he didn't want it to be traced to him.'

Maybe Russell got the idea from the movies. Because it's an old-fashioned approach; kind of quaint. These days it's easier to set up a fake email account, if you want to disguise your identity.

'The windfall that Nicky told us about,' says Jayden. 'Maybe this is it. Russell was asking someone for money.'

'And that's what got him killed?' breathes Ally.

'Maybe Shoreline Vines was the meeting point. But it went wrong.'

They look down at the letters on the sideboard. The discarded fragments.

'Al, Russell knew the story about Frank killing someone.'

'He did.' Ally furrows her brow. She touches the tip of her finger to the leftover letters. 'Shaun said Russell never mentioned that story again. But maybe he stored the information away until he saw the chance to use it.'

'Look how neat his flat is, Al. Empty, even. I think Russell was someone who only held on to the things he wanted.' The idea grows in Jayden's mind. 'You've seen those bank statements. Russell was heavily into his overdraft. And losing his job at the call centre, he didn't exactly have much hope of getting out of it anytime soon. He needed money. Plus, that monthly payment he was making – that was always in there, no matter how bad his finances were, which made it an ongoing pressure, on top of everything else. Shaun said Edwin was bragging about the millions they were set to receive. Shaun told Russell, and maybe Russell saw the opportunity?

Basically, it's the same line of thought as Russell going to the vineyard to ask for his dad's job back. Only . . . a different ask.'

'So you think he blackmailed the Harpers? Gosh, that's a huge accusation.'

And Jayden doesn't like it, but it works.

'Shaun knew Russell had his struggles,' says Ally, 'but he said he was never involved in anything illegal. That's why he couldn't believe he'd steal a quad bike.'

'Shaun's a loving dad. Of course he wants to believe the best of his son. Plus, think about it, if Russell and his dad were close, he'd have been gutted about the way the Harpers treated Shaun after Frank died. So, the blackmail's not just financially motivated, it's emotional too.'

Ally's deep in thought. 'So . . . if Russell was threatening the Harpers, why on earth didn't they go to the police?'

'Why do you think?'

'Because Shaun's story about Frank is true.'

'Exactly.'

Ally shakes her head. 'So, they all know? About the letter, or letters, from Russell, and the old story about Frank?'

'Not necessarily. Perhaps only Ruth does. Or maybe she confided in her sons. But if none of them have said anything to the police, then either they know the story's true or they're worried that it might be. Because of the timing with Celine's visit, maybe they just don't want to run the risk of any bad press. Even if it's nothing more than rumour.'

'That's lot of maybes,' says Ally.

'Yeah, I know. It's total speculation. The whole thing.'

From the cut-out letters in the bin, to Russell remembering his dad's story, to there even being a body in the first place.

'And we're going to have a hell of a job proving any of it.'

Ally nods. 'A hell of a job or . . . impossible?'

'Not impossible.' Jayden rubs his hands together. 'Okay, here's what we do. We'll talk to Nicky again. Just sound him out on this line of thought. Then I think we've got to fill in the police.'

'Before we talk to Shaun?'

And it's a difficult one. Because Jayden has a feeling that Shaun will shut down if they suggest that Russell was involved in anything illegal.

'We need to keep Shaun onside. There might still be things he could tell us.'

'Going to the police with this isn't going to keep him onside, Jayden. He trusts us precisely because we're not the police.'

'But we know things that the police don't, things that could make a real difference to their investigation. If we could pool resources . . .'

'We could risk losing Shaun's trust. Especially as our theory paints his son as a blackmailer.'

'He wants answers, Al. And sometimes they're not always easy to hear. We've been here before, haven't we?'

Inconvenient truths. They divided Jayden and Ally during the JP Sharpe case, and he won't let that happen again.

'And the one thing we know is that we've got to agree a way forward together, right? So I reckon we talk to Nicky again, and see where that gets us. Then we make a plan.'

'Agreed,' says Ally.

Jayden hears his phone buzzing in his pocket. It's a landline number he doesn't recognise – but the voice, he does.

'Jayden, am I disturbing you?'

'Oh, hey, Bernard. Not at all. You okay?'

'My wife is right about a lot of things, including my fine memory.'

Jayden turns to Al. Pops a thumbs up.

'Go on.'

'It just needed to be jogged by a little more lunchtime wine, that's all. *In vino veritas* – you've heard that one, *oui?*'

'I've heard that one, Bernard.'

'So, it came to me on the drive home. Frannie was driving, it goes without saying.'

'Sure.'

'The man I spoke to in Mousehole, about his missing brother. He was Spanish. I said that, yes?'

'You did, yeah.'

'From Barcelona. The missing man's name, it was Eric.'

'Eric. Are you sure?'

'I'm certain. His surname . . . that I couldn't tell you. But I remember Eric, because my favourite player at the time was Eric Cantona.'

'Yeah, he was my dad's too, once upon a time. Until he left us for Old Trafford.'

'Of course. He played for Leeds.'

'For ten months.'

'And then never looked back.'

'Yeah, okay, thanks for that. I'd like to say us Leeds fans don't hold grudges . . . Anyway. This is useful. A Spanish man called Eric.'

'Does it help?'

'It helps.'

'*In vino veritas*, Jayden. Remember that.'

And at that, Bernard hangs up.

Ally's face is lit up. 'I heard all that. We have a name.'

'Eric from Barcelona.' Jayden puffs out his cheeks. 'I mean . . . hats off to Bernard for the memory feat, right? But . . . he's not giving us more than any of those names I looked at online yesterday.'

Less even, because they were all people known to have gone missing in Cornwall or Devon. And with surnames.

'No one knows if this Eric ever actually ventured beyond Torquay . . .'

Ally nods.

'But the thing is, Al, this info's come to us.' And Jayden realises he's doubling back on himself. 'What I mean is . . . we've got to follow it up. No question.'

'Because sometimes the stars align,' says Ally quietly.

'So, let's head back to The Shell House and go down a rabbit hole to Barcelona. You in?'

47

'Well,' says Celine, 'I'm impressed. Shoreline Vines has a wonderful future – and, as you already know, I would love to be part of it.'

The tour of the vines has wrapped, and Edwin holds out his hand for her to shake. Celine sees that the bruising across his knuckles is deep purple now. When she returned to the farmhouse earlier, Edwin was complaining to his brother. Celine could hear him in the lounge as she removed her boots in the porch.

As if I'd be parading around a bashed-up hand if I was trying to hide the fact I'd been in a scrap with Russell Tremaine. To which Owen replied, somewhat ominously: *It doesn't matter what we do or don't parade. They've got our DNA now.* Uncertain laughter followed, but she couldn't tell which brother it belonged to. And honestly, nor did Celine care.

'I'm only glad,' says Ruth, 'that you haven't been unsettled by the police intrusions this weekend, Celine.'

'They're only doing their job. It's unfortunate, of course, the young man who died. But from a business perspective, it's no pollutant.'

Celine smiles her most reassuring smile, and Ruth returns it with one of her own.

'With your investment,' says Ruth, 'the vines are safe. In fact, I rather think they'll flourish.'

Celine sees Owen wandering across the yard then; his shoulders are hunched, hands in his pockets. 'Excuse me one moment,' she says, then strides over to intercept him. 'Any luck?' she asks in a low voice.

She can feel Edwin and Ruth watching them both.

Owen looks confused for a moment, then resets himself. 'Yeah, sorry. Miles away. No, no luck. There's a few boxes of Dad's stuff up in the attic. I went through the ones with books in, but there's nothing with a dedication to you, Celine.'

Celine grits her teeth. 'Ah, but you could miss it. I think my mother just wrote "To my darling daughter". And it would be in French, of course.'

'Sorry, but there was nothing like that. I went through the lot. Easy enough, as Dad wasn't a big reader. I'm sorry to disappoint, Celine, but we don't have your book.'

Celine's concern, before she came, was that it had fallen into Ruth's hands. But from Ruth's behaviour, it's obvious that isn't the case. She could leave now and forget all about it, but that's not her style. In business, she's tenacious, ruthlessly efficient, meticulous. And what is this trip, if not business?

Owen makes to walk on, but Celine sets a hand on his arm. She makes a rapid calculation. 'Listen,' she says, 'I know it'll be in one of those boxes. I'd ask to look myself, but as you know, I really don't want to upset your mother. Remember, this deal, it means a lot to me too. I don't want to risk her . . . mixing emotion with business.' Celine looks at him pointedly, and she knows he's reading between the lines. 'How many boxes are there?'

'Three.'

'If I give you an address in St Ives, could you organise for the boxes to be delivered to me this evening? It would mean a great deal.'

And she puts an extra weight on those words, *great deal*. Because Owen wants her investment every bit as much as Ruth and Edwin do. She has a feeling that if you cut Owen, he'd bleed Shoreline.

She watches him hesitate, rubbing his jaw with his hand. She realises then how tired he looks.

'I know they're your father's things,' she says coaxingly, 'but I'll take great care of them. And I'll courier them directly back to you.'

Owen looks back to Edwin and Ruth. They're standing by her car, affecting to admire it. But they're clearly trying to listen in, because what on earth could Celine have to say to Owen that they can't hear too?

'Okay, sure,' he says, finally.

She takes out her phone, performs a fast sequence of taps. 'There, I've sent you the address.' Then, in a loud voice, designed to carry to the eavesdroppers, 'Thank you, Owen. I know your father would turn in his grave to hear me passing judgement on the grape varieties he lovingly chose. But with the effects of climate change, I do think you could consider other possibilities. You can take the girl out of Provence, but you can't take Provence out of the girl, and all that.'

Owen shrugs, says, 'We'll give it some thought.'

His play-acting is a little half-hearted in Celine's opinion, but she squeezes his arm and says, 'Your father left his vines in good hands with you, Owen.'

She walks back to Edwin and Ruth, says, 'I'm sorry, I had to pester him about grapes.'

'You can always pester me about grapes,' says Edwin. 'I am head of the winery, you know.'

'Ah, but it's Owen getting his hands dirty with the vines, *n'est-ce pas?*'

Edwin gives a short sharp laugh. 'He doesn't get his hands dirty doing anything.' He cups his hand, calls out to Owen's retreating back, 'Hey, do you, brother?'

48

Down in the dunes, the sunset is masked by clouds as dense and immovable as mountains; giant, darkening purple formations, with occasional bursts of silver. The tide is high, and waves hit the shore in a fury of white water; the beach pushes back with indifference.

Ally watches from the veranda of The Shell House, as inside Jayden is on the phone to Nicky Ballard. Fox patters up and down the boards and she bends to stroke his ears. He turned down a walk, which isn't like him. Instead, her little dog was content to nose around the garden – and now, by the look he's giving her, he's ready for his basket by the fire again.

Nice work if you can get it, Bill would say.

As they go back inside, Ally eyes the table where she and Jayden would usually settle. How this spot has changed. Ally can picture Evie down the years: bouncing in her highchair; blowing out birthday candles; her pencil case split open like a seed pod as she did her homework. And Bill: candlelit suppers; fish and chips wrapped in brown paper; slow weekend mornings when he wasn't on duty, newspapers spread across the table, crispy fried bacon and racks of toast. Then, the between time; this is how Ally has come to think of it – after Bill, and before Jayden. The house aching with quiet. This table – with its time-worn oak, its nicks and dents – a constant reminder of those who were missing.

As a workspace for a detective, Ally's table has taken on a new identity these last two years. But there's something about Bill's little office – the room she was half-afraid of – that makes her feel connected, as if the dots of life and death are joining, and perhaps the lines are more blurred than anyone'd think. She hasn't said this to Jayden, though he's open-hearted enough to go with it.

'To the thinking room?' he says now.

'To the thinking room.'

Settled at Bill's desk, Ally opens a new page in her notebook. Beside her, Jayden's in the easy chair, one leg hitched over the other. The lamp sends its \warm glow.

'So, what did Nicky have to say?'

'The police have spoken to him too, which means Mullins took my tip about Russell's potential good fortune seriously, though Nicky just told them it was probably gambling. They also asked if he had any idea why Russell was at the vineyard. Nicky said the same thing. No idea.'

'What happened when you broached our blackmail theory?'

'Nicky thought I meant someone was blackmailing *Russell*. That's where his mind instinctively went, despite all of Russell's money talk.'

'Unless he's covering for him.'

'True, but I don't get the feeling he is. By the way, that monthly payment from his bank account? It's to his dad.'

'To Shaun?'

'Nicky said when Russell stressed about money, part of that was because his dad is in an even worse position. Work's hard to find round here, especially off-season. So ever since Shaun lost his job, Russell's been sending him money every month.'

Ally looks down at the page in her notebook. A son supporting his father through thick and thin. Could someone like that also be capable of blackmail?

'I know what you're thinking,' says Jayden. 'Everything we're hearing is that Russell was a decent guy. So I asked Nicky if, theoretically speaking, he thought Russell could ever go in for blackmail. And he thought about it, then said . . . here wait. . . I wrote it all down.' Jayden reads from his notebook: '"Russell was a risk-taker. And he was always glass half full. No matter how many times he got knocked down, he'd get back up again. If he thought he had a surefire way to get some money, and it wasn't going to hurt anyone? Then yeah, maybe he would go for it. I'm not saying he did, but maybe he was capable of it. More capable than other people, anyway."' Jayden claps the notebook shut. 'Nicky's words.'

Ally quietly nods. 'Perhaps blackmail isn't all that different from gambling. It's risky. And it's opportunistic.'

'Exactly. If Russell saw an opportunity to get some money from the Harpers – not hurting anyone as far as he's concerned, because it's not even their money at this point, it's part of a huge investment – then maybe he would go for it.'

'He'd be prepared to gamble . . . even if other people would think it immoral. And illegal.'

And Ally thinks of Shaun again, who's so sure his son wasn't a thief.

'Yeah, and as to the immoral bit, Russell reckoned the Harper family's morals are all over the place, so that's not a factor, is it? At best they sacked his dad, at worst Frank killed someone.'

'And they're still covering it up, Jayden.'

They sit for a moment, looking at the four names of the Harpers up on the board: Ruth, Owen, Edwin, Karensa. Who knows and who doesn't?

'Okay,' says Jayden eventually, 'I think we can draw a line under Nicky. What he's told us basically supports our theory about Russell. So . . . ready for that rabbit hole to Barcelona?'

'Okay, Barcelona. How do we get there?'

'By good old-fashioned legwork, Al. Well, internet old-fashioned, anyway. Googling any possible combination of "1995, missing man, Eric, Barcelona, Cornwall".'

Bent over their laptops, they hardly notice as, outside, the sky sinks towards darkness. Ally takes off her glasses and rubs her eyes. The sound of the sea presses closer, The Shell House an outpost, wind cracking over the dunes.

Jayden looks up. 'Got anything?'

She shakes her head. 'Nothing relevant, anyway.'

An obituary for a recently passed elderly man in Penzance. An *Antiques Roadshow* reference. A smattering of articles about the same footballing Eric that Bernard talked about.

'Me neither. Let's try different spellings. Like Erik with a *k*.'

'Okay.'

Still nothing.

'What about if we tried in Spanish?' says Ally suddenly.

'Al, *yes*.' Jayden's fingers move fast across the page. 'Translate it. *Persona desaparecida*. Okay, now we're talking.'

Ally gets up and goes to sit beside Jayden. He shifts his screen so she can see it too, entry after entry in a language they can't understand. He hits 'Translate' on the page, and it turns to English.

'Oh,' says Ally, 'there are so many.'

And she feels a pang of sadness, thinking of these lost souls.

'Looks like Erik is a short form of Enrique,' says Jayden, eyes moving over the screen. 'So we need to try Enrique too. Hold on. Bernard said the guy came from Barcelona, but he went travelling in the UK, and the postcard from Devon was the last they heard from him. So he'd have been reported missing to the British police, not the Spanish. He might not even be on a Spanish listing. Let's try again in English.' He taps in *missing person, Enrique, Devon and Cornwall, 1995*.

As Jayden hits the third entry in the search results, a man's face fills the screen.

'Enrique Delgado,' says Jayden.

'Last seen in Torquay, in August 1994.'

'In 1994?' says Jayden. 'That's a year earlier than Bernard said.'

'Perhaps he got the year wrong.'

'No, he wouldn't have. The reason it stood out to Bernard is it's the day he proposed to Old Fran. Even if he got confused, she'd have corrected him.'

'So the man was searching for his brother the year after he went missing?'

'It makes sense,' says Jayden. 'At first you think the police are going to solve it. Then time goes on, you realise there's a limit to resources, manpower, public interest. So, you take matters into your own hands.'

'You walk the streets of Mousehole handing out flyers, even if you've no evidence that your brother even crossed the Tamar,' says Ally.

They both sit quietly for a moment, looking at the face of Enrique Delgado.

Young; just twenty-two. Short dark hair and wide brown eyes. Good-looking, by anybody's estimation.

'I'm going to call my mate Fatima,' says Jayden. 'See if she's up for checking the file. I want to know if the police traced Enrique Delgado beyond Torquay. And if they had anything else on him.'

As Jayden goes out to make the call, Ally opens a new web page. Since beginning the detective work, she's spent more time on the internet than in her whole life before that. Sometimes it doesn't feel so different to wandering the shore, eyes peeled, feeling the thrum of possibility. Lifting a drape of weed or a length of driftwood, just in case there's treasure beneath, like the delicate mouth of a cowrie; the pearlescent mosaic of a top shell. Or a detail that changes the course of an entire investigation.

She copies and pastes the name *Enrique Delgado*, this time with *persona desaparecida* and *1994*, and a list of search results fills the screen. There's the same statistics of appearance and timing, but then halfway down the page, something catches her eye. She clicks on it and sees the headline.

> ¿Has visto a mi hermano? Enrique Delgado, conocido como Eric, está desaparecido desde agosto de 1994.

She hits translate: *Have you seen my brother? Enrique Delgado, known as Eric, has been missing since August 1994.*

Ally scans through the pages of the website. It's altogether different from the others they've seen. Rather than a listing on a police agency or charity site, it's a direct appeal from Enrique's brother, Max Delgado. There are numerous pictures of Enrique, and a full biography describing his studies, hobbies and interests. He was a keen amateur artist; an engineering student at the University of Barcelona. There's a map of his possible travels in the UK that summer in 1994, based on postcards or possible sightings in London, Oxford, Bath and Torquay. *My brother likes to be alone*, Max writes, *travelling with his camera, his sketchbook. He is quiet, intense. He does not start conversations with strangers or join random parties. But how is it possible that no one saw him? That no one remembers him at all?*

The quiet desperation of the brother's words; the use of the present tense. And the footnote saying the website was last updated seven months ago – meaning he's still looking. Ally sits back in her chair, cradling her coffee cup in her hands. Her mind spins.

Is there really a body buried beneath the vineyard? And, of all the missing people, of all the needles in haystacks, could it be

Enrique Delgado? A person just as real as Russell; just as missed and mourned by his loved ones.

Solving this decades-old case suddenly feels every bit as urgent as solving Russell's death. And not just because the two might be connected.

49

'You've got to love Fatima,' says Jayden, as he returns to the thinking room. 'Said she'd been waiting all day for someone to ask her to look up a missing person's file from thirty years ago. And she was so glad that that person turned out to be me.'

He always enjoys his one-time training colleague's line in sarcasm. Jayden knows he's pushing it asking her, and would never want to get her into trouble, but it's a cold case. Cold case rules are different, right? Fatima pulled the file while she was ribbing him about life in the country, or, to use her phrase, *the arse end of nowhere.* And as she demanded to know why Jayden wasn't hanging ten on his surfboard yet, the facts of the Enrique Delgado case were loading on to her screen.

It didn't take long, because the information was light.

Enrique Delgado's passport was stamped at Dover in August 1994. There was evidence that he used his bank card in London to change money. There were possible sightings in Oxford and Torquay. And then nothing.

'The last reported sighting ties in with the postcard Enrique's brother received,' says Jayden. 'He was seen on Torquay pier, late at night. It's not a hundred per cent reliable; apparently the witness had been out drinking, and honestly, you glimpse a tall, dark-haired guy in passing, lots of people could match that basic description, right? Anyway, the working theory at the time was that he likely ended up in the water and drowned.'

'But a body was never found,' says Ally.

'A body was never found.'

'Which is why his brother is still campaigning to find him,' says Ally. 'Look.'

And she turns the computer screen to show him Max Delgado's website. Jayden nods as he takes it all in.

'Nice find, Al. But . . . the trail still ends in Torquay. There weren't any sightings of Enrique Delgado in Cornwall.'

'It doesn't mean he wasn't here. Remember in his postcard he wrote "next stop Cornwall". How many of us really pay attention to the people we pass in the street? Look, his brother says that he was quiet, kept himself to himself.'

'I know, but he would have stayed somewhere. A youth hostel or a campsite or hotel or whatever. Even if it's informal, and you're paying in cash, there's a check-in process.'

'He could have been wild camping.'

Jayden nods. 'True. But. . . here's the thing, Al. His brother was asking around in Mousehole, and that's why this has come to our attention, right? But beyond that one line in the postcard, there's nothing to say he came to Cornwall. And there's less than nothing to say that he had a link to Frank Harper.'

Talking to Fatima always serves as a reminder of the cold, hard facts.

Why this guy, Jay? You got something on him? Because you clear this case, there's plenty more where he came from.

Basically, a kinder version of Cliff's wild-goose-chase comments.

Ally sighs. 'But Jayden, look.'

She clicks through the website, pulling up a page that shows Enrique's intricate pencil drawings, displayed by a brother wanting to show that Enrique was more than a statistic; more than dark-haired, six foot two inches, last known sighting Torquay.

'I know we've little to go on, but we've got to tell the police about Frank Harper. If somebody's buried at Shoreline Vines, there's a family out there who needs answers.'

'I hear you, Al. I just can't see them bringing the diggers in. Even if we tie it to the blackmail theory and Russell's death.'

'But it's their job to investigate.'

And Jayden knows it should work like that. But even in Porthpella the police have their hands full; resources are stretched. And, really, is this any more than hearsay?

'Enrique Delgado was a good artist, you know,' says Ally. 'There's something very real about these pictures. Look how he captured people.'

Ally slowly scrolls through.

'Hold on,' says Jayden. 'Stop at that one.'

'This one?'

Jayden leans closer to the screen.

'Do you know who that reminds me of?' he says. 'Celine.'

But Ally only met her for a couple of minutes. Jayden spent most of an evening in her company.

'There's another of the same person, I think.' Ally scrolls down to a pencil drawing; a young woman sitting at a café table in a summer dress. A cigarette in one hand, a coffee in the other. 'See, that's her again, isn't it?'

'Okay, that one *really* looks like Celine,' says Jayden.

And he feels that thing, that indefinable *flicker* of something. Possibility?

'Al, Enrique was in the UK in 1994. That's the same summer as Celine.'

And Jayden knows how ridiculous it sounds, because how many other people were also in the UK that same summer? Erm, around sixty million – plus tourists.

'Forget it. I'm just seeing things I want to see.'

'No, wait,' says Ally. 'Trust your instincts. I looked earlier and there's plenty about Celine Chevalier online. Maybe there'll be a picture of her when she was younger.'

Jayden starts tapping at his laptop. But for all the entries about Celine's business ventures, the photographs of her smiling at this opening or at that dinner, there's nothing nostalgic. Even when they find an interview in a business magazine, and she briefly talks about growing up in Aix-en-Provence, there are no pictures from that time.

'I suspect that Celine hasn't changed very much,' says Ally. 'And you're right, she's distinctive.'

They compare two pictures side by side: Enrique's line drawing, and a close-up of Celine at a business awards dinner that's dated ten years ago.

'My God. The shape of the eyes, the smile. Jayden, I can see it.'

'The cheekbones,' says Jayden, excitement jumping in his voice. 'It's her. Isn't it?'

They click back to the website, but after the café picture, Enrique's drawings are of buildings, a bridge, a vase of flowers. *My brother studied engineering*, Max Delgado writes, *but as you can see, he is also a talented artist.*

Jayden taps *Celine Chevalier* and *Enrique Delgado* into Google but nothing comes up.

'She wouldn't have been called Chevalier back then,' says Ally. 'I read that she's been married twice.'

'But if Enrique was a friend, or a boyfriend, Celine might have been involved in the campaign to find him more recently. I don't know when she became Chevalier.'

Jayden gets to his feet, starts pacing.

'Alright, this is crazy, but let's go with it. If Enrique and Celine knew one another, that not only potentially puts him in Cornwall, but it puts him at Shoreline Vines. Or Shoreline Farm, as it was then. So, we've got to establish a link between the two of them. Something that's more concrete than these drawings.'

'And presumably we can't go and see Celine and ask her if she ever knew a Spanish man called Erik?'

'I reckon not.'

But Jayden holds it in mind for a moment. While the drawing at the café is intimately observed, Enrique could simply have been a people watcher, and Celine just a passing stranger. But that would be even more of a coincidence – and Jayden isn't into coincidences.

A thought lands. A total starburst.

'Al! Celine was in Spain before she came to the Harpers.'

Ally's hand goes to her mouth. 'Jayden, was she really?'

'Yes! Ruth said it last night. She made some quip about hoping Celine would teach her kids Spanish as well as French, but it came to nothing.' Jayden holds up his fingers. 'Jeez. Okay, that's three links. This drawing that looks a hell of a lot like Celine. Thirty years ago, they were both in the UK. And Celine had recently spent time in Spain. The second two are non-debatable.'

'But it only works if the first is non-debatable too,' says Ally. Then, 'And, Jayden, think of the timing – Russell blackmailing the Harpers just as Celine is about to visit. Could he have stumbled on the connection somehow?'

'That would be . . . wild.' Jayden takes a deep breath. 'Okay, look. We can't take this to Skinner as it is. We need to *directly* link Celine Chevalier to Enrique Delgado.' He glances at his watch. 'Al, I'm going to call Cat. Let her know we're on to something here. Alright for us to push on through?'

'Absolutely. I'll get the coffee on.' She gets to her feet. 'We need Celine's maiden name, don't we?'

'Yeah, we do. And the frustrating thing is, Ruth would know it.'

'From when Celine was their au pair. Of course. Could we somehow coax the info out of Ruth?'

'I don't want to give the Harpers any reason to think we're on to this.'

'Agreed . . . Hold on, I'm sure Celine mentions a brother in an article I read. Not by name, just in passing. That's a way in, isn't it?'

Because he wouldn't have changed his name.

'It's a way in,' says Jayden. 'Al, find that brother.'

50

Saffron didn't plan to end up at The Wreckers, but when she closed Hang Ten, after the world's slowest afternoon, she didn't especially want to go home. And then Mullins messaged her – *Mullins!* – saying he was stopping in for a pint and did she want to join him.

Mullins has never asked her for a drink. Back in their school days, Saffron probably would have run a mile if he did; he was your basic lunk at the back of the class, lobbing spit balls and sniggering at anyone who wanted to listen to what the teacher had to say.

The guy's come a long way, it's got to be said. He's almost a friend. A mate, for sure. So why not have a drink? All she's got waiting for her at home is Broady, and right now that's more complicated than she wants.

Mullins? Not complicated.

Broady phoned Saffron earlier – just after Wilson hung up on her – asking if she'd had a rethink about Hawaii, because surely it was only a heat-of-the-moment thing, her saying she couldn't go. And because he was the second man in a row to tell her what she was thinking – the second man she cared too much about, as well – Saffron was probably a bit harsh in her response.

Is this about us? Broady said to her, his voice unusually quiet.

No, it's not about us. It's about showing up for Wilson.

Even though Wilson didn't want her to.

You don't owe him anything, babe. You know that, right?

Funny. He said the same thing.

But Broady didn't get it. Of course she wants to spend the winter surfing in Hawaii. She's hardly going out of her way to choose wintry Porthpella, a dead café and an ill dad over big waves, sunshine and the company of her boyfriend, is she?

'Mate,' says Mullins, sliding into the booth opposite her. 'You look like I feel. Or is it the other way round? Anyway. Beer?'

He's wearing a rugby shirt. The tang of his aftershave makes her want to sneeze. The tip of his nose is faintly red.

'Beer.' She nods. 'Cheers.'

Mullins does a quick drumbeat on the table, then gets up again and heads to the bar. He pulls a hanky from his pocket as he goes, blowing noisily.

Saffron settles back and closes her eyes. She lets the low burble of The Wreckers wash over her. This time of year, it's quiet, and she knows almost all the faces. A handful of old-timers; those two artist guys who live down the coast; a woman who came into Hang Ten earlier with her grown-up kids. Tucked in her booth, facing away from the rest of the pub, Saffron doesn't need to turn on a smile for anyone.

'So, before you ask,' says Mullins, putting down a pint in front of her, 'we're making headway on the case.'

'Nice.'

He drops into the seat opposite, lowers his voice conspiratorially.

'In fact, I think we'll be making an arrest tomorrow.'

'Have you told Ally and Jayden?'

'I've given them too much already,' he says with a wink. 'Got to keep some surprises up my sleeve.'

'Okay.'

'Mate, you really are off-colour. Aren't you supposed to be lecturing me about working together? The greater good or something?' His face suddenly changes. 'Have you and Broady broken up?'

260

'Why would you say that?'

'I don't know, wishful thinking. *Joke!*'

Saffron looks down at her pint before she realises Mullins isn't filling the silence. She flicks a glance at him. *God*, she thinks. *He's serious.*

'It's Wilson,' she says, feeling a sudden urge to move the conversation away from relationships. 'He's having more tests, but it looks like cancer.'

Mullins's pint is halfway to his lips, and he stops; lowers it.

'Oh, it's not, is it?'

She nods, and her eyes straight away fill.

'Saff, I'm sorry.'

'It's stupid, because . . . I mean, I know he's my dad, biologically speaking, but it's not like we've spent a load of time together.'

'Doesn't matter though, does it?'

'No,' she says quietly. 'It doesn't.'

Mullins takes the top off his beer. 'Bloody cancer,' he says, with just the right amount of anger. 'It can do one, can't it? It can bloody do one.'

Saffron smiles; gestures to his lip. 'Erm, froth moustache,' she says. 'Kind of takes from the tough talk.'

Mullins dips to his pint again and this time sticks his nose in it. Grins like an idiot.

'Better?'

She laughs. 'Yeah. For sure.'

Mullins wipes his face on his sleeve.

'It's not definite, but it's looking like prostate. I know that's . . . I don't know, one of the better ones, that's what they say, isn't it? But . . .'

My mum.

'I know. You've been here before.'

Saffron blinks. Just occasionally, Mullins surprises her.

'So anyway, I think I'm probably going to stick around. You know we were heading to Hawaii for winter? But I think I want to stay. I'm going to stay. I've told Wilson I'm staying.'

'That's really nice of you, Saff. I bet he was made up.'

She doesn't say anything, just gives a small smile.

'I'd do the same,' he says, splitting open a bag of Scampi Fries, pushing it across the table. 'You want to be here, don't you? This sort of thing. If you can.'

'That's what I think.'

'And I bet your fella doesn't care about ditching the trip, does he? It's not like you can't go surfing here in winter.'

'Oh, Broady's still going to Hawaii.'

She sees the way Mullins's face changes. Then how he quickly hides behind his pint, says, 'Oh, course. Sure.'

'I'd never ask him to stay.'

'Course not.'

But Saffron can read Mullins like a book, and the look on his face says she shouldn't have to ask.

51

Celine sits on the floor of Castaway, surrounded by the limited book collection of Frank Harper. What she's looking for isn't here.

Most of Frank's books are paperbacks, spines cracked and pages yellowed with age. There's poetry, and that sits with the Frank she knew – A. E. Housman, John Clare, Dylan Thomas; male voices, writing of the countryside. There's W. G. Grace's *Classic Guide to Cricket*. Several books on winemaking. *A Year in Provence* by Peter Mayle.

This last volume gives her pause. Did Frank's mind turn to Provence after she left? Or did this interest in southern France predate Celine's arrival at the farm? Somehow, she doubts it. She knows very well the effect that she had on Frank Harper.

Among Frank's books there are two notebooks: one that's never been written in, the other with notes from a winemaking conference in 2002. She flicks through it, desperate really. As if looking for a clue that she'll never find.

It's not here.

She stands and goes to the window, trying to process what this might mean.

Frank would one hundred per cent have kept it. Why? Because he categorically told her that he would. And, in the whirlwind of emotions at the time, how Celine felt about him keeping this piece of her was the least of it.

She looks out beyond the terrace and the lights of St Ives shimmer back at her. A fishing boat is making its way out of the harbour towards the dark open water. Its lamps are burning, and it looks so vulnerable as it lifts and drops over the waves. She thinks of the men inside, men like Frank, earning their living from the land and the sea, subject to the grace of the elements. Tough men, because you can't be anything but.

Celine would have liked to have seen Frank tend the vines. To say to him, *You did it then?* That slow smile, and the shrug: Cornish, not Gallic. *Yeah, I did it.*

She steps out on to the terrace, and immediately feels the buffet of the wind. *Just you try and knock me down.* All around her are signs of life, although far fewer than in the high season, probably. She thinks of the families behind those lit-up windows; the children sleeping in their beds; the couples closely entwined. The transactions of their days a far cry from those of Celine's neighbours in Chelsea, but the essential things – the living and the dying – are perhaps not so very different.

The French and the English have the same expression – to be born with a *une cuillère en argent dans la bouche*, a silver spoon in your mouth. But that's not Celine. She's worked hard for everything she has – and yes, she includes the marriages in that – fuelled by a desire for forward motion above all else. *Je ne regrette rien*: if Celine has a motto, an anthem, it's that.

She leaves the vista and goes back inside, to the emptied boxes and scattered possessions of a man she knew thirty years ago.

Celine doesn't resent Frank; he was her saviour, after all. But perhaps all these years he's been her incarcerator too. She didn't realise it at the time, because at nineteen she was laughably naive.

Pouring out heart and soul to the pages of her diary, night after night.

Not a book, like she told Owen, but a notebook.

She remembers writing that first diary entry, the day she arrived at Shoreline Farm: *Le père des enfants, Frank Harper, est charmant. Je ne m'attendais pas à ça.* Because she didn't expect the children's father – a man twice her age, a farmer in the back end of nowhere – to be quite so charming, did she?

Now Celine takes out her phone and taps out a message to Owen. Then she changes her mind and phones him instead. When he doesn't answer, she leaves a courteous but emphatic message on his answer machine.

'Owen, if it isn't too much trouble, I shall come to the farm tomorrow morning to look in the attic for myself. I suspect the book I'm looking for is among the miscellaneous items you mentioned. As you know, I wish to be respectful to your mother, so you should arrange for the house to be empty. Perhaps take your family for a celebratory breakfast, along the coast, to raise a Bloody Mary to our partnership? I hear the Sandcastle Hotel is good. I shan't need more than half an hour. I'll come to the farm at nine o'clock. If you leave the key by the door, I'll let myself in. You'll never know I've been, but I will be grateful to you, Owen. Just as I know your family is grateful to me.'

She's stretched out on the sofa, having poured herself a second glass of Veuve Clicquot, when Owen messages her. She holds the bubbles in her mouth for a moment, hesitating before opening his reply. But no one refuses Celine Chevalier – including Owen Harper.

If her teenage diary is at Shoreline Vines, she'll find it. Then she'll destroy it, as she should have done thirty years ago.

52

'Celine Auclair!'

It's a cry of triumph from Ally, and Jayden whoops in response. He's immediately at her side.

'You sure, Al?'

'I'm sure. Look. Bruno Auclair, that's Celine's brother.'

Five years ago, Bruno Auclair was competing in a triathlon, fundraising for a children's charity. In the list of supporters, Celine Chevalier has donated five hundred euros and left a comment wishing him well: *Allez, mon frère!*

Those three little words are all they need.

They zoom in on the picture of Bruno Auclair.

'Same eyes, Al, same cheekbones.'

'And it's the right region. The triathlon's on the Côte d'Azur. That's Provence.'

Jayden cracks his knuckles, rubs his hands together. 'Alright then. Celine Auclair. Let's do this. Ah . . .'

Ally watches as Jayden clicks through page after page of Celine Auclair search results. A jeweller in Lyon. A visual artist in Lausanne. Students, lawyers, musicians, teachers.

'So it's a common name, apparently,' he says.

'Try Celine Auclair, Barcelona.'

This time they get an attendee at a medical conference in 2023. A jazz musician's concert at a venue called La Cueva. Jayden adds *1994* to the search terms. They both lean close to the screen and hit the 'Translate' button again.

'Try that one.'

'It's a newsletter from a university sports club,' says Jayden. 'Football, tennis, volleyball, swimming. It goes on and on. Match results. Fixtures.'

'Team lists,' says Ally.

'Team lists, Al,' says Jayden. 'Let's go through them. There's got to be a hit in there somewhere. And . . . boom, there it is. Celine Auclair played tennis for the University of Barcelona.'

'Jayden, we've got it!'

'"Exchange student Celine Auclair's convincing two-set victory over Lucia Fernandez of Girona University, 6–3, 6–2." What would we do without this translation tool?'

'Go through a dictionary in a painstaking but rather satisfying way.'

'We'd have to buy one first.'

'Evie did Spanish GCSE. I bet I have her copy in the attic somewhere.'

'Okay, so we get the book down from the attic, and after several hours we get to a pretty sketchy translation. Hang on, think of all the online trawling we've done to get to this point. It'd be hours and hours and *hours*.'

'Or we'd consult a Spanish speaker. Find an expert.'

'Know any Spanish speakers in Porthpella, Al?'

'I think Wenna and Gerren went on holiday to Lanzarote a few years ago,' Ally smiles.

'Yeah, okay, so we have options. But . . . seeing as we live in the twenty-first century, how's about we settle for Google?'

Ally sits back in her chair. 'Jayden, have we really just found a link between Celine Chevalier and Enrique Delgado?'

'No. We've found a link between Celine Chevalier and Barcelona.'

'Surely that's enough?'

She watches as Jayden taps in *Celine Arnaud Enrique Delgado Barcelona*.

Nothing comes up.

'Yeah, that was just for kicks. Al, it's enough. We can put Celine Chevalier in Barcelona at the same time as Enrique Delgado. That *cannot* be random. If Enrique was last seen in Torquay, but had plans to visit Cornwall, he must have been coming to see Celine, right? Maybe they were friends, maybe they were even girlfriend and boyfriend. But it can't have been a coincidence.' Jayden's eyes are bright. 'Because that would be crazy.'

And Ally agrees that it would, indeed, be crazy.

'So, now we've got enough to take to the police,' she says. 'More than enough, surely.'

Jayden looks at his watch. 'It's coming up on eleven on a Sunday night. I don't think Skinner would appreciate the call, do you?'

'Perhaps not. But what if Celine has left the vineyard?'

'I'm sure she's left. To be honest, I'm kind of surprised she stayed on the next day. But she's easily trackable.'

Ally turns from the computer screen and slowly takes off her reading glasses. Outside, the wind's getting up. She can hear it tearing through the marram grass, pushing at the walls of The Shell House. By morning the dunes will have shifted; a drift of sand heaped outside her door like a snowbank, every window ledge coated too. Tomorrow, the high winds are forecast to turn to gales.

'Why do you think Celine is here, Jayden?' she asks quietly.

'Yeah, I'm wondering the same. If she was friends with Enrique, or she was his girlfriend, maybe she's here because she's looking for him too.'

Could it be that thirty years ago Enrique came to Cornwall and never got to see Celine? That something happened to him here, and he ended up buried on the farm: a hit-and-run on the coast road, one dark night? An accident with some farm machinery? And Frank Harper, frightened of the consequences, kept it hidden.

In a night of speculation, this seems no more far-fetched.

In all that Ally's read of Celine Chevalier, she's a private person. In the press, she talks business, not her personal life. If she had a friend or a boyfriend who went missing, perhaps it's not surprising that she hasn't talked about this loss publicly.

Ally voices this to Jayden, and he nods. 'I agree. But as a person of influence, you'd think she'd want to use her platform to find him if they were close.'

'But it was thirty years ago. She must presume he's dead.' A thought lands. 'With the investment, who approached who first?'

Jayden raises his eyebrows. 'Interesting question. Go on . . .'

'Well, what if Celine approached the Harpers? What if, after all these years, she's put something together, and thinks Enrique made it as far as Porthpella? She might be pretending to want to invest, just to gain access to the vineyard.'

Jayden grins. '*Ally Bright*. So, you're saying they're laying out the red carpet for Celine, but all this time she's doing some sleuthing of her own?'

'How was she at the dinner?'

'She's the first millionaire investor I've met,' laughs Jayden with a shrug. 'Aren't they all a bit shifty?'

'When we saw her walking in the vines, what do you think she was doing?'

'Stretching her legs,' says Jayden. 'Giving the Harpers space to answer questions with the police. Or . . . yeah, maybe scoping things out. But Al, Celine must have infinite resources. If she really thought that there was a connection between Enrique and the Harpers, she'd be paying top dollar for a private eye. Or she'd be going straight to the police.'

'Maybe she's someone who likes to get things done for herself. That's how she comes across in these articles. Incredibly self-motivated, self-reliant.'

'The ultimate go-getter, huh? And now she's after Shoreline Vines. Al, I really want to talk to her, but . . . it's got to be Skinner first. We'll go and see him tomorrow. If he hears us out, there's no way he can't see that we're on to something.' Jayden gets his phone out. 'I'll message Mullins now though, let him know. Might as well get him onside early.'

'Jayden, if Russell was blackmailing the Harpers about a body buried at the vineyard, and Celine is only here because of Enrique, then Russell's death was utterly pointless, wasn't it?'

'Yeah. His blackmail would have had no value whatsoever. But Russell didn't know that. And neither did the Harpers.'

Ally thinks of Shaun alone in his dark cottage, sunk beneath the weight of his sorrow. For all the work that she and Jayden have done here, she finds herself hoping, perversely, that none of it turns out to be true. That Frank spun Shaun a tall tale, and Russell died in a tragic accident with cattle.

Jayden interrupts her thoughts. 'Al, if Russell was killed by one of the Harpers to keep him quiet, then that shows the lengths that someone up there will go to. Because it's never been just about losing the investment; it's about protecting so much more.'

'A thirty-year-old crime. Which means if we're right about Celine's Enrique suspicions . . .'

'. . . then she could be in danger too.'

53

Owen loiters in the hallway, checking his watch. When he floated the idea of a celebratory breakfast at the Sandcastle Hotel, he felt Edwin's scrutiny. Fair play, because since when does Owen suggest family outings? *My treat*, he said, at which Edwin clapped him between the shoulder blades – harder than necessary.

'We've a lot to celebrate after what this family's come through,' says Ruth. She clacks over the flagstones in her heels, pearls swinging at her neck. 'All that we've achieved, too. And you boys know how I love a good breakfast. Best meal of the day.'

One Mother's Day, when they were small boys, Owen and Edwin made a fry-up for their mum. They rose early, using the stove for the first time on their own. Owen stood over the eggs while Edwin spurted ketchup in an approximation of a heart shape. Just as everything was ready, Owen had the idea to add some primroses to the breakfast tray and bolted outside to pick a handful. When he came back, the kitchen was empty. Edwin had taken the tray up without him. He galloped upstairs but he was too late. There was Edwin, tucked in bed beside their mum, chewing on a bit of toast and grinning with such nasty triumph that Owen wanted nothing more than to lay into him with his fists. *Look what Edwin made me!* Ruth trilled, as behind his back, Owen folded his fingers around his pathetic little bouquet, crushing the tender stems to death.

'Right on, Mother,' he says now. 'Best meal of the day.'

'Karensa's not feeling great,' says Edwin, shrugging on his jacket. 'I doubt you'll lure her out.'

'No, she's coming,' says Owen. 'I just spoke to her.'

Edwin narrows his eyes. 'You appear to have better luck with my wife than I do.'

Karensa might be coming, but she's in a strange mood. Yesterday she said she wanted the truth out, but today she's gone in on herself; fixed as a whelk. Just now, she could hardly bring herself to look at Owen. And when he briefly squeezed her shoulder, she flinched. Karensa has never, ever shrunk from his touch. But he couldn't delay things by talking to her; Celine Chevalier has them on the clock.

Owen's head spins with all the things he's balancing. The extra beers last night, on his own in the silver bullet, didn't help.

'Kedgeree cures all ills,' says Ruth in a singsong voice.

Owen glances through the pane, out across the windswept yard. While there's no danger of Celine rolling up ahead of time, he wants to hold up his end of the bargain, which is to clear the house by nine o'clock. It wasn't a threat, the way Celine framed the request, but the subtext wasn't far off. Whatever this book is, it has a lot of meaning for Celine. Owen doesn't want to think about what that meaning is, but then who's he to talk?

He hears Karensa's footfall on the stairs and looks up. She's heartbreakingly beautiful in a red jumper, her dark hair tied with a white ribbon. He's never said, *I'd do anything for you, Karensa*, but he's thought it often enough. What good's thought without action though? Owen has a horrible suspicion that he might be a coward. He wills her to look at him, to smile, but she doesn't. Her face is a white wall.

'You do look rather peaky, dear,' says Ruth. 'But don't worry, you'll perk up.'

'I'm glad Owen persuaded you,' says Edwin, throwing an arm around his wife and kissing her on the cheek.

'Personally, I'm interested to see what the fuss is all about with the Sandcastle. I should think it's a case of style over substance,' says Ruth with a smile. Her negativity has levity today.

'I think it looks wonderful,' says Karensa, stiffly.

A thought suddenly comes into Owen's head: what if Karensa thinks he's called this breakfast to announce their relationship to his family? Surely, she must know that's the last way he'd do it. And never without discussing it with her. He didn't want to tell Karensa about Celine's request, because it comes with the suspicion of his dad's affair. And Owen can't make it look endemic – the wandering eyes of Harper men.

'Won't be a patch on what we're going to do with Shoreline,' says Edwin.

His brother pushes past him and out the door, just as a police car pulls into the yard. Owen sees Edwin stop dead.

'Oh, for the love of God,' says Ruth.

'They can't be back,' whispers Karensa.

'Yeah, this isn't going to work,' says Owen, and he hustles out the door, goes striding towards the car.

The officers are slow to emerge, and Owen can't work out if that's deliberate, or they're just running on basic procedural, nothing-to-see-here energy. Behind him he hears Ruth mutter, 'It's Tweedledum and Tweedledee again.'

'Morning,' says Skinner. 'You all off out?'

'As it happens, we are,' says Ruth. 'What do you want?'

'A word with Edwin here,' says Skinner. He's unsmiling. 'I say "here", what I mean is down the station. Edwin Harper, I'm arresting you on suspicion of grievous bodily harm.'

273

'GBH?' Edwin blinks. 'What?'

And it's Ruth that Edwin looks to – always the mummy's boy.

'That's ridiculous. Just who is my son supposed to have grievously harmed?'

'Russell Tremaine,' says Mullins.

'Russell Tremaine!'

And the way she pronounces it, with such distaste, makes Owen glad of the small mercy that Shaun isn't here to see this.

'I'm sorry, but we don't understand,' he says, stepping up. 'Edwin had nothing to do with Russell. He was found here, that's all.' He looks to Karensa, then quickly back to the officers. 'On what grounds are you arresting him?'

'We're not obliged to say,' says Skinner.

'And you're not obliged to say anything either, Edwin,' says Ruth, grabbing hold of his hand. 'Don't utter a word without a lawyer. Not one word.'

'Mum . . .' Edwin starts.

Ruth squeezes his hand. 'Darling,' she says. Their own brand of call and response – one Owen's never had a part in.

'Russell Tremaine was trampled by bullocks,' Owen says, turning back to the cops. 'Clear as day. The bloke was covered in hoof marks.'

'Yes, he was,' says Skinner. And then he holds up the cuffs. 'I repeat, Edwin Harper, we're arresting you on suspicion of grievous bodily harm. You don't have to say anything . . .'

'Oh, for goodness' sake,' cries Ruth, her voice shrill as a chainsaw. 'This is preposterous. What possible reason could my son have for hurting that man?'

As PC Mullins takes Edwin's arm, Owen's aware of a movement at the gates. Does he catch a flash of a red coat? He checks his watch. It's five past nine. He looks back to his brother, his mother.

And his lover, standing there with her hair flying, her hands covering her mouth. Frozen as an ice sculpture.

It strikes him then – a feeling as unarguable as a gust of wind slapping the side of his face.

Karensa knows something.

'You're just going to stand there and do nothing while your brother's arrested?' cries Ruth.

She suddenly looks very small, and very old. Owen's never thought of his mum as vulnerable before; not even when their dad died.

'What are we supposed to do?' says Owen, as Edwin disappears inside the police car.

'Sit tight,' says Skinner. 'I'm told "don't leave town" is a cliché, but I still find a use for it every now and again. And it goes for all of you.'

The slam of doors. The rumble of the engine. Then they're gone.

The yard is silent for three beats, four, then sound pushes back in. The whistle of the wind. The flap of the tarpaulin. Somewhere, a stray barn door squeaking on its hinges. Owen looks to Karensa and his stomach lurches. She's frozen to the spot; her hands still covering her mouth.

'Karensa. . .' he begins.

'Never mind her,' snaps Ruth. 'Owen, I need to talk to you in private.'

'There's nothing Karensa can't hear.'

'Owen, please,' says Ruth. 'I need you.'

And the genuine appeal in his mum's voice cuts him to the quick. When, in Owen's whole life, has she ever said that to him?

'I'll be in your godawful little caravan,' says Ruth, striking out across the yard. Her coat fills with wind, and for a moment she looks like a ship, her sail billowing behind her as she's propelled in the wrong direction.

Owen turns back to Karensa – he wants to say something, anything – but she's vanished.

54

Mullins is waiting for the kettle to boil. He's making Edwin Harper a cup of tea, and he's got no intention of it being a good one either. He'll briefly show the hot water the teabag, slosh in the milk, and that's your lot. Now, who says Mullins doesn't dispense justice?

His phone buzzes in his pocket.

'Jayden?'

'Mullins. Did you get my messages?'

Mullins can hear Jayden's impatience, and he puts on his high and mighty voice in response. It's one of his favourites, and he doesn't get to use it half as often as he'd like.

'Yes, Jayden, I did get your messages. But at midnight I was getting my beauty sleep. And this morning we were a little bit busy making an arrest.'

He suddenly has an image of Jayden from back in the summer, kneeling beside a dying man, his hands clasped over his chest. While he, Mullins, just stared in horror. Jayden's never once said a thing about that; never made himself out to be the big man, when anyone can see that he is.

It's why Mullins told Jayden about the boot prints on Russell's body.

'Is it to do with Russell?'

'Yes, it's to do with Russell. And if you're after Skinner, he's going to be busy with the suspect all morning, I'd say.'

'Mullins, who have you brought in?'

'Edwin Harper. We got a DNA hit. Look, I can't talk now. I'm supposed to be in there.'

Delivering this cup of crappy tea while Skinner does the interview.

'But, Jayden, if you and Ally have got an angle on this, I reckon Skinner would be open to hearing it. You've just got to pick the right moment, mate. And this morning ain't it.'

'What's the charge?'

'GBH.'

'Not murder?'

'Newsflash, you can't charge animals.'

Because what the pathologist couldn't tell them was whether the fatal blow was delivered by man or beast. Not that Edwin Harper knows that.

'Ally and I are going to come down to the station.'

'Don't do that,' says Mullins. 'It's a waste of your time.'

'I'll say I want to make a statement.'

'Jayden, listen. If you and Ally want to do something useful, go and check on Shaun Tremaine. He saw us carting Edwin off.' Mullin rubs his nose. 'I get the feeling there's not much holding that bloke together. Reckon he could do with a shoulder. Or at least be kept out of trouble.'

Because the last thing they need is a call to say Tremaine Senior has been mouthing off up at the farmhouse again; swinging punches too.

'We think this is bigger than what happened to Russell,' says Jayden.

'Oh, you do, do you?'

'Mullins, we think there was blackmail involved.'

'Blackmail, huh?'

'We've had some information that there might be a body buried at Shoreline Vines. From thirty years ago. We think Russell might have known this too.'

And it's all Mullins can do not to laugh. How do they cook up this stuff? Just when he's starting to trust the Shell House Detectives – more than that, go out on a limb, risk his own neck by sharing details of confidential cases – they go and take it that bit too far.

'Alright, Jayden, you can stop now. We've got an actual suspect to interview about an actual crime. And like I said, I'm already late.'

'Mullins, wait. Just hear me out. Ally and I went into this wanting the answer to one question: why was Russell Tremaine in that field? We haven't got that answer yet; in fact, it's opened up a whole bunch of other questions.'

'Brilliant. Nice one. Great stuff.'

'But a picture's starting to emerge. It's hazy but . . . we can kind of see it. And we need to share it with you. It's too big not to. That herd of bullocks? They're the least of it.'

Mullins pulls open the door, phone wedged between his ear and his shoulder, Edwin Harper's rubbish mug of tea slopping in his hand.

'Look, soon as I get a minute, I'll tell that to Skinner.'

'I've left a message for him too.'

'Of course you have.'

'And Mullins, we'll go up to see Shaun now. That's a good call. But . . . what Ally and I have affects your interview with Edwin. In fact . . . No, scratch that.'

So even Jayden, Mr Self-Assured, isn't one hundred per cent backing his own horse this time?

'Mullins, what Ally and I have affects *everything*.'

55

'Gus, I can't believe you made these.'

Neither can Gus, because there was certainly a point in the process when he questioned his ability to see it through. He has never rolled, nor folded, so much pastry in his life. And he never considered, for one second, how much butter went into the making of a croissant. It's enough to make your arteries clog just thinking about it – and your mouth water.

Ally dips her head to the tin and inhales.

'My goodness, they're warm.'

'As soon as they were out of the oven I galloped over the dunes. And . . .' He rummages in his bag, produces a jar of jam. 'Lashings of apricot, wasn't that what you said? The finest White Wave Stores could muster.'

Ally squeezes his arm. 'What have I done to deserve this?'

Gus shrugs. *Oh, just existed.* 'I know how hard you're working on this case.'

'Let me get the coffee on. You'll stay, won't you? I can't possibly eat them all.'

'I'd love to.'

It's his first breakfast at Ally's, and he helps lay the table. A blue-and-white-striped butter dish – *oh dear God, not more butter* – two spoons for the jam. Two china plates, delicately scallop-shaped.

'I haven't seen these before,' he says, holding one up.

'I keep them for special.'

She passes him a glass of orange juice, and they chink. Then she brings the cafetière to the table, and Gus carries the mugs. Just as they take their seats across from one another, the sun breaks out from behind the clouds, bathing the whole scene in soft light.

'Well, this is glorious,' says Ally.

'I'd say,' says Gus. And his heart sings.

From somewhere deep in The Shell House, Ally's phone rings. She waves her hand. 'It can go to voicemail.'

But then, ten seconds later, it's trilling again.

'I'm so sorry. I'd better just . . .'

'Of course. I'll put the lid on the tin. Keep them warm.'

While Ally's gone, Gus takes a sip of coffee. He looks to the wide window and watches as dark clouds screech across the bay, blotting out the timid sun. It's as if someone's flicked a switch, and abruptly The Shell House falls into gloom. He looks around for a lamp.

'Oh Gus, I'm so sorry,' says Ally, coming back in. 'That was Jayden. I have to go.'

And that gloom switch is flicked inside of Gus too.

'Edwin Harper's been arrested, and we're worried about Shaun.'

'Of course, of course. Edwin Harper, eh?'

Ally rests a hand on his shoulder. 'Gus, you went to so much trouble. This was just . . . lovely.'

'Oh, it was nothing. They'll keep. In fact, take them with you. For you and Jayden, and Shaun. Shaun might want one. Nothing like a fresh-made croissant when . . . someone's been arrested for your son's . . .'

He stops. He's talking absolute nonsense.

'Gus, you must stay. Finish breakfast. Enjoy the coffee.'

'So, you think you won't be long then?' he says hopefully.

'I honestly don't know.' Ally bites her lip, and the fact she looks so sorry is consoling. 'But please, don't feel you have to rush off. Just . . . pop the key under the pot on your way out.' She smiles, points to her sleeping dog in his basket by the hearth. 'Fox will be glad of the company.'

◆　◆　◆

After she's gone, Gus carries on eating his croissant rather mournfully. Then, slowly, he starts to see the positives. Ally trusts him enough to be here without her. To carry on sitting at her table, as if breakfasting together is an everyday occasion.

Imagine if it was.

Gus looks to Fox in his basket and realises he's not there. He didn't slip out when Ally left, did he?

'Fox?' Gus calls. 'Fox!'

But there's no patter of paws in reply.

Gus suddenly feels an acute sense of responsibility. For all his hopes, and Jayden's achievements, it's Fox who is Ally's most treasured companion. Gus can't lose him on his watch. He stuffs the last of the croissant in his mouth – now it's cooled, it tastes a little greasy, if he's honest – and gets up.

'Fox! I'm not into hide-and-seek, you know.'

Gus wanders down the hall. The door to Ally's bedroom is open. He knows Fox likes to jump on Ally's bed when no one's looking. He peers in. The bed is neatly made, with a cornflower-blue bedspread and white pillows. On her nightstand there's an old-fashioned alarm clock, a lamp, a couple of books, and a pair of reading glasses. And on the other side – Bill's side – just a lamp.

Gus steps inside the room. *That's alright, isn't it?* He bends down and looks beneath the bed, just in case Fox has nipped under there. One of his old cats used to spend most of the day under the bed, hiding from Mona, probably; Gus would have done the same if he could.

When he draws himself up, his back creaking, he notices the wardrobe door is open. Ally's wardrobe. It's bright white, like the rest of the room, and a straw hat hangs from the handle.

Inside, he can see men's shirts. He can see suit jackets. Not Ally's wardrobe then, but Bill's.

Despite himself, Gus is drawn to it like a moth to a flame; he opens the door wide, just to feel the full burn. There are formal shirts, cotton casuals, chequered weekenders. A couple of pairs of cord trousers. Dark suits; decent quality too.

Everything kept. Everything saved. As if, one day, Bill is coming back.

Fox barks and it makes Gus jump out of his skin. The little red dog is standing in the doorway and Gus could swear he's sending him an accusing look.

'There you are, then,' he says. And he knows it's time to go.

Gus clears the table, the joy with which he helped lay it earlier quite gone. He washes the mugs and plates; carefully dries them with a tea towel. He doesn't look for where they live in the cupboards – he doesn't fancy opening any more doors – so instead he leaves them on the sideboard. When all is neat, when all is just as Ally has it, he looks to the photograph of Bill; the one over the fireplace, where he's wearing his striped barbecue apron, grinning like the happiest bloke in the world.

Gus wants to be more for Ally; God knows he wants it more than anything. But not before she's ready. For it would be a terrible thing – for them both – to get that wrong. And all those clothes in the wardrobe? Well, Gus isn't stupid.

And shouldn't he count his blessings? To have found himself in paradise in later life and have such a friend as Ally by his side. To have dodged death by the skin of his teeth, when others – far better men – didn't; couldn't. He takes a deep breath and nods to Bill, and it's as if Bill nods back. A mutual understanding, through time and space.

What they already are is enough. For now, it's enough.

Gus gets his coat and leaves. He battles back over the dunes, the wind stinging his eyes.

56

'You're telling me Edwin had a fist fight with Russell the same morning he died? Mum, how could you not tell the police. It's just . . . it's so stupid.'

And Ruth has been called a lot of things in her life, but never stupid. She absorbs the insult because she needs Owen now. Needs him like she's never needed him before.

She's inside the godforsaken sardine can that Owen insists on calling home. It's always baffled her, that he'd rather live here instead of the house he grew up in. Ruth suspects it was Edwin marrying, the mantle of the household being passed. Perhaps Owen imagined a farmhouse full of children and wanted to cut and run before Karensa started churning them out.

'Don't you see how suspicious it looks? Not saying anything? When, what, hours later, he's found dead on our land?'

Ruth's lips are pressed firmly together. She blows through her nose, just like one of those burly, skittish bullocks that ran all the way over Russell Tremaine as if he was nothing at all.

Nothing.

Ruth feels a pulling inside her chest. *Not again.* She thinks of the panic attack that came out of nowhere the other day, leaving her like a fish gasping on land, flicking her useless tail. She, Ruth, doesn't panic. But her youngest son, her dear darling boy – that foolish, foolish boy – has been taken away by the police, and what on earth can she do about it? She parts her lips. Sucks in air.

'Does Karensa know what Edwin did?' says Owen.

'Karensa?' Ruth gives a taut laugh. 'Absolutely not. What a peculiar question.'

Owen rubs his face with both hands. 'It's because of the quad, isn't it? Edwin was so sure Russell stole it. And he thought he could punch the truth out of him, did he?'

'Edwin has always had a powerful sense of right and wrong,' says Ruth. 'He'll tell the police about their scuffle. And it was no more than that, by the way.'

Ruth's hand goes to a cushion. It's a feminine sort of thing for Owen to have in this otherwise undecorated space. She rubs her thumb against its quilted edges.

'You sure about that, Mum? Because if the police know about it, they've got it from somewhere. Russell's not talking, is he? It'll be the post-mortem. Forensics. And if they've made a link with Edwin, that's more than a scuffle. Grievous bodily harm, they said.'

'Edwin will set them straight.'

'If Dad . . .' Owen stops himself. Chews at his thumb.

'If Dad *what*, Owen? If he was here to see your brother protecting the vineyard, standing up for what's right?'

'Since when has violence been the answer? He drilled that into us. Always.'

'Yes, he did, didn't he?' And it's acid on her tongue. 'I wonder why that was?'

Owen stares at her.

'Your precious father. Who never once put a foot wrong.' The anger's rising in her now; rising like a damnable tide. 'What an extraordinary privilege you enjoyed, growing up believing that. What a gift I gave you. Yet have you ever appreciated it?'

The confusion is all over Owen's face. Cartoonish question marks might as well be forming in the air above him. She's being cruel now, but hasn't she shown enormous forbearance, down the years? And, in certain lights, Owen is so like Frank; especially now, with those sorrowful, tormented eyes. She can't bear to look at him.

'Of course you haven't, Owen. Because you have no idea. No idea of the sacrifices I've made. Your brother though? He knows.'

Ruth's so close to telling him. She feels the crackling truth of it racing through her veins.

'I had to tell someone, Owen. And I chose Edwin. Not you, but your little brother.'

'Mum . . .'

Owen's voice is cautioning, as if she's nothing but a stiff wind on the *Shipping Forecast*. A gale warning. *Ruth Harper, moderate becoming rough.*

'Your precious father died, and you ran away to France, of all places. But Edwin, he stayed. He helped me face the storm. The absolute mess of our finances. And I know what you're thinking; I know it's your view that Edwin only made things worse, but at least he tried. Because he loves this vineyard more than you'll ever know.'

'I love this vineyard,' says Owen quietly.

'All this devotion you claim to have for your father, and yet it's Edwin who puts himself on the line.'

'You never said you needed my help.'

'You never once offered it.'

'Edwin was married. He was settled here. He . . . No one else seemed to miss Dad like I missed him . . .'

And Ruth stands up at that. She towers over her son – and that's how she feels, like a tower; not one of strength, but like one of those chimneys up on the moor; a crumbling reminder of former greatness; an absolute goddamn ruin – and her fingers curl into fists.

286

'He was my husband. And I stood by him.'

Owen drops his head.

'For better or for worse, I stood by him. But what do you know about marriage vows, Owen? Your brother is in a police cell. And if they press him, if they push him, there are secrets . . .'

That pull in her chest again; her breath coming short. She sucks, breathes, sucks, breathes.

'Mum, if Edwin just tells the truth, he'll be—'

Ruth Harper. Severe gale 9.

'You want to help?' she cuts in. 'You want to help this time, instead of running away?'

She stares down at Owen and it's like there's some war raging beneath his skin. He's her son, her own flesh and blood, but she doesn't know him well enough to even guess at what that war might be. Brotherly rivalry, probably. That tired old story.

'I want to help,' he says eventually.

Ruth looks away from him, out the window and away down the skeletal vines – row after row of them. Beyond is the tall pine, the ship's mast, watching over the entire spread. The tree that people spin ghost stories about. Stories that are nowhere near as wild as the bare-boned truth.

She has no choice but to tell him.

'Then you listen to what I've got to say. Because if you really loved your father, you'll do what I'm about to ask you. For him. For us. You'll do it for this place, Owen.'

57

Jayden drives fast along the lanes to Yew Tree Cottage. The wind hurls handfuls of rain at the windscreen, and it hits the glass like shale. They pass Shoreline land, the rows of gnarled vines, looking dead as disco. As they pull in at Shaun's place, Jayden cuts the engine. He looks at his phone for the twentieth time.

'Still nothing, Al.'

After talking to Mullins, Jayden waited ten minutes, then left a long voicemail on Skinner's phone. He laid out his and Ally's thinking – clearly, rationally.

So Celine Chevalier, he concluded, *if she's on to the Harpers, I wouldn't be surprised if she's still in Cornwall. That she hasn't gone back to London at all.*

Now he and Ally climb out of the car. The wind pushes at their backs as they head to the cottage door, but before they can knock, it flies open. Shaun stares out, a haunted expression firing across his features. Jayden's eyes drop to the gun in his hand. A shotgun. An ancient-looking thing – but no less deadly.

'Shaun,' he says, his voice, calm, level. 'How are you doing, mate?'

Jayden's had the de-escalation training. He drops his shoulders, adopting a casual pose. But at his elbow, he feels Ally stiffen.

'Are you okay, Shaun?' he says.

Shaun's eyes dart from Jayden to Ally and back again.

'Police with you?'

'No,' says Jayden. 'It's just us. Is it alright if we come in?'

'Shaun, your information really helped us,' says Ally gently.

And to anyone who didn't know her, they'd think she was cool. But Jayden can hear the tightness in her voice. Has she even seen a gun in real life before?

'I was cleaning it,' says Shaun, looking down at the weapon. 'I've got a licence. I keep it locked.'

'Sure,' says Jayden. Then, 'Shaun, okay if we come in? We'd like to tell you what we've found out.'

Shaun steps aside, holding the shotgun close to his side like a soldier ready to march.

'I'll lock this back up,' he says, his eyes down.

'Great,' says Jayden.

As they go inside, Ally briefly squeezes Jayden's hand. He glances down the empty lane behind them. The yew tree's shaking in the wind, its massive branches lurching as if it's a city-centre drunkard looking for a fight. It suddenly feels very lonely, this spot, with only Shoreline Vines up the track. Beyond, the sea is a band of angry grey.

'How about I make us some tea?' says Ally.

And Shaun agrees that, yes, a cup of tea would be just the job.

'Edwin,' says Shaun, 'I saw him. Sitting in the back. He had his head down, but I saw him alright.'

'You haven't been up to the vineyard though, no?' says Jayden.

They're settled in the cottage. Tea all round. Shaun fiddles with his pouch of tobacco but makes no move to roll a cigarette.

'Thought about it,' says Shaun. 'I'm not saying they murdered my boy, but I know they're part of it. Whatever happened, they're covering it up. I know it.'

'How do you know it, Shaun?' says Jayden carefully.

'I feel it,' he says, and rubs his hand over his heart. 'They're lying up there.'

Jayden glances to Ally and she nods.

'That story you told us about Frank, about the buried body, we think it might be connected.'

Shaun's eyes are bleary. He looks bone-tired.

'You think I should have reported it at the time, don't you? Way back when Frank first said. But I just . . . I don't know. It was so hard to believe, in a way. And I just didn't want to get involved. S'pose I figured I had a lot to lose, if I stirred up trouble.' His voice cracks. 'Shows what I knew then.'

'Shaun, can you remember any more of what Frank told you about it?'

He shakes his head.

'And Frank didn't give you an idea of who it was? Or why? If it was an accident or . . . intentional.'

'I told you, no.' Shaun's fingers trace the rim of his mug. 'But I trusted Frank. So, make of that what you will.'

'Shaun, you said you and Frank had the conversation twenty years ago. But is it possible that Frank was going further back in the past. Maybe, ten years before that?'

'The memory was fresh, that's all I know.'

'What was his relationship with Celine Chevalier like?'

Shaun snaps his head up; confusion clouds his face. 'The money woman? Frank passed two years ago. He never met her.'

'She was an au pair first. At Shoreline Farm, thirty years ago.'

'I don't know about that.' Then, roughly, 'What's this got to do with my boy though?'

Jayden looks to Ally. She's distracted, her eye caught by something outside the smeared pane of the window.

'Al?'

'A tractor,' she says. 'Or . . . more of a digger.'

Shaun moves to the window. 'They've got the front loader out.'

Jayden rubs his sleeve on the pane of glass and watches as the green tractor, with its front scoop, tracks up the hillside. Shaun nudges in beside him, a pair of ancient-looking binoculars in his grip. Were they already to hand, Shaun holding up his outpost with his shotgun and binoculars? As the tractor climbs, an uneasy feeling builds in Jayden. When he first moved down here, when his head was a mess, he'd have distrusted a feeling like this, but now he knows it's instinct – and he goes with it.

He slips his phone from his pocket; still nothing back from Mullins or Skinner.

Shaun's fiddling with the latch on the window; it sticks, then opens. A cold gust blows in as he holds the binoculars to his eyes.

'It's Owen,' says Shaun.

'Is it usual,' asks Ally, 'to have the front loader part?'

Shaun shrugs. 'Up on that top field? They've no beasts to feed. Not these days. Shifting something, I expect.'

Jayden and Ally swap a look.

'What is it?' says Shaun, lowering the binoculars. 'You think he's up to something?'

'The tractor's stopped by the tall pine,' says Ally.

'The one from the old story. The ship's mast,' says Jayden.

'Fairy stories,' mutters Shaun. 'Ghost talk.'

But the binoculars are back up.

'Is he digging, Shaun?' asks Ally.

'Reckon he is.'

'Al,' says Jayden. 'Edwin's been arrested. Owen's out with a digger.'

291

Ally nods. And Jayden doesn't need to say it: Owen Harper is moving the remains; the remains of Enrique Delgado, if they're right.

He takes out his phone again. Still nothing back from Skinner. He needs to call this in, but it's a question of timing. Because it's no crime to take a tractor and dig up your own land. Jayden needs Skinner to understand the full story – but the DS is in an interview room.

Jayden peels away, tries Mullins's mobile. It goes to voicemail.

'I don't know about you, Shaun,' says Ally, 'but I could do with another cup of tea.'

Shaun turns to her, the binoculars hanging from his neck.

'Keeping me out of trouble, are you? While Jayden goes and sees what Owen Harper's digging up? That the idea?'

Shaun's tone is gruff, but it's not antagonistic. Is it safe to leave Ally? If Jayden was in any doubt, he'd never do it.

'But I really could do with that tea,' she smiles. 'Are there any of Saffron's brownies left?'

Shaun gives a low laugh. 'No chance.'

Then he rests a hand on Jayden's arm. It's the only time Shaun's touched him, apart from the punch.

'Now, look. If you think what's going on up there has anything to do with my boy, anything at all, then I want to be in on it.'

And if Jayden was in his shoes, he wouldn't want to be on the sidelines either.

'Thing is, Shaun, if you come with me, Owen will smell a rat.'

He's not sure he's ever used that phrase before, but it's one of Cliff's favourites. And in the barns at Top Field Camping, you can smell rats, for real.

'Let's tell Shaun where we're up to, Jayden,' says Ally. 'It's time, don't you think?'

And she's right. Because Jayden doesn't want Ally to be put on the spot, once he's gone up to the field to see Owen. He doesn't want her to feel like she has to start talking – and for Shaun to hear that word *blackmail* and freak out.

And he did answer the door with a shotgun.

So, they tell Shaun what they've put together: the story of the body buried at Shoreline Vines; Russell's anger at the Harpers mistreating Shaun; the timing of Celine's visit; Russell's talk of something big in the pipeline; the cut-out letters in the bin in his flat; fortune favouring the brave. They tell him calmly, carefully, without judgement or sensation.

He listens quietly, his head bent. When Jayden finishes, Shaun stands with his fingers knotted, as though in a muddled kind of prayer. The silence stretches.

'That's what you're thinking, is it?' he says, finally. 'That it was Russell who started it.'

'Russell didn't start it, Shaun. If you track it back, Frank started it.'

'And Frank told me. But I never said a thing. Head in the sand, wasn't I?' His mouth drops, as he tugs in a breath. 'I'm paying for that now. If I'd gone to the police . . .'

But that kind of thinking will ruin him.

Jayden goes to change the tack of the conversation, but Shaun runs on. 'And, what, the Harpers found a way to silence Russell? They killed him to stop him talking? Threw him in with the steers?'

'All we know for sure is that the police have made enough of a link to arrest Edwin for GBH. Shaun, you asked us to find out why Russell was in that field. And this theory explains why he was at the vineyard – so we're close. But it is only a theory. It's not fact. Not yet.'

Shaun drops into a chair, sinks his head into his hands. Ally sits beside him, a still, reassuring presence. Somewhere in the room a clock ticks. Outside, beyond the smeared pane, Owen's digger is at work. Jayden tries to stay steady for Shaun, but inside he's bouncing on his heels, wanting to be out and up that hill.

Shaun says something that Jayden doesn't catch. He leans closer, says, 'Say that again.'

'I said . . . it could be that. With Russell. If he thought that he was . . . on to a winner. And, if it didn't hurt anyone. Not anyone who didn't deserve it, one way or another.'

He lifts his head up, and there are tears in his eyes.

'Go and see what the hell Owen's doing, Jayden. I'm alright here. We're alright, aren't we, Ally?'

'We're alright,' she says.

And as Jayden heads out the door, his phone finally rings.

58

In the farmhouse, Ruth sits at the bottom of the stairs. Her restless fingers pick at the worn old carpet. This was the very spot where Frank died. By that point his body was stormed by malignant cells and, too weak to even hold his footing, he fell – never to get up again. *Perhaps a mercy to go that way*, people said, but Ruth didn't see it like that.

She closes her eyes, battling to find an inner strength.

Right now, her son is in a police cell, saying God knows what. Without her by his side, Ruth has no idea how Edwin will hold up under questioning. Or if those loose lips of his – his desperate need to prove himself – will sink their ship.

But her other son is, perhaps, showing her what he's made of after all. As soon as she told Owen about the body, he agreed that they had to get there before the police. And Owen knew his father better than anyone.

The ship tree, he said, the pine. *Dad never trucked with that old story. Maybe that's why.*

Bury a body in the very spot where a centuries-old yarn says one lies? Perhaps Frank would do that.

Ruth leans on the banister, pulls herself to her feet.

She hears a noise from high up in the house then, and pauses, her head cocked. Karensa, probably, having snuck back into her bedroom. As Ruth and Owen were talking in private, Karensa was likely on one of her long walks, hurrying like a startled deer. Does she care that her husband has been arrested? No, she's making it about her – Karensa's stresses and anxieties. She was never made of stern enough stuff for Shoreline.

Ruth starts up the stairs, ready to give her daughter-in-law a piece of her mind.

'Karensa?' she calls. 'Is that you?'

As she climbs, a feeling builds in Ruth's chest. Not the panicked yanking of earlier, but a throbbing unease.

'Who's there?'

At the top of the landing, Ruth listens again. She hears a muffled crash – and she knows where it's coming from. She breaks into a fast walk, her feet creaking the boards. She stops at the tiny door that leads to the attic, an oddity of this battered old farmhouse, running on to a narrow, perilously winding staircase. She waits, listens. Blood roars in her ears.

Someone is up there, in the attic.

For an absurd moment, Ruth imagines the ghost of Frank. But doesn't he know that they're trying to protect the vineyard's legacy? That when Owen unearths Frank's secret, it's not to judge – *by God, I've done enough of that* – but to make them unimpeachable.

Galvanised, Ruth pushes open the door and yanks the light-pull, but nothing happens; the bulb's gone. She places her foot on the first step, then stops. Who would be here in the dark? Perhaps it's her imagination after all.

But then a blinding light shines in her eyes and Ruth cries out. She covers her face with her arms, ducking as if from a blow.

'Oh, come on,' says a voice she recognises. 'I'm not going to hurt you, am I, Ruth?'

59

'I never meant to hurt you, Saff.'

Broady sits at the counter, a bright yellow smoothie in front of him. It's way too happy a drink for the expression on his face.

When Saffron got in from The Wreckers last night, she found that Broady had gone back to his place. He left her a note saying *I got it wrong. I'm sorry. Love you*, with a drawing of a hibiscus flower. A really bad drawing of a hibiscus flower, but he'd coloured it in and everything.

'It's just . . . all that stuff you went through last Christmas, the way that Wilson blew so hot and cold . . . I don't want you to have all that stress again.'

Saffron's behind the counter in her usual spot, her arms folded across her denim apron. Outside it's still blowing a hoolie, the sea a churning mess.

'It's different this time,' she says.

Is it though? The way Wilson ended that call with her. *Not cool.* What if that's how her dad's going to handle this? Pushing her away, because he's afraid to let her in. She's grown-up enough to read between the lines, but still, wouldn't it be nice not to have to?

'He doesn't think I should stay either, by the way.'

'Who, Wilson?'

Saffron nods. 'I called him yesterday.'

'What does Dawn think?'

'I haven't asked her.'

But Saffron can guess. She would reassure her that they're totally fine. Dawn's a tough cookie – and generous with it.

Broady stirs the straw round and round in his drink. Outside, the wind whistles; a loose shutter bangs. She should go and secure it really, but Saffron feels like if she moves, then the current of the conversation will shift. And she knows she needs to hear him out.

'Whatever you want to do, I'm with you on it. I'm with you *in* it, Saffron. That's what I should have said right away. You stay, I stay.'

And as soon as Broady says it, she realises how crazy it sounds. Is that because her expectations are different with him? Saffron knows that when it comes to her and surfing, she'd never ask her boyfriend to choose. She wouldn't expect Mullins to understand, but when two surfers get together, it's always an open relationship with the sea.

'No way, Broady. You have to still go.'

'I thought about it, babe. But it wouldn't be fun.'

'Those North Shore waves wouldn't be fun?'

He runs his hand through his hair; hair that's already sun-bleached, already half salt. She knows just how his tan will come out in Hawaii, his laughter lines running deeper than ever. She knows how he'll look paddling out among the giants, then jumping to his feet, at one with the board, the wave. And she wants those things for herself too. But not at the expense of doing the right thing.

'Alright, forget fun. It just wouldn't be right, Saff. Those North Shore waves will wait. We've got loads of winters ahead of us.'

And what if Wilson hasn't? That's the bit he doesn't say. That's the bit they're both thinking.

Saffron leans across the counter and kisses him. She kisses him for a long time, trying to close her mind to everything else.

'Oh hey, your business plan,' she says, eventually. 'Did you wing it to Celine Chevalier?'

'You bet. No word back though.'

Outside Hang Ten, the wind howls like a mad dog.

60

'Alright, so Edwin admits there was a bit of a set-to,' says Skinner. 'Says he caught Russell in one of the barns and figured he was casing the joint for what else he could steal.'

'Except it wasn't Russell who stole the quad bike,' says Jayden.

Jayden's walking up the track, his eyes on the tractor at the top of the hill. The wind's blowing offshore and straight into his face, so he keeps his head dipped, cups his hand around the phone.

'You have no proof of that,' says Skinner.

'I can't prove a negative, no. But I know he was out partying in Newquay the night it was taken.'

'Well,' says Skinner, 'Edwin says he challenged him, and they had a scrap. Russell was getting the harder end of the bargain, Edwin admits that much, so he did a runner. That's when he ended up in the field of bullocks.'

'Instead of going down the track to his dad's house. Or into the vines. Both of which were closer. Oh, and Russell was scared of cows. Like, *really* scared. Did you know that?'

'Yes, I know that. The post-mortem shows Russell took multiple blows to the head – mostly bovine-inflicted, but also consistent with falling against a hard surface. It's possible he was confused, Jayden, and never meant to end up in with the cattle. But whatever Edwin says, there's a boot-print-shaped bruise on Russell's body.

More than one. It was a proper beating, meanwhile Edwin's walked away with barely a scratch, apart from across his knuckles. We're not going to let him slip our net. You know what else we found on Russell? Traces of yeast in the weave of his jumper.'

'Yeast is used in winemaking.'

'Bingo. Mullins and I have been reading up on a little process called disgorging. Getting the sediment out and sticking the cork in, to you and me, Jayden. That's what Edwin was up to when he came across Russell. And it's a messy business. No wonder there was transference of yeast to the victim.'

And Jayden's letting Skinner run on, focusing on the parts of the puzzle that make sense, thanks to forensic evidence and a suspect's account. But he's waiting for him to say *about your message*.

'About your message, Jayden.'

Jayden's suddenly quite nervous. For all that he rolls his eyes about Skinner's modus operandi, his respect for the guy has grown over the last months. Vice versa too – and not before time. Even if it's grudging.

'You and Ally broke into the victim's home and rooted through his rubbish bin.'

'With his dad's blessing.'

'That's irrelevant.'

'It's very relevant. And access wasn't restricted. Is it now?'

Skinner hesitates. 'Yes, it is now. We'll be bagging that evidence. And hoping we can see past the prints of you and Ally Bright.'

Jayden nods. This means they're taking it seriously. And if they're taking the blackmail story seriously, they're taking the body at the vineyard seriously – because there's no blackmail without the bones.

'What about the basis for the blackmail?'

'It's one hell of a shaggy-dog story, Jayden. We need facts, not assumptions.'

'But assumptions can turn into facts. And it had to be something substantial for Russell to take the risk.'

'He's a gambler. Though I expect you know that too.'

'Pretty small-time bets though. Something like this is different. But it's bang on, right? Because otherwise the Harpers would have reported it.'

'What, like they reported their missing quad bike, you mean? Oh no, sorry, they hired you and Ally for that.'

'Owen hired me and Ally. And he didn't throw in a side case of blackmail, if that's what you're getting at . . .'

'Where are you now, Jayden?' Skinner cuts in.

'Mullins suggested we drop in on Shaun. In case he was agitated, seeing Edwin arrested.'

'He did, did he? And you're still with Shaun, are you?'

Jayden turns on the spot, trainers squelching in the damp ground. The vines swoop in orderly lines down the hillside. At the top there's Owen's tractor, moss green against the grey sky. The towering pine.

'Not exactly.'

'Tell me you haven't confronted the Harpers with this blackmail stuff.'

'No.'

'Well, don't. Save us something to do,' Skinner grunts. Then, 'This Spanish bloke you're on about. We've run the file.'

Jayden's eyes are on the vehicle, the lift of its front scoop. He wants to hear everything Skinner has to say, but he also needs to keep moving.

'There's no evidence he even crossed the Tamar, Jayden. Last seen in Torquay.'

We told you that.

'But okay, it's worth the conversation, because of the Chevalier connection. The very tenuous Chevalier connection, mind. Here's a number: 1.62 million. Population of Barcelona.'

'But police don't like coincidences, do we?' And Jayden wants to bite his tongue. *We.* Before Skinner can throw out a smart remark, Jayden goes on. 'Look, Owen Harper's got his digger out. I'm watching him now.'

Skinner breathes heavily. 'He's out digging?'

'Of course, it could just be another coincidence . . .'

'Alright,' says Skinner. 'Keep him under surveillance.'

'I was going to talk to him.'

'Like hell you're going to talk to him.'

'He doesn't know Ally and I are in this. He hired us for the quad bike, right? And now a load of machinery's turned up in a barn in a warehouse in Bodmin. Why don't I tell him you've recovered a Honda that matches the description of theirs.'

'What, stall him?'

'If he unearths the remains, he could destroy them.'

'I can't just click my fingers and get a warrant to dig up Shoreline Vines, Jayden. And I can't go arresting all the Harpers based on your shaggy-dog story. Our best bet is to question Edwin around the blackmail angle. And get a warrant to search the farmhouse.'

'They could have destroyed evidence there too – or be about to. You can fast-track a warrant, right?'

'I know what I can do. Listen, if you want to be useful, stop talking to me on this thing and hit your record button instead. Film Owen doing whatever he's doing.'

'Digging up the remains of Enrique Delgado?'

'Just hit record, Jayden. And don't get yourself seen.'

61

'Celine? I don't . . . understand.'

'Your bulb's gone,' says Celine. 'Highly inconvenient. But I found a torch in one of these boxes. Frank helping me from beyond the grave, perhaps.'

Celine shines the torch in Ruth's face again and she blinks.

'But what are you doing here?'

'Come up and I'll explain.'

Celine watches Ruth slowly climb the steps then sink down on to a chair. The woman holds her hand to her chest and suddenly she looks incredibly frail. And confused.

'I cannot begin to imagine what is happening,' she breathes.

'I saw Edwin get arrested earlier,' says Celine. 'I thought that man died by accident.'

'He did. The cattle.'

'Then why the police?'

'They fought beforehand.'

Celine shrugs. After all, this isn't her concern.

'Ruth, I'm looking for something that's mine. You were supposed to be having a celebratory breakfast at the Sandcastle. Courtesy of Owen.'

Ruth stares at her. *If looks could kill.* That's the phrase that comes to Celine's mind as Ruth speaks. Frank had no such murderous expressions in his facial range. He was an open book: wide eyes and a strong jaw, just like his eldest son.

'You're manipulating Owen too now, are you?' Ruth pushes her fingers to her eyes. 'There's nothing of yours here.'

'My diary,' says Celine. 'I left it here. Actually, Frank took it from me.'

'Frank took it?'

And Celine can guess the thoughts now running through Ruth's head. Was Frank seeking titillation? Or some confirmation that his own feelings for Celine were returned? Ruth's probably fretting that it was both. *Well, let her.*

'I need it back, Ruth. Are you sure you don't have it?'

'Don't be ridiculous.'

That percentage breakdown: words, audio, body language. Ruth is telling the truth.

'If you're trying to pretend that things happened differently, and you want the diary to prove it, then you're out of luck,' says Ruth wearily.

Before Celine came here, she was afraid of how much Ruth knew. Now she realises that Ruth's understanding of what happened that summer – the whole basis of her emotional blackmail – is nothing more than an approximation. How embarrassing, for her husband to have kept so much from her, for so long.

Celine can't help smiling – however grimly.

But the missing diary is a problem. Over the years, she's fantasised about coming back to Porthpella to wrest it from Frank, because it was the power play that she never saw coming. Nineteen-year-old Celine – naive, green as a new shoot – believed Frank when he said he'd never use it against her. And, despite appearances to the contrary, that much is apparently still true.

'Celine, you're indebted to my husband. Which means you're indebted to my family, to this land, for ever more. While you and I are having this ridiculous conversation in here, Owen's out digging.'

'Digging?'

'I need to know if he's looking in the right place.'

'I have no idea what you're talking about,' says Celine coolly.

Ruth jerks her head up. 'You know exactly what I'm talking about.'

Celine holds her gaze without falter; she is an ace, an absolute ace, at poker.

'Then why did you reply to my letter?' Ruth's voice is rising. 'Why are you investing?'

'Because I spent some memorable months in your home, I enjoyed your hospitality, and now I'm in a position to help your business financially. Just as I do with many other businesses. You've seen my portfolio.'

'You're lying.'

'What do you want me to say? That I came all this way to try and find a teenage diary of mine? Is that more believable to you, Ruth?'

'You were in love with my husband.'

'Not at all. Though I suppose he was in love with me. Don't worry, Ruth, just a little in love. As so many men were.'

'Not just a little.'

'But doesn't it make you feel better, to reduce it?'

Ruth's hands go to her head, fingers ripping through her hair. She looks, in the feeble torchlight of the attic, incredibly old.

'I asked Frank why you left so suddenly, and he wouldn't give me a straight answer. But we women always know. Then, when his conscience got the better of him, he told me what really happened.'

'Go on, I'm fascinated.'

'I thought I wanted to know. But . . . then I didn't want it at all. Not one bit of it.'

'Fiction, Ruth,' says Celine. 'Rest assured.'

'Frank said he saw the attack out by the barn. A man forcing himself on you. Frank pulled him off, but he didn't know his own strength. Somehow, the man fell and struck his head. Frank was trying to do the right thing. That was all. And you, you were hysterical, Celine.'

Celine holds Ruth's eye. She doesn't say a thing, but she thinks, *And you hold that against me? Woman to woman?*

'It was an old boyfriend of yours. Stalking you, all the way from France.'

Spain, actually.

'And he found you at our farm. Accosted you. Frank knew how the police would interpret the death. Frank as the jealous lover. This foolish old farmer, falling for the French au pair and going toe-to-toe with her handsome ex-boyfriend.'

Celine shakes her head. 'Oh, Ruth. This fiction.'

'I filled in the blanks with that last part. The truth is, Celine, Frank was weak. Not physically – that man's death was evidence of that – but he was scared of what he'd done, and he saw a way out. Frank buried him here on the farm. Perhaps you even helped. He buried that man, and he thought his secret, your secret, was safe. Because this has always been Harper land. Always has been and always will be.'

Ruth looks up at Celine. Her eyes are furious.

'He said you were horrified at the death. But you were glad to see him gone, this man who followed you from France.'

From Spain.

'That you'd been scared. Defenceless. Frank was your rescuer, your white knight, wasn't he? Galloping in on his horse, to save a damsel in distress. Do you have any idea how it feels, to live

307

knowing that your husband's desperate desire to impress, to protect, means you're forced to live with the most grotesque of secrets?'

'And you've kept this so-called grotesque secret all these years?'

'Not for you. For him.'

'But Frank died two years ago. Why not go looking for me then?'

'You changed your name.'

Twice over.

'But you found me in the end,' says Celine. 'Still, it was a risk, Ruth. What if I've had a change of heart? What if I no longer see Frank as someone who saved me, but someone who should have faced the consequences of his actions. There is such a thing as a posthumous reckoning.'

Ruth shook her head. 'I know the way you used to look at my husband. Before, and after. You might not have been in love with him, but you liked him a great deal.'

'And doesn't it shame you, to exploit another woman's vulnerability? To use my worst moment against me? So much for the sisterhood, Ruth.'

'Don't talk to me about the sisterhood, when you were carrying on with my husband.'

'I was nineteen, Ruth. Just a girl. I was naive.'

'I don't think someone like you is ever naive.'

And it shouldn't matter to Celine, to hear another woman say something like that. But it does. Despite her hardening, despite every one of her immaculate barricades. In this moment, Celine hates Ruth Harper. And that mask of hers – the mask she's crafted from ashes, three decades in the wearing – threatens to slip.

She breathes.

'Go on then. Tell me how you found me. I've been wanting to ask you that, but it hasn't seemed . . . appropriate.' Celine gestures to their surroundings. 'The gloves are off now though, aren't they?'

'After Frank died, he left us with a financial mess. I was going through his papers . . .'

How could Ruth not have found the diary?

'. . . and I came across a wine industry magazine from ten years ago. Perhaps on some unconscious level I thought it unusual that Frank kept it, so I leafed through it and . . . I saw your face. Part of a line-up at an awards dinner. Barely wearing a little black dress. I recognised you instantly. You'd aged, of course. And the Chevalier part was new.'

'My second husband.'

'Well, there we go. You did well from the divorces, I presume?'

'I've worked for every penny I have.'

'I looked you up, Celine Chevalier, and I saw what you'd become. An angel investor. Your enormous wealth. I knew then that you were the person to help us. Frank never allowed me to believe that you were indebted to us. He said that it was his own action that he was covering up, but I knew it was all for you. Would he have waded in like that, in any other situation? But I put up and shut up, because I loved him, and I loved what we were building here. With the vineyard, we'd turned the farm around. But it was failing. It is failing. We need money.'

'Or you'll be forced to sell. And, as you subtly pointed out in your original letter, the diggers would no doubt come rolling in – and who knows what they would find?'

Ruth nods, her lips pursed. 'If you don't invest, then your secret is as good as out. We can't protect you any more.'

'Just going with this story, this fairy tale . . .' Celine takes a breath. 'Did Frank ever tell you the name of the man who died?'

'No.'

'You didn't ask?'

'I didn't want to know. What was done was done.'

And, despite everything, some part of Celine applauds Ruth for her compartmentalising skills.

'Owen's out with the digger,' says Ruth, 'but it's a needle in a haystack. If the police break Edwin . . . we're all ruined. You'll be charged with aiding and abetting.'

'There's nothing to connect me, Ruth.'

'Tell me where he buried the body. I know you know.'

'Truly, I don't,' says Celine, folding her arms across her chest. 'You know, the wonderful thing about being powerful is that the truth doesn't matter any more. The truth is whatever I decide. My lawyers, my incredibly expensive lawyers, will see to that.'

Celine sees Ruth's face transform.

'You owe us.'

'I don't owe you anything. Frank? Maybe. But not you.'

Or not even him. Frank thought he was protecting her, but perhaps the greatest kindness would have been to have stood by her; to have supported Celine as she told her story, with all its truth and severity. It's too late for that now though. Celine feels tears burning and swipes them away. *I will not cry.*

She's suddenly taken by a gust of recklessness.

'Ruth, I was never coming here to invest in your vineyard. All I wanted was to reclaim what was mine. But it seems to have disappeared, and so, therefore, shall I.'

At that, she moves towards the stairs, turns. 'Your son. Edwin. He was a snotty-nosed whining brat. Not like Owen. I liked Owen.'

Ruth's on her feet. Her face is laughably furious, and Celine can't help poking the bear.

'Did Edwin hurt that man, Russell Tremaine? It wouldn't surprise me. I saw him pull the wings off a butterfly once, just because he could.'

Celine expects Ruth to launch into an impassioned defence, but instead she hurtles forward, fast as an arrow. Their bodies clash, and Celine – despite being younger, despite being stronger – falls backwards. As she slams into the wall, she gasps and doubles over. The torch slips from her fingers and rolls across the floor. Ruth darts to grab it, then she's slapping down the stairs, banging the door behind her. The torchlight goes with her.

Celine hears the unmistakable sound of a key turning in the lock, and her heart misses a beat.

She has always been afraid of the dark.

62

Jayden shifts his position, tweaking the angle of his phone so the view is uncluttered by undergrowth. The vines themselves were useless cover, so he looped around and came in from the side, edging close to the tall pine and the digger.

Owen sits high in the cab, hunched towards the window as the scoop churns the earth. There's no doubt the guy's looking for something. And Jayden's recording his every move.

Jayden's attention is so focused on Owen, and getting the recording, that it's as if Karensa comes out of nowhere. Suddenly she's standing in front of the tractor, waving her arms around, more animated than Jayden's ever seen her.

Owen cuts the engine. His face, as he climbs down from the cab, is impossible to read.

Jayden keeps recording. Without the roar of the tractor, it's dead quiet on the hillside – even the wind has dropped. The tang of diesel hangs in the air.

'Owen, what the hell?'

Karensa's voice is clear as a bell. Jayden slows his own breathing, minimises the rustles; he never reckoned on recording dialogue.

Owen pulls his coat off, pushes up the sleeves of his chequered shirt. He's breathing hard, a shovel in his hand now. Beside him,

Karensa looks very small in her big winter coat. Her long hair flies across her face, but her voice is clear; precise.

'You need to tell me what you're doing.'

'I'm trying to fix this mess. For Dad.'

'But . . . Owen, he's dead.'

Owen plants the shovel in the ground. 'What about Edwin? Are you protecting him?'

'Not for one second, but . . .'

'When he was arrested, I saw your face, Karensa. You looked like you knew it was coming.'

Karensa grabs hold of his shoulders. 'Owen, we made this happen. All of it.'

'What are you talking about?'

'So, Edwin attacked Russell? You know what that means, don't you?'

Owen shifts from foot to foot. His body language says that yes, he knows. Karensa sees it too.

'Russell told Edwin about us. But you'd already worked that out, hadn't you? Russell must have gone straight to tell him after seeing us in the vines. And Edwin . . .'

'Karensa . . .'

'It makes sense. *Horrible* sense. Edwin would have hated, absolutely hated, someone like Russell even suggesting that I wasn't faithful. That you were—'

'Karensa, stop. Russell Tremaine was blackmailing Mum,' says Owen. 'That's what this is.'

She shakes her head. 'What? No . . . It's us, it's—'

'Russell said Dad killed a man thirty years ago, and that he buried the body on the vineyard. He threatened to go to the police if Mum didn't share the investment. He was asking for two hundred thousand, Karensa.'

She gives a blurt of laughter. It sounds like a seabird's cry.

While Jayden's internal monologue shouts *we were right!* his phone-holding hand stays steady.

'But that's crazy. Then Ruth should have let him go to the police!'

Owen shakes his head. He looks intently at her. 'Mum said she couldn't do that.'

Karensa steps back.

'No. Owen, surely . . .'

'It was an accident. Dad was trying to stop an assault. He never meant to hurt the guy. I don't even know who it was, but . . .'

'But you all knew about it? All these years?'

'I only found out this morning. But Edwin already knew.'

Karensa covers her mouth. 'And Russell's death?'

'Another accident,' says Owen. 'Russell confronted Edwin, and Edwin said there was no way they were going to pay. But he was between a rock and a hard place, because if Russell did go to the police, this place would be torn up.'

'Torn up? Like this, you mean?' She gestures to the mounded earth; the shovel in Owen's hand.

'And we could forget about investment. We could forget about any kind of future, because who wants to buy wine when the terroir is a boneyard?'

And it sounds like Owen's still working through it all; processing, rationalising.

'Mum said Edwin tried to negotiate with him, but Russell wasn't having it. That's what happened, Karensa. It's nothing to do with us. They came to blows. Russell ran off, took a wrong turning and ended up in with the bullocks.'

For a moment there's no sound but the gusting wind, and Jayden's own breathing. His eyes go to the record button that's still flashing red, the seconds ticking on.

'And you believe that?' says Karensa. 'Because I don't. Not for a second.'

314

63

The wind pushes at Karensa's back, but her conviction has sprung roots, and she feels taller, stronger. After months of being buffeted by high emotion, wrenched this way and that by desire, confusion, guilt – finally, Karensa's standing firm.

So, Owen wasn't lying; he really hadn't noticed that Russell caught them together. *Thank God.* That's the trouble with guilt; it swashes in and colours everything. No, Owen was oblivious, and Russell carried on up the track and met with Edwin. And whatever else the two of them were discussing – blackmail? Bones beneath the vines? It's no crazier than the places her own thoughts have gone lately – Karensa is certain that Russell told Edwin what he'd just seen.

Edwin's wife and his brother, kissing in the vines.

Karensa didn't know Russell, but she could imagine how someone might want to make Edwin feel small. Because Edwin has spent his life doing it to other people – including her.

She closes her eyes, and she can see, with absolute clarity, Edwin losing it; hands curling to fists. *My wife? And my brother?*

There was a moment yesterday when Edwin looked at Karensa with such scrutiny that she withered inside. *Why do I feel like there's something you're not telling me?* he said. So, Edwin knows about her and Owen then. He's known for days. And the only reason he hasn't confronted them is because of what he did to Russell. The ugliest truth – on top of so many ugly truths.

She takes a breath and looks Owen straight in the eye.

'If Russell told Edwin that he was being cheated on, he'd have killed him for it.'

Perhaps there was glee in the way Russell told him; perhaps there was triumph. Edwin Harper cuckolded? Yes, Karensa could see people round here enjoying that one. She knows how her husband struts about Porthpella, how he's always playing the big man. What they wouldn't reckon on would be Edwin's reaction. *Karensa and Owen? What?* How the news would destroy him – then he, in turn, would seek to destroy.

She feels a sob rising as Owen reaches for her. His face is all tenderness.

'Karensa, no. It was the blackmail.'

How can Owen understand? He's nothing like his brother. Edwin is obsessed with what people think of him; who beneath all that façade, that arrogance, has a paper-thin ego. The slightest nick, and it's shredded.

'I know you want us to tell Edwin, I know you want us to be out in the open . . . but if this is some twisted wishful thinking, then . . . don't do it to yourself. It doesn't help anyone, it—'

'Wishful thinking?' Her mouth drops wide. 'My God, Owen. You think I *want* this?'

'I'm sorry. No. *No.* That was stupid. What I mean . . .' Owen kicks at the ground. His cheeks are wet with tears, while her own, she realises, are bone-dry. 'Karensa, all I want to do is save Shoreline. Dad made this place. He made it something special. This land . . . it's sacred. Whatever Edwin did, whatever he knows, or doesn't know . . . it was the bullocks that killed Russell.'

'And you think Edwin didn't stand by and watch?'

Owen leans against the side of the tractor, rubs his face with both hands. 'I just need to find the bones. Then it's unprovable. Dad's dead and . . .'

And she can't believe he's back to this.

'Are you going to dig up the whole vineyard, Owen? Then what? A bonfire? I mean . . . my God. You do this, you're as bad as Frank. You're as bad as Edwin.'

'It was an accident, Karensa. Dad was just trying to help someone—'

She can hear the pain in Owen's voice, and she can't stand it. But she can't stop herself.

'Who? Who was he trying to help? And what about Edwin? What was he doing?'

Karensa's words rain down on Owen like blows. She hauls in a breath; tries to soften her voice, because she loves this man, she does. And for once in her life, she knows, unequivocally, what the right thing is to do.

Even if it'll end them.

'Owen, Russell died because of us. Because of us and our lies. I'm going to tell the police. Finally, I'm going to tell someone the truth. Whether you come with me is up to you.'

64

Ruth stands in the hallway, one hand resting on the wall. She's knocked a picture askew; her breath comes in staccato gasps. Behind her, above her, she can hear Celine hammering at the attic door.

The liar. The cheat.

Locking Celine in was a bad idea, but Ruth couldn't stand her laughing, leering face. Celine never intended to give them a penny? This fact is like a dagger twisting between Ruth's ribs. There are so many consequences to this revelation. At best they'll be a laughing stock, the local business with ideas above their station, who thought they'd caught the eye of a Londoner with money to burn. And what about at worst? She can't think of what they'll lose.

Oh, Edwin. Her darling boy, her stupid boy, who tried to protect them and is now in a police cell. Ruth imagines shackles, rats, and dark, dripping corridors. Such is her tumult. What if they keep him? Throw away the key?

Bang-bang-bang from up in the roof.

Ruth closes her ears to the racket and pushes open the farmhouse door. The wind slices her face as she flounders across the yard. She and Owen are the only ones who can save things now.

From here she can see the tractor winding its way slowly down the edge of the top field. Does that mean he's done it? Found the bones? Owen surprised Ruth with his willingness to dig, but perhaps he isn't so different to them after all. Her heart lifts a little.

As the tractor draws closer, Ruth squints. The cab is crowded. As it passes the hedge, she sees Karensa in there too, riding high beside Owen. Karensa's arms are wrapped around Ruth's eldest son, her head resting on his shoulder.

Ruth's hand goes to her mouth. She makes a strange noise: a splutter; a choke.

She has no doubt, no doubt whatsoever, of what this is. Perhaps she's always known, on a subconscious level. The fact that Owen can hardly bear to be in the house he grew up in. The way his voice softens when he speaks to Karensa: a voice Ruth's never had come her way, nor anyone else's – not even Frank's.

Ruth stands in the yard, wind whipping at her back, her hands clasped to her mouth. So many betrayals, one on top of the other: the prison cell; the liar in the attic; the bones beneath the vines; and now Owen and Karensa. An Old Testament fury rises in Ruth. And this fury feels so much better than panic. It is so much more productive. She hauls her uneven breaths into line. *In and out, in and out.*

Russell Tremaine's cocksure face looms in her mind's eye. His sticky-tape letters were pathetic, but his blackmail landed, didn't it? She couldn't ignore it. Because what he said was true and, two weeks ago, Ruth had an awful lot to lose.

Not any more though.

Ruth plants one foot in front of the other, until she's out of the yard and on to the track. There's one person left to blame for this. One person who whispered to his feckless son that, once upon a time, Frank Harper killed a man.

Ruth's rage is a piston engine as she heads for Shaun's cottage. And this time? She has nothing left to lose.

65

Ally watches as Shaun tosses another log on the fire. She hopes it won't be long before Jayden comes back. It's not that Ally's uncomfortable being left alone with Shaun, but his agitation is clear. He jabs at the logs with a poker and sparks fly.

Charlie the dog has settled at her feet, and she bends to stroke his ears. The wind pummels down the chimney with a strange whistling sound; smoke blows back into the room and her eyes sting.

Shaun still hasn't answered the question Ally asked. The question that sent him out of his chair and to the fire. He turns to her now, poker in his hand.

'You're right,' he says slowly. 'I do know their land. I worked every inch of it alongside Frank. But Owen knows it better. He loves the vines. I'll say that for him. The terroir – that's the word they use – the terroir is the most precious thing for him. That's why he lives in that caravan, I'd say. To be close to it.'

But does it mean Owen knows where to look for a body? There's been no word from Jayden and the tractor's moved from the top of the hill. Shaun tosses the poker on to the hearth, where it lands with a clatter. Against Ally's legs, Charlie doesn't shift at the noise. He knows there's no threat from his master.

'Try thinking of Frank over the years,' she says carefully. 'Was there a part of the vineyard that he treated differently? That he avoided, or the opposite, even . . . a part that he tended more carefully. I think people are unconsciously drawn to the places that matter. It's like saying to a child not to stare at something unusual: they can't help themselves. We keep going back and back.'

Shaun sinks into a chair. 'My Russell loved the beach. Scraggy patch it is, that's where I met your mate. The bald bloke.'

'Gus.'

'Gus. That's it. It's more shingle than sand. Big boulders, crumbling cliff up behind. The waves go at it even on a still day. No kind of beauty spot is what I'm saying, but Russell would tear about on it like he'd landed in Eden. As a boy, if he was troubled, that's where he'd go. He'd take his worries to the water.'

'That's what I've always done too,' says Ally. Then, 'Where did Frank take his worries?'

'Frank was always whistling. You'd think it was because he was free as a bird, but there was always something more to it, I thought. Like he didn't want to be alone with his thoughts rattling around. Like, whistle a happy tune, to keep the unhappy ones away. That was Frank, I reckon.'

Shaun has a faraway look in his eyes. Ally tries to follow.

'What about Frank's favourite part of the farm, where was that?'

Shaun stops suddenly; cocks his head like a dog. 'That's the gate banging. That'll be your Jayden.'

And Ally feels a thud of anticipation. What news?

Shaun's getting to his feet when the door to the sitting room swings wide.

'Ruth.'

And the way Shaun says it, it's as if he's a little afraid of Ruth Harper. And Ally doesn't blame him. Because this Ruth Harper – fury pooling on her face like oil on water – doesn't look anything like the woman Ally met a few days ago.

'This is cosy,' says Ruth, her sneer taking in Ally, the fire, the mugs of tea. 'Isn't it? Very cosy.'

Danger stirs in the room, clouds deepening and darkening. Charlie feels it too; the dog growls, then slinks against the wall.

Ally's eyes instinctively go to the poker that's lying haphazardly on the hearth, and memories of what happened at Rockpool House in the summer rise unbidden. She knots her fingers in her lap; feels the press of her wedding ring. She wills Jayden to come back.

Ruth is looking at them both. It's a calculating look, as if gauging how much they know – and how much trouble is due.

'Well, I know you're lying,' she says, fixing on Shaun, 'when you say you had no idea what your conniving son was doing.'

Shaun's face is deep red. 'Lying?'

'You were in on it together, weren't you?' She paces, and her jaw's working as if she's chewing something. 'So, what's your strategy? That's what I can't understand. You still think we're going to pay, do you? If you hush up, we pay up?'

Shaun looks to Ally, and she gives the briefest shake of her head. *Don't rise.*

'No idea what you're talking about,' he says, his voice as mechanical as a robot's.

And if Ally needed proof that Shaun has only ever told the truth to her and Jayden, this is it: his lie couldn't fool a child.

Ruth moves in fast, like a magpie stealing a trinket.

'Oh dear, you're about as convincing as your son. Because for all his grand threats, he folded like a piece of paper.'

Threats? *We were right.* Ally holds her breath.

Wind howls down the chimney; the fire spits in the grate.

'I'd like you to leave,' says Shaun quietly. Behind him, Charlie growls again.

'What are you going to do, now he's dead? When do you make your move, Shaun?' trills Ruth.

'You need to go,' says Shaun. 'And that's me asking nicely.'

'Because there's no money. We're ruined, and that's all thanks to you and your boy.' Ruth's attention switches to Ally. 'You're listening awfully hard, Ally Bright. Aren't you?'

'Shaun would prefer you not to be here,' says Ally carefully. 'I think it's best . . .'

'Best? Oh, there's nothing to be salvaged here. Nothing. No best.'

The dog whines.

'Charlie,' says Shaun gently. 'It's okay, boy.'

And Ruth bares her teeth. She growls back, in a pitch-perfect impression of the dog – only far meaner. There's something dreadful about it.

Charlie's hackles go up, more from anxiety than aggression. But Ruth swears at the animal and kicks out at it. The dog yelps; cowers. Before Ally knows what she's doing, she's out of her chair and pulling Ruth away.

Ruth spins around. She laughs in astonishment as she looks down at Ally's hand on her coat.

'Oh, the dog, is it?' she says. 'The useless dog. Well, we all have our buttons.'

Ruth kicks out again and Charlie howls. Ally grapples with her. Ally has never grappled with anyone – not as a child in the playground, certainly not as a woman. She pins Ruth's arms and pushes her against the wall.

'What on earth are you going to do with me now, Ally Bright?' Ruth taunts.

She realises then that Ruth doesn't care. She's beyond it.

'Shaun, call the police,' says Ally. 'Report an intruder. Animal cruelty.'

Shaun hurries from the room as Charlie cowers in the corner. Should she drop her hold on Ruth? Ally strains to hear Shaun's voice. Could the police already be on their way, if Jayden spoke to Skinner?

Out of nowhere, Ally feels an astonishing pain in her head. She stumbles backwards, her vision blurring. Her legs appear to fold and the next thing she knows, she's on the ground. Was she punched? But how would that be possible, when she was holding Ruth's arms?

She hears fast footsteps, receding then loud again. Shaun's voice saying, 'Don't move.'

And Ally thinks he's speaking to her. She blinks her eyes open, head spinning. She can taste blood.

'I said, don't move. Or I'll shoot.'

Ally's vision fizzes, her eyes stream. She can just see Ruth with her hands up. And Shaun with his shotgun trained on her.

'Shaun, no,' Ally breathes. But her head's clanging, and when she tries to get to her feet, she can't do it. She grabs hold of a chair, and by sheer determination she hauls herself up.

'You hurt my friend. You hurt my dog. And you, or one of your lot, hurt my son.' Shaun's voice splinters. 'Killed my son.'

'Take your shotgun to the cattle field, Shaun,' says Ruth. 'Do your worst.'

And Ruth doesn't sound in the least afraid.

'Though they're flighty, those bullocks. It really doesn't take much for them to startle. And once they're running, well, you'd best keep out of their way. They don't know their own strength, you see. I wouldn't have said they're malicious animals, but territorial? Well, I suppose we all are, when push comes to shove. We all protect what's ours.'

'Russell was already dead when he wound up in that field,' says Shaun. 'Wasn't he?'

His hands are steady on the shotgun, though his voice falters.

'Oh no, he was breathing,' says Ruth. She has her hands in the air and, with one, rather primly tucks a lock of hair behind her ear. She smiles. 'Just.'

And if there's anything that'll tip Shaun over the edge, Ally knows it's that smile of Ruth's. Her face is throbbing, and at the very edges of her vision there's a glittering constellation of tiny stars. Ally knows that if she leans into the panic, those stars will fill her sky completely; the ground will tilt. And she won't be able to stop this.

'Shaun,' she says, trying to keep her voice steady, 'don't rise. It's what she wants.'

'I just want the truth,' he says.

The shotgun wavers in his hands.

'And we'll get it,' says Ally. 'But properly. With the police.'

Ruth laughs. 'Oh, Ally. Your faith in the system is touching. Is that the continuing influence of your dear departed husband?'

Ally dabs a finger to her nose. It comes away bloody. Her head starts to spin again, but somewhere in the background she can hear a car engine.

'Yes,' she says. 'It's Bill. And it's Jayden. It's Tim Mullins.'

There's a rap at the door. A shout, 'Police!'

'And it's Detective Sergeant Skinner,' she says.

Beside her, Shaun lowers his shotgun.

Skinner crowds into the room, and Ally's knees give way. As she drops, she thinks, *Faith? Yes, Ruth. I have faith.*

66

Jayden follows the path of the tractor all the way back to the yard. As it rumbles through the gate, he slips to the side of the abandoned holiday cottage build. He watches as Owen swings the vehicle in a full circle and brings it to a stop. At the smell of diesel, the size of the thing up close, the sharp teeth of its massive scoop, a memory flashes in: The Drop, last Christmas, the metal beast surging towards him; Jayden's leap of faith.

But he feels no threat this time. After hearing Owen's exchange with Karensa, Jayden's sure the older Harper brother is innocent of what's gone on at Shoreline Vines. Okay, so he went digging for the body, but Karensa stopped him from seeing it through. What their next move is, though, is anybody's guess. Face Ruth?

Jayden watches as Owen steps down from the tractor, then reaches up his hand to help Karensa down. It felt uncomfortably intimate, observing their exchange. His phone is weighty in his hand. He knows Skinner will say the recording is gold – if it's admissible.

If Karensa's right, Russell's death wasn't accidental. They were right all along. *Hell of a cover-up.* Whatever happened after the fight, only Edwin knows. Edwin and, possibly, Ruth.

Owen flicks a look at the farmhouse, then folds his arm around Karensa and walks away with her. They go out of the side gate, and down towards the field with the silver bullet. Jayden's about to follow when his phone vibrates with a message. *Mullins.*

Where are you? Skinner has Ruth. I'm on foot.

What does Mullins mean, that Skinner has Ruth?
He taps a message back:

I'm in the yard, watching Owen and Karensa. What's going on with Ruth?

Jayden watches the three dots, indicating that Mullins is typing.

She attacked Ally.
But she's fine.
Seriously, she's fine.

Owen and Karensa are crossing the field, getting smaller with every step. Jayden doesn't even think of following them any more. Ruth isn't there. Ruth is with Skinner. Ruth attacked Ally. Jayden steps out from his hiding place, just as Mullins enters the yard.

'Mullins, what the hell's going on?'

'Easy, Jayden. I told you, Ally's fine. And Ruth Harper is in cuffs. Shaun Tremaine's stopped waving his gun about.'

'*What?*'

Mullins explains, then says, 'We're going to nick Owen and Karensa too. Want to join in?'

'They're headed to the caravan. Mullins, for what it's worth, I think they're innocent in this.'

'It was only Edwin's DNA on Russell. Ruth's clear too.'

'I wouldn't be so sure about Ruth. The way Owen was talking, she's the one in charge around here.'

As they pass the open barn, Jayden does a double take.

'Celine's car,' he says. 'A silver Porsche, right?'

Mullins stops; sniffs the air like a dog. 'What's that doing here?'

Jayden runs his hand along the bonnet. 'It's cold,' he says. 'It's been parked a while.'

He looks around the space, eyes adjusting to the gloom. Most of the Harpers' outhouses have been repurposed, housing wine equipment, great vans and bottling machines, but this is the kind of random barn that Cliff specialises in. Is this where the quad bike was stolen from? They didn't get to ask even the simplest of questions before Russell's fate took centre stage. At the rear there's a cracked stone sink, some complex-looking piece of spiked farm machinery, and a wheelbarrow.

Jayden goes over to the barrow. There's a residue of water pooled in the bottom, as if it's been left out in the rain. He squats beside it, eyes running over every inch.

'Are you sending CSI up here?' he asks, turning to Mullins.

'Yeah, they're on their way.'

'Ally and I think Russell was unconscious when he was put in that field.'

'I know you do.'

'So, Edwin would have had to get him in there somehow. This wheelbarrow's worth looking at. I think it's been recently hosed down.'

Jayden takes out his phone and shines the torch beam on the underside. There's what looks like a tiny fleck of rust. And another.

'But not that thoroughly. Mullins, see that – that could be blood.'

Mullins bends down to look. 'Put money on it, would you?'

'I'd put a CSI on it, that's for sure. What about finding a match for the boot print?'

'We're working on it,' says Mullins. 'Easiest thing in the world, though, to ditch a pair of shoes.'

Jayden straightens up. He pictures the fight unfolding, here in the barn or in the yard. Russell's body bundled into the wheelbarrow then taken into the field. *Every contact leaves a trace.* Edwin's been arrested on assault charges, but forensics could make it murder.

Just like Enrique Delgado was murdered. Jayden looks to Celine's Porsche again.

'Ally and I know who Frank killed. What if Celine does too?'

'Yeah, yeah, Enrique Delgado. You told us. Come on, Owen and Karensa are waiting. Not exactly Bonnie and Clyde, but if I don't get them nicked, Skinner'll—'

'But think about it. Celine could be in danger. If Ruth's lost it . . .'

'Ruth's definitely lost it, mate.'

'So, what was the trigger point? She's been a cool customer so far, right?'

'Arresting her son. That'll do it.'

Jayden looks to the farmhouse, and its sullen granite face stares back at him. If Russell was beaten to near death for blackmail, what would they do to Celine, who knows their worst secret too?

'I think we should check inside the house for Celine.'

Mullins shoots a look across the field, then says, 'Yeah, alright. But let's make it fast.'

Jayden surges ahead as, behind him, Mullins radios Skinner.

The door isn't locked, and Jayden steps into the farmhouse. The hallway's gloomy; faintly damp. It feels very different to the night when they hosted their party here. The Harpers thought they'd got away with it then; they thought that all they needed to do was keep impressing Celine.

'Celine!' Jayden calls out.

There's a beat of silence, then a thumping sound comes from deep in the house.

Jayden turns to Mullins. 'Hear that?'

'Blimey. You called it. Come on, let's go.'

Jayden takes the stairs two at a time, Mullins following fast behind him. Jayden knows this rhythm: two cops moving through a building, fast and focused. He pauses on the landing – listens. Another round of thumping; a muffled shout.

'Is she locked in or what?' says Mullins, pushing beside him.

'This way. Celine!'

They turn down the hallway, the rug slipping beneath their feet. The noise is coming from the end, and it sounds somewhere higher in the house. Is there a third floor? They can hear a scream now too, the panic tangible.

'I reckon that's a French accent,' says Mullins. 'It's got to be her.'

Jayden sees the tiny door and moves fast towards it. He opens it, but when he tries the light, it doesn't work.

'Let me go first,' says Mullins, reaching for his torch.

And though he doesn't want to, Jayden steps aside.

'It's tight,' says Mullins as he makes his way up, the torch beam playing off the close walls.

Jayden follows. Celine's piercing cries get louder; a voice that's lost control.

'Police,' calls out Mullins. 'It's okay, Celine. Oh hey, the key's in the lock. Easy . . .'

Mullins turns the key, and as he pushes open the door Celine bursts out, a scream at her lips. She immediately loses her footing on the narrow stairs.

Mullins catches her, but as Celine struggles in his arms he drops the torch. The light disappears. In the swamping darkness, Jayden tries to reach up to support Mullins, but the stairs are too steep, too narrow, and in the dark he feels Mullins stagger. Fall.

Then it's dominoes.

Slow-motion dominoes. Absurdly, Jayden has time to think – *we're falling, we're all three falling* – as they crash in a heap at the bottom of the stairs.

And it's Jayden who takes the crushing weight of everyone.

67

Cat's out walking with Jazzy on the beach. Her daughter wanted to see the snow, and neither she nor Jayden are very good at saying no to her, so even though Cat was cosy at home on the sofa, she bundled on her big coat – her coat that she can only just zip up over her growing bump – and the two of them headed down to the beach.

It's not really snow, but sea foam, flying through the air in an all-white flurry. Jazzy charges ahead in her red wellingtons, screaming with joy. The wind whips her daughter's voice from her, and Cat pulls her own bobble hat down over her ears. It's not cold, but wow, it's blustery.

She's amazed she even hears her phone ring over the roar of the wind, the explosion of the waves. But when Jayden's out with Ally, Cat always has one ear trained on her phone. Call it old habits dying hard. It was the same when Jayden was on duty in Leeds. And the night Kieran died – the night Jay phoned her, crying – all her worst fears were realised. Since then, there's been knife fights, cliff drops, more life-and-death situations than Cat ever thought were possible in her childhood dreamland of Porthpella, the place she naively thought of as a safe harbour for their family.

But for all the peril, she knows what Jayden has found here with Ally Bright is something rare; perhaps even precious. Not exactly a conventional route to making detective, but since when have they cared about that? And Cat's not sure she's ever seen Jayden happier. So, she's not afraid for what lies ahead for them, and this little baby who's growing inside her. Jazzy's little brother. Jayden's son.

She pulls out her ringing phone and frowns, not recognising the number. She turns from the wind; cups her hand to speak.

'Hello?'

'Cat? It's DS Skinner.'

And her heart drops.

68

Owen hears the sirens wailing along the coast road. He sticks his head out the caravan door and watches hedgerows tilt in the wind, the beech shimmering and shaking, its golden leaves flying. The sea beyond is pewter. How can such a beautiful place harbour such secrets? And how can their secret, his and Karensa's, be the cause of so much destruction too?

Because despite Owen not wanting to believe it, he does; Russell's hardly innocent, but the violence that Edwin unleashed on him had Owen's name on it. And that's a guilt he must live with.

'More police?' says Karensa, her hand on his shoulder.

'That's an ambulance.'

Earlier, Owen stopped his shovelling by the pine tree. He brought the tractor down from the hill and came back here with Karensa to talk it out. Not like on the windswept hillside, where words were flung haphazardly, emotions gusting; this time, quietly, steadily. Re-finding their natural rhythm.

They didn't care where Ruth was in that moment. She could have been on the moon.

Owen knows how close he came to going along with his mum's plan. Anything to save the vineyard, to keep Dad's secret buried. And for what? Family loyalty? Even Owen can see the hypocrisy in that. The very first time that he looked at Karensa for a beat too long – which was basically the first time Edwin introduced her to him; it might not have been love at first sight for Karensa, but it was for Owen – he should have realised he was giving up his right to be here. Upending the ground beneath the whole place, too.

Owen's father killed a man and covered it up. His mum knew all about it. Edwin knew about it too – eventually. When Russell tried his luck with blackmail, he pushed it too far.

These are the facts.

Did Edwin deliberately leave Russell to die? Did he stir up the cattle, to finish the job he'd started? Owen wouldn't put it past him. Not if Edwin knew about him and Karensa. And not if Russell – scrappy little Russell Tremaine, with a mouth on him, a nerve on him – was the one to do the telling.

When Karensa tells the police everything, Owen will be right there beside her. That is his decision: to stand by the woman he loves. Even if it's at the expense of his family.

'Ambulance,' he says now. 'Coming up the track.'

'Oh God, what now?'

'I don't know, but let's go and find out.'

As they step from the caravan, Karensa holds out her hand and Owen takes it. He holds it firmly as they walk towards the blue lights.

'No hiding?' she says.

'No hiding.'

They need each other now, more than ever. Big emotions swirl inside of him. His brother, his mother, his lover – and whatever the hell his beloved dad did thirty years ago. He wants everything out in the open, once and for all. Whatever the cost. As they cross the field, the land sinks beneath his boots. The wind gusts in the treetops.

Shoreline Vines. This beloved, broken place.

69

Ally and Shaun are on the track to the vineyard. Ally's whole face aches, but she's moving fast. With perfect animal intuition, Charlie keeps pushing his nose into her hand.

Shaun glances down. 'Friend for life you've got there.'

'He's lovely,' says Ally.

And there must be something in her voice, because Shaun briefly touches her shoulder.

'Don't go worrying. That detective bloke, Skinner, he says Jayden's fine. The ambulance is just to be on the safe side. You know that, eh?'

And what a kindness, that Shaun should think of her, amidst all that he's lost; amidst the brutal truth that's emerging.

'I know. *Thank you.* Shaun, how are you faring?'

He hesitates. 'When all this is laid to rest, it'll help.' Then, quietly, 'I suppose you and Jayden think I'm daft, sticking my neck out for Russell, saying there was no way he'd nick that quad. And all the time he was up to something worse.'

'We don't think you're daft, Shaun.'

'You want to believe the best, that's how it is with your kids. And you never stop loving them, no matter what mistakes they make. I loved that boy like nobody's business, Ally.'

She thinks of the framed picture in Russell's flat, in pride of place on his chest of drawers – the little three-person family of Granny, Dad and son – and her heart clenches. She doesn't know what to say. But then Shaun speaks again.

'That's why it hurts so much, isn't it?' he says. 'Because of the love.'

Because of the love.

'You're right. That's just what it is.'

They walk on, heads bent, feet in step.

'Talking of hurting,' says Shaun, with a quick laugh, 'I can't believe Ruth Harper nutted you.'

'Is that what it's called? Good lord. Nutted!'

'Nasty piece of work. The way she was talking . . . I think she might have . . .' His voice breaks. 'You know what I'm saying, don't you?'

'I know what you're saying.'

It was the way Ruth described the bullocks. Ally thinks Edwin killed Russell, and that his mother helped him cover it up.

'She always had that son of hers under her thumb,' says Shaun. 'Edwin's always been the favourite, but it's a mixed blessing, that, I'd say. All he ever wanted to do was please her. Frank saw how it ate Edwin up, how much her opinion mattered. But I suppose in their own way that was Frank and Owen too.'

Shaun strokes his dog's head as he speaks.

'Me and Russell, it being just the two of us, there was never any rivalry. Never any pressure. We were always thick as thieves.' He gives a sad smile. 'And I know full well what I just said, by the way.'

Ally thinks again of Ruth. The way the woman growled at the dog. Headbutted Ally. Laughed in the face of Shaun's shotgun.

'Shaun, I wouldn't be at all surprised if Ruth was the one pulling the strings.'

'They'll get that out of her, will they? The police?'

'We'll make sure they do.'

The farmhouse is just coming into view, the ambulance parked askew in the yard.

'What Frank told me, all these years, I hardly gave it any thought,' says Shaun. 'And that's because I trusted him, Ally. Respected him. I suppose I thought that whatever happened, it would have made some kind of sense. I know how it sounds, but you didn't know Frank. I should never have spoken a word of it to Russell, I know that much. That's where all this started.'

'It was Frank burying the body instead of going to the police. That's where it all started, Shaun. You can't take any blame for what happened afterwards.'

'I've been thinking of it, though. Frank wasn't the kind of bloke to hide from his mistakes. He wasn't a cover-up merchant. If Frank killed someone by accident, he'd have owned up to it.'

'He could have been frightened. A panicked decision that he couldn't come back from.'

Shaun shakes his head. 'No, I've been thinking about them all. Edwin, Ruth, what they did to my Russell. All the different ways that could have happened. But with Frank, I reckon if someone died at his hands, and he hid it, then he'll have done it on purpose. The killing, I mean. It's going to sound strange but . . . he was honourable like that. If you get what I mean.'

'You mean it's more likely that he set out to kill someone, than it being an accident and he covered it up?'

'That's it, yeah. Do you see where I'm coming from?'

The yard's in view now. Ally can see Jayden standing beside the ambulance, a blanket draped over his shoulders. Mullins is close beside him. Celine Chevalier is talking to another police officer who Ally doesn't recognise.

White-suited CSIs surround the barn.

The wind must be blowing in their direction, because Ally hears Celine say, quite clearly, 'No, I don't want to press charges on this occasion. I'd sooner put the ordeal behind me.'

A sudden thought lands. Ally trusts Shaun's assessment of Frank. It's considered, informed. So, what possible reason could an honourable man have for not owning up to another person's death?

'What if he was covering it up for someone else? Shaun, given what you know of Frank, is that a possibility?'

Shaun stops. 'I'd say that's possible. In fact, I'd say that's more likely.' He shakes his head. 'I never thought of that. What, you're thinking of Ruth?'

'Perhaps Ruth,' says Ally. 'Or perhaps someone else.'

Celine's voice continues to carry.

'It was such a foolish over-reaction on my part, but I've been afraid of the dark since I was a girl. I lost all perspective. I can't apologise to these young men enough for my slip. I'm more than happy to pay for private healthcare or offer other compensation.'

Celine turns a glittering smile towards Jayden and Mullins. Ally sees Mullins look back; his cheeks are as red as two apples.

At that moment Jayden turns. He lifts an arm to wave and grimaces – then quickly grins. But as Ally reaches him, his face changes.

'Al, what happened to you?'

'Jayden, never mind me. Skinner said you've broken your ribs. That you were lucky not to—'

He shakes his head. 'Cracked, worst case. I'm all good. I just can't walk too fast. Or get up too quickly. Or laugh. Or cough. Honestly, other than that, it's all great. But you – your nose, your lip . . .'

'Ruth nutted me,' says Ally. 'I believe that's the terminology.'

'Al, don't make me laugh, seriously. It kills.'

'Mrs Bright,' says Mullins. And he does that at times of stress – reverts to formality. 'It's my fault. Poor Jayden took the hit.'

'Mate,' says Jayden. 'You'd have done the same for me.'

'I did take a mean whack on the elbow though. The trouble with you as a cushion, Jayden, there's not enough padding.'

A paramedic touches Ally lightly on the arm. 'Would you like me to look you over too, love?'

'Oh, I'm fine. The sergeant assured me my nose wasn't broken.'

Once he'd bundled Ruth into the police car, Skinner was gentle, and really very kind to Ally – and to Shaun. All of which came as a surprise.

You'll want to lock that back up, sir, he said of the shotgun. *Immediately.* Then, *We'll get you your answers about your boy. One way or another.*

Shaun was still wielding an offensive weapon, even if the gun wasn't loaded. But given the circumstances, isn't that just the kind of thing Bill might have overlooked too?

The paramedic feels Ally's nose gently. 'And the sergeant was right. You're a lucky lady.'

'Skinner scared the hell out of Cat by phoning her,' says Jayden.

'Jayden,' says the paramedic, 'given where the pain is I don't think an X-ray is necessary, not unless you want one.'

He shakes his head. 'Thanks, but I'm good.'

Ally sees Celine look over. She murmurs something to the officer, then joins them.

'I feel terrible for the fuss,' she says to Ally and Shaun. 'These boys were wonderful though, coming to my rescue. And you must be Shaun? Shaun, I'm so sorry for your loss. What a terrible thing. I don't mean to rush off, but I'm already late, and—'

'Sorry, madam,' says the officer, cutting in, 'but you've got the wrong end of the stick. We need you to come with us.'

'I've given you my statement,' says Celine, still smiling.

'We need you to come in for questioning at the station, madam.'

'I'm already very late for a meeting,' she says. 'I've spent more than enough time in Cornwall.'

'Just standard procedure,' says Mullins, his hand rubbing his elbow. Then, 'Ah, there you are. We were just coming to see you.'

Owen and Karensa are in the yard, their hands clasped tight together. Ally and Jayden glance at one another; Jayden raises his eyebrows.

'We'd like to make a statement,' says Karensa.

And Ally thinks how purposeful she sounds. Owen, beside her, stares down at his boots.

'Alright,' says Mullins. He's looking a little flustered by this filling yard, but then spies Skinner on the approach. 'We'll get that organised down the station,' he says, his voice louder.

Ally leans close to Jayden, whispers, 'Has Celine said anything about Enrique?'

'Not a word,' says Jayden.

And that's the detail Ally needs, to be sure. She takes Jayden's arm and quietly leads him away.

'You've got something, haven't you?' he says, face illuminated.

'I think Frank was covering for Celine.'

70

The wind rages all afternoon and into the night. And down the station there's raging too.

Edwin swears he barely touched Russell Tremaine. Ruth says she never took the blackmail attempt seriously. Celine has never heard of anyone called Enrique Delgado. Owen and Karensa are the calm ones. They want to help, but all they have is supposition. Plus, they're sleeping with each other, so are they the trustworthy type?

Mullins yawns as he fills the kettle. They're getting nowhere fast. Skinner skids a mug over to him.

'Fill her up, will you?' And he sounds jaded. 'I don't know, Mullins, it makes sense on paper, this story of Ally and Jayden's. But we can't prove a thing. Beyond making the GBH charge stick on Edwin, that is. And Ruth for ABH.'

Mullins taps the spoon on the rim of the mug.

'That's not in the least bit annoying, Mullins,' says Skinner.

'Sarge, do you buy that Edwin being told about Owen and Karensa's affair was what tipped him over with Russell?'

'It's fair to say it won't have gone down well. Especially if his blood was already up . . .'

They're yet to question Edwin on this point, because Owen and Karensa's statements were at the back of the queue. Skinner's suggested they hold on to it, and use it at the next cross-examination.

'Alright, so we've got a double motive for Edwin,' says Mullins. 'The blackmail situation, and his wife's affair. So, what if we soft-soap him a bit? If his mum cajoled him into duffing up Russell, then he could help himself, couldn't he? And help us get Ruth.'

Skinner frowns; strokes his moustache. 'I think someone has mummy issues. He's never going to sell her down the river.'

'But what if Edwin was, erm, led to believe that Ruth was selling *him* down the river?'

Skinner doesn't throw it out.

'And Celine,' says Mullins, 'she's flat denying any knowledge of any incident at all, back in the day. And claims never to have met a Spanish bloke called Enrique Delgado. There's got to be an angle with her.'

'She's one smooth talker, but I don't trust a thing she says. Reckons she was up in that attic looking for some book her mum gave her. My foot.'

'And the thing is, she had no idea Ally and Jayden had worked it out about Enrique Delgado. Because if she did, she could have pretended to be the avenging angel they first thought she was. Not the killer they reckon she is now.'

'Exactly.' Skinner rubs his chin. 'But it would take a good deal of work to connect her to Enrique. And she knows that.'

'We need those flipping bones.'

'With DNA analysis we could confirm the identity, but it's still a long road, Mullins. And the department's not going to foot the bill for a digger, even if we make a cracking case for it. In the meantime, Celine's flash lawyer will make sure she's untouchable.' Skinner takes his coffee from Mullins. 'Hey, chin up, son.'

Mullins juts his jaw. He's surprised by the feeling that pulses through him, but maybe he shouldn't be, by now.

'Ally and Jayden worked hard on this one, sir. They put themselves on the line.'

'They always do, Mullins,' says Skinner.

'Jayden's got a couple of cracked ribs, thanks to me.'

'Thanks to Celine Chevalier, technically.'

'And Ally got herself nutted by a stark raving mad woman.'

'She did. And she lived to tell the tale.'

'Yeah, on that, they're headed down the station . . .'

'Ally and Jayden?'

'I thought they might want to . . . give statements.'

Skinner's caterpillar moustache twitches. 'Statements, eh?'

And Mullins's thinking is that Ally and Jayden have a way of viewing people – they see past all the front – and maybe, just maybe, they'll hold the key to Edwin and Ruth.

'You're getting a little bit ahead of yourself, Constable Mullins,' says Skinner, cracking his knuckles. 'Thought we needed the extra firepower, did you?'

Skinner's phone goes and he answers it in his usual way, barking his own name into the receiver. He nods, says 'good' twice, then 'right'.

'Forensics are in. They found traces of Russell's blood on the underside of that wheelbarrow. Must have made a pig's ear of getting him in it.'

Mullins shakes his head. 'Jayden called that.'

'They did a better job of hosing it off though. No prints.'

'What, none?'

Skinner shakes his head. 'And all that blood trace means is that the wheelbarrow was nearby.' Skinner holds up a finger. 'But! A single fibre from his jumper was caught in the metal.

And that's our money shot, Mullins. Russell Tremaine was in that barrow.'

'Or his jumper was,' grumbles Mullins.

Skinner runs a hand through his hair. A hand that, Mullins notices, is finally without its wedding band.

'We need confessions to make this watertight.'

Mullins decides to make his play. After all, it worked quite well when he mentioned bringing Ally and Jayden in on it. Skinner actually called them 'firepower' – and maybe it wasn't even sarcastic.

'Can I tell you what I think, Sarge?'

'Enlighten me.'

'Ruth was shouting her mouth off in front of Shaun and Ally, but she clammed up the minute we got her in here. For my money, Edwin's the weak link.'

'I don't disagree with that.'

'So, what if with Edwin we present a scenario of how things happened, and kick off by saying "We've been talking to your mother. And we put it to you that . . . et cetera." He'd read between the lines, and I don't think he'd like it if we made out that Ruth wasn't backing him.'

Because if they can get Ruth, or Edwin, or the pair of them, on a murder charge, then that would open up Enrique Delgado again. And they could make the case for the diggers. Do a proper job of it, not Owen's panicked shovelling.

'It's not the worst idea I've heard.'

Which in Skinner speak, is basically a high five. Or a Shell House knuckle-bump.

'A play like that though, we've got to get the psychology bang on, Mullins. Like you said, Ally and Jayden have a bit of extra insight here . . .'

◆ ◆ ◆

It feels cosy having Ally and Jayden down the station; like they're one big team. It's very different to the first time, back when Ally came to interview a lunatic suspect at said suspect's request. Mullins didn't know what to make of them, meanwhile Skinner had them down as busybodies, annoying amateurs playing detective. Well, the sergeant's eaten humble pie enough times since then. Not enough to turn him actually humble, mind; Ally and Jayden are detectives, not miracle workers.

'I like Mullins's idea,' says Jayden.

And in this moment, Mullins really likes Jayden.

'It's about figuring out their weak points,' he says.

'That's it,' says Mullins. 'Hit them where it hurts.'

'So with Edwin, where does it hurt?' says Ally.

Skinner's staying on his feet, a bid to hold on to a bit of power, probably.

'Edwin Harper reckons he's the bee's knees,' says Skinner. 'He's that arrogant, he thinks he can shrug off an assault charge. Maintains there was a scuffle, but that boot print belongs to someone else. Said Tremaine was the kind to get in scraps. We've had no luck in matching the print to an actual boot.'

'Edwin strikes me as rather brittle beneath that arrogance,' says Ally. 'It's the way he looks to Ruth when he talks. I noticed it at the farmhouse.'

'And if Russell did break the news to him about the affair that morning, that's huge,' says Jayden. 'Edwin will have hated hearing it from Russell, of all people.'

'Especially if he was already harbouring his own suspicions,' says Ally.

'Owen and Karensa think Edwin had no idea about them,' says Mullins.

'He will have,' says Skinner. 'Deep down you always know. And then Russell comes along and confirms his worst suspicions.

No doubt in a less than gentle way, because he's throwing it in with the blackmail chat. That's a combination that'd push anybody's buttons.'

'Plus, he's a right mummy's boy,' says Mullins. 'We've got to push those buttons too.'

'Ruth gave herself away at Shaun's, didn't she, Al? We think she's directly involved.'

As Ally recaps how it unfolded – Ruth's taunts about the cattle; her sense of control, even though she was obviously a total lunatic – Mullins has to agree.

'Ruth Harper as puppet master,' says Skinner. 'I'll buy that.'

'Edwin's facing the more serious charge on account of his DNA,' says Jayden. 'Add that to the forensic evidence on the wheelbarrow, and we – I mean, you – could build a murder case. Meanwhile Ruth walks away with an assault charge for the attack on Ally. Once he's locked up, and has the time to think about it, that's going to feel all kinds of unfair to Edwin.'

'So perhaps we focus on the pressure that his mother's put him under,' says Ally. 'How much he's been carrying, not just in the last two weeks since he's known about the blackmail, but before that too.'

'Ruth Harper as puppet master,' says Skinner again. 'It's got a good ring to it. Poor little Edwin manipulated, and now he's taking the fall. And he's lost his wife, to boot. Alright then.'

'I think it's important not to make him feel small though,' says Jayden. 'He doesn't want our pity. Especially given the Owen and Karensa situation. If we go in too hard on that, we run the risk of losing the Ruth angle. This is about her conviction too.'

'He does have a petulant side,' says Ally. 'Perhaps it's about appealing to that.'

'Get his nose out of joint,' says Skinner. 'Well, I'll do that with pleasure.'

'Make him think his mum's laughing all the way to her freedom,' says Mullins. Then, quietly, 'No one likes being laughed at.'

'What about Celine?' says Jayden suddenly. 'You know what we're thinking there, right?'

'Yes, yes, that she's a killer. But don't go getting ahead of yourselves,' says Skinner. 'Celine Chevalier has a top-drawer lawyer incoming.'

71

Jayden's been here before, on the other side of the one-way glass. Not out of uniform though. And not in this station, invited in by Devon and Cornwall Police. Alright, invited in by Mullins – who appears to be stretching his wings – and tolerated by Skinner.

'I feel like I'm watching television,' says Ally, beside him.

And 'watching' is about right. They'd never be allowed in the actual interview, even though Ally nailed it here way back with their first case. Proved herself a master interrogator, surprising everyone, including herself.

'Do you wish you were in there?' asks Ally, turning to him.

'I don't know,' he says, honestly. 'Do you?'

Ally shakes her head. 'I prefer it this way. Skinner really listened this time, didn't he?'

Jayden grins. 'Now who's the puppet master?'

They fall quiet as, on the other side of the glass, Skinner starts talking. Through the speakers, his voice booms.

'Your mother said you lost control, Edwin.'

Skinner's voice is matter-of-fact; there's no goading. But Jayden immediately sees a flicker at Edwin's jaw. Hitting him where it hurts, as Mullins put it?

'You used to do it as a child. Owen was always the steady one and you – you were the wild card. If there was a fight, you started it.'

'Rubbish.'

'You wanted to talk Russell round, but when that didn't work, you lost it. Because that's what you do, isn't it, Edwin?'

'No.'

'Was it Russell telling you about Karensa and Owen? Was that the tipping point, on top of everything else? Because it can't have been easy, hearing a thing like that from someone like him. And at a moment like that.'

'No. Wait . . . what?' Edwin jerks his head up. 'What did you say?'

'Owen and Karensa. Russell saw the two of them together. And I expect he took a bit of pleasure in enlightening you . . .'

Edwin's completely still. His face is suddenly very pale.

Jayden looks to Ally. 'He doesn't know, Al . . .'

'Oh, that's it, is it?' says Skinner. 'You're going to pretend you don't know what I'm talking about.'

'You're talking rubbish,' says Edwin, with an angry shake of his head. 'It's a cheap shot to . . . Who told you this? Not Russell, because that guy is dead, so who? Shaun? Stirring things up? Pathetic.'

'Karensa. And Owen.' Skinner calmly takes a sip from his mug. Meanwhile, fifty different emotions cross Edwin's face, until he's left with just one.

He drops his head into his hands. The man's heartbroken.

Beside him, Mullins looks through the glass to where Ally and Jayden are sitting. Bites his lip as if he's the one in trouble.

'Always smart-thinking, though,' Skinner says, unflinching. 'Your mum did say that too. You thought if you put Russell in the field with the bullocks you could stir them up, so it'd look like an accidental death. Cover your tracks. Clever.'

'No.'

And this time Edwin speaks so quietly they can barely hear.

'We've found the wheelbarrow you used, Edwin. Russell's blood is on it.'

Edwin looks up. His eyes are red.

'Whatever you say to us here, we've got enough to charge you.'

Jayden isn't sure if this is true. Though, to be fair, Skinner doesn't clarify the charge.

'Here's the thing, Edwin. You didn't just lose your temper in the heat of the moment. You masterminded a brutal killing. That's a whole other level. You'll be going away for life.'

Ah, okay, he's clarifying the charge. Bold.

Edwin rubs a hand across his eyes.

'You won't be there to celebrate your mum's seventieth, or her eightieth,' chips in Mullins. 'You'll be behind bars.'

'We've got her under arrest too, you know,' says Skinner. 'She was devastated when she worked out what really happened. She's very disappointed in you.'

Jayden glances to Ally. Skinner's really laying it on now, but after the Owen and Karensa revelation Edwin's got about as much fight in him as a deflated balloon.

'She assaulted Ally Bright. Not seriously; she'll be bailed in a heartbeat. But your mum acted entirely out of character, and that's on you too.'

Jayden watches Edwin drag in a breath. He can feel the torment coming off the guy now, great waves of it crashing through the glass. This is it. *The breaking point.*

He touches Ally lightly on the arm; counts down, 'Three, two, one—'

'Out of character? For my mother?' says Edwin, his voice high as a bird's. 'I don't think so.'

72

It should feel stranger to Ally to be here, but it doesn't. Because Edwin Harper just accused his mother of, to use Skinner's words, masterminding the murder of Russell Tremaine. And at that moment, Mullins looked directly through the glass towards Ally and Jayden and nodded at them.

Not a wink, or a laddish grin – or any of the things she might once have expected of Mullins – but a discreet acknowledgement of their part.

After the Edwin interview, they regroup.

'That was tough to watch,' says Jayden. 'Edwin had no idea about Karensa and Owen.'

'So those guys gave themselves away for nothing,' says Skinner, with a grim laugh. 'Big of them, I suppose.'

Did Ally feel pity stir, as Edwin crumpled before their eyes? In truth, she didn't. Because Edwin beat Russell until he was unconscious, and his only remorse was for the fact that his mother was shirking all blame for what happened next.

Ally and Jayden agree that the way to get to the heart of the matter with Ruth is to demonstrate an understanding of her good – air quotes – intentions.

'It'll be the last thing she expects,' says Ally.

'Make her feel seen,' says Jayden.

At which Skinner rolls his eyes, says, 'All these new expressions. I see her, alright. And I don't like her one bit.'

'She wanted to protect her son,' says Jayden. 'That parental instinct is powerful.'

'The way she spoke at Shaun's house, I don't think she was at all surprised that Edwin snapped. I do wonder if that was her plan all along. For that negotiation to turn to confrontation. Possibly even to . . . silence Russell.'

'Agreed, Al. But in the interview, I think we take her by surprise. Play it the opposite way.'

Incredibly, Skinner doesn't correct the 'we'.

'I see where you're coming from,' the sergeant says. 'Doing the last thing she bloody expects. So, we'll be on her side. Alright, Mullins?'

Mullins flicks a glance at Jayden. Then, a knuckle-bump. 'Let's do this,' he says.

◆ ◆ ◆

Ruth's hair is as sculpted as a jockey cap; her cheekbones are sharp as blades. She looks at Skinner with nothing short of a sneer.

'Ruth, how were you to know that Edwin would spin out of control when you asked him to talk to Russell?' says Skinner.

Ruth stares back at him. Mistrust flickers across her features.

'You were only trying to fix things,' says Skinner. 'But you ended up with a far worse problem. A devastating problem, for a mother.'

Ruth lifts her chin. 'Don't talk to me about "devastating". Sitting there in your cheap suit, just ticking your boxes.'

'You sent Edwin in coolly, calmly, but he was neither of those things, was he? When Russell wouldn't play ball, Edwin couldn't stop himself. He let you down. Again. For all Edwin's efforts since your husband died, he just keeps falling short, doesn't he? That must be very difficult for you.'

'You've changed your style, Sergeant. Suddenly you're telling me how I feel. Have you reconsulted your manual. A touch-feely twenty-first-century one?'

Behind the one-way glass, Ally looks to Jayden.

'Gosh, she's tough. I don't know if she'll crack.'

'She's furious,' says Jayden. 'Remember, she laughed at Shaun's shotgun and headbutted you, Al.'

'She kicked Charlie.'

'When Ruth thinks people are against her, she thrives. But when Skinner acts like he's on her side? I still think that's the right call.'

On the other side of the glass, Ruth takes a sip of water.

'But you've always stood by Edwin, haven't you?' says Skinner. 'You've always championed him. You let him lead the way with your investor.'

A fresh burst of anger crosses Ruth's face. Whatever happened between Ruth Harper and Celine Chevalier in that attic, it was fury that propelled Ruth to Shaun's cottage. And it's fury that's propelling her still.

'And when Edwin lost his temper with Russell, when he crossed a line that he couldn't step back from, you came to his rescue. Only your son doesn't quite see it like that, Ruth. He said it was your idea to put Russell in with the bullocks. Edwin said that's all on you.'

Ruth laughs. A short, sharp bark.

'Russell was badly beaten by Edwin – the post-mortem told us that – but he was still breathing when he went in that field, Ruth.'

'No one put Russell anywhere. He went in that field all by himself.'

'Forensics say different. The wheelbarrow you used was hosed down, but not very thoroughly.'

Ruth's face is impassive. She falls quiet – and it stretches.

'All I can think,' she says, eventually, 'is that my son was very scared. That he panicked . . .'

So as soon as there's forensic evidence she's pivoting?

'And you wanted to protect him, Ruth.'

She shakes her head.

'Look,' says Skinner, 'I'm a parent.'

Behind the glass, Ally looks to Jayden. 'Is he?'

Jayden shakes his head.

'Doesn't matter if they're fully grown, they're your babies still,' says Skinner. 'All Edwin was trying to do was look after the good name of the vineyard, of your family, and stand up to someone he perceived as a bully. He never meant for it to go so far.'

Ruth's jaw juts. She looks hard as Cornish granite.

'It was too late for Russell,' says Skinner, 'anyone could see that. When you put him in that field with the bullocks it wasn't about ending a life, it was about saving a life, wasn't it? Saving your son.'

Out of nowhere, a tear rolls down Ruth's cheek. 'Anyone would have done the same,' she says, her head held high. Another tear falls. 'If they had the courage.'

And they've got her.

But instead of sending Jayden a triumphant look, Ally looks down at her palms. Because for Ruth to see killing Russell as an act of bravery is perhaps the worst thing of all.

73

'I call that a job well done, Constable,' says Skinner.

Mullins is pulling his coat on. It feels like a job well done to him too. Apart from Celine Chevalier: no hat-trick for them there. Her lawyer zoomed in in his Maserati and zoomed out again just as fast – only with Celine in the passenger seat. Even with Ally and Jayden's detective work – leading all the way back to a tennis team at the University of Barcelona, and a pretty damn realistic drawing of Chevalier as a young mademoiselle on Enrique's brother's website – they were told they didn't have a leg to stand on.

'How much do your reckon Celine was paying for that lawyer?'

'More than you and I make in a year, Mullins.'

Celine said that Ruth trying to implicate her in the blackmail was ridiculous. That the only reason she considered investment in the farm was because of the time she spent there as an au pair, and how much she'd liked Frank. She knew nothing about a dead body. Said it must have been a story Russell cooked up, and Ruth was unstable enough to lose her head and believe him.

So why is Ruth trying to implicate you now? they asked. *What does she have to gain by doing that?*

Celine shrugged. *All I can think, Officers, is that Ruth is upset that I changed my mind about the investment. That and the fact that she always suspected her husband was a little in love with me. See, there are two reasons. I expect the third is that she's just not a very nice person.*

And even Mullins couldn't argue with that one. But still, why does he feel like this case is one big jigsaw puzzle and they've done it all – shedloads of blue sky, too – but there's just one piece missing. Bang in the middle.

'I expect you're after a pint, are you?' says Skinner. 'Meeting up with Ally and Jayden?'

'Jayden's gone home to his wife. And Ally's having dinner with Gus.'

'All on your own then, are you?'

Mullins shrugs. 'Lone wolf. That's how I like it. Unless you wanted . . .'

'I'm getting this done then I'm driving out to see Shaun Tremaine, tell him what's what. Poor bloke.' Skinner sighs. 'I expect Owen and Karensa are shacked up in the farmhouse now. Nothing to stop them, is there? Alright for some.'

He continues to tap at a report. Mullins zips up his jacket.

'If you really want to know about Gran Canaria, I put my foot in it, Mullins.' Skinner's not looking at him as he says it; he's still facing his screen.

'Sarge?'

'Fellow guest. Divorcee. Lovely woman. I can't remember how to read the signals, that's the trouble. Egg on my face, so I cut my losses.'

'Erm . . .'

And Mullins has no idea what to say. They don't do personal chit-chat. So, he thinks of Hippy-Dippy. What would Hippy-Dippy do?

'You sure read the signals in the interview room though, Sarge,' says Mullins. 'I know that much.'

Skinner slowly turns round. His moustache twitches with a half-smile. 'You're right there, Mullins. Though we had a bit of help on that front, didn't we?'

And Mullins grins at the thought of Skinner acknowledging the part that Ally and Jayden played. Not least because wasn't it Mullins's idea, to bring them in? So, it's a pat on the back for him too.

'Ruth and Edwin,' says Skinner, 'when the chips were down, they hung each other out to dry without so much as a second thought. Lovely stuff, eh, Mullins? Now get out of here before I find some paperwork for you.'

74

Jayden is back home, and he's making that long-awaited spaghetti bolognese for his girls. Jazzy has already expressed the opinion that so long as he stays at home with them in future, *then no one will fall on top of you*. To be fair, she has a point.

After the action at the station, Jayden and Ally wanted to drive over to see Shaun, but Skinner said that announcing the charge was firmly police business, and they could do whatever *hobnobbing and gladhanding Shell House Detectives do* in the morning; to which Jayden replied he didn't know what either of those things were, but fine.

Since then, they've had a further update from Skinner: Celine's hotshot lawyer got her out of there in under half an hour.

Now Jayden has a wooden spoon in one hand, and his phone in the other, as he and Ally go over the latest. The bolognese simmers on the hob.

'Al, there's no evidence to connect Celine. Her line is that Ruth trying to implicate her is just sour grapes because Celine changed her mind about the investment.'

They need that body. Because without Enrique Delgado's remains, there's no way of proving that he was ever in Cornwall.

'Jayden, I don't understand why the police can't send the diggers in. Do the job properly.'

'Budget. Resources. It's a huge space to search. Plus, priorities. Because even though Ruth is accusing Celine of being complicit, even she says it was Frank who did the killing. So, it's a cold case with a dead prime suspect.'

They don't have all the answers, but Celine being directly involved in Enrique's death, as implicated as any of the Harpers – perhaps even directly responsible – makes sense. But proving it? That's something else.

'The good thing is, Skinner's confident he'll get his convictions for Ruth and Edwin based on the recorded confession and forensics,' says Jayden. 'And that's what we need for Shaun.'

It's hard though, to be so close to the full truth.

'So, Ruth's maintaining that they thought Russell was already dead when they put him in the field?' says Ally.

'Like that makes a difference, right?'

'It's almost as if she has a strange code of honour. That if Russell was already dead, what would it matter? Except to spare Edwin.'

While his and Ally's tactic worked – painting Ruth as the caring mother, the great protector, determined to fulfil her role at any cost – Jayden's not sure there's even a scrap of truth in that. Ruth was flattered into the admission, but Jayden suspects she's a far colder prospect.

Nevertheless, Edwin's a thirty-something man, responsible for his own actions.

When Jayden imagines Jazzy as a grown woman, he just can't do it. Already he wants to hold on to this version of her – the version that slips a hand into his own as naturally as a foot into a shoe. Who laughs at just about anything. Who knows nothing of the horrors of the world. But his tiny daughter will be a big sister in just a few months, and that he can picture: fun, loving, authoritative bordering on bossy.

Jayden steps back from the stove and looks through to where Cat is sitting on the carpet with Jazzy, the pair of them stacking Duplo. Their heads – one blond, one dark – are bent together. Cat's bump is perfectly round. He thinks of their little boy to come and, despite himself, the image of Russell Tremaine as a child jumps in. That blond buzz cut, the roguish grin. Skinny legs in wellies and towelling shorts.

What lengths would Jayden go to keep his children safe from harm? He'd go all the way. But sometimes, even then, it's not enough.

'So, we'll go and see Shaun tomorrow morning?' he says to Ally.

'Yes, first thing.'

Outside the window, the wind's tearing through their little garden. The old apple tree, with Jazzy's swing on it, is leaning dangerously. He briefly wonders how deep the roots go.

'How's this wind down in the dunes?'

'Gus keeps thinking someone's trying to get in. The sand's flying at the windows.'

Gus. Ally said she'd asked him round this evening. He pictures the pair of them by the fire, sharing a bottle of wine – probably not from Shoreline Vines though. Jayden smiles to himself, thinking back to his chat with Gus a few days ago. *Go Gus*, he thinks. *Go Ally.*

'You stay cosy, okay?' he says.

'Oh, we will. And you too. Good night, Jayden.'

He sets down his phone and gets back to the bubbling bolognese. He feels a tug at his leg.

'How long, Dadatz?'

Jayden squats down to his daughter – gingerly, what with the ribs. 'Oh, we're back on calling me Dadatz now, are we? When we want something? Ten minutes, babe. Tops.'

Jazzy whoops, like ten minutes tops is the best news ever. Then she runs back to her Duplo.

Cat calls to him from the carpet. 'Weston, you'll always be her Dadatz. Even when she's old and grey.'

They share a sweet smile. But the thought of Jazzy in this world without them to protect her – however old she is, however grey – breaks Jayden's heart clean in two. But for now? He stirs the bolognese. And counts his lucky stars.

75

After Detective Sergeant Skinner leaves, darkness settles around Shaun's cottage. He sits in the quiet. He wouldn't call it peaceful, but it's bearable, and Charlie's stretched out at his feet. The fire is lit.

So Ruth and Edwin Harper have been charged with Russell's murder. At that news, Shaun shook the copper's hand and thanked him.

Ally and Jayden will be out to see you in the morning, Skinner said. Then, *They played their part.*

And no one needs to tell Shaun that. Other people might have been first through his door, but it was Ally and Jayden who stayed. Maybe that's as much as anyone can hope for when the worst happens. That people are kind.

And that justice is served.

Now, Shaun checks his watch. Russell's friend Nicky is due any minute. He's bringing a couple of pizzas, a six-pack, and Russell's favourite film on DVD. Even though Shaun's not sure this pizza, this beer, this film, is what he feels like, he's not sure it's *not* what he feels like either. *Nine films*, Nicky said. *The first* Rocky *ones, then* Rocky Balboa, *the three* Creeds, *after that. What if we do one a week?* And Shaun figured that'd take him to Christmas and into the new year, and maybe it's not the worst idea, to have a thing like that.

See, kindness. It's a comfort to know that Russell had a mate like Nicky.

There's a knock at the door and Shaun goes to get it.

But instead of Nicky Ballard it's a tall, dark-haired woman in a long red coat. She's wearing sunglasses, even though it's getting on for pitch-black.

Celine Chevalier.

'Hello, Shaun. I won't come in. I've got a flight to catch.'

And he's not sure what he'd do with Celine Chevalier standing in his living room, so whatever this is, the doorstep's fine by him. He wants to ask her what the hell she wants, but he's got some manners in there somewhere, so he just waits. And tries to stop the confusion from messing up his face.

'I hear Ruth and Edwin Harper have been charged with the murder of your son.'

'That's right.'

'I'm sorry for your loss.'

He nods.

'If it wasn't for the prospect of my investment, it wouldn't have happened.'

'No, but what Russell did . . . that was him.'

'I was never going to give the Harpers any money. I wish your son had known that.'

Shaun blinks at her. *She* wishes? You could fill a book with the things Shaun wishes.

But, really, there's just one.

Celine hands him a bag – a gym bag with a sports logo on the side.

'I don't know how much Russell was asking the Harpers for. Money doesn't fix anything, in my experience. What's broken stays broken. But . . . it does make some things easier.'

The bag weighs a ton.

363

'I just have one question before I go,' says Celine. She takes off her sunglasses, and Shaun's surprised to see her dab at her eyes. 'I don't suppose Frank ever gave you a diary for safekeeping, did he?'

She suddenly looks very young; very young and very sad.

Shaun shakes his head. He finds two words: 'Sorry, no.'

And with that, Celine Chevalier turns and walks down the path. She gets into the back seat of a sleek black car, and it drives away up the lane.

Shaun leans against the door frame, the bag heavy in his hand. He looks up at the night sky. The fast-moving cloud reveals a slip of moon – a perfect silver crescent – then it's gone again. Quick as a trick. Or like it was never really there in the first place.

76

Gus checks his watch. 'I think I should probably be heading back,' he says.

But the fire's crackling, and there's still a glass of wine each in the bottle. Spanish, mind; not Shoreline Vines.

'Really?' says Ally. 'Are you sure?'

Gus nods. 'I'm attacking the book again. I've rather let it slide these last months, and my DI Larkin's been feeling rather neglected.'

The doctor told him to limit screentime if it was bringing on headaches – and, it seemed to Ally, Gus was rather relieved to take a break from his 'ink slinging', as he calls it.

'Oh, you're back into it, are you?'

'With both feet, Ally. Which might account for the clumsy typing,' he laughs.

Ally joins in. But as Gus gets up – casts around for his scarf, and that knitted hat he's taken to wearing which gives him the air of a fisherman – she feels a swell of disappointment. They were cosy here, the pair of them. The three of them, she should say, Fox in his basket, curled as neat as a whelk.

'Go careful out there, Gus,' she says.

The wind booms across the dunes, and Ally knows nights like these. Autumn storms, with waves as tall as high-rises, slamming the shore. Gales so fierce they lose invisibility, taking up sand, shingle, palm fronds spinning through the air like spears. In all this, you'd be forgiven for thinking The Shell House was as insubstantial as a house of cards, but it's stood the test of more than forty winters – and that's just with her and Bill. Gus's All Swell, a less substantial dwelling by anybody's reckoning, will be bearing the brunt of this weather.

'In fact . . .' she says, 'I'm a little worried about All Swell.'

'Oh, join the club,' he laughs. 'I'll be going to sleep with a hard hat on.'

Ally thinks of Evie's room, a guest room now. And then she thinks of her own room. She's suddenly aware of her heart beating in her chest.

'You'd be more than welcome. To stay, I mean.'

Gus is knotting his scarf, and she sees his hand pause. But then he carries on.

'Ah, now that's very kind,' he says, pulling on his hat next. 'But . . . I'll be grand.'

Ally is used to a certain tentativeness with Gus, but in this he sounds quite certain. He steps towards her, and his face is all kindness as he studies hers.

'Ruth Harper,' he says, touching a finger to her cheek. 'She really did a number on you.'

The tenderness in his voice. So why won't he stay?

'Oh, it looks worse than it is. Jayden said I was lucky she didn't break my nose. Or split my lip. That happened to a fellow officer of his once.'

'Teeth intact?'

Ally smiles. 'Teeth intact. Lips intact.'

Gus leans forward and drops a gentle kiss on her forehead; so light you could almost miss it.

'Good night, Ally,' he says. 'And thank you for having me.'

◆ ◆ ◆

Ally wakes to silence. After the last few days, where the wind has been a constant presence, it's the rarest thing. She sits up in bed and can hear the sea – but only just. It's low tide, and the waves are shushing in at a distance.

She settles back on her pillows and gently touches her nose, her lip, with the tips of her fingers. She checks her watch: it's half past seven in the morning. Late for her.

She'll let Fox out to do his morning business, brew some coffee, and think about the day. The immediate aftermath of a big investigation always feels strange to Ally. There's a resettling. Usually she craves quiet and solitude, but something's different this time. The case doesn't feel finished. Or, perhaps it's because of Gus.

She wanted his company last night. Whether in the guest room, or on the sofa, or even here, in this room. This feels like a simple fact to acknowledge, but Ally suspects it isn't. Because a lot of the time she's content on her own. This is her status quo, her "new normal", as they say. And she has Fox, doesn't she? She'll always have Fox.

Ally sets her coffee pot going and wanders out on to the veranda, her little dog nudging her ankles. He's been lazier lately, enjoying the warmth of his basket, so she's glad to see that his lust for his first morning run is intact. She stands on the veranda in her dressing gown, watching him nose about the dark garden. Out over the water the sun starts to rise, turning the sea to liquid gold. The empty beach shimmers like a lunar landscape. Empty only from a distance, that is. After coffee, she'll pull her boots on and walk the strandline. See what's come in on the tide.

Ally breathes it all in; there's no place she'd rather be.

And then she remembers.

She asked Shaun a question – what Frank's favourite place on the farm was – and he was about to give her an answer when Ruth Harper burst in, and everything changed. How could Ally have forgotten until now? She can hear Jayden's voice: *You were nutted, Al!* Maybe. But she and Shaun walked up the track together afterwards too, Shaun mulling on Frank's honour, leading to Ally's breakthrough thought that he'd been covering for someone. Covering for Celine Chevalier. But Celine's hotshot lawyer had held no truck with that, and the police couldn't keep her. She walked free – for now.

And in all the time that followed, Ally forgot to ask again.

Behind her in the house, the coffee pot's whistling. She takes it from the stove and then phones Shaun. He answers straight away. She apologises for the early hour, and says she knows they're going to see him shortly, but that this couldn't wait. She reminds him of the question.

'Ah yeah,' he says, 'I thought about that last night too. I was halfway to giving you an answer, wasn't I? Frank's favourite place was at the top of the farm.'

'The pine tree where Owen was digging?'

The ship's mast from the old ghost story; the land that the digger was tearing at.

'No, further along the ridge. There's a bit of a dip, with a nice old beech tree. You wouldn't notice it really, as everyone's eyes go to the tall pine instead. But Frank liked it up there. Always said it was a good tree, that beech. I remember the kids wanted a tree house in it at some point, but he wouldn't let them. Said it wasn't right to go knocking nails in it.'

'He wouldn't let them have a tree house?'

'Oh, he did build them one. Frank could never say no. But down near the lane instead.'

Interesting.

'Shaun, when Jayden and I come over this morning, do you think you could show us the beech tree?'

'Course. Are you going to bring that little dog of yours this time? I wouldn't mind meeting him.'

Ally looks to where Fox is crashed out in his basket again. 'I'll bring him,' she says.

'Mind how you go though, I wouldn't be surprised if there's a fair bit of debris in the lane. Haven't had gales like that in a long time.'

Ally messages Jayden straight afterwards:

How are the ribs? Could you manage one last trip to the vineyard?

His reply is instant:

Sure. What are you thinking Al?

Her fingers hover. What is she thinking? That if they stand beneath the canopy of the beech tree, they'll get a feeling, rising from the earth, as to whether a man is buried far below?

I'll explain on the way, she types. Pick you up in 15?

77

Saffron looks over at Broady's sleeping form. When his eyes are closed, his lashes look extraordinarily long; his streaked blond hair is fanned out on the pillow. He sleeps like a man without a care in the world. She knows this isn't true, though. His younger brother, Caspar – currently off-grid with someone, somewhere – was supposed to be one of the first people taking part in the Blue Project they set up last summer, designed to improve mental health through surfing. But he never showed. *It is what it is*, is Broady's line.

But while there's wisdom in acceptance, Saffron believes in action too. Because if you can't do anything, do *something*. She doesn't know what that something is with Wilson yet, but at least she'll be around to work it out.

She pads down the stairs just as a package is pushed through her letterbox. It lands with a clunk on the mat. She picks it up, immediately recognising the handwriting. Last time, his letter didn't even make it to the postbox.

She opens the door, just in time to see Wilson heading rapidly for the gate. He's in his big yellow coat, the one he's worn for a lifetime in the wheelhouse, wrestling *Night Dancer* through heavy weather.

'Hey,' she calls. 'You weren't even going to knock?'

He stops, hand on the gate. He's wearing a dark knitted beanie, his grey beard neatly trimmed. He looks like a burglar, caught in the act.

'Sorry,' he says, 'didn't want to disturb.'

'You're not,' she says. Then, 'You couldn't.'

He looks down at his boots.

'What's this then?' she says, holding up the package.

He walks back up the path. He looks sturdy enough. But appearances can be deceptive, she knows that too well.

'Just something I thought you could do with.'

She raises her eyebrows. Pulls open the padded envelope. It's a book; a travel guide.

'But I said I wasn't going,' she says.

What, he was just going to drop this and leave?

'Read inside. There's a note.'

Saffron opens the book. It's called *Best of Hawaii*. Inside the front cover, he's written a message.

To Saffron, I want you to go so I can picture you there. And so that I can look forward to hearing all your stories when you get back. Your loving father.

Her eyes fill.

Wilson shrugs. 'I haven't earned the right to have a say in what you do. Not even close. But if I thought you were staying here because of me – even just a small bit – that wouldn't sit right, Saffron.'

'What if it sits right for me?'

He shakes his head. 'You've got the biggest heart. And I'd say that's all your mum, because I know it's not me.' He gives a little laugh. 'Dawn would back me up there.'

'You're crazy about Dawn.'

'And she's with me every step of the way in this, Saffron. I'm not saying I don't need you, but I've got Dawn. And Trip. And those two damn dogs.'

'How are the dogs?'

'Good for nothing.' Wilson grins; gestures to the wide band of sea behind them. 'Saffron, every single time we lift anchor, and pitch out into all of that, what we're doing is we're travelling hopefully. Hoping for the catch. Hoping to make it back to shore. Hoping for hope's sake.'

'That's different,' she says quietly.

'I don't get out on the boat like I used to, but I'm still travelling hopefully. It's deep in me, see. All of life's out on that water, Saffron, and you've got to keep charging towards it. Don't be still. You can be still when you're dead. You get a chance to go to some kind of a beautiful spot like Hawaii, you take a running jump at it. For both of us.'

'But what if —'

'I croak? We'll cross that bridge. Could happen to anyone of us, any time, couldn't it? Don't go making me special.'

She shakes her head. 'I don't mean that, I just mean . . . what if you could use the company?'

On the dark winter days.

'Oh girl,' he says, folding her into his arms. 'I could always use your company. You know that. But you'll be giving me something important by getting on that plane.'

'What's that?' she says into his coat.

'The chance to do the right thing by you at long last.'

Saffron stays in this hug. It is, she realises, the first one he's ever given her. Eventually they break apart.

'Now go and get that bloody sunshine,' he says. 'And catch me a wave while you're at it.'

78

Jayden climbs gingerly out of the car at Shoreline Vines. It's the moving, that's the trouble. If he could just stay completely still, these ribs of his would be fine. Though he said the opposite to Cat earlier, when he was negotiating his exit pass. *Movement's good, babe.*

'Here,' says Ally, offering him her hand.

Jayden takes it gratefully. 'You've got a killer bruise coming there, Al.'

'I know. I can't FaceTime Evie. She'll be on the first plane.'

'To shut down the Shell House Detectives?'

'Don't joke.'

Beside them, Shaun looks over to the farmhouse. They called first at Yew Tree Cottage, and Shaun shook their hands; thanked them. *For everything,* he said, *and even then, that's not enough.* And then he went and pressed a wad of money into Jayden's hand.

Will that do it? he said.

Shaun, said Jayden, *we can't take this.*

Payment for services rendered. For you and Ally.

But we didn't ask for payment. And even if we did, this is way too much.

Shaun looked as if he were about to say something, then changed his mind. Said, *You'll take it, or you'll look ungrateful. Now, are we going up to that beech tree or what?*

Now, Charlie noses about in the yard, Fox pattering along beside him like they're old mates. They thoroughly investigated one another back at Shaun's cottage, in the way that only dogs can, and now they're inseparable.

There's no sign of either Owen or Karensa.

'Should we knock?' says Ally. 'Or go to the caravan?'

'Look, Owen's coming,' says Shaun, nodding to two figures in the distance, side by side and striding this way. 'And Karensa. They've been out clearing debris, there was a tree down at the bottom of the track. Told you the gales did some damage.'

The lanes on the way up to Shoreline Vines were scattered with broken branches. It's the calm after the storm now though, and the sky is true blue. Sunshine draws out all the autumn colours. It looks like the landscape is on fire.

'Have you and Owen talked?' says Ally.

'Yeah, we've talked,' says Shaun. 'It's alright. Overnight, he's lost a mother and a brother. I figure that gives us something in common.'

But he does have Karensa. Jayden wonders if Skinner has told Owen and Karensa that their relationship played no part in what happened between Russell and Edwin. Jayden decides he'll leave that one to the sergeant.

His phone rings, and he moves away to take it.

Mullins. They called him on the way over; told him their hunch about the beech tree.

'Mum and son murder charge not enough for you, Jayden?' Mullins says now.

'Come on, it's the final piece of the puzzle and you know it.'

'Celine's untouchable.'

'Not if we find remains.'

'And not if, of all the missing persons, it's this Enrique Delgado. Yeah, yeah, I get it.'

Jayden watches Owen and Karensa click through the gate. Owen shakes Shaun's hand. Ally glances back to Jayden, her face a question, and he gives her a thumbs up. Together they head on up to the top of the field, Jayden following behind.

'Got to go. I'll stay in radio contact, Mullins.'

'You do that.'

The uneven ground makes Jayden's ribs throb, and he's glad of a chance to go slow.

If Ally is right, if Shaun's intel is sound, if they get very, very lucky, then the investigation will open – and Celine will be a 'person of significant interest'. And she'll really need that expensive lawyer of hers then.

Jayden looks up, hearing someone exclaim in the group ahead. Even at a distance he can see that the tree they were heading for has been wrenched from the earth. Its roots are exposed and the ground around it is scattered with stray branches. Owen's digging from yesterday ends just a few metres away from it.

Jayden watches as Shaun's dog catches a large branch between his teeth and tries to run with it. Fox explores the base of the tree, barking. The two dogs turn in circles, yapping. It's a dream come true for them. He sees Karensa take a stick and throw it, and Charlie chases it. Fox stays by the upturned tree – then jumps down, disappearing from view altogether.

Jayden pauses. It's a steep climb, and if he breathes too hard then he feels it in his ribs. He's glad Cat can't see him. He probably should have stayed on the sofa today, but Shell House rules are that you follow hunches.

He watches Ally get down on her hands and knees beside the beech tree. And there's something about the way she does it:

solemnly, like she's kneeling in church or something. Jayden can't see Fox, but he can hear him barking. Shaun's beside Ally. And Owen too. Karensa spins from throwing the stick for Charlie, and Jayden sees the expression on her face change. Her hands go to her mouth.

Ally rocks back on her heels and turns to him. She nods.

As Jayden gets to her, they look down into the earth together; see where white bone shows beneath dark soil.

'Jayden,' says Ally, softly. 'We've found him.'

79

THREE DAYS LATER

They're waiting outside Hang Ten when it opens. There's a note on the door saying it's the last day of the season – and what a day it is. The kind of autumn morning that feels like a gift to Ally, but then, don't they all? Inland, the hedgerows blaze with fire-bright colours, but down at the beach it's all serenity. The sea is its bluest blue, the sky a paler wash, with streaks of cloud darting over the horizon. A spry breeze, nothing like the gales of the other night, holds the waves up just so: the water's dotted with a handful of surfers, bobbing, dancing, exploding in the white water.

'You don't want to be out there?' says Cat to Saffron. 'We can hold the fort here.'

'Dawn patrol,' grins Saffron. 'And it was epic.'

They settle at the tables. Fox turns circles as Saffron offers him a bone-shaped biscuit, and goodness knows he deserves it, after the part he played at the beech tree. Pelting about with his new friend Charlie has taken years off him. *Perhaps we could walk them together from time to time?* Ally found herself saying to Shaun. And Shaun said that if a dog walk in Porthpella means passing by the place where Saffron sells her brownies, then that's okay by him.

Three days have passed since they found the bones. Owen's digging destabilised the ground up there on the ridge, but it was the gales that tore up the beech tree – and exposed just the smallest nick of bone for Fox to see. The officials came, with their blue-and-white tape and masks and great big toolkits. They dug up the remains, so carefully, so respectfully. With testing, they'll work out the identity of the deceased, but Ally and Jayden know already.

Shaun told them about Celine coming by with the money – and her mention of a flight to catch. It's Jayden's theory that Celine thought they were getting too close for comfort, though with her resources she might be anywhere in the world by now. Sipping cocktails on a beach; secreted in a palatial villa. But Shaun said she didn't look like a woman who was getting away with something. *She just looked sad.*

For all that they tried, Shaun wouldn't hear of taking his payment back. *Help the next person who can't afford it*, he said.

'How long to go now, Cat?' asks Gus, taking the top off his flat white.

'Four months,' says Cat. 'Though Jazz came early so . . . who knows, maybe a bit less. All bets are off, right, Jay?'

'Big time. We're ready for anything.'

But it's a good thing there's no baby to be cradling just yet. Jayden needs a few weeks to heal, thinks Ally. The other night he went in for the X-rays after all, as the pain wasn't easing. *That's how it goes with ribs, apparently*, he said. *The doc says it gets worse before it gets better, and time is the only healer.*

And they've both heard that before somewhere.

'I, for one, can't wait to meet the little chap,' says Gus, fond as a grandad. 'Roll on spring.'

Saffron turns the music up and Hang Ten fills with the lilting voice that Ally now knows is Sister Nancy. Earlier, Saffron told Ally about Wilson – that he's just been diagnosed with prostate cancer.

Apparently they're just going to watch and wait, said Saffron. *No treatment yet. He's calling it a win.* Her face was uncertain. *Is that a win, Ally?*

And given the circumstances, given the infinite ways that life has of pulling the rug from under us, given how Saffron, more than anyone, knows how it can be otherwise, Ally nodded her agreement; then folded Saffron into a hug.

He says he and Dawn might even catch a plane to Honolulu. Meet me and Broady at Waimea Bay. I think *he's joking . . .*

Now, Saffron's dancing behind the counter. A vision of joy and abandon, and Ally's heart swells to see it.

Just then, the door opens and it's Mullins. Mullins in jeans and a jumper, with a grin as wide as they come.

'Morning, all,' he says. 'What's cooking?'

Saffron rolls her eyes, a special gesture she reserves, Ally has noted, just for the constable. But then she says, 'Bacon sandwich, Mullins?'

'With brown sauce, obviously,' says Mullins. 'Might as well stick an egg in while you're at it, Saff?'

'Might as well, hey,' says Saffron, as the rashers hit the griddle.

Sister Nancy sings 'Bam Bam', and Jayden's daughter joins in, striking her spoon on the table. Over the top of her head, Jayden smiles at Ally and Ally smiles back.

They hold the moment, as around them Hang Ten swirls with merriment: Gus and Mullins debating the merits of ketchup versus brown sauce; Cat and Saffron talking waves, and the swell to come.

They've done it: another case cracked.

Yesterday, Jayden said that Owen had been in touch to say that he and Karensa are leaving Shoreline Vines. The future of the vineyard is uncertain once again.

Ally notices Mullins go up to collect his order, rather than waiting for Saffron to bring it to him.

'It's like a party in here,' he calls out. Then, 'And you're smiling again. Good to see, Saff.'

'It's the last day of the season.'

The sandwich that's halfway to Mullins's mouth pauses. 'What?'

'You didn't see the sign on the door? Mullins, we're going to Hawaii. Wilson said I've got to. He's okay for now.'

Mullins nods slowly. Then he carries on where he left off and takes an enormous bite.

'That's great, Saff,' he says through his mouthful. 'I'm really pleased for you. Especially about Wilson.'

As he turns away, Ally is surprised by the look on Mullins's face. But perhaps it confirms what she already half suspected. They'll all miss Saffron this winter, but Tim Mullins more than most.

'So, Al,' says Jayden, coming to sit beside her. 'Apparently, we're not done here yet. My father-in-law said he'll give us the double murder, but we're still not up to much if we can't get Owen Harper his quad bike back.'

'He did not say that, Ally,' says Cat. 'Honestly, Jay's favourite pastime is pretending Dad's down on him.'

'Yeah, well,' says Mullins, 'he's got a point. It wasn't in that Bodmin haul. The only Honda Fourtrax from that lot belongs to some riding stables near Redruth.'

'So, case . . . not quite closed after all?' says Ally. Then, 'Do you want to keep going on it today, Jayden?'

Then she looks to Gus. They've talked about one day packing a Thermos and getting a few coast path miles under their belts. And all today, the weather's set fair.

'Actually,' says Ally, 'I can't imagine Owen's that bothered about his quad bike after everything else.'

'Right answer, Al,' says Jayden. 'And that's exactly what I told Cliff.'

'How about that hike then, Gus?' she says. 'Could today be the day?'

Another direct invitation. But nothing like her one before.

'Oh, I don't know about a hike. It'll be more of a saunter, really.' Gus grins. 'I'm game if you are, Ally.'

A saunter. A slow wander, destination uncertain. But grateful for every step.

Yes, that feels right.

Ally reaches down to Fox, who's sound asleep across her feet. She strokes his soft ears, murmurs, 'Have you got the legs for a saunter, old boy?'

Fox doesn't stir right away, but then he looks up. And the twinkle in her little dog's eyes says yes. Today, he's got the legs for it.

Epilogue
TWO YEARS PREVIOUSLY

Frank sits in front of the fire in his study. The doctor's verdict, and all that it means, is still settling. The end is nigh.

Frank knows that in due course he'll need to consider his wife, his sons, the vineyard, the mess he knows he's made of the finances, but right now, he thinks of Celine.

He meant it all those years ago, when he told her that her secret was safe. Frank saw the way that man went for Celine out in the barn, and he knew how it would have ended too.

Now, he turns the diary in his hands. He's kept it hidden at the back of his desk drawer for twenty-eight years.

He opens it and reads over her final entry one last time. It's in French, of course, but he painstakingly translated it. He knows just what it says.

> *Enrique found me here. I couldn't believe it when I saw him at the farm. When I said I wanted nothing to do with him he tried to hurt me. To force me. He had me up against the barn, and I was struggling, trying to scream, his hand over my mouth was disgusting, but somehow*

I fought him off. When he chased me, I took a spade and . . . stopped him. I stopped him. Frank found me. Crying. Shaking. I told him how afraid I was. Not of what Enrique was going to do to me but of what would happen to me now. The price I would pay for protecting myself. For fighting him to the death. Frank said that it would be okay. He said he would take care of it, and I let him. I don't know if it was the right thing, or the wrong thing, because nothing makes sense any more . . .

Frank closes the diary. It was cruel of him to ever take it from her. Celine turned to her diary to try to make sense of the horror, not thinking of the danger of it falling into the wrong hands and scuppering them both. They should have burnt it together there and then. But, instead, Frank told Celine he needed it for insurance; in case she ever had a change of heart, he wanted it to be clear that he had nothing to do with the killing of Enrique Delgado. But the burying of him? The concealing of his remains, for twenty-eight years? Yes, that's on Frank.

That Celine trusted him with this diary of hers broke his heart. *Okay, Frank, I understand, but please know I would never betray you.* And God knows, where she was concerned, Frank's heart was already in tatters. A family man with a crush on a young woman half his age? He knows how pathetic that makes him. But apart from the pleasure of being in her vicinity, Celine gave him the idea for the vineyard. She told him he should take their ordinary old farm and turn it into something different. Something wonderful.

So, Shoreline Vines is down to her. And for all that they're floundering now – a couple of bad harvests will do that, a plague of blackfly, his own not-quite-sturdy hand on the finances – they've had some good times. The 2018 vintage with their medal-winning sparkling Pinot Noir was their best ever. Frank wonders now if it's to be their swansong.

He was weak, telling Ruth about the body he buried all those years ago. But he was sunk in a depression, and it just stumbled out of him. At least he spun the story differently: an accidental killer afraid to own up to his mistake, rather than someone doing something selfless out of love for another woman. He doesn't feel good about deceiving Ruth. But then he doesn't feel particularly good about anything these days, so add it to the list.

The one thing Frank does know is that his family loves this vineyard – and they'll never sell it either. His wife and Edwin enjoy what they see as the status; it doesn't take much to be a big fish in Porthpella. But Owen? Owen loves the vines. Every inch of this terroir. Although Owen doesn't know its every secret, because if you love someone, you protect them, don't you?

Frank slowly gets up from his chair, the diary in his hand. He'll take Celine's secret to his grave, just like he said he would. The grave that's a good deal closer than he ever imagined.

Frank tosses the diary into the grate. It takes a moment for it to catch, but then the fire engulfs it. A riot of colour. He watches it burn until it's blackened and ashen. No matter who comes looking for it, they'll never find it now.

That's his first job done. His next is to talk to Ruth. Call it a pre-death wish, because regardless of the kind of man Enrique Delgado was, his parents deserve to lay their son to rest, instead of being stuck in the purgatory of having no answers. Frank will, of course, keep Celine's name out of it. He'll simply tell the police that he thought the man was an intruder; that he was defending his property. And Frank will take whatever consequences come his way, because isn't he dying anyway? The hard part will be explaining himself to his boys; he's not sure he'll have the words for that.

Frank closes the door to his study and shuffles along the hallway. He sees Ruth standing at the top of the stairs, dusting a picture; a gilt-framed photograph of the vineyard.

He takes the stairs slowly, because he's weak now, and by the time he makes it to the top he's wheezing. Unsteady on his feet.

'What is it, Frank?' she says, her face already set to impatience. 'What do you want now?'

Ruth won't like what he wants to do, but Frank hopes that she'll understand it. A man's last request for peace – not just for himself but for others too.

'I've made my mind up about something,' he says.

But as he tells her his intentions, Frank sees Ruth's expression change from brewing storm to all-out fury. He sets a hand on the banister to steady himself; to steel himself.

'I'm sorry, Ruth, but you can't stop me.'

His wife tucks her duster in her apron pocket and takes a step towards him.

'Oh, Frank,' she says, her hands reaching for him, 'I think you'll find I can.'

ACKNOWLEDGEMENTS

Thank you for joining me on this fourth Shell House Detectives adventure. I hope you enjoyed reading it as much as I enjoyed writing it.

Thank you to my fantastically supportive agent, Rowan Lawton, at The Soho Agency. I'm so grateful for all you do, along with the brilliant Eleanor Lawlor and also Helen Mumby on the TV side.

At Thomas & Mercer, I'm incredibly lucky to be working with the editorial dream team of Vic Haslam and Laura Gerrard. I truly couldn't ask for more passion, vision or intuition. Big thanks, too, to all at Thomas & Mercer, including Gemma Wain, Sarah Day and Rebecca Hills. Marianna Tomaselli's cover illustrations continue to be a total joy: thank you for bringing the Shell House world to life with such style.

Thank you to my friend Lucy Clarke and my husband, Robin Etherington, for weathering my first draft and giving such helpful feedback. I'm so appreciative of the energy, wisdom and fun that you both bring to the process. Lucy, this book is dedicated to you: whether we're swapping voice note chats, or writing together beachside, it's always luminous. Thanks are also due to Emma Stonex, who read a later draft and whose thoughtful response gave me just the boost I needed for the final stages; your generosity is boundless.

As I was busy writing this novel, *The Rockpool Murder* was published, and I'm very grateful to the amazing writers who read early copies and offered words of support. Big thanks to Rosie Walsh, Kate Riordan, Libby Page, Emily Koch, Emma Stonex and Lucy Clarke for such sparkly quotes: your ongoing enthusiasm for the series means so much, and always fuels my writing.

Thank you to my CSI friend Zoe and my police constable friend Oli, aka 'the professionals'. You're both brilliant, and I truly value your advice. Any procedural inaccuracies are down to me.

Thank you to all at Polgoon Vineyard near Penzance, especially Bronwyn Phillips, who gave me the most fantastic tour one wet November day and indulged my slightly loopy questions about murder among the vines. Any similarities between the fictional Shoreline Vines and the wonderfully real Polgoon are entirely coincidental.

While we've shared many Cornish holidays as a family, a solo writing retreat in St Ives was crucial to the writing of *The Death at the Vineyard*. Thank you to my husband, Robin, and my son, Calvin, who always wave me off on such trips with love, encouragement and generosity of spirit. I know how lucky I am to have you.

Lastly, thank you to my dear family and friends. For everything, always.

ABOUT THE AUTHOR

Photo © 2022 Victoria Walker

Emylia Hall lives in Bristol with her husband and son, where she writes from a hut in the garden and dreams of the sea. She is the author of the Shell House Detective Mysteries, a series inspired by her love of Cornwall's wild landscape. The first, *The Shell House Detectives*, was a Kindle Top 10 Bestseller, with the rights being optioned for TV. *The Death at the Vineyard* is her fourth crime novel. Emylia has published four previous novels, including Richard and Judy Book Club pick *The Book of Summers* and *The Thousand Lights Hotel*. Her work has been translated into ten languages, and broadcast on BBC Radio 6 Music. She is the founder of Mothership Writers and is a writing coach at The Novelry.

Instagram: @emyliahall_author

X: @emyliahall

Follow the Author on Amazon

If you enjoyed this book, follow Emylia Hall on Amazon to be notified when the author releases a new book!
To do this, please follow these instructions:

Desktop:

1) Search for the author's name on Amazon or in the Amazon App.
2) Click on the author's name to arrive on their Amazon page.
3) Click the 'Follow' button.

Mobile and Tablet:

1) Search for the author's name on Amazon or in the Amazon App.
2) Click on one of the author's books.
3) Click on the author's name to arrive on their Amazon page.
4) Click the 'Follow' button.

Kindle eReader and Kindle App:

If you enjoyed this book on a Kindle eReader or in the Kindle App, you will find the author 'Follow' button after the last page.